SCRAPPLINGS

CHILDREN OF THE DRAGONS

ANAMAT BOOK ONE

AMELIA SMITH

ISBN-13: 978-1-941334-21-8 ebook

ISBN-13: 978-1-941334-22-5 paperback

Published by Split Rock Books

Cover and book design by the author.

Cover image is a detail of "The Tower of Babel" by Pieter Bruegel the Elder, ca. 1563.

For more information or to sign up to the author's mailing list, visit:
www.ameliasmith.net

Table of Contents

Prologue: The Lost Land..1

Chapter 1: Darna's Discovery.................................5

Chapter 2: Crossing the Hills................................23

Chapter 3: The Walls of Anamat.............................41

Chapter 4: The Ballad of Ara and Enat....................58

Chapter 5: A Shelter..75

Chapter 6: The Box...95

Chapter 7: Cereans..115

Chapter 8: Nira..129

Chapter 9: The Tongues of Anamat.....................142

Chapter 10: The Commission..............................158

Chapter 11: In the Governor's Palace...................178

Chapter 12: On the Run.......................................197

Chapter 13: The Boys Take their Share.................218

Chapter 14: Giri, Again..234

Chapter 15: Iola at the Gates...............................251

Chapter 16: Darna and the Boys...........................265

Chapter 17: Midsummer Night.............................289

Epilogue: Entering the temple.............................310

Author's Note...316

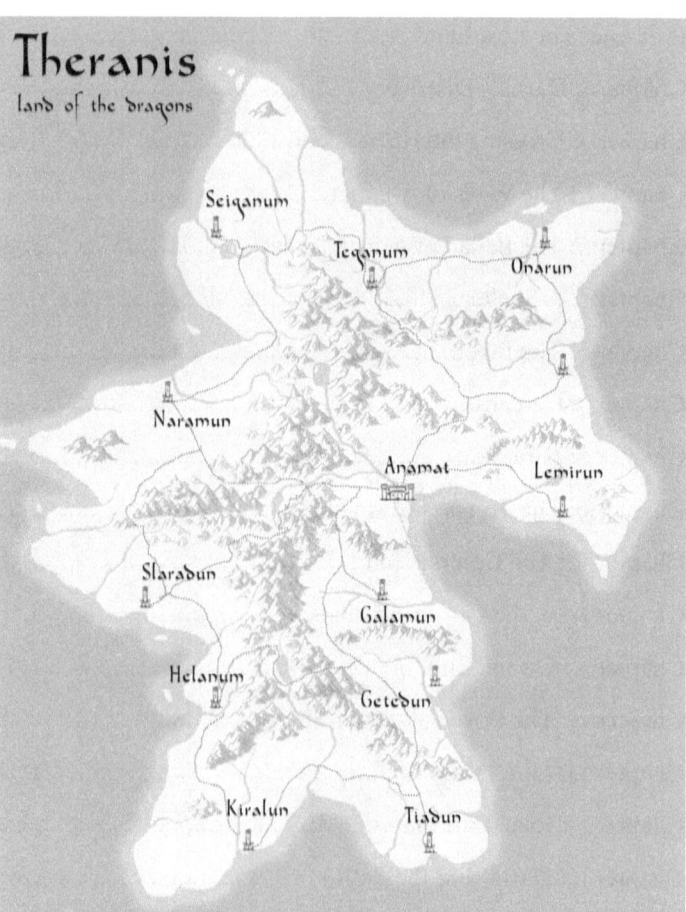

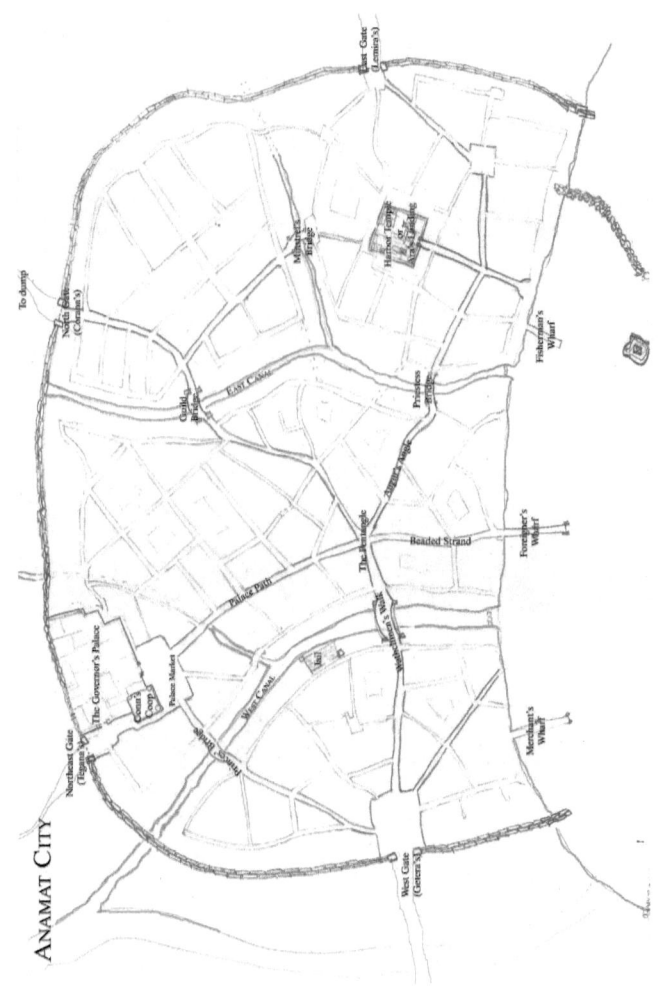

ANAMAT CITY

Prologue: The Lost Land

The man who rowed up to the shore was not young. His boat was so small that he could haul it up past the high water mark single-handedly, albeit with visible exertion. He overturned it on the rough grass and looked around. Was this the place? If his reckoning was correct, it could be the southern province of the forgotten land. It appeared to be deserted.

On the promontory near where he'd landed, the peak of an old stone building showed above the waves – some kind of fortification. He'd almost run aground on another bit of stonework farther out. The fields nearby looked like they might have been tended once, and a long, even depression with slightly different vegetation could have been a road, a hundred years before. The slanting afternoon light showed differences between parts of the forest, too, newer growth against older woods. Only bird calls sounded. He set about making camp – it was late, and it had been a long three days' row from Calandria's furthest outpost, through waters only fools would brave.

§

The blade at his throat woke him out of a deep, dreamless sleep. His limbs were heavy, but his throat tightened with fear. He swallowed to calm himself before he opened his eyes, but he could not see who wielded the blade, only smell them;

pinewood smoke, sweat, and grease.

"So there are men here," he said, hoping that the language he chose would be understood.

"Women, anyway."

She didn't let him up. She'd taken one hand and pinned it behind him such that if he moved anywhere, it would send jolts of pain down his spine. He knew that trick and how to counter it. He let her keep that arm and ignored the momentary agony to let his other arm drop to his side, then rolled over. By the time he was on his feet the blade was in his own hands.

The woman sat back. "Where did you learn that?" she asked.

"From my grandmother, when I was a boy."

"Long time ago, wasn't that?" she said. She was at least as old as he was and her clothes were little more than skins.

"Are you one of the bandits?" he asked. "Did they survive the fall?"

"No one survived the fall, just as no one survives landing on these shores. The ghosts of the dragons steal their souls."

"Do they?" he asked. Despite the deplorable condition of the woman's clothing, he could see that she was well-fed. She certainly wasn't dead. He didn't feel very dead, himself. His muscles were tired from the long row, yes, but he felt very much alive. "You don't look like your soul has been stolen."

"Ah, but I was born here. You weren't. Don't tell me you haven't heard the stories. That amulet you wear looks Cerean."

He clutched the bronze amulet that hung from a string around his neck. "This? It was a gift, and yes, I have been to Cerea. It is a remarkable place. Not exactly comfortable, but remarkable even so, the greatest civilization on the seas. Calandria is more beautiful, but Cerea's empire is vaster."

"They don't want the world to remember what they destroyed," the woman said.

"Of course not, and those who remember it are all gone. Nothing remains."

The woman gave a little smile. "Not much." Her gaze took in the whole sweep of the land around them. Her eyes narrowed as she turned back to him. "What do you know of it?"

"My grandparents said that they sailed from there, when they were young. They could only tell me some of the story, not what happened after the end, though they say that Darnasa of Tiadun would know, if she lived."

Something in the woman's expression changed. ""Your grandparents? Do you know what their names were?"

"They took new names in Enomae, but they told me that when they lived in Anamat – not for very long, I'm afraid – they were called Eppie and Kinner. They were very old when they told me that, and I wasn't much more than a boy."

"Ah, the last apprentice and the scribe boy."

"You know of them?"

"I heard the stories,"

"It seems that I've come to the right place, then."

"The right place to throw your life away, especially if you're wearing a Cerean amulet."

He frowned down at the amulet. A good friend had given it to him for protection on his journey. If it would put him in danger here, there was no need to keep it. He took out his knife, cut the string, and threw the amulet away from him. The woman nodded.

"I'm old," he said. "Soon, I won't be able to row so far. I wanted to know what remained here more than I wanted to live to see Cerea again."

"Good," she said. "Then I'll tell you, but I don't know that we'll let you leave these shores with our story."

"I don't mind," he said.

"Come back to my camp then," she said. "We won't kill you yet, and the dragons-to-be are still sleeping in their shells."

He nodded. He knew that much. The last of the priestesses had told him that they would sleep for a long time. He missed those old women for their stories and the tales of beauty that they wove. When he became old enough to understand, the thought that they'd prostituted themselves horrified him. He said as much to the last of them, the one who'd come to tend the shrine. She'd laughed at him.

"You don't understand anything, young man," she'd said. "The women of Cerea never had such power."

She'd died soon after that, before he could ask her more. She'd been beautiful until the end, always wreathed in flowing scarves. He blinked and begged pardon as he realized that the rough, fur-clad woman before him had said something.

"I am at your service," he said to her. "Are you the chieftain here?"

She shrugged. "Gather your things and follow me, if you want to know."

§

Chapter 1: Darna's Discovery

Theranis lies at the heart of the seas, a verdant land, a gem among nations. Its people were once our people. If we can persuade them to leave off their womanly superstitions, they will lead us to immeasurable wealth.

– A letter from a Cerean merchant

Darna looked out across the bay from the rise beside the root cellar. A square sail peeked over the white-capped waves beyond the watchtower, the first ship to approach since the winter weather had calmed. It was a foreign ship, with red and white stripes running up and down its sails, not like the plain red sails of the fishermen or the white and yellow sails of Anamat traders who brought baskets and cloth that nearly glowed with dragonlight in their beauty. Darna squinted at the foreign ship then opened her eyes to the sky, hoping to glimpse the dragon. She only saw Tiada when she was outside of the keep walls and alone.

Light danced around the edges of the scattering storm clouds, hinting at places where a dragon might fly. The sun lit a patch of farmland and a bit of the road to Anamat, then Darna looked back up just in time to glimpse the dragon's wing cutting through the clouds. Perhaps it was a sign.

Tiada, the dragon of Tiadun, was all colors of the rainbow and of fire. She swooped low, churning the clouds in her wake, making a hard rain fall out over the bay. The sight of her warmed Darna, and though Tiada flew back behind the cloud cover, for a moment she felt that all was right with the world.

"Hey!"

Darna turned at the sound of the boy's voice, but not soon enough. A clod of mud hit her on the shoulder.

"Gotcha!" the boy stuck out his tongue. Darna shook herself off and looked down at what was left of the clod of mud. It wasn't enough to throw.

"What were you doing, staring at the sky?" he sneered.

"Nothing."

"Oooh, like a priestess!" he teased. He had a sack in each hand and he waved them like scarves, swinging his hips and mooning his eyes.

Darna tightened her grip on her stick, but as soon as she took a step forward he stopped and sneered at her again. "Oh, I forgot. You can't be a priestess 'cause you're ugly and a cripple! Ha!"

"At least I'm not stupid like you," Darna muttered. He wasn't much bigger than she was, but he was a bully who thought that coming from the keep's town made him more important that villagers like Darna.

"What did you say?" The boy dropped one of the sacks in the mud and picked up a hardened pat of cow turd and positioned himself to throw.

"Why are you here?" Darna said.

"Check up on you," he said with a shrug. "Cook sent me. Said to tell you to get two more bags of parsnips." He threw the bags at her.

Darna circled back around to the door of the root cellar. It was barred with a thick plank, too heavy for her to move. The boy had turned to watch the approaching ship and was picking his nose. She called to him to help her. Together, they opened the door just far enough for Darna to slip in, but he stayed outside, watching the ship. He was afraid of the dark.

She made her way down the steps by feel, one hand on the grimy rock wall, the other clutching her stick. At the bottom she straightened. If she stood tall, her head just reached the ceiling. Perhaps now she was old enough to make the journey to Anamat, where the last true priestesses lived, where even guildsmen saw the dragons, and where she might find an apprenticeship and learn to craft beauty out of stone and dragonfire. The ship's arrival meant that it was spring, the traveling season. If only the city weren't so far away.

The light from outside drifted dimly down, so that the shelves of earthenware jars and crates were only just visible. Darna filled the sacks with parsnips then stopped to listen. The boy was whistling, but no one else was coming, not that she could hear. She felt along the back of a shelf and shifted a loose stone aside. Her pouch was still there. She emptied the beads into her hand and counted them.

She rehearsed the value of each one, found on lucky days while sweeping the great hall or dropped by a careless guardsman in the kitchen yard. One small bead would buy a loaf of bread, another a half day's journey in a farmer's cart, or a bowl of stew. A tiny bead was worth less than that, but six of them were worth a small bead, and six small beads or a middling would get her halfway to Anamat. They said that it was five or six days' journey to Anamat but it would probably take her twice as long, limping as she did. She had enough beads for four days' food, but she could scavenge, or even stop at temples and hope that they wouldn't try to draw her into the priesthood before she'd even seen the city. She would wait one more year.

The door above shifted and Darna startled, dropping two of her beads to the fioor, both small ones, not the tiny ones. She scrambled for them.

"Hurry up," the boy said from up above. "It's starting to rain again."

"It's dry down here," Darna said, teasing him for his fear of the dark as she ran her hands across the fioor, searching for the dropped beads.

"No thanks," the boy said. "I'm going back inside."

"Didn't you say you were supposed to help me carry?" The bags were heavy. She'd have to go back to get the second one. Her hand touched a bead, and caught it before it rolled away.

"What are you doing down there?" he demanded. "You take half a day to get anything out of that cellar."

"Nothing," Darna said. She tucked the found bead into her pouch. She'd have to find the other one later. She was just reaching in behind the jars to hide the pouch when the boy stepped through the door above, blocking the last of the daylight.

"Hurry up!" he said.

She couldn't find the stone. She tucked the pouch under her belt and hoped that no one would notice it.

At the top of the steps, the boy took the cleaner bag of parsnips. He sprinted away through the rain while Darna struggled to push the door bar back into place, leaving her to limp through the downpour with her heavy, muddy sack.

At the corner by the back entrance to the stable yard, there was a little overhang. Darna paused to rest, catching a last breath of free air before she went back to the kitchen and more barked, never-ending orders. She sat down on the bag and closed her eyes, remembering the dragon's fiight through the clouds, the promise of the road to Anamat. She just didn't have enough beads.

A jangle of metal on metal and the snort of a horse startled her. The prince and his men were coming in from the hunt, riding up the broad road into the stable yard. The horses picked their way nervously across the mud. Darna sat as still as she could, wishing she could be invisible to them, horses and men alike.

The prince was a man of middle years, still strong, but with graying hair, dark circles under his eyes, and pale skin. He rode a black horse which set him above his companions in height, though he wasn't a tall man when he stood on his own. His brother, the taller of the two, rode a small brown mare. He was undefeated in the keep's tournaments. The prince judged the tournaments, rather than joining in himself. The royal brothers were accompanied by the game warden, who rode a mule and carried a longbow across his back. His eyes flicked around the courtyard, wary of enemies or looking for quarry. Darna was too small to interest or threaten him.

"Tell the steward to be sure the chambers are prepared for our friends," the prince said to his brother.

"Of course, brother." The noblemen and the steward rode on and Darna edged closer to the wall. She'd been kicked by a horse two years before, when she'd first arrived at the keep. Since then, she'd kept her distance from the beasts, but she didn't want to draw attention to herself by hurrying away.

"Shall I tell the priestesses to prepare themselves?" the game warden asked.

The prince frowned. "I think not," he said. "It is not their custom."

His brother laughed. "Nonsense! Who doesn't enjoy a good romp?"

"Our Cerean philosopher says it is a blasphemy to all his countrymen."

The game warden laughed. "I think the tutor prefers – "

The prince's horse shied, startling the beasts on either side of him and almost unseating the prince. A stable boy ran up and took the reins, glaring at Darna.

The prince, who had not seen her until then, glanced her way for a brief moment.

"Back to your work, idler!" the game warden said.

Darna scurried away as the three men dismounted, handing their mounts' reins to the stable boy.

§

Back within the kitchen's oppressive walls, the cook railed at her for getting the bag muddy, even though it hadn't been her fault.

"I'd lash you but I don't have time," the cook said. "Peel these. I'll lash you in the morning."

Darna settled into her usual corner and began peeling, the sharp knife edging under the knobbly skin until it inevitably slipped and cut the root in half. She tried to concentrate. An unfamiliar woman's voice sounded from the passage to the great hall.

"And why won't he see me?" the woman demanded.

Darna couldn't hear the mumbled reply.

"Tomorrow?" the woman said. "That will have to do, though he may regret it."

Darna looked up just long enough to see a priestess enter, then bent back to her task, moving the knife slowly, trying not to let it slip. The blade did slip, it always did, but this time it was because someone moved her stick. The priestess who'd just come in sat down beside Darna. The kitchen stank of smoking grease and garlic but a cloud of incense followed the priestess, wrapping around her like a silken scarf.

"Darna, is it?" she said. "You remember me, don't you?"

Darna didn't look up. She shrugged noncommittally and picked up the next unpeeled root. She couldn't remember the priestess. They were all the same to her, letting her know that she wasn't fit to be one of them, crippled as she was. It was just as well, though. The last thing Darna wanted was to lie down for petitioners and preen for courtiers and guardsmen.

"We had not heard from your mother in a long time," the priestess said, "not since she left our temple for the hills. We were preparing her funeral rites when a message came to us. I consider it to be her dying wish."

"What does that have to do with me?" Darna said. "When she left me, that village couple became my family. Now I only have Tiada. The dragon is my parent. That's what they all say." Darna had been fostered by a childless couple in the village for a few years so that they would have an heir for their farm, but then they'd had a baby, and another and a third. Darna didn't want to be a stupid farm wife anyway. She'd heard that her birth mother had gone into the hills, but how could it make any difference? Priestesses weren't supposed to have babies.

The priestess sighed. "If you listened, you would learn something, something which might be very interesting to you."

Darna shrugged. "I never knew my mother. I don't see how it could make any difference if she's alive or dead." She dug her knife into the next bit of root and it stuck. When she pushed harder, it overshot its mark and tore a hole in the edge of her tunic.

The priestess waited.

"You have a father," she said, after a while.

"My mother was a priestess. I have no father."

The priestess took a moment to look around the kitchen. No one was paying much attention to the two of them.

"There are changes in the air," she whispered. "If you were a boy, your father would surely recognize you, despite our traditions. He might do so even though you're just a girl. He needs an heir, he needs to show that he can sire a child."

"Just a girl? The chieftain of that village has three sons and two daughters," Darna said. "I have to finish peeling these."

"But the prince does not."

The priestess's statement hung in the air. To be the daughter of the pale, sickly prince. What would they say in the kitchen? The prince's daughter could make the cook cower, not the other way around. She would be able to get revenge on all the servants who had slighted her or thrown dung at her. She would be beholden to the prince for everything, trapped at Tiadun keep. She would still have to bow to him and do whatever he and his mistress planned for her. Still, she would have fine clothes, do no work, and probably have a Cerean tutor of her own, teaching her to read and reason in the way of the rulers, without regard for the dragons.

If she were stuck in the keep and surrounded by people all the time, she would never see the dragon again. She knew it in her bones. If she took another parent, Tiada would leave her. She wanted to see Tiada again and to see Anara if she could. She didn't want to be one of the dragon-blind, even if it meant a life of comfort. Besides, the whole idea was absurd.

"Well?" the priestess said. "Shall we go to him now?"

"I don't see what he'd want with a daughter, even if he had one," Darna said. The prince had red hair, too. Not as bright as her own, but on him everyone admired it instead of teasing him. People would admire a wart on a prince.

"He could make you head priestess in another province," the priestess said, "or a keep mistress."

"I don't want that," Darna said.

One thing he would not do would be to let her run free. Anamat waited for her, she was more sure of it than she'd ever been. It was home to the dragons' children – that's what the minstrels said. She wanted to see the beauty of its streets and of the many graces of Anara. The keep had none of that. She hated the place. She would not be chained to it.

"You're a fool. You will never be a priestess without his influence," the priestess said, pursing her lips. She was probably as dragon-blind as the prince himself.

"Why would I want to be?" Darna threw a dirty parsnip in with the peeled ones.

"You are obviously unsuited to this work, in any case." The priestess sniffed at her mutilated pile of parsnips. "I will go tell him."

"Don't," Darna said.

"I promised your mother that I would," the priestess said.

"Why should she care?" Darna complained, so loudly that some of the other servants turned to look. "Why would he?" she added more quietly.

"She was your mother," the priestess said. "She suckled you through your infancy, and she always waited for word of you."

Darna doubted that. She'd certainly never heard anything about it.

"As for the prince," the priestess whispered, "if it is known that he has sired a child, he will be better able to fend off his brother's ambitions. I saw him as a youth. I am older than he is. You look very like he did before he became a man."

Darna shook her head. Now, of course, despite the red

hair, he looked nothing like her. People admired him, or at least flattered him.

"And there's this," the priestess said. "The princes have begun to pay some heed to this new Cerean philosophy. In it, the father's seed has all the making of the child, the mother is just the passive vessel."

"The Cereans also say that the dragons aren't real, or that they are demons. Who could believe that?" Darna asked, exasperated, wondering how the priestess could favor Cerean philosophy over the dragons' ways, even if she was dragon-blind.

Darna stood to walk away. Her father was less than nothing to her, even if he was the prince. She didn't care that the keep mistress hadn't borne him an heir. The child of a village priestess could mean nothing to him, even if he had visited her once. All sorts of men came to the priestesses. If they did bear babies, it was a shame and an accident, a sign that they were not performing the rite in earnest. How could her existence mean anything at all to them?

"He would value you," the priestess said.

Darna shook her head. If by some chance she did mean something to him, it could only trap her forever.

The priestess stood, brushed a few parsnip peelings off her formerly immaculate robes, and swept out of the kitchen, taking the scent of incense with her. Darna was left with the garlic and muddy peelings and less than a handful of beads in her pocket. She considered the prospect of being the princess of this provincial keep for the rest of her born days.

"To Na's fire with him!" Darna cursed. She felt faint, queasy. She had to get outside. She dropped her work, scrambled to get her stick, and ran. The cook shouted after her but it didn't matter. She had to escape. She wanted as little to do with the prince as possible. He fed the servants meager rations even at harvest time. The keep cramped them all together, grating against each other, one complaint fast on the heels of the last, from the prince right down to her, the least of the servants.

Once outside, Darna slowed down. Tiada was nowhere to be seen. Near the privies, a few guardsmen were gossiping over dice, but they didn't look up as she hurried past.

She made for a lookout point just beyond the keep wall. The foreign ship had drawn closer. She could see its hull now and almost discern the movements of the men on the decks. The prince had a Cerean tutor in the court, but the Cerean rarely appeared outside the prince's private quarters and never spoke to servants, so the ones who came at trading season were still a novelty. Their ship looked far larger than the one that had come the year before on its way to trade in Anamat.

Darna looked up and glimpsed a tip of Tiada's wing through the clouds. Then the dragon flew back up and out of sight. No one else in Tiadun ever saw the dragon, except possibly some temple-bound priestess. She would probably never meet another person who could see the dragons as she did unless she went to Anamat. There, maybe someone might understand why she stared at the sky and not condemn or pity her for it, even if they did pity her for other reasons.

The foreigners' ship swung toward the shore. Incense spiraled up from the priestesses' shrine to appease the dragon as her enemies sailed closer. In the town around the keep, people climbed up onto their rooftops to watch the foreigners approach. With all the people running up and down through the keep and the town, it would be a good time to slip away, but Darna was hungry. She resolved to go to the kitchens to steal some bread, even if the cook walloped her and she had to dodge that village priestess with all her unlikely and pointless tales.

§

When Darna returned to the kitchen, the cook scowled and ordered her back to work. Messengers ran back and forth to the lookouts, carrying news of the ship. Darna cut and washed and carried and fetched and looked over her shoulder for the visiting priestess until she was ready to collapse. As soon as she could slip away, she slunk into her sleeping place in the corner of the kitchen. She curled up but sleep was impossible. The cook and her minions worked on into the night, arguing about the foreigners. Darna closed her eyes. Fragments of dreams danced behind her eyelids, dreams of some distant land, barren and empty. The clatter of pots broke her out of her reverie again and again, but still she pretended to sleep. She needed to think.

At around midnight, a horn sounded from the keep's front gates. Darna woke to discover that the servants had deserted the kitchen, leaving only one old woman nodding on her stool by the cooling hearth. Darna limped out the door. She skirted around the keep the long way to avoid the other servants and so she could slip into the receiving yard unnoticed, through a gap in the wall behind a storage shed.

The half-moon was rising by the time the Cereans marched up through the town. The priestesses had prepared their shrine, laying out the cloth on their soft altar. They had bathed and lit lanterns to imitate dragonfire. Townspeople and servants left their beds to gawp at the procession of foreign sailors.

Darna scrambled onto a wall between two of the other young servants. The boy next to her was covered with soot and ash from cleaning the guest-chamber hearths. Across the courtyard, the prince stood on the temple porch. It raised him above the heads of the gathered throng, flanked by his brother on one side and his Cerean tutor on the other. The game warden was nowhere to be seen – probably making pressing his unwelcome attentions on one of the older maids. The prince was old but not ancient. If Darna did have a father, he could be about that age. The visiting priestess in the kitchen claimed to be older than the prince, but her hair was still dark, not yet streaked with white. Maybe she dyed it. The prince wore a permanent sneer. Darna looked away as his eyes turned in her general direction – not that he was looking at her, of course. Servants grouped around the keep's gate. Out in the streets, a baby howled. Darna craned forward, as curious as everyone else to see the approaching foreigners.

The Cerean sailors entered the gates dressed in tunics dyed varying shades of brown, except for the two men in the lead who wore blue. They all stood taller than the Tiadians.

"They're tall," said the boy beside Darna as the first rank entered the castle gates.

"No, they're just wearing tall boots," Darna observed. They also wore slouchy caps and tunics with the arms cut away to reveal broad, muscular shoulders. The procession halted as its leaders bowed to the prince. Torchlight flared along the shrine wall and its curtain rippled, but the priestess – if she was there – waited to reveal herself.

The Cerean in the lead turned to the man behind him and whispered something. The prince whispered something to his tutor, who spoke to the ship's captain. Murmurs ran back through their ranks as the shrine's curtain swung aside. Clouds of incense wafted out, but still the priestess did not appear.

"What are they doing?" asked a girl below Darna. She hopped up as far as she could, but she was too short and the top of the wall was already full.

"They're supposed to go make the offering," Darna said. "The prince is inviting him forward, but he's not moving. There's another Cerean stepping up. I wonder why the captain won't make the offering."

"They're strange, even that tutor. I always thought," said the boy. He pushed a little to get a better look, almost making Darna fall.

"Stop that," complained the girl on Darna's other side.

Darna regained her balance, muttering an apology to her neighbor and pushing back to reclaim her spot.

After many murmured speculations, the priestess emerged clothed in flowing scarves, moving with the grace of the dragons. Instead of admiring her, the Cerean sailors looked down at their boots. Some of them clutched their amulets. A few at the back of the group made warding signs.

The keep guardsmen stiffened, spears ready. The Cerean captain took an offering box from one of the men behind him. There were two boxes, and they argued, pointing at one then the other. In the end, he took the smaller one. The crowd grumbled.

"They don't have dragons in Cerea," said the girl next Darna. "That's what I heard."

"Everyone knows that," Darna said. Legend held that the Cereans had killed their dragons a long time ago. Since then, the land of Cerea had been nearly barren, while Theranis was still lush with the dragons' blessings. In any case, the Cereans didn't have priestesses. The captain looked like he didn't even know how to make a proper offering, something all adult men in Theranis knew and looked forward to. A few of the sailors looked up from the toes of their tall-heeled boots and from their clutched amulets to stare at the priestess as if she were as strange and miraculous to them as a living dragon would be.

The priestess chanted while her two attendants played on a flute and a small drum. Their music mimicked the sound of the dragon's breath, the force of creation. The priestess started moving, inviting that force into her body. Her robes fluttered around her like wings, like the wind.

One Cerean sailor grabbed his crotch. The man beside him jabbed him with an elbow. The priestess beckoned to the captain, and the prince urged him up the steps to the shrine doorway, while the tutor stood back, frowning. The prince's brother smirked. The curtain closed behind the priestess and the Cerean captain.

The people of Tiadun keep whispered to one another as they waited.

After a little while, a different priestess appeared from behind the temple. She wasn't one of the ones who lived at the keep; it was the one who had come to the kitchen earlier to talk to Darna. Why hadn't she waited to speak to the prince at his regular audiences? She could hardly have picked a worse time to approach him. Darna cursed under her breath.

The priestess slipped through the ranks of guardsmen to the prince's side. The prince ignored her while his brother shifted uncomfortably and the Cerean tutor clenched his jaw. She raised her eyebrows, in that way priestesses do, and the prince grudgingly nodded for her to say her piece. The murmur of gossip swelled.

"Priestesses don't like foreigners," said one of the townspeople below Darna.

"Can't say I do, either," another responded.

"... should know better."

The priestess whispered in the prince's ear, turned, and pointed straight at Darna.

"Wha'd ya do this time?" the boy beside her asked.

"I was born," Darna grumbled. "Go away."

The prince shook his head and Darna let out her breath.

The priestess spoke again, more insistently but not loudly enough to be overheard over the subdued sound of the crowd, but the Cerean tutor did hear, and whatever she'd said made his eyes grow wide. He sprang to the prince's side, pressing his palms together and fixing Darna in his gaze. The prince's brother hissed something at the guard beside him. Darna felt the breath stolen from her lungs. The prince looked at her. He looked with a kind of desire, as if this kitchen girl had suddenly turned into some piece of iron with magical powers. Darna could not breathe.

She looked up. Even here on the wall, uncomfortable as it was, she had clear view of the skies, of the stars, or the dragons. That was what she wanted, all she wanted, only to see the dragons fiy, even if it meant a dangerous journey to a distant city. She wanted to prove herself and to be free, free of the keep, its kitchens, and its unseeing towers. She wanted to be in that place she'd heard of in the minstrels' songs, where she could become whatever it was that she was meant to be and where she would still be the dragons' daughter.

"I have to go," she said to herself. Then she turned to the boy beside her. "Help me over the wall."

"Where you going?" he asked.

"If I stay here, I'll hit you!" Darna shook her stick as if the prince and his court weren't all staring at her.

A few of the guardsmen had turned to look in Darna's general direction, too. Just then, the head priestess of the shrine emerged alone. She raised her eyebrows. The prince hurried to her side. He bowed to the priestess then followed her into the temple, looking back over his shoulder toward

Darna, scowling as always.

"Now!" Darna hissed. The boy gave her a boost and she scrambled up, over the tiled roof of the stables. On the far side, she dropped her stick onto the ground, falling after it with a thud. Her leg hurt from the landing, but she could walk and that was all that mattered now. A horse whinnied. She dragged herself to the pasture gate, hoping against all odds to reach the hills unseen and, before too long, Anamat.

§

Chapter 2: Crossing the Hills

*In the beginning, the great dragon Na lay down on the sea,
stretched himself out across its surface and made a land of his
body, nesting the eggs of other dragons all around him. He
hatched them one by one, from Anara to Salara. Forests took
root on Na's slopes, and the moving part of the dragon
retreated to the hollow earth, leaving his body to become the
land itself. One day he will shift the land again. We did not
know that we were living in the time of legends.*

– A letter from Enomae

arna's heart thundered. She heard raised voices from
the courtyard: the priestess, and the prince's brother.
The Cereans babbled. She ran as well as she could.

Somewhere, an owl hooted. Darna struggled up a slope
and into the orchards. She followed the paths until she reached
the woodlands, then walked under the shadow of the trees with
the moonlit road just in sight, all night long. At dawn she
stepped out into the open and looked back. The villages were
waking, roosters crowing, farmers letting their cattle out to
pasture. The keep lay like a discarded pebble beside the bay, its
blue and orange pennants flapping in the wind. Beyond it the
Cerean ship sat at anchor, sails furled tight.

Darna's legs were tired, her ankle sore, and her belly
sharp with hunger. She'd had no time to take bread from the

kitchen. She had nothing but those very few small beads. Ahead of her, the road disappeared into forested hills and the mountains beyond. Darna's stomach growled. She leaned on her stick and thought. A cart clattered along the road above her and she dove into the underbrush, taking refuge in the soft brown leaves under a bush. She held herself as still as she could, waiting until it passed.

It was after midday when she woke. She was thirsty and her stomach growled. At least she had the paring knife that she'd absent-mindedly stuck in her belt the night before. She waited and watched until the sun sank into the hills and torchlight flickered from the keep towers. There was a village nearby. She crept around the backs of its cottages until she found a crust of old bread on a garbage heap and a dipper by a water trough. She ate and drank then she walked on, setting out along the long road to Anamat.

§

Looking back, she wasn't sure how she had survived that first part of the journey. She was hungry all the time. She stayed away from the road in daylight and dodged the villages as much as possible, eating only what she could steal from the fields, unripe berries and bitter raw greens. She searched the edges of farmyards for eggs, and when she found one she poked a hole in it with her knife and sucked out the gooey contents raw. She drank from streams and from wells. She picked from scrap heaps, and she stayed away from the temples.

Every hobbling step brought her closer to Anamat and carried her further from the keep. She slept in short spurts, day and night. She looked for places the dragonlets guarded, which seemed to be safer from wild beasts. Dragonlets were the geniuses of small corners of the world. To Darna, they looked to be about the size of a dog or a large cat. They kept her silent company, hovering at the corners of her vision even when the great dragon was nowhere to be seen.

On the third morning, Darna looked back at the low fields of Tiadun for the last time. They were an irregular patchwork of bright and dark green laced with glistening brooks. Sheep baaed in nearby pastures. A farmer turned his team of oxen as they plowed a field. Even the dirt looked like something a person could eat, not like the rocks of the mountains ahead. She thought of turning back to take what the prince would give her, a position of some power, some subservience. There would be food, but she would never see Tiada again, and never see Anara at all. She spat over her shoulder and forged ahead.

It was harder to find food in the mountains, but once she had passed the border temple she didn't feel the need to hide as much. The herders and bandits who camped in the mountains owed nothing to the prince. She did hide once, when a caravan was passing. She overheard the drivers saying that they would reach civilized lands again by full dark. She trailed them, falling further and further behind and she stubbed her toe midway through the afternoon which slowed her down even more. At dusk, she thought she could see green fields ahead, but she'd found a good overhang to sleep under, so she waited.

In the morning, she had to go through a narrow pass. A dust-encrusted man crouched on a ledge handing over the path.

"Going to Anamat, are you?" he asked.

Darna grunted in response.

"Did your ma give you beads for the journey."

"Got no ma," Darna said.

"Sure, they all say that."

Darna shrugged.

"So you got no beads?" The bandit raised his eyebrows, considered her stick, her torn cloak, her general thinness. It was clear that she didn't have anything worth stealing.

The bandit whistled. Another whistle answered him. "Go on then," he said. "We won't bother you."

A half-dozen bandits emerged from their hiding places above the road, waving to her and talking to each other, waiting until a wealthier traveler came their way.

Then, quite suddenly, she entered Getedun. She'd seen no dragonlets for a whole day, but now one scuttled across the road. It was different, with unfamiliar markings, and unlike the Tiadun dragonlets it shied away from her.

§

Darna entered a farmland bounded by low hills. High, craggy mountains loomed to the west. A crossroads lay ahead, with a signpost and a girl standing still at its center. The girl stayed exactly where she was, turning only a little to look at Darna as she approached. At one corner of the crossroads, a spring burbled and there was a carved stone bench and a shrine beside it. In the shrine sat a plump dragon carved of malachite: Getera. The girl poured out the last drops of water from her water skin into the bowl under the dragon's statue then refilled it with water from the spring and drank.

Darna considered going around the crossroads to avoid the girl, but she was thirsty, and it was only a girl. Millet and wheat sprouted in the fields all around. Smoke blew in from a village a little way to the east, and a bit of roof poked out of the trees in the wooded area off to the north. A farmer rolled his cart down a road beside a stream. The cart creaked away into the distance and the roads were silent again apart from the tap of Darna's stick and the shuffle of her feet.

The crossroads signpost was made of cedar from the mountains, tall and dark red-brown with designs of flowers, writing, and arrows carved on its top. The girl was looking intently at it when Darna came up to her.

"What's that sign say?" Darna asked, her voice cracking a little from disuse.

The girl looked over her shoulder. "Me?" she squeaked.

"Of course you," Darna said. "There's no one else here, is there?"

"You mean I'm not invisible?" the girl asked.

Darna wished she hadn't said anything. People might think that she was odd for staring at the sky, but at least she didn't think she was invisible.

"Where are you going?" the girl asked Darna. Straight, dark hair fell across her face, curling a little at the ends. It didn't even reach her shoulders, which meant she was a servant or a peasant, not a chieftain's daughter or one of the princes' kin. She was taller than Darna and looked like she had been well-fed, though. She was older, too, maybe as much as sixteen, which was nearly old enough to be a priestess. She wasn't one, though, at least not yet. Darna tried to edge past her.

"I'm just going where everyone goes," Darna mumbled. "To Anamat."

"But which way is it? I don't know what the sign says but I heard that Anamat was over three ranges of mountains."

"Like that one?" Darna asked, pointing toward the craggy peaks.

The girl shook her head. "No, that's way I came, from Helanum. I..."

Down the road from Tiadun came a sound like muted, distant thunder.

"Shush!" Darna said.

The girl was listening too. "What is it?" she asked.

"Horses," Darna said. The girl was a fool as well as crazy if she didn't know what a horse sounded like. That, or she came from a village that princes never visited.

"I gotta go," Darna said. "Don't tell them I'm here!" She dove into the bush, flattening herself on the prickly twig-covered ground. The girl followed her.

"What are you doing here?" Darna said. "You don't have to hide from them."

"But why do you?" the girl asked.

"It's just in case. Who are you anyway?" Darna demanded. "Are you going to Anamat?"

"My name is Myril. I came from Helanum, and I'm going to Anamat too." As the horses walked slowly toward them, she told Darna her story, or at least some of it.

§

Myril looked back at her village from Helana's last shrine, at the edge between the green woodlands and the dry hills. The shrine was a simple stone pillar with a niche for an amethyst statue of the dragon. Myril had a pouch of small beads, a loaf of bread stuffed with olives, and two boiled eggs. She had eaten three boiled eggs the day before, on her way up from the village. The people at the market said that it was three days' walk to the next valley, if all went well. Myril left a piece of the bread and a bead at Helana's shrine then stepped into Na's country, leaving behind everything and everyone she'd ever known and loved. If only she could have stayed, but her sister needed to stay more than she did.

As she entered the mountains, Myril thought of the children's stories about how the dragons had made the land. Na's crags cut a hard line against the ice-blue sky and pines loomed over the rocky path. Myril's feet hurt, and she longed to be home, and not alone. Until the day before, she'd always been with her mother or her younger sister. Her sister was sickly and simple-minded. She wasn't strong or clever enough to survive the journey to Anamat, even though custom dictated that younger daughters and sons should leave their villages and go to the city, or at least to the keep town. Myril had gone in her place, and she had chosen Anamat over the keep.

Exhaustion and homesickness dragged at her, but she kept walking. Her footsteps echoed in the silent, deserted pass. She ate the last of her bread and drained her water skin. The only people she saw on the mountain trail were a pair of guardsmen arguing over the last drink in their fiask and a man with a mangy donkey, slouching toward Helanum. She hid from them, and once they'd passed she followed the track on toward Getedun. A few birds fiew overhead, not enough to ease her loneliness.

Myril didn't know the names of the coarse herbs growing in that rocky landscape, or which were good to eat. As the shadows lengthened and the air chilled, she began to look at the small, coarse seedlings and wondered if they were worth prying from those rocks. Some of them looked a little like the greens a donkey might graze on, but none were the herbs that Myril knew from her mother's cooking pot. She found no streams, no water of any kind. The snow was sparse and far away, up steep and treacherous-looking slopes. Myril was tired. She wanted water and food. She wanted to sit down by the fire and stir the pot, to see if the kittens were hunting mice yet, to help her sister plait her hair, to mend a skirt. Could she go home, or be a servant in the keep? There she might at least see her family again.

The sky darkened ahead as if it might rain. Myril wished

she could find a shrine or a cave to shelter in for the night, a
corner in which she might imagine herself at home instead of
in a barren, exposed wilderness.

Just as the setting sun touched the peaks above with rose-
colored light, Myril glimpsed blue between the rocks ahead, a
tiny lake of melted snow. She climbed over the rocks heading
straight toward it as if it might disappear if she went around by
the path. She bent her head to the lake and drank like an
animal, then with cupped hands. Finally she filled her water
skin with the cold, clear water.

She closed her eyes, breathing a prayer of thanks to
Helana. It was what she had always done, but now she had
crossed into Na's realm. When she opened her eyes, she saw a
familiar-looking fungus peering out from behind a rock. She
went to look more closely. Yes, it was just like a kind that she
knew from the woods. She also found a rocky overhang where
some hermit or traveler had cleared the sharp pebbles away to
make a sleeping place. She gorged herself on the mushroom,
which tasted more bitter than she thought it would, most likely
because she had no fire on which to cook it. In any case, she
was too tired to think of such things.

Myril slept. At first, she did not dream. The stars wheeled
above in their accustomed orbits. The moon rose, casting the
landscape into sharp relief of gray on black. In her dreams, the
rocks began to move away from her, leaving her on a limitless,
barren plain with only that small lake before her. Somewhere
in the distance, something screeched. A hawk? A cat? A
dragon? Whatever it was, it woke her.

The lake swam in moonlight, but instead of reflecting the
night sky above, it glowed a pale orange color, as if it were a
rising moon bound to the earth. Behind Myril, the rocks
moved again, prodding her toward the water against her will.

"Come," a voice said. That was the dragon. "Have you been unfaithful to me, priestess?"

"No," she breathed. She couldn't manage to say that she was no priestess, only a very young woman.

"It is the other who may betray us. See that she doesn't."

Myril turned to look behind her, half expecting to see a person emerge from those rocks, but as she turned the dragon seized her by the scruff of the neck and pulled her into the glowing lake.

The shock of cold water hit her, stealing her breath. A moment later, all was dry and warm. The dragon Na stood before her in his lair, his form made of smoke and stone. A tendril of that smoke wrapped around Myril, taking her mind with it as it poured into the earth. For a flash of a moment, she saw the bones of the land laid out in every detail, then the cavern below, where all the dragons meet, then nothing.

Myril woke at dawn on the shore of the lake, cold to the bone and wet. She felt sick. The mushrooms churned in her stomach. At least she wasn't hungry. The lake looked ordinary again in the daylight, just an icy reflecting pool ringed with hardy plants and wasteland. She clutched her knees to her chest and shivered, closing her eyes, trying to recall what the dragon had shown her. Even then, so soon after waking, the details slipped away.

As the sun rose, a hermit priestess came down from some hidden place higher up. She wore the rags of what had once been a ceremonial gown; her hair was knotted and flew in all directions. Her face was only slightly softer than the landscape and as full of deep shadows.

Myril opened her mouth to speak, but the priestess made a sharp cutting motion to silence her, then pressed her lips together with one hand and pointed a shaking finger at Myril.

Then the priestess pointed to the lake and gestured again.
Though she used no words, Myril understood that the hermit
was under a vow of silence, and that it had something to do
with Na. Perhaps she should stay silent, too. Myril sensed that
Na still lay under the surface. She shivered all the way through
her bones.

The things that Myril had seen in the lake, the simple but
unheard-of feat of seeing Na himself, had changed something
in her. She didn't relish the solitude any more than she had the
day before, but it was as if her desire to go back home to see
the people she'd loved all her life had died in that lake. She
was dragon-touched. Now that Na had marked her as the
dragons' own and she knew that she would not escape the
temples entirely, and she dreaded that fate without
understanding why.

The hermit priestess ushered Myril back onto the path
through the still-swimming landscape. She gestured that Myril
should stay to the path, that the rocks would hold their places
unless she went astray. If she did step off the path, then Na's
bones would bury her. Myril wished she had someone to walk
with, to keep her from drifting off into another lake and falling
into that realm again. She had seen Na. No one ever saw Na.

She walked through that day, with her mind still half full
of the strange sight of the dragons' realms. By midday the
mountains were softening into forested hills. She passed a pair
of travelers and instead of hiding she walked on, but they
didn't seem to see her. The wind went through her. The next
morning, she reached the crossroads.

§

Darna and Myril lay under the bush as the prince's men
approached. The men had no hounds, only horses, but those
were frightening enough. In the open fields they could never

run fast enough to escape those hooves, though in the forest they might have a chance. Myril stole a glance at her new traveling companion. She had left pieces out of her own story, and the other girl would certainly do the same. She could see that Darna would be easy to spot, with her flaming red hair, her staccato gestures, and her stick. Lying there on her stomach, in the shadow of the bushes, she looked as if she would be able to walk as well as anyone, but on the road she'd leaned heavily on the stick. One of her legs *was* a little shorter and thinner than the other, but only slightly.

The three guardsmen, riding heavy-hoofed horses, paused at the crossroads. A young squire rode pillion behind one of them. He jumped down to fill leather buckets with water.

"She must be on the Anamat road," said one of the guardsmen.

Another, the eldest of the three, shook his head. "She's weak. She'd never go so far."

"We can't have missed her," said the last of them.

The squire looked around, as if noting the number of hiding places around them, even in the fields.

"In case we have, we should tell Getedun's men. They'll hold her for us, if she's still in those mountains."

The horses drank noisily as the guardsmen readjusted their livery.

"To Getedun keep, then?" the middle guardsman said.

The men nodded, except for the squire who was busy gathering the buckets and folding them into the saddlebags, now that the horses had drunk.

"There's a good tavern a short ride down the road to Anamat," the youngest of the guardsmen said.

"And a better one on the way to the keep. We can stop at the one you like on our way to Anamat, after we send out the alert here."

The squire remounted and the guardsmen rode away.

Darna exhaled. Quietly.

"Why are they looking for you?" Myril asked.

Darna sat up and brushed herself off. "Who says they're looking for me?"

Myril just shrugged.

"I guess it's obvious," Darna admitted, "what with me hiding like this, and being weak, like they were saying."

"You don't look weak," Myril said.

Darna pushed her way out of the bush and tapped one foot with her stick. "I limp. Can't walk right. The bone's all knit together wrong."

Before Myril's sister was born, her mother had been apprenticed to the village midwife. She was still called on, from time to time, to help with healings if the midwife was busy, and the case wasn't so grave that it needed a healer priestess. Myril had learned some of the healing arts from her by listening and watching as she helped.

"May I look at it?" she asked.

"I don't see why you'd want to," Darna said, but she pulled her tunic up and stuck her leg out. The bottom part of her right leg looked a little thinner than her left. The knees were the same. She had a lumpy part on her right thigh, where the bone seemed to have turned.

"How did it break?" Myril asked.

"Boar ran me down," Darna said. She looked over her shoulder, down the road to Getedun keep. "I'd better get back into the woods."

"I'll come with you," Myril said, "but I'm hungry."

"So am I," said Darna. "But I got three eggs this morning. I've got two left. Want one?"

She extended an egg to Myril, a duck's egg. Myril turned it over and tried to crack it on the stone bench beside the water spout.

"Don't do that!" Darna said.

"It's not raw, is it?" Myril asked.

"Of course it is. They don't lay 'em cooked. I'll show you," Darna said. "I figured it out days ago." She tunneled back into the bush and emerged a moment later with two sharp twigs. She took one, jabbed it into her egg, swirled it around, then drank the contents.

"I'd rather have it cooked," Myril said.

Darna shrugged. "It's better than nothing."

"It is," Myril conceded, "and better than..." She looked back at the mountains, thinking of the mushroom she'd eaten the night before. Her dreams had felt more real than waking life, but the dragons looked as real to her as the land did, so she knew that most would say it was an illusion.

She shook herself out of her reverie. "I wonder if we can get something cooked, maybe from that tavern on the Anamat road?" The smoke from the place in the pines up ahead promised cooking fires, pots of stew, or even bread.

"You, maybe," Darna said. "I gotta stick to the forest. Raid a farmer's yard for eggs when I can. Can't be seen. They'd find me."

Myril looked at her closely. "Why are they looking for you?" she asked again.

Darna looked at her feet. "Maybe I stole something?" she said.

It was a weak excuse. What could a girl steal that would be worth the expense of sending three horsemen after her on a quarter-moon's journey? The traces of her dream, or whatever it had been, echoed as if hinting at some hidden truth beneath

Darna's words, a truth she wasn't even aware of as she constructed her small lie. "You haven't stolen anything, yet," Myril said.

"It doesn't matter," Darna said. "Maybe I'll see you in Anamat." She struck out, veering away from the road, out into the stubbly fields, toward the woods and harder walking.

"Wait!" Myril said.

Darna hesitated.

"I'll come with you," Myril said. "We're both going to Anamat. We should go together, watch each other's backs, help each other find food."

"I can make it there alone," Darna said. "I know I can. I have to."

"I need company," Myril pleaded. She didn't want to face the mountains alone again. She would go mad if visions of Na stalked her in those hills with no one to pull her out of them.

Darna looked down the road to Getedun keep, where the dust of the horses' passing had already settled, leaving only their hoof prints and a pile of steaming manure.

"All right," she said at last, "but I won't blame you if you change your mind."

"I won't," Myril promised. "Now let's see if I can buy some bread, or even a cooked egg."

"I haven't got any beads if that's what you're after," Darna said as they set out along the road.

"I have a couple of beads," Myril said. "What's your name?"

"I don't want to tell you and it doesn't matter, anyway. Let's just walk a while, first."

"It's lonely, walking alone," Myril said, "and there are bandits. It's still a long way to Anamat. We could take turns keeping watch at night. I'd feel safer."

"With me? No, you wouldn't. I'd just slow you down, see? I'm a cripple."

"I'm not in a hurry."

"Well, just for today, then," Darna said. "But if I slow you down, go on ahead."

"Which way should we go?" Myril asked.

"Well, the guardsmen said this was the Anamat road, and they went the other way, so let's go," Darna said. "Besides, they said there's a tavern up ahead. Could you go in and buy us some bread?"

"I don't really like taverns," Myril said. "I heard that you can get bread from temples, but I haven't passed any yet."

"Neither have I, thanks be to Na," Darna said.

Myril shivered.

"I think I'd rather go into a tavern," Darna said.

Myril said nothing more until they reached the tavern. Shoulders square, she went in and soon emerged with a dusty loaf of bread as well as all her beads. That night, they found a place to sleep under an ancient, spreading rhododendron. When Myril had fallen asleep, Darna slipped out from under their shared blanket, taking her cloak with her. The moon shone a dappled light through the leaves and a warm breeze blew in from the south. Darna tip-toed to the edge of the bush and was about to slip through the wall of leaves when Myril woke then rolled over as if she'd been only stirring in her sleep.

Darna still wasn't sure of her. She stepped out from under the leafy boughs. There, sitting on a rock and blocking her path, sat a sullen dragonlet. It said nothing – Darna never actually heard dragonlets speak – but it was clearly standing in her way, telling her to go back. Darna sighed and went back to lie down again beside Myril.

§

Darna hadn't been looking for a companion, but Myril was quiet and good at finding food. On the second day, she cooked up a bitter concoction and made Darna wash her hair in it, turning the red curls into dull brown locks so that the guardsmen would have one less thing to know her by. Myril probably could have found enough for both of them to eat even without the piles of bread left out for scrapplings at the taverns and roadside shrines. They walked all the way through Getedun and Galamun together, up to the next ridge of mountains. Darna wasn't sure why Myril stayed with her.

They were climbing through a mountainside pasture when Myril gasped: "Look!"

Darna saw a dragon swoop up into the open sky, shining like the evening star. "She's beautiful," Darna said, forgetting for a moment to pretend not to see.

"And a good sign, too." Myril smiled. "And you see them, too?"

"See what?" Darna said.

"Getera, Tiada, Helana, maybe even Anara."

Darna shook her head, but Myril knew if she hadn't guessed already and she didn't seem to mind. Would there be others in Anamat who could see dragons? Darna had always hoped that there would be, but now that it was so close she wasn't sure any more. She would feel too exposed. Could they keep her secret? She glanced back, but the dragon had flown on, leaving a dragonlet standing beside the road to watch over them.

As they came down from the hills, the city's rooftops glistened like a mound of red and blue jewels, dotted here and there with gilded temple spires, shining in the sun. It was laced with canals which looked like liquid opal from the distance. It was a living being, a work of art, far more than just a collection of human dwellings and places of commerce. Anamat sat on the shore of a turquoise bay with green fields and orchards spread around it all the way to its thickly wooded hills.

Darna stopped in her tracks. "There it is," she breathed. "There it is."

Myril's hands trembled even as she marveled at the sight. "I guess we'd better go on," she gulped.

"Better?" Darna said. "Of course we'll go on!" She laughed and hurried ahead until a pain in her leg slowed her down and she looked over her shoulder one last time, back toward Tiadun. The priestess and the prince's men had not caught her yet. She prayed that Anara's valley would keep her safe. Myril ran to catch up.

As they walked down the valley the road grew busier with people on foot, donkeys, and lumbering oxen. A messenger on horseback bearing brown and gold livery galloped past. Bread was laid out at the shrines for passing scrapplings but the villagers shooed them along if they lingered.

The valley was too wide to cross in that afternoon, so they rested in an orchard for the night. Sheep grazed lazily around apple trees and bees buzzed through the branches. Darna breathed it all in, peaceful in the purple evening light.

"It's nice here," she said, thinking how much better the city would be.

Myril nodded, her eyes closed lightly as she listened and smelled. "I could stay right here."

"Well, I couldn't. Anamat, the city. That's the place to be."

"I don't know anything about it," Myril said. "I've never even been to the keep town, just to the market in the next village down the road. There were so many people there I couldn't hear... couldn't hear the dragonlets."

"You know, it's not normal, hearing dragonlets," Darna said.

Myril shook her head. "In the legends, they say that most people did in the old days. I never met anyone else who saw them until I met you, except for a wild woman, an old priestess who lived in the mountains."

"I don't like people to know that." Darna worked her mouth around, looking for the right words. "When I was young, something happened to me and maybe I saw dragons, or maybe not, but the people who took me to the castle told the priestesses that I'd had visions of them. The priestesses didn't care, they didn't believe it and they laughed at me. Besides, I don't know if I really see them anyway."

"But you do," Myril said.

"It doesn't matter if I do," Darna said. "Don't tell anyone. I don't want them thinking I'm crazy. Being a cripple is bad enough."

"I won't say anything, then," Myril promised. "Let's just go to sleep. We'll be in the city by tomorrow night."

Darna spread out her cloak. She had good soft grass and moss to lie on, and she should have fallen asleep right away, but instead she lay watching the apple blossoms bob and sway in the night breeze for a long time, hoping to dream of Anamat.

§

Chapter 3: The Walls of Anamat

Let these walls make of the city one house, a house of
learning and of craft, a temple and a shelter for Anara and
all the dragons' children.

– The Chronicles of Theranis

They reached the western gate to Anamat city late the following morning. The gray granite walls were taller than most houses and they sparkled here and there with brighter stones. Along the top, a guardsman paced. In the market outside, vendors covered their wares and turned their backs to the road.

"What's going on?" Darna asked one of them. "Aren't you still selling?"

"Not now," said the farmer, without looking up. "It's midday. Gate's closing." He rolled his cart a little distance away from the thoroughfare.

"Closing?" Darna echoed. "But why?" Somewhere inside the city, a bell rang, its tone so pure that it seemed to carry out to infinity, as if it would not fade with distance, though she hadn't heard it the day before. As it rang, all movement and commerce stopped. The people in the market closed their eyes and bowed their heads until the sound faded. Even the dogs seemed to be listening for the sound of Anara's wings cutting through the air overhead.

As soon as the bell stopped ringing, it all picked up where it had left off. The vendors and travelers moved toward their midday cook-fires, the donkeys yawned. Darna sprang into action, too. She stumbled as fast as she could through the last stretch of the market. The massive city gates, made of oak as thick as a man, slammed closed a hand's breadth in front of her. Watchmen barred the gate from the inside as Darna threw herself against it, beating her fists on the solid planks and bolts.

"Get away, scrappling!" one of the watchmen ordered. "It opens again after midday."

Darna's fists fell to her side. She'd been in such a hurry to get to the city that she hadn't let Myril stop for food all morning. They'd only eaten a few old, withered apples in the orchard where they'd slept. Myril rested a hand on her shoulder and led her away.

"Come on," she said soothingly. "Let's sit over here. It won't be long." She led Darna behind the row of vendors to a shady spot by the wall. There was a log there, not a bad place to sit except for the ants.

"It's not fair," Darna said, brushing an ant off her foot and shaking out her tunic.

"Well, I suppose it's what they always do," Myril said. "Besides, they said that the gates would open again after midday. Where you came from, did the keep gates close at midday?" Myril asked.

"I suppose they did," Darna said. "It's just... I just wanted to walk right in."

"You will," Myril said.

"It's like you don't understand!" Darna said. "Do you even want to be in Anamat?"

Myril shook her head. "It's noisy, but... but this is what I had to do."

Darna shook her head and looked away. The skies were clear and empty, not even any birds in the midday sun, just the dull stir of flies and dust near the ground. The city wall wound around keeping them out.

Darna fidgeted. "Look, I've got to go pee," she said. "I'll be back."

Myril nodded, still gazing back toward the southern hills. Darna picked up her stick and checked to be sure that her pocket was still firmly attached to her belt. She wandered around a bend in the wall and found a secluded spot behind the next watchtower.

She squatted down. When she was done, she noticed a small stream coming out from behind the next tower. She went down to it to wash her hands and had a poke around the culvert where it flowed under the walls. The tunnel was blocked by an iron grille. She kept poking until something moved – a dragonlet. Its eyes shone laughingly at her and it ducked around the grille, showing her a space where moments before she had seen only stone.

Not all dragons had dragonlets. Some, like Na, kept themselves to themselves, but Anara was so bountiful that she filled her land with reflections of herself, small dragon forms tracing her veins in the earth and flitting over the surface. Like the great dragons, they were invisible to most people. Before leaving the keep, Darna hadn't seen a dragonlet of Tiada in almost a year. she'd even begun to wonder if they still existed, or if she'd imagined them.

She climbed out of the culvert and back toward Myril, but as she rounded the corner she heard an unfamiliar child's voice. Myril was talking to two strangers, a girl and a boy. The girl was radiant – both of them were. The girl had midnight

black hair and alabaster skin. She sat perfectly straight, as if
something were lifting her from within. The boy was golden-
brown, warm like a fire, drawing Darna closer, but she
hesitated.

"My friend should be back soon," Myril said.

Darna stepped back toward the culvert. She looked for
the dragonlet and the gap in the wall, but it was gone as if it
had never been there at all.

She returned to the shaded log.

"Do you know how to get in?" the boy asked Myril.

"They're going to open the gates after midday."

"Looks like after midday to me already," Darna
complained, coming up on them quickly, as if the boy might
disappear like the dragonlet had. His eyes were brown but
bright and he was perfect in every proportion. He began to
smile at Darna but stopped with the welcome half-formed and
turned to the girl beside him.

"This is Iola," he said. "She's ridden a dragon."

Iola blushed. She leaned into the boy and gazed up at
him, all but fluttering her lashes. She clung to him.

"And I'm Thorat," the boy said. "I came from Onarun,
but I suppose none of that matters now."

"No, it doesn't. Darna." She stuck out her hand but the
boy only nodded to her. She sat back down on the log while
Myril asked the too-beautiful Iola how it was that she had
ridden a dragon.

They passed a water skin around and Iola told her story
as they waited for the gates to open, blushing and mumbling as
she spoke.

§

Rain dripped onto her blanket through the shed roof. Iola
rolled her bedding into a dry patch at one end of the loft and

lowered herself down among the goats. She took her cloak and fished her comb out from the straw of her sleeping loft then tip-toed away from the sleeping house. She passed the cottages at the end of the village and followed the path to the spring.

Iola had been to the market at Teganum keep once, the year before, but apart from that she had never ventured beyond the village and its patch of woodlands. A thousand people lived clustered around Teganum keep. She hadn't known that there were so many people in the world, though she'd heard that there were a hundred times more in the city of Anamat.

When she came home from that market, her parents had made her live in the goat shed. They acted as if they'd brought her home by mistake and forgotten where to put her. Iola was old enough to go out and herd the goats, weed the garden, or collect firewood, but they never asked her to do any of those things. They treated her as if she were only in the way.

Iola settled down on the spring's mossy bank to comb out her hair in the lingering drizzle. Her reflection wavered in the water. If she waited quietly by the spring, and maybe hummed a little when no one could hear, sometimes Tegana would fly down from the mountain heights and roost in the forest nearby. Years ago, only once, she'd run home to tell her mother that she'd seen the dragon.

"Don't frighten the babies!" her mother had scolded. "And don't lie!"

"But I did see her! And Tegana's not frightening," Iola objected.

Her mother had looked at her as if she were some kind of dragon-spawn herself and handed her the peelings to dump beside the garden.

The rain slowed to a mist as dawn progressed into

morning. Iola sat by the spring, wondering when the others would wake and come to fill their buckets. She slipped into the undergrowth to wait in case Tegana fiew by. She climbed into the boughs of a shadowy beech tree, hiding in its branches.

After a little while, she heard footsteps coming up the trail and the clatter of water pails.

"Setting off in the rain like this!" It was her mother's voice.

"Do you think she's finally gone?" Iola's older sister asked.

"She's not in bed," Iola's mother said, "but I wouldn't count on it until tomorrow. You know how she is."

"Sneaking out of work," her sister complained.

"It's about time she hied off to that city," Iola's mother said. They reached the spring and set their buckets down on the board beside the pool. Iola's sister filled her buckets. "If she doesn't go soon," her mother continued, "I don't know if we'll be able to save enough grain for your wedding this harvest time."

"Again? You promised me. This year." Her sister heaved her buckets onto the board while the other two were filling. "I'll tell her she has to go."

"No, don't do that!" her mother said. "She must go on her own. If she can't figure out that much, she'll never make it out of the valley, though goodness knows you only have to follow the path. Ah, that girl is so lazy! The sooner she goes to the temples, the better."

"The temples? But they're supposed to be like palaces! What would they want with Iola?"

Iola sat very still, willing them not to see her, if they even bothered to look. Her pulse pounded in her ears.

"Why?" Iola's mother responded as if it should be

obvious. "Well, she's a pretty enough girl. Better them than us. Come on." Iola heard the board creak as her mother and sister lifted their buckets again and set off on the path back to the village. Iola clung on to her branch and sobbed.

§

After the last straggler filled her buckets at the spring, Iola went down to the water and washed the tears from her face. As she drank from the wooden spout, she noticed that someone, certainly not her mother, had left a loaf of yesterday's bread on the board. She would need it. Maybe one of their neighbors had left it when word had spread that she was gone. Everyone knew that she liked to sit by the spring and look at the reflections in the pool, and most of them had been kind enough to her until the past year.

Iola took the bread and put it under her cloak. The sky was clearing. Up the hill, beyond the spring, a blessing shimmered through the leaves: Tegana's wing. It glistened, half a shade brighter that the green of the surrounding leaves.

Tegana's head swung around to watch her approach. The dragon's eyes rolled toward her, their molten gold shifting as she gazed at Iola.

So you're coming to us at last. The dragon seemed to smile.

"I-I-I don't know," Iola stammered. "Coming to where?"

To Anara's place, Tegana said. *You all go there.* Tegana's head drooped a little. *Spend the night at my temple, that way.* Tegana pointed her wing up the hill, toward a little gap in the ridgeline, a pass.

Tegana took a step toward Iola, and Iola reached out her hand to stroke the dragon's neck. She'd seen Tegana before, but never this close, never speaking to her or touching her, at least not since she was very small.

"Is it far?" Iola asked.

Ah, you're a real one. Tegana leaned her head over Iola and reached one clawed leg around her. *Hold on.*

Iola was enveloped by the dragon. It happened so quickly that she didn't have time to panic. In the distance, she heard the stroke of an axe on a tree trunk. Tegana's flesh cooled at the sound, and Iola shivered. With a whoosh, the dragon bolted up through the trees and into the sky.

The dragon rose above the trees and the earth spread away below. The village was behind them and out of sight already. They arced over the ridgeline. Down in the distance, Iola saw a bulky stone building jutting up from a rocky hill in the middle of a cultivated valley. A gleam of sun on metal caught her eye: Teganum keep. Tegana skirted the valley, flying low next to the hills. Iola felt her snarl and hiss in the direction of the keep.

That prince grows greedy. Tegana's nostrils flared, exhaling an acrid smoke. *There will be another soon.* Iola coughed and blinked as the dragon's smoke swept past her. The dragon held her close with a net of energy that cradled her like a baby. Iola hadn't felt so safe and warm in as long as she could remember, even though she was careening through the sky like a bird. She could not feel fear, but only wonder and delight in this sudden flight. They flew over the trees into another, smaller valley, and Tegana plummeted into a clearing.

The feel of stony ground beneath her feet woke Iola back to her everyday senses. Tegana released her and backed away, sidling toward a small cave, a gateway in the hill behind her. Iola held out the loaf of bread she'd found by the spring. She had to give the dragon something, and it was the only thing she had. Tegana's head looped down and she took the bread with her sharp teeth. The teeth were translucent and glowing and the bread disappeared in a puff of smoke, like incense.

The dragon nodded once to Iola then folded her wings back and slipped into the earth. Iola caught a glimpse of the tunnel beyond, a narrow way into the dragons' realm. Its brightness lingered as the dragon faded down, sending back hints and scents of that other place. As the gate closed, the dragonfire quieted until it looked almost like an ordinary cave mouth except for the faded traces of offerings hanging from the branches around it.

Iola stood in a clearing in the forest, not unlike the land near the spring in her village. People came here, leaving offerings for the dragons that most of them could not see. Sometimes they spoke as if they didn't believe that the dragons were even real, but the dragon had carried her halfway across the province. She hadn't known such a thing was possible. For all the frightening childhood tales she'd heard of dragons, she'd never heard of a person, however small, being carried away by them and living to tell the tale. There were other tales, of course, tales of whole flocks of sheep consumed in a night, or cows' milk gone dry when a village neglected its offerings, but the people of Iola's village gave their part in season, unthinking.

What was it that Tegana had said? Something about spending the night in her temple? Iola sat down at the edge of the clearing and closed her eyes, wishing that she could have followed the dragon into that other world under the earth.

She must have slept, because when she looked up, the sky was tinged with sunset colors. Someone had left flowers and bread at the altar in front of a small carving of Tegana. The statue was much finer than the wooden idol in the village shrine. The flowers wilted against the stone. Beyond the altar, a path wound down into the forest. Iola hurried along it, anxious at every crack and snap of twig, every rustle in the darkening forest. Her stomach complained, and she began to feel a little faint. She hadn't eaten since the night before, and that had been a thin meal.

By the time she reached cultivated land the almost full moon was rising. The path widened into a broad processional way, leading to a shining white building as large as Teganum keep itself. The path took her to a gate in its wall. Weeds sprouted there, as if it hadn't been opened in a long time. Iola followed the wall around to a well-traveled road in front of the building where she found a gateway into a welcoming courtyard. Iola looked once over her shoulder as she entered the temple, uncertain of her welcome. Across the valley, Teganum keep perched on its rocky hill. Somewhere beyond it was her village, but she would not look back there. How could she mourn that place, now that she had flown with the dragon?

§

"The priestesses at the temple told me to go to Anamat," Iola said, "so here I am."

Iola's story should have been impossible, but no one doubted her sincerity. Could she really have spoken to and flown with a dragon? Seeing Tiada in the distance had been so rare and strange that Darna had hidden it for fear of being mocked, but it was nothing compared to what Iola had done, what she could do. Iola's family and village had driven her away, and why wouldn't they? She was more than a little dragon-touched. Darna had hidden her ability to see the dragons. After all, she lived in the world of humankind. Iola was different. It was as if she couldn't imagine any world other than the dragons.

Thorat didn't care that Iola was crazy, either. He gazed worshipfully at her, as if her vision of the dragons were something to be revered, as if he, too, could live in the story she told. He believed her with every pulse of his being.

Myril shook herself as if trying to wake up from a dream. She reached for Iola's hand. Thorat stopped her.

"I'm sorry," he said. "I know that you mean her no harm –"

"Of course she doesn't," Iola said. She looked into Myril's eyes. "You have fiown with them too?" she asked.

Myril looked confused, and she was still sitting gape-mouthed when the bells rang out a moment later. The bells, the clear, vibrant bells, filling the air and throwing open the gates, saving Myril from answering Iola's question.

Darna jumped up. Thorat and Iola startled back a bit when they saw her stick fiy up, but she ignored them. She charged to the gate, past the farmers' carts lining the road, past the mercenary guardsmen coming in from the provinces, past the lame goats and packs of firewood bound for the city's kitchens. Myril and the others struggled to catch up.

"Wait," Myril said. "Let's go together."

Darna shrugged her hand off, straining forward with the throng. Her foot got tromped on. She kept her pocket tucked under her belt with its one last bead hidden deep in its folds. Thorat and Iola followed with Myril – they all looked a little lost. Darna paused. She didn't know where she would go once the gates opened, either. She let them close in around her.

The tide of traffic carried them in through the gates. The watchman who had ordered Darna away earlier looked down his nose as they passed. Darna scowled back at him. Thorat strode in with his head high, Iola and Myril close behind him, shrinking away from the crowds. It was a little like the market days at the keep, only there was so much more. She prepared to plunge ahead.

"I want to go to the temple." Iola's voice was quiet, but as clear as the bells.

Darna didn't want to go to the temple, but they would have bread, and she was hungry. She looked around for a hint of direction. The city walls blocked the way behind them, and in front and to the sides was such a crush of buildings that Darna could only tell where the streets lay by the movement of the crowd across the square. The shops surrounding the square were two or three stories tall, with stone walls variously plain and whitewashed. Their tiled roofs rested on polished wood beams with painted ends. The carved and colored shutters of the dwellings above the shops opened to let in the afternoon breeze.

Someone pushed them from behind, a city watchman. "Move along!" he barked.

Thorat looked back at him. "Where's the temple?" he asked.

The watchman shrugged. "Which one? You're too young for it, anyway." He laughed. "Move along."

"Which temple?" Iola echoed as they were edged out of the center of the traffic.

"There's more than one, then," Myril said.

They were standing right up against a shop as its shutters swung open, folding back into a clean-swept room floored with polished tiles. The shop had cakes and sweets in baskets and on shelves, more than Darna had seen anywhere, even on a feast night from far away, and there they were, within arm's reach.

The baker seemed amused. He looked at them each in turn and raised his left eyebrow. "Welcome to Anamat, green scrapplings," he said. He held his lips tightly together and his eyes squinted a bit, as if he were holding back a laugh.

"Move along or I'll fine you for disrupting commerce," said another city watchman, coming up from behind them.

"Fine us what?" Thorat wondered under his breath.

"They're not disrupting anything yet," the baker said, waving the watchman away.

The watchman frowned at him, shrugged, and moved on.

Darna kept staring at the cakes. She couldn't help it.

"Where is the temple?" Iola asked.

The baker regarded her a moment before answering. "You'll be wanting the harbor temple, or Ara's Landing as it's properly known. They have the best bread – apart from what mine would be, if I had a dragonfire oven." He chuckled. "Easiest way – follow that street down to the harbor, go along the shore, to the left, until you see the processional way. Ask there how to get around the back, and go tomorrow morning. They only give out bread in the mornings."

The baker gave Thorat a packet of crisp pancakes, slightly burned around the edges, and pointed them on their way.

"Let's go then," Darna said, forging ahead. She barely thanked the baker, only turning to give him a nod as she dove into the throng.

The other three struggled to catch up as the crowds closed in around them. Iola clutched Thorat's cloak. They just managed to keep Darna in sight as she battered her way through the crowd.

Iola craned her neck up to the sky as she followed, looking for Anara.

The street widened ahead as it entered the next square, an intersection bordered on one side by a moss-banked canal. The crowd mingled and milled across it, going every which way, confusing even Darna's sense of direction. She picked a current of foot traffic, hoping that it would carry them to the harbor. She followed it down a narrow lane, through a maze of stores and houses and workshops, down across the canal and through some more streets. They emerged at the end of the street, near a long dock stretching out into the harbor. The sandy shore was less crowded than the streets. Darna spotted a log to sit on and started toward it.

"How does she know where she's going?" Iola asked Myril. Then she noticed that they'd reached the shore. She stopped in her tracks, marveling at something on the horizon.

It took the rest of them a moment longer, but then they all saw Anara with her wings spread over the ships' masts, soaring across the sky and disappearing into the horizon.

Iola still stared wistfully toward the spot where Anara had disappeared. Darna shuffled impatiently. The day was slipping away.

"A temple!" Iola gasped.

Darna followed her gaze. It was a small shrine, a single room tucked behind an arch of carved wings. A priestess stood there, robed in red gauze, regarding the crowds impassively. Her kohl-black eyelashes fluttered and her lips shone red with glaze. She was one of those priestesses who offered petitioners little more than common coupling, a shadow of the true rite. She seemed to have abandoned all but the barest trappings of devotion as she measured the passing men with her gaze.

Iola moved toward the shrine, drifting sideways across the road, her eyes locked on the dragon's statue in the shadow of the arch.

"Be careful!" Myril said. Iola didn't hear her. People stepped aside for Iola, who moved as if she were in a trance.

Thorat darted after her, grasping at her arm. "We're going to find bread to go along with these pancakes."

"I'm hungry, too," Darna said.

"But this is a temple," Iola said, shaking Thorat off. "They'll have bread here."

They weren't looking at that sort of temple. The curvaceous priestess had just sighted a sailor.

"Come," she said in a singsong voice. "Make your offering to the goddess-dragon of Anamat!"

The sailor looked around, as if to be sure she wasn't talking to anyone else, then looked her over before moving closer. Iola cut in front of him.

"Child!" the priestess chided. "Do be careful where you walk!"

"But isn't this a temple?" Iola asked. Thorat and Myril hesitated, not wanting to haul Iola away against her will, but not sure how to make clear what she could not see for herself. Darna rolled her eyes and began to walk away.

"To be sure it is." The priestess smiled weakly. "But we offer no shelter here. We are only a small sisterhood..." The sailor, annoyed, had turned away. "Sir! If you please?"

"But – " Iola persisted.

"Come!" Myril caught her arm. "Let's go find the temple the baker told us about. They'll have bread there."

The priestess, who was pretty enough when she smiled, scowled at the sight of the sailor disappearing around the bend in the road. She held her temper in check until Myril and Thorat herded Iola away.

"Stupid green knees!" the priestess muttered as they left.

"I don't understand," Iola complained. "Surely all temples – "

"No, some are different," Thorat said as he led her away.

"It's true," Myril said, taking Iola's other arm. Back at the shrine, the priestess was rearranging her robes, preparing to lure in another petitioner.

They scurried to catch up with Darna who slowed as they reached another marketplace, an open square facing the harbor. Along the shore, sail-menders and barrel-makers worked in sheds and warehouses stood with their doors open to let in the afternoon light. A cluster of people stood by the low sea wall to watch a girl singing. Darna made a move to join them, but Myril tugged on her sleeve.

"Can we go?" she said.

"All right," Darna sighed. She looked over her shoulder as they walked away. As they reached the edge of the square, a woman with a market basket lurched against her neighbor. The person next to her pushed back, then another one shoved someone, until everyone seemed to be jostling everyone else.

A wiry boy rode the center of the confusion, slipping his quick hands into pockets. His eyes flickered to one side and he disappeared just before a city watchman strolled up, one hand on the hilt of his short sword. The crowd thinned to let him pass.

The singer, a young girl about Iola's age, stood on a barrel. She looked desperately around the crowd, then jumped down and picked up her basket and emptied its contents into a cloth, tucked it under her belt, then scrambled out of the watchman's sight. The watchman scanned the edges of the crowd.

"Come on," Thorat said.

"Right," Darna agreed. She led the others into a narrow alley before the watchman looked their way.

"Do you think..." Myril whispered. "Do you think that's allowed, picking pockets?"

"Maybe it wouldn't be so hard," Darna said. "That watchman was slow. I wouldn't do it like that, though."

"Hey you!" The boy, the pickpocket, appeared suddenly

at the mouth of the alley. "This is my turf. Scram, green-knees. Find another place to pick up beads and bread."

Thorat stiffened at the challenge, but then the boy noticed Iola.

She shuffled her feet and looked up at him with her wide, clear eyes. "Where should we go?"

He had to catch his breath at her beauty, but with an effort he recovered his customary sneer. "I don't care," he said. "You find something over that end of the harbor. Don't think anyone's claimed the spot under Fisherman's Wharf, not yet this season anyway. Just keep away from here. This is our turf."

He disappeared and the watchman strode past, barking at everyone in his path:

"Move along now!"

They strolled along the bustling shore until they found a log lying on a quiet stretch of sand. They watched the harbor and ate the burned pancakes they'd gotten from the baker. Iola dozed. Darna didn't even notice that she was falling asleep, but when she woke she had a crick in her neck and the sun was setting.

"Shall we go find the temple?" Myril asked.

Darna shook her head. "Too late now," she said. "We can find it in the morning. Besides, we're here. Anamat."

Small boats came and went from the trading ships through the evening. Other scrapplings darted along the shore, looking for pockets to pick or begging for work. The light faded and stars winked to life while seagulls cried, circling like dragonlets. The four green scrapplings curled up together to sleep in a half-sheltered spot under the wharf, with gentle waves lapping on the sands at their feet.

§

Chapter 4: The Ballad of Ara and Enat

*Ara left the chieftain in his stronghold, she left the low and
settled land.*
*Ara walked with her feet on the ground and her eye on the
heavens.*
*She left the tilled and fertile ground for the mountains of Na
and Enat followed.*

– The Story of Ara and Enat

Darna woke in the chill of dawn. The city and harbor
were quiet, with only the caw of seagulls and the distant
rattle of carts over cobblestones to break the silence. Myril
slept at her back, just as she had during the journey to Anamat.
Beyond her, Iola and Thorat dozed.

Darna sat up to look around, knocking her head on the
underside of the dock. She stifled her cry – she didn't want to
wake the others up. Sunlight struck the sides of the buildings
on the far edge of the harbor. Nearby, a small blue-gray
dragonlet emerged out of the waves. It skittered up the sand,
leaving no footprints, and curled at Iola's feet. In her sleep,
Iola sighed, smiled and snuggled closer to Thorat. The
dragonlet tucked its head under its wing, ignoring everything
and everyone but Iola. Why? And for that matter, why was
Thorat so entranced by Iola, too?

Myril had been a good companion on the road, but Darna

didn't want to watch Iola swan around looking at the sky. She eased away from the others and got up to look around at the waking city. Steam and smoke rose over the tiled roofs, spiraling through the morning fog. Piles of scrapplings yawned in its doorways and blind alleys. At the far end of the harbor, people squatted where the tide would carry their waste away.

Darna considered the lay of the land. As she walked along the shore, she noticed a narrow alley that winked into view from behind a barrel. She tried it, and that was the beginning of her exploring into the maze of Anamat's hidden ways, the ones that ran beneath and between the public thoroughfares and only appear to those who can see them. She followed the hidden way, catching glimpses of dragonlets as she went over rooftops and through alleys. Her path crossed the fortune-tellers' street, where signs of moons and stars hung from every window ledge. At the foot of the street, an arched bridge crossed a canal, and across that bridge she found a market full of secondhand scrap peddlers with their sheds packed close together.

Eventually, her path emerged onto an open road, across from a long white wall. A little further along the road was a gate where about two dozen scrapplings stood, waiting for their bread from the priestesses' dragon ovens. It was the back gate of the harbor temple itself. The bread smelled a thousand times better than the bread on the road had, even better than the baker's pancakes. Darna joined the huddle, pressing her face to the gate.

"Hey, green-knee!" someone said.

Darna turned around slowly.

"Where'd you come from?" demanded a tall girl.

"Who's that, Nira?" asked another girl.

The big girl, Nira, poked Darna in the shoulder. "So,

green-knee, where'd you come from?"

"Provinces, same as anyone else." Darna shrugged.

Nira's frown deepened. "No. Just now. Didn't see you come up the road. What's your game?"

Darna shrugged and looked down, as she always had with the cook in Tiadun keep. She fumbled with her stick.

"Cripple," Nira pronounced, as if she were very clever to have noticed Darna's stick. "You'll be a beggar. All cripples are beggars."

"Yeah," one of her hangers-on chimed in. The smaller children, ragged and skinny, gathered around their ringleader. They drew closer, sensing a possible fight, a bit of entertainment.

"Are you a beggar?" Darna asked Nira.

"Of course not!" Nira snorted. "I'm a scavenger. This is my gang. They all do what I tell them."

Nira was a bit older than most of her gang. "What guild are you going to join?" Darna wondered aloud.

Right away, she knew that it had been the wrong thing to say. Nira's nose twitched and her mouth moved around, as if searching for words. Her followers looked smug, even with their nervous eyes and ragged clothes.

Nira still hadn't found anything to say when suddenly they all turned their attention to something behind Darna. She turned to see three Tiadun guardsmen and a squire were rounding the corner, the same ones she'd seen at the crossroads where she'd met Myril.

She dove into the growing crowd of scrapplings and searched for a place to hide.

"Over there!" the squire said, pointing toward Darna.

As the guardsmen turned to look, Darna found a gap in the nearest wall. She disappeared into it.

"I don't see anything," said one of the guardsmen.

"She was just there!" the squire said, baffled.

"There wasn't anyone there," said one of the scrapplings.

"Well, if there was anyone there, they're not any more," said a guardsman.

Darna's hiding spot provided no way out except back onto the street, so she listened intently.

"We're looking for a girl, a cripple with red hair," the oldest of the guardsmen said. "She's about thirteen years old, but small."

The scrapplings mumbled and gave a collective shrug.

"What about that new girl," one of the younger voices piped up.

"Shut up, Elna," Nira said. "That girl had brown hair. She couldn't have been older than you, either, and you're what? Nine?"

"Twelve," Elna grumbled.

The older guardsman cleared his throat. "The prince of Tiadun is offering a reward for the return of this girl. He promises a position in his household to the boy who brings news leading to her return, or a reward of twelve gold beads."

The guardsman held out a money pouch. A few of the scrapplings eyed it curiously.

"Show us," said one of the boys.

The whole gaggle of scrapplings formed a circle around the provincial guardsmen. The guardsmen spoke in undertones among themselves. Finally, the older one settled the pouch into the broad palm of his hand and carefully untied the knot.

"Over there!" shouted Nira, pointing frantically in the direction opposite Darna's hiding place. The guardsmen looked up, and a gang of boys rushed them, knocking sharp elbows into knees and flailing wildly with sticks which appeared out of nowhere. The guardsmen reached for their bronze swords, but the beads scattered. The scrapplings cleared them from the cobblestones faster than the fiats of the guardsmen's blades could reach them.

The temple bell chimed, the gate opened, and the scrapplings retreated into the courtyard, laughing.

The guardsmen followed them to the gate, where a priestess barred their way.

"You may not enter at this gate," she said firmly.

The elder guardsman straightened his tunic and sash. "They stole our property," he said.

The priestess shook her head. "It is inside our gates, and therefore is temple property now, if those who carry it would offer it."

"They won't," the guardsman said.

"The children of Anara are our sacred charge," the priestess said. "The law says we must give them sanctuary, even in their mischief."

"The law should be changed!" said the younger guardsman, but he let his sword drop. The two other guardsmen also moved to sheathe their weapons. The squire hung back, eying the scrapplings who were busy tearing into their morning meal.

"The law stands, and it is temple law inside these gates," the priestess said. "Besides, you should know better than to ask the children to inform on one in their midst. They too have laws."

"Wouldn't know it to hear of them," one guardsman said. "Bunch of thieves."

The guardsmen regrouped and trudged away. The squire looked back over his shoulder, as if wishing that he could join the scrapplings, too.

§

Darna sneaked in and got her share of bread as soon as the guardsmen were gone, but she stayed close to the wall, didn't talk to anyone, and slipped away into an alley as soon as she could. If the Tiadun guardsmen were looking for her, she didn't want to be out in the open any more than she could help. She would have to find the others later, preferably when the guardsmen were gone.

The alley she'd found went north until it reached a set of stepping stones across a small stream. From there, another passageway led into a quiet courtyard. Darna sat down to eat on a sunny stoop next to a flower pot full of blooming daisies, out of sight of the main streets in and out of the courtyard. Her loaf of bread was still steaming. As she was eating, a boy a few years older than her came along with a leather satchel and set it down beside the corner shrine. He took out a string, a bronze stick, and an elaborate contraption of wood and metal. When he'd set that up, he took out a wax tablet and a stylus on which he made some markings that Darna couldn't see.

"What'cha doing?" she asked.

The boy jumped. "I didn't see you there. Scram, we don't like scrapplings in the guild quarter."

Darna had her stick on her lap and her belly was full. She didn't feel like scramming.

"I'm just eating my bread."

"So? You're still a good-for-nothing scrappling."

"And what are you, then?"

"Apprentice, can't you tell? Planners' guild," he said proudly.

"What do the planners do?" Darna said.

"You're awful green," he said. "We make the bridges and walls, make sure the shrines look right, all the complicated

building. Builders just do the houses, and whatever we tell 'em
to."

The boy's measuring tools lay half-in, half-out of his
satchel, gleaming in the sunlight. Darna wanted to touch them,
to use them, to know what they meant. She wanted to know
what those tools were for.

"How do I get to be an apprentice?" she asked.

"You? A planner? You'd be lucky to get a maid's job at
the palace."

Darna rose to her feet, ready to strike with her stick, but
the boy was so intent on his work that he didn't even notice.
He kept talking, and she lowered her stick back to her side.

"Most of us, apprentices at the planners', we're from
Anamat. It costs ten gold beads for your first year, twenty if
you can't read. So that's why we don't take scrapplings.
Thieves and illiterates."

"But..." Darna stammered. "But I thought only priestesses
read. Men do, too? Guildsmen?"

"'Course we do," the boy said. "Stupid provincials."

"I'm not a provincial any more," Darna said. She had no
idea how she would get twenty gold beads. What size of gold
bead? What kind? If the price on her head was twelve gold
beads, and she could get that somehow... No, it would never
work.

Just then, a dragonlet emerged from the shrine. It looked
at her then spread its wings and drifted over Minstrel's Bridge.

"What are you looking at?" the boy said, looking up just
as she was staring at the sky like a dragon-touched priestess.

It took Darna a moment to answer. "Nothing," she said.

"If I didn't know better, I'd say you were dragon-
touched. 'Course hardly anyone sees dragons any more," the
boy said. "My name's Tevan. What's yours?"

"Darna," she said. "What's that about no one seeing dragons?"

"I don't know. The guild... Never mind. It's different if you see dragons, but you're just a scrappling." Tevan shouldered his bag and walked off down a narrow lane before Darna could ask how it was different. Probably not in a good way.

Darna considered following him, but the dragonlet had promised gold with its wings, and she needed gold, twenty beads' worth, if she was going to buy that apprenticeship. She could hide her dragon-sight if she needed to, she always had. She could get better at hiding it, and she would get the beads, somehow.

She glimpsed the dragonlet again at the next corner and followed its lead into the hidden passages around the northeast quarter of the city. She emerged in a thicket outside the city wall just in time to see Nira and her gang disappear up a dusty road toward some hillocks a little distance outside the city. Pale, thin brush dotted the low slopes. A faint smell of rot hovered over the shabby market outside the northeast gate, but it was a dry kind of rot, not the pungent smell of the canals. A cart carrying scrap rattled by. The Anamat peasant who drove it tipped his head when he saw Darna but said nothing.

From the shade of a market stall, Darna watched the peasant's cart lumber on into the dumping ground. Nira's gang scattered across the hillocks, sweeping the area for bits they could re-sell. Darna followed at a distance, keeping behind carts, stalls, or bushes in case Nira and her gang looked back. There were riches in that dump, she was sure of it. After a while, she limped away to look for Myril, Iola, and Thorat.

§

Myril, Iola, and Thorat reached the temple after the

breadlines had closed, but while there were still a few scrapplings lingering around. One of the boys invited Thorat to come to the East Market with him and Iola urged him to go, but he promised to meet them back by the dock before sundown. After that, Iola and Myril drifted through the streets, tugging a hand here and there in hopes of a bead as they'd seen the other scrapplings do. Myril wished she didn't have to touch anyone, but the streets were so crowded that she couldn't avoid it. When she did, their memories and feelings sometimes leaped into her. They weren't always bad, but it always made her shiver, as if she'd just come up again from the waters of that pool in the mountains. At least she had Iola by her side, so that she wouldn't drift away entirely.

Along the lower reaches of the canals, the smell of tar, wet hemp, and sealed barrels mingled with incense and steam. Further up the hill, a neighborhood of counting houses had air full of the dry whiff of ink and parchment. Myril and Iola approached the palace through the jewelers' quarter with its hot metal, and past the dusty clothiers' halls. Iola only seemed to notice the street-corner shrines, and gazed up at the sky in between as if she were indifferent to the life of the city.

"There aren't as many dragonlets here," Iola observed as they climbed toward the palace. "I saw more back by the harbor."

Myril nodded absently. Up ahead, a crowd gathered around a minstrel. "Let's go listen," she proposed. It would be something to do while they waited for Thorat to meet them.

Iola blinked and cocked her head to listen. "Yes, let's."

They found a place to stand on the edge of the crowd. The minstrel was singing a ballad about Ara, the first priestess.

In this ballad, Ara journeyed into the mountains of Na, retreating after the weary work of seducing the first chieftain, the progenitor of the princes and governors. Through her arts, she helped the dragon-blind and power-greedy chief see the light of the dragons, if not the dragons themselves. Then Na called, inviting her to view his wonders, to rest in the cradle of his mountains. She braved the wilderness and wild beasts, even the first bandits. She longed for her consort, Enat, who had stayed in Anamat to guard Anara from the thieves of future generations.

Ara nearly froze on the mountain passes, but finally she reached Na's own valley, a nest of warmth between the mountains. She saw his treasures laid there, open to the sky, and then Na opened up the clouds. It rained for a very long time. Ara recorded every treasure as it sank into the water from the rain falling into the valley. The puddle grew to a pool, then a pond, until it finally became a lake. Ara cried, and her tears became a stream, flowing out of that lake and down to the river which courses through Anamat valley.

That lake came to be known as the Eye of Na, and it still weeps, making a river that binds Na's wilderness to Anara's gentler lands.

When the minstrel concluded his ballad, he swept off his hat and passed it along the first row of the crowd. His gaze settled on Iola, and he beckoned to her. Myril nudged her forward.

"Greetings, young girl." The minstrel smiled. "Would you do me the great favor of passing the hat through the crowd? I will give you a share of the collection."

"I don't know," Iola blushed and looked back at Myril.

"Go ahead," Myril said. Their timid attempts at begging hadn't yielded much, and she was hungry.

Iola and Myril turned around to face the crowd while the minstrel climbed back onto his perch and tuned his harp a little, tempting the listeners to stay for another tune. "Let this beautiful child gather in your beads, and she, like the great priestesses of Anamat, will ensure that my song continues."

He winked at them as they wound their way through the listening crowd. Heavy beads, far more of them than Myril had seen in beggar's baskets, dropped into the hat and disappeared though its false bottom. They were rounding the back of the crowd, just out of sight of the minstrel, when it all went wrong.

"Hey!" A brown-haired girl with crooked front teeth launched herself at Iola. "This is my beat. That's my minstrel." She grabbed the hat and tried to pull it out of Iola's hands.

"But he said –" Iola's voice protested weakly, but her arm pulled back with all her might. She was stronger than she looked. Myril jumped in and tried to pry the other girl's hands away.

The minstrel crossed the crowd in two strides. The audience rearranged itself to watch the tussle, keeping their hands over their pockets. The minstrel grabbed the girl with the crooked teeth by the scruff of her neck.

"You weren't here," he hissed. With his other hand, he pried her fingers away from his torn collection hat. "I don't have to play along with your squabbles."

Iola tugged Myril's elbow. "Let's go," she whispered.

Myril looked over her shoulder. A wall of scrapplings had formed around them, at least half a dozen of the girl's friends, including some burly boys who snickered and dusted off their knuckles.

"We can't," Myril said.

The minstrel shoved the crooked-toothed girl back toward her friends. "Scram," he said.

The scrappling gang stood their ground. One of them ran around and started toward the minstrel's harp.

"I said scram!" the minstrel shouted as he lunged to protect his harp. He held it to himself and looked desperately over the heads of the crowd. "Watchman!" he called, but there was no answer.

Myril joined hands with Iola and they turned to run.

"Think you're so pretty?" The girl blocked Iola's way, her crooked teeth protruding in a sneer.

"Out of our turf," one of the boys added.

They circled around, pushing and grabbing at the girls' tunics. One girl tugged at Myril's belt, but she jerked free before her pocket came loose. The biggest of the boys raised his fist to strike.

Later he became an accountant, no thanks to Darna's stick.

It came swinging as if out of nowhere and cracked across the boy's unguarded wrist. He howled. Though there was only one of Darna and she was small, she had the advantage of surprise and a ready weapon. She used her stick like a scythe, sweeping the knees of the little gang. The minstrel looked on, one sweaty hand clutching the pillar of his harp, guarding it until a city watchman appeared.

"Watch!" the crooked-toothed girl warned.

Her gang scrambled into the alleyways, disappearing instantly.

Darna, Iola, and Myril looked at each other in the sudden calm. A heavy, gloved hand landed on Darna's shoulder.

"These scrapplings causing trouble, minstrel?" the watchman asked, raising his eyebrows.

The minstrel opened his mouth then pressed his lips together. He looked at Iola. "No," he said. "Not those. The troublemakers went that way." He pointed in the direction opposite from the way that the crooked-toothed girl's gang had fied. Perhaps he needed to keep peace with them so they wouldn't sabotage his next performance.

The watchman yawned. "You shouldn't call if we can't make an arrest, you know," he said to the minstrel.

"I thought you might get here in time."

"They steal your beggar's cap?" the watchman teased.

"It's not begging," the minstrel bristled. His hand went into the cap as if to prove his point. He handed the watchman a small bead. "Thank you for your trouble."

"Oh, no trouble at all," the watchman shrugged, inspected the bead, and strolled over to the far side of the square where he slouched against a shady wall and yawned.

"Are you with them?" the minstrel asked Darna. "If so, you'd better stick together. Where's your quarter?"

"Our quarter?" Myril asked.

Darna cleared her throat. "We're new, just got to the city yesterday. Where do you think we should go?"

The minstrel shook his head. "I don't know, but in my days as a scrappling..." His eyes gazed out at nothing for a moment, and he plucked one string of his harp. "There was a good place near the mouth of the East Canal. It's far enough from this gang, anyway."

Then he smiled at Iola. "You *are* a beautiful child," he said. "I had a very good collection. Here." He handed her a large, wave-patterned bead with dots of gold along one orbit. It was the best bead the girls had seen yet.

"That's a middling tailor's bead," he said. "Spend it wisely."

§

Myril embraced Darna as the minstrel walked away. "Thank you!" she said.

"I was just up here, you know – wandering by," said

Darna, pulling away. "I have to go, though. They're looking for me."

"Who's looking for you?" Iola asked.

Myril shook her head to discourage Iola's question. "It's almost sundown. Let's go back to the dock."

Darna tapped her stick on the cobbles. "Sure. Let's get out of here before those scrappers come back."

"Where were you?" Iola asked her.

"Oh, here and there," Darna said. She looked over her shoulder. "Did you see any Tiadun guardsmen?" she asked Myril.

"No, why?"

"They were at the temple this morning."

"The ones from the crossroads?"

Darna nodded, and Myril stopped. She stood as still as the stones for a moment, listening.

"I think they're inside the palace," she said. Darna had noticed Myril's ability to hear far-away things on the road to Anamat, but now that they were in the city her hearing seemed even stronger, as if Anara's city guided her to what she needed to hear, just as it guided Darna to the places she needed to discover.

"We'd better go further away in case they come out," Myril said.

Darna didn't need to be told twice. She set off at a fierce clip and Myril dragged Iola out of her reverie of sky-gazing.

"What happened to that boy, Thorat?" Darna asked as they crossed a small square. A couple of scrapplings looked out at them from a shady begging spot.

"He went over to the East Market to do something with those boys," Myril said, gesturing to the beggars that they were moving on, and that they wouldn't tread on their turf. "We're going to meet him now, aren't we?" she said. "Won't you come with us?"

Iola nodded and even smiled at Darna.

Darna looked away. "All right, but just down to the harbor."

"The minstrel said to stay with us," Iola said. "Anara said so too."

Darna rolled her eyes. "She did, did she?"

Iola just nodded, as if it were the most ordinary thing in the world to say that she knew what the dragon was thinking, that Anara had special plans for her, or for any of them.

"I guess I'll come, then," Darna said, not quite ready to contradict Anara, even if the direction she gave came through Iola. "Besides, my hair's starting to show red again, I saw it in a reflecting pool, and I was wondering if you could dye it again."

"If I can find some walnut bark," Myril said.

Iola sighted a shrine. She gazed down at the brightly colored bead in her hand, then back at the shrine. She started toward it, mesmerized by the small statue of Anara in the nook.

"Iola!" Myril reached out to stop her. "You can't!"

"Of course I can!" she said. She tried to pull away, to leave that whole big bead to the priestesses, when it was enough to feed three or four scrapplings for a quarter-moon. A cart rattled down the hill, crossing between Iola and the shrine and slowing her headlong rush to give the bead to the priestesses.

"See," Myril said. "That's a sign. We might need that bead."

"It's just that the shrines..." Iola sighed. "In the village, there was a shrine, but not like that." She moved as if the shrine were pulling her in, as if it might swallow her. Darna joined Myril in holding her back, then she let go.

"Do what you want," Darna said. "It's not my bead, but what I think is, we go to the temple for bread, the temples don't come begging to us, right? Not until we join guilds or something. That's how it works."

Iola opened her mouth as if to say something, but then she nodded at Darna. "You're right. Scrapplings don't have to give to the temples." She put the bead back in her pocket and looked longingly back at the shrine's gilded carvings, its glossy-tiled roof shining in the sun, the incense and ribbons curling in the wind. She took Darna's hand as they walked away.

When they reached the harbor, Iola let go of Darna's hand and just gazed out at Anara's island, on the edge of the sheltered waters. It was a gateway to the dragons' realm, so foreign ships and merchants steered well clear of it, but local fishermen set offerings in the waves to float onto its shores.

"There's Thorat," Myril said, pointing to his graceful figure striding toward them through the crowds.

Iola turned her gaze from the dragon's island to smile on Thorat as he approached.

"I got some beads!" he boasted. "Let's go get some stew!" Then he noticed Darna. "You're back," he said.

Darna cocked her head sideways and squinted at him. "So are you."

"Of course. I pledged myself to guard Iola here, at least until she enters the temple." He startled as the words tumbled out, as if he'd said too much.

Darna frowned. "Why?" she asked.

Iola gazed adoringly at Thorat. "He saved me," she said.

Thorat shook his head. "Na saved you. But listen, I'm hungry."

"So am I," Darna said. "I'm always hungry."

"Me, too." Thorat grinned at Darna, making her blush. Then he took Iola's hand again and Myril led them all, following her nose.

§

Chapter 5: A Shelter

If you catch a tiny bead, six is the number of that you'll need.
When you catch them all, then they roll into a small.
If the small is not enough, one and five is middling stuff.
Middlings gather in a dozen to grow into a large one, cousin.
  – Children's rhyme

They found an old woman stirring a big iron cauldron on an open fire at the end of a side alley and sat there, eating stew while Thorat told the story of how he'd met Iola.

The people of Thorat's village sent him off on the road to Anamat with their blessings and a good handful of beads. He had a full pack of provisions, including the best of the past summer's dried apricots, and a sharp knife at his side. He slept in farmers' sheds and on temple porches. Everywhere he went, people wished him good fortune in Anamat. He crossed the thin range of hills between his home province of Seiganum and Coradun. Three days later he entered the mountains surrounding the Anamat valley.

The path from the northern provinces to Anamat was well traveled, and consequently well known to thieves. Thorat had been warned about them, but he didn't worry much. He had little to steal, and the people he met along the way had been kind. On his first night in the mountains, he found no temple or herdsman's hut to shelter him, but there was a dense piney bush with dry leaves underneath which was comfortable and dry enough. The journey had been easy, but he didn't have any idea what he would do once he reached Anamat itself.

At dawn, a noise woke him, an eerie screech of glee, followed by a girl's voice, clear and enchanting.

"But Tegana told me to go to Anamat, to be a priestess there!"

Thorat sat up.

A man laughed. "You're in Na's country now, and all dragons keep to the same lair in harvest time. You'll meet Anara, if that's what you want."

"But Tegana said to go to Anamat," the girl repeated.

Thorat peeked out through the boughs of his shelter. An old woman in a goatskin tunic and two bearded men, clad in lion skins and carrying cudgels, surrounded a young girl. She was thin and dressed in rags, but her skin was like moonlight, her eyes green like the growing spring grass, or an emerald, or the sea on a sunny morning after a storm. Thorat stared at her.

He also knew that they were not in Na's country, but only on its borders. They were still in Coradun. He could even see Corana's shrine through the boughs on the opposite side of the bush. The girl looked around frantically, as if she feared there might be more bandits, and not as if she expected help to come. Then her eyes lit on the shrine and she straightened to her full height, which made her look stronger, despite her thin limbs.

"Tegana said to go to Anamat," she repeated.

The old woman cackled. "Na says you're coming with us," she said, patting the girl's shoulder. "Come along, dearie. Na needs priestesses, too. He hasn't had a young one in a long time."

The girl looked at the woman, puzzled. "The priestesses

at the temple said I was too young."

The taller man, the one with brown hair and a beard, guffawed while the other, shorter and darker-haired, leered at the girl's budding breasts.

"And we say you're not."

The girl kicked the taller man in the shin, a sudden and unexpected move. Thorat tightened his grip on his knife. He had to stop them, but how?

"Come on," said the darker man. "We shouldn't be lingering this long by the road."

The other two grunted assent. The old woman and the taller man grabbed the girl's arm to propel her up the hill. The girl looked back and saw Thorat, still mostly hidden in the bush. Their gazes locked, his green eyes matching hers for a moment. It was as if she were suddenly rooted to the spot.

The tall man tugged, unable to move her, and the old woman grumbled.

"Little fool," she said, "don't you know Na will go easier on you if you don't fight us?"

She's not fighting Na, she's fighting you! Thorat thought.

The girl's gaze broke away and whatever spell had been cast between them was broken. Her resistance gave way, and the big man who'd been straining to move her stumbled forward and nearly fell.

"Na's blood," he cursed as he regained his balance. "Let's get away from that path!"

Thorat watched them go on up the hill toward the rocky peaks. The girl's eyes haunted him. What did they want with her? She was beautiful and so delicate. He was about to follow when he saw an old man coming up the path, leading a donkey. The man had a thin beard and his donkey was heavily laden with parcels.

Thorat poked his head out of the bush. "Sir?" he said.

The old man looked around, searching high and low, until Thorat broke all the way out of the bush. The donkey sidestepped, startled, and the old man's rheumy eyes settled on him.

"You could have gave me a fright," he said slowly.

"Sir," Thorat whispered, "I need your help."

The old man backed off a step. "I got no beads, it that's what you're after, and nothing but seed barley and a couple of empty jars in these packs."

"No, no," Thorat said, looking over his shoulder toward the peaks. "There's a girl. Some rough-looking men took her up there and –"

"Were they bandits?" the man asked, alarmed.

"I think so."

"Thank you for the warning and I'll be on my way," the man said, goading his donkey back to a walk.

"But we have to help her!"

The man shook his head. "I don't. I'd be no threat to them besides. Bandits would only eat my poor donkey and take the rags from my back. Any sensible man knows not to trouble the bandits. Bad luck, it is."

Thorat stared at him. "You won't help her?"

The man didn't even look at Thorat as he walked away. The donkey stumbled off around the bend as fast as his master could drive him, a shambling walk. Thorat listened closely. He could still hear the bandits, so he followed the faint sounds up through the forest. He began to wonder how he would find his way back to the path, but he knew that he had to catch the girl's eye again, to help her get away somehow and back on the road to Anamat.

The bandits went up through thin places in the

underbrush and over pine-needle-carpeted slopes, all the way up to the tree line where the sky opened and only a thin skin of soil covered the mountain's bones, tufted with tiny flowers and soft grasses. He'd never been so high up. He looked behind, over the tops of the trees. Ever so far away, the azure sea sparkled in the sun. He hadn't seen the sea in over five days, not since the morning he'd set out from home. The forest below looked trackless, impenetrable, and for the first time he wondered whether he would reach Anamat at all.

At the sound of a shout from above, he ducked behind a rock. He peeked out to see the that bandits were still high above him on the slope, climbing slowly with the reluctant girl between them.

"Almost there now," one of them said. On the open mountainside, he could hear them from far away. He stole quietly after them, moving as quickly as he could from one bit of cover to the next.

As the sun reached the height of midday, the bandits entered a narrow gouge. There, Thorat could approach more closely, and besides, the bandits had begun to argue among themselves.

"When will they be here?"

"Sunset, maybe earlier."

"Well, I don't want to wait. I say we offer her now."

"We should all be here."

Thorat's heart hammered. There were more of them? He wasn't sure he could prevail against the three of them even with the girl's help, and with more it would be truly impossible. Even the old woman was taller than he was, and the girl looked very small indeed, even if she did have some magic,.

"Tie her there."

"But I'm told to go to Anara," the girl said.

Thorat crept up to the edge of the defile and looked down. What he saw took his breath away, and nearly unseated him from his hidden perch. In the little valley, such a narrow, cramped place, a spring bubbled. Its mossy banks were carpeted with every kind of flower on the mountainside and more, in such profusion that they seemed like a soft bed in rainbow hues, as inviting as anything. The girl lay in the midst of it, looking bewildered, with her hands bound before her. She craned her neck. A little further away were some bushes covered with jewel-like berries, unnaturally early: the berry bushes lower on the mountain were only just in bloom.

"May I have a berry?" the girl asked.

The bandits looked at one another and shrugged.

"I don't see why not," the old woman said. "Old Na will take her anyway."

The short, dark man approached the girl and leaned over her. He leered a little, but stayed further away from her than he had at the beginning. "They're Na's berries," he said. "To feed the dragon. He makes jewels of 'em, see?"

He jerked his head, indicating the far corner of the defile. The girl struggled to sit up.

Thorat looked, too. Not too far from where he crouched, the narrow mouth of a cave opened into the mountain. It wasn't just any cave, though. Its mouth was ringed with crystals, like luminous teeth. The ground before it was smooth, polished as if by fire, with more crystals and jewels scattered at the edge of the rising rock walls on either side.

"We've been looking for a long time for a fit sacrifice for Na," the woman said. "You eat his berries, he'll kill you, but he'll feast on you for us, so..." She spread her hand toward the berries and smiled. The dark-haired man untied her wrists. The girl stood, shook her head, and walked straight toward the crystalline cave, forgetting the berries. Thorat could tell that it wasn't a place that humans were meant to enter. Even a priestess would stop at the brink, if she dared to go that far. The girl's gaze was fixed on something deep inside. It was his last chance.

The bandits shrank back, confused by the girl's eagerness to be consumed by the cave. Thorat took that moment to race to her side, tumbling into the ravine with his drawn fish knife in one hand and his satchel in the other. He landed at her side as her eyes lit up again.

"I'll go to Na, then," she said, to no one in particular.

Thorat shook his head and stepped forward to draw her attention away from the cave. "No, you're for Anara, that's what you said. I'm going there, too."

The bandits stared slack-jawed at Thorat.

"What, did Enat drop out of the sky?" the old woman said after a long moment.

"Stop it with your legends," the tall bandit said, reaching as if to silence the woman, but stopping the gesture half-way.

"He can only be a meddler," the short one said, creeping further away from Thorat, up the lower end of the valley. "He's just another scrappling gone astray, isn't he?"

"We can sacrifice him, too," the tall one said. He stepped toward the would-be priestess and her boy defender in a brief show of bravado, but the woman dragged him back.

Overhead, the sky darkened and a streak of lightning cracked down onto the rocks above the cave, sending a volley of crystals down onto the ground around the girl's feet. They shone on her, making her bright with the light of the dragons' realm.

The girl looked up to the sky and spoke, her voice

reverberating like a trumpet blast, out of all proportion to her body.

"Let us go," she proclaimed. "'Go to Anamat,' Na says. 'Have your fill of Anara's ways and come at last to me.'"

Then the clouds cleared as suddenly as they had come, and the light of the dragons receded back into the cave. The girl was just a small, ragged child again, not even a woman, not yet a priestess.

Thorat bowed down to her. "I will protect you, if I can," he pledged.

The girl's teeth were chattering and she shivered. "The dragons protect me," she said.

Thorat nodded. "I see that, but – but I would stand by you, too."

She took his hand and pulled him to his feet. "My name is Iola," she said. "Let us go together."

"To Anamat," Thorat said.

And so they set off down the mountain. Thorat brandished his fish-gutting knife and glared at the stunned bandits. They let him pass, watching anxiously as thunderclouds swept away over the peaks.

§

At the end of Thorat's story, they walked back toward Fisherman's Wharf, where they'd slept before.

"We need a place to shelter, something better than that dock," Darna said. The sand had been damp from the harbor's waters and the dew leaked down from above.

"The minstrel said that there was a place he remembered on the East Canal," Myril said.

"Let's have a look, then," Thorat said.

Darna led the way. They took a couple of turns and

skirted through the back alleys, keeping the East Canal nearby. A long warehouse, extending all the way up to the canal, forced them around and across the main road, but at the next hidden alley Darna found a way down to the canal side. A bit of old ash puffed out from under the struts of a broad bridge, where that same main road crossed from the fortune-tellers' quarter to the neighborhood around Ara's Landing. She crept closer along the opposite bank.

A pair of eyes stared at her from the darkness. A dragonlet. Behind her, Iola gasped. They had to go back up to the road and cross the bridge before climbing down the rocks to a sheltered cave with a smooth floor. Thorat and Myril, who were taller, had to duck to get under the protective arch of the struts and into the vaulted space underneath. It felt like a spring house, with the evening light reflecting off the water.

"It's lovely," Myril said. She investigated the crannies at the back. "It's dry, even back here. Someone left a clay pot, too." A thick wall of brush and brambles blocked the upstream side, cramping the space.

Darna tugged at the tangled mass. "If we moved this it would be a lot lighter."

Thorat agreed, and they spent the last of the daylight clearing the space which would be their campsite through the rest of the trading season, the short interval between the homes they'd come from and whatever role they found at Midsummer, whether as novice priestesses or in the guilds, if Anamat would take them. If not, some scrapplings went back to the provinces, but Darna would not think of that. When the sky darkened, they curled together to sleep, with Darna and Thorat flanking the group and Myril and Iola tucked in between.

§

The next morning, they all went to the breadlines together, with Myril listening for any sound of the Tiadun guardsmen and staying close to Darna. A boy named Pannen invited Thorat to come out to the East Market again, so Myril decided to stay with Iola while Darna went scavenging.

After the breadline, Myril and Iola looked for a begging spot, finding one in a market near the harbor where Iola could gaze at the statue of a sea dragon in its shrine. They gathered beads and news of the city, to buy or find an apprenticeship if the temples didn't chose them. That first day, they got three tiny beads and a small one. Not much, but it was something.

They carried on like that for a few days until, one morning, someone shoved Darna at the breadlines. It was Nira, the big girl who'd said she would be a beggar.

"What are you doing here?" Nira demanded.

"Getting bread, same as anyone else," Darna said.

Nira's lip curled and she set her fat hands on her hips. "Stay out of my turf, cripple," she said. "Stick to begging with your little friends."

"Oh?" Darna said.

Pannen sauntered up, with Thorat behind him. "Back off, Nira."

"Who says I have to?" Nira said, raising one eyebrow at him. Then she turned back to Darna. "You stay away from the dump, and from the East Market, hear?"

Darna tightened her grip on her stick.

"East Market isn't your turf," Pannen said to Nira.

"Not now, but maybe..." Nira said.

Darna backed away as a look passed between the two older scrapplings.

"Fine," Pannen said. "Stay away from my market, then, anyway," he told Darna, shrugging.

Darna gave him a cursory nod before she walked away. Why did Nira's gang follow her? Surely they'd be no worse off alone.

Myril tugged at Darna's sleeve. "You can come begging with us today," she suggested.

Darna and followed them, for lack of a better plan. They set up their begging basket and Darna fidgeted all morning long. Iola sat quietly, watching the sky or gazing rapturously at the clay statue in the shabby corner shrine. It was a poor place, full of riggers and rope-makers and some shipwrights.

"Can't we beg somewhere else?" Darna said.

"Maybe it will be better in the afternoon," Myril said.

Iola nodded. "Besides, there's a –"

"A shrine, I know there's a shrine," Darna said. "It's been staring me in the face all morning. There's a hand's-length split in the beam that holds up the side roof, three hands'-breadth over from the pillar, where the gilt is wearing thin, and there's a loose cobble four over from that farmer's cart there and I'm –"

"Shh," Myril said.

"I'm tired of this market." Darna stood up. "There must be something better to do than just sitting here. I'm going."

"We'll see you back to the bridge at dusk, won't we?" Myril asked.

Darna nodded as she walked away. The market really wasn't much. The West and East Gate markets were the best in the city, and there was another good one outside the palace, but she avoided that one because there was too much chance of seeing someone from Tiadun keep there. She thought about going to the West Gate market, but the watch was thickest in the West Market.

Darna sat down for a while on an empty crate beside one

of the docks, then she hauled it up the sand and stuck it in a quiet corner to pick up on her way back to the bridge, if it was still there. It looked like it would be good firewood if it dried out. She picked up a bit of rope too. It was too short to do anything with, but she saw another piece a little while later and tucked it under the fold of her tunic.

A little further along the shore, she spotted a group of riggers at work on an old ship. She wandered by.

"What are you doing?" Darna asked one of them.

He just grunted and ignored her. He was doing something with an awl and a couple of pieces of rope, attaching the two pieces together.

"Bug off," he finally said.

Darna stuck out her basket for a bead in hopes that he wouldn't realize she'd been watching him work, wanting to steal his guild secrets.

"I don't have any beads," he grumbled. "We're working here."

"Get out," said the woman working next to him. She was doing something similar, but she was working with a needle. "You wouldn't go into a guildhall and beg now, would you?"

Begging around the guild halls couldn't be less profitable than the morning in the market had been, Darna thought, but she said nothing and walked away from the riggers. Soon the midday bell rang and the riggers packed up their tools. On the shore, the market stalls closed and people gathered around their fires to cook. Darna took her bread from her pocket and tore off a chunk with her teeth, but a bit of rope had gotten stuck in it. She had to spit that out, along with the half-chewed mouthful of bread.

She looked at the two pieces of rope in her hand. One was about twice as thick as the other, and made of nine strands, while the smaller one was just three twisted-together pieces of twine. Even if she had an awl, she wouldn't be able to do what the riggers had been doing.

Groups of guildsmen and a few merchants were moving toward the taverns for the midday meal. The riggers headed toward one place, the merchants toward another. She followed a group of merchants, holding out her basket with one hand and limping a little extra.

A merchant dropped a small bead into the basket. "Now scram," he said.

Darna nodded and gave him a bow. A moment later, a group of about a dozen men approached the tavern. She limped out to intercept them. One of them said something but Darna didn't understand a word. They wore crunched caps, tall boots, and a strange, oily hairstyle. Cereans.

One of them was laughing and another was already reaching into his pocket for a bead, so she stayed despite her first impulse to run away. The Cereans looked almost friendly. She knew that they were enemies of the dragons, but these men carried no swords, and there was a bead in the man's hand, a shiny bit of blue glass with a yellow band. Darna reached out for it and made her bow.

He said something to Darna, but she didn't know what the sound meant. She echoed it, puzzled. He laughed at her, then repeated the word again. She echoed the sounds once more. He reached his hand toward her and she backed off.

§

Darna avoided the Cereans the next day, begging instead from Theranian merchants and Anamat guildsmen along the harbor. She only got one tiny bead – the other beggars who worked the harbor front had spotted her, so she spent half of the time keeping out of their way. She also spied on the riggers and picked up a few more bits of rope. At midday, she found herself near the same tavern again with the Cereans coming up on her. She thought she'd try her luck with them once more, and shouted their word at them.

"Greetings, beggar," one of them said in the language of Theranis, but with an odd accent.

The word must mean something like "greetings," Darna thought. She repeated it to the others and they nodded. She followed them toward the tavern.

At the door, they paused to talk amongst themselves. One of them gestured to Darna to come in with them. She hesitated. Taverners never let scrapplings in. Of course, they didn't let foreigners in either – but whatever was in there smelled good. Darna followed the Cereans in. The tavern had whitewashed mud-brick walls and low, smoke-blackened beams holding up the roof. A little light peeked through the roof tiles, which probably leaked when it rained. There were a half-dozen round tables circled by benches and tree-trunk stools. One table was set a little bit apart, for the foreigners. With grunts and gestures, the Cereans invited Darna to sit on a stool at their table. She sat facing the kitchen door, sure that she would be tossed out as soon as she was spotted. The taverner ambled out.

"What next?" he huffed. "What are you doing here?"

Darna shrugged. "They said... They said that I could come in with them."

The taverner raised a questioning eyebrow at one of the Cereans, who nodded and smiled. He was just a little bit taller than the others, with a bit of gray in his hair.

"Very well then," the taverner said. "Soup?"

The one with the gray hair asked his friends something equally short, translating to the Cerean word for soup. Sighs and nods went around the table. They didn't know how to ask for anything else, Darna realized.

"They always get soup?" she asked the taverner.

"Sure they do," he said. "I don't know why. They're getting some for you, too."

"Oh." Darna grinned, fleetingly. "What are they doing here?" she asked.

"Trading, I suppose."

"Oh."

"Their beads are as good as anyone's, and I charge 'em double. I'll just throw yours in."

"Soup?" the gray haired man cut in.

The taverner nodded. "Right, soup it is, then." He ducked into the kitchen.

§

That was the beginning of Darna's midday hours with the Cerean sailors. They bought her a midday meal, and as the taverner said their beads were as good as anyone's, and more than she was getting elsewhere. She learned their words for things, mostly food, and started helping them ask the taverner for the thicker stew, and the stuffed bread, and fruit. She didn't understand much of what they were talking about, but she learned to count up to ten and their words for greeting and parting.

She ran errands for them and in between she sometimes begged with Myril and Iola in the market. While Iola gazed at the sky or at the shrine, Darna frowned at the passersby even when they dropped beads into her begging basket. She kept thinking about the dump, and all those piles of treasure lying hidden there, guarded by Nira and her gang.

Thorat spent his days in the East Market with Pannen and his gang, but returned to the bridge by full dark every day. He was the only person who could turn Iola's attention away from the dragons for more than a moment.

One morning at the breadlines, Thorat waved to the girls from across the courtyard. They waved back and started to walk over to join him, but Pannen and Nira were there, too. Nira had her hand on Pannen's shoulder and put her lips up to whisper some nonsense in his ear. He blushed.

"Let's get going," Darna said, tugging Myril away.

Iola started to protest, but Darna and Myril whisked her away. Still, Darna felt restless. She sat down behind her begging basket, but soon gave up and went looking for the Cerean sailors. She went around to all the taverns, walking the harbor front with her beggar's basket under her arm. When the bells sounded, she wandered over to their usual tavern.

"You again?" the taverner grunted. "Your sailor friends left this morning."

"Friends?" Darna snorted.

"Well, patrons or what have you. You can't come here any more."

"I've got a bead for stew."

"All right, just this one last time," the taverner said. "In the kitchen yard."

Darna circled around the back of the tavern, and the taverner met her at the door with a smaller-than-usual bowl. "I won't charge you, just don't come back," he said. The yard was muddy, but the pigs were kept in a high-walled pen which looked sturdy enough. Darna kept her eye on them, though.

The taverner stood over her, waiting for her to finish, as if she might steal the battered wooden bowl.

"Where did they go?" Darna asked.

"Their captain has them working on the ship, outside the city," the taverner said. "They had to make some repairs, and they'd spent their allotted time here in the harbor. It's better that way, keep them away from the temples."

"Why?"

The taverner snatched the bowl away, even though there was one more good spoonful in it. "I have customers to attend to," he said. "Go on, out of my yard."

Darna grumbled as he shooed her away and forgot to thank him for the soup. She would just have to try to find other customers.

§

By listening at the breadlines, Darna had learned that Nira and her gang usually came back into the city before the gates closed for midday, then sold their goods in the afternoons. When the gates opened after midday that day, Darna made her way out to the dumping grounds.

She skirted around the back of the farmers' stalls in case some of Nira's gang had lingered there then out through the dry hillocks out toward the dump. A few carts were carrying garbage out of the city. They moved slowly, their wheels catching on the muddy ruts in the road. Darna followed one at a distance. It had some scraps of broken wood on top, but something shone underneath. She was concentrating so hard on keeping out of sight of the cart that she didn't even notice she was being followed. At the very edge of the dump, she heard a pebble roll down the slope behind her, hesitated for a heartbeat, and walked on. She ducked behind the next thin bush and squatted to hide. She looked back. A thin boy shuffled up the slope behind her, then startled back.

The boy was just as scrawny as Nira's hangers-on, but he wasn't one of them. Besides, he was alone.

Darna walked back to the last rise and looked down. There he was, a small boy with a strange, scrunched cap pulled down to hide his eyes. A Cerean?

"Hey you!" Darna hissed, in her own language.

The boy jumped like a startled frog.

"What are you following me for?" Darna asked.

He shook his head. "No, no... not... follow." He struggled for the words.

"Who do you work for?" Darna asked. It made no sense that a foreign boy would be in Anamat alone, especially so far from the harbor where foreigners usually stayed.

"Work?" he puzzled. "I... no... no one?"

Darna didn't believe him, but it didn't seem likely that he would answer any questions. A loud clang of metal, closer to the city walls, reminded her that she needed to keep out of sight in case one of Nira's lackeys was lingering around.

"Well scram, quit following me," Darna said.

The boy stared at her for a long moment then scampered away, sidling toward the city like a little reptile with none of the grace of the dragons.

Darna crept across the mounds of the dump, listening for pursuit and following the distant sound of the cart. It creaked into a hollow and shifted its load with a sharp clatter, tumbling it into the rest of the mess, then rattled away.

She waited to make sure that the boy was gone before she slid down to investigate the fresh pile of scrap. Then she forgot all about the strange Cerean boy for a while.

§

After that day, Darna usually went out to the dump after midday. Nira's gang scavenged first, but they just skimmed the surface, picking up anything shiny, even if it was worthless. They never found the best bits. Darna dug deeper.

She soon learned that best scrap usually sat a few layers down, and it didn't all shine. She found blocks of iron-hard wood for ships and pieces of metal that no one had known what to do with, but which the metalworkers' guild could melt down for ingots. Once, she even found a gold piece, covered with clay. That was the kind of thing that Nira's gang would miss. Darna felt like she could spot a good haul from all the way across the dump, under five layers of rotten wood and a full half-moon passed before Nira even noticed that things had changed.

At night, Darna gathered with the others under the bridge and they shared their take from the day. In the East Market, Thorat spent the day with Pannen and his gaggle of followers, tipping carts or running errands for the marketers. Darna didn't talk much about her scavenging, but she counted her beads and if all went well, she might have enough to buy an apprenticeship at one of the lesser guilds, maybe the potters or the weavers, where they still took on scrapplings from time to time. Not the planners, though. If it turned out that she couldn't buy any apprenticeship at all, then maybe she could steal away on a foreign ship and escape Tiadun's clutches forever, but in foreign lands she wouldn't see the dragons. No, she wanted to stay in Anamat, she had to.

Iola and Myril kept to their spot in the market and usually begged enough to buy some evening bread. They had enough, and so did most other scrapplings, though some of the ones who came from the near provinces went back to their home villages even before Midsummer.

When the day's begging was done, Iola would go out on a stone jetty in the harbor, and watch Anara circle overhead. Myril sometimes saw the dragon before Iola did, but not often, and she'd never seen Helana so often. She wondered if it was Anara's strength that made her visible, or whether the thing that had happened to her in the mountains had opened her sight. Then again, maybe it was Iola's presence that revealed the dragon in her flight across the evening sky.

The dragonlet under the bridge grew plump and vivid as the moon turned, sitting by Iola's side in the dusk.

§

Chapter 6: The Box

The legends say that once, a long time ago, the Cereans were like ourselves. Three, perhaps four dragons lived in their land, filling it with good things. But they neglected their dragons, who faded away into the hills and withdrew their power from the earth. Perhaps some day they will rise again, not like the dragons of Enomae and Ganat, who were slain forever by the ones they call heroes.

– A merchant's logbook

Darna sold the things she found at the dump along the harbor while Nira sold hers near the East Market and to the lesser guilds. Nira didn't even notice that someone else was scavenging on her turf until the next full moon had come and gone. One morning, Darna sold a good axle bolt to one of the small shops in the eastern part of the city, braving Nira's territory. Nira finally noticed. She approached Darna at the breadline the next morning.

"Hey cripple! What do you think you're doing?" Nira demanded.

Darna shrugged. "I don't have to answer to you."

"If my gang find you out at the dump, you're going to be crippled all over again," she threatened.

She reached out to grab the front of Darna's tunic, but Darna slipped out of her grasp as Pannen walked up, distracting Nira long enough to let Darna wander away and get her bread.

"My sentries find you out there, you'll pay!" Nira yelled, once she noticed that Darna was leaving the breadlines. All of her followers stared after Darna.

Darna took her stash of the previous day's pickings and had a fine morning of trading in the eastern part of the city again, just to irritate Nira, then she set out for the dump.

Darna tiptoed and balanced her way across the rubble. Having a stick was an advantage when it came to scavenging. She could use it for balance and also to poke under things, to feel around without getting cut by the odd bits of metal here and there, and to avoid running her hands into something rotten. Other scavengers carried sticks when they were out in the dump, too, but theirs weren't as sturdy.

Darna found a broken cart a little way in to the dump. Nira's gang had already picked through its load, but they'd left most of the cart where it was. Darna tapped on the shafts, sounding out the metal parts in between the layers of rotting wood. The bed of the cart was thoroughly broken up, but some of it was thicker than the rest. She tapped to see if any of the thicker parts were hollow.

She heard nothing from inside the cart, at first, but she did hear someone scrambling up the hill behind her. She backed away to hide under the cart just in case in case it was one of Nira's lackeys, but no one came.

She was thinking about going on to search elsewhere when something rattled inside the cart. She was lying right under the place where the driver would have been. If there were a hidden stash, that would be it. She wormed her crowbar between two boards and pried. Sure enough, a big chunk of dusty wood fell out. She turned her head and squinted her eyes against the falling debris. The wood cracked, and with another shower of dust a few beads spilled out, bouncing off her face on their way to the ground. A piece of parchment fluttered down after them. She picked up what she could and crawled out from under the cart to tally her find.

They weren't good beads, just provincial clay, but small beads were better than none. She stuffed them into her sack. She was contemplating the piece of parchment, wondering what to do with it, when she heard a footfall behind her.

A dirty, black-haired girl peered at her. "Darna? Is that you?" she said, squinting.

"What's it to you?" Darna replied.

The girl shrugged. She was one of Nira's hangers-on. She squinted as if she was nearsighted – not a very good trait for a sentry.

"Nira said, make sure that girl Darna never comes out here," the girl said. "This is her turf, our turf."

"It's the city dump," Darna said. "Who said she could have it all? She should be in a guild by now anyway. She's too old to be a scrappling."

"She's keeping this turf," the girl declared, evading the question. "They... We're the scavengers here. You stick to the market scrap piles. We'll get you!" She stayed way back at the top of the hill as she made her declaration. She didn't even have a stick with her. Darna felt the heft of the crowbar in her hand. The girl was even smaller than she was. It wouldn't be a fair fight, but if the whole gang came for her that would be another matter.

The girl backed away a step, but then she turned her attention to the sack in Darna's hands. "Whaddya get?" she asked. She scuttled down the hill toward Darna, feeling her way over the rubble.

"Nothing much," Darna said quickly as she set her crowbar aside. "What's it to you?"

"Sure you didn't. Whaddya get?" the girl repeated.

"No business of yours," Darna said. "Unless..." She stopped to think. "What did Nira give you to watch this place?"

"Half. I'm getting half her share of temple bread," the girl said.

"That's all?" Darna said. "You must eat a lot of temple bread, then. You look pretty skinny."

"It's better than village bread," the girl said.

Darna thought that was the stupidest thing she'd heard all day. Of course temple bread was better than village bread.

"I tell you what," Darna said. "You quit scrounging and spying for Nira and help me dig stuff out and carry it back to the city instead. I'll pay you in beads." She reached into her sack and pulled out three of the small clay beads – Onarun beads, by the look of them – and held them out to the girl.

Her jaw trembled. "Nira won't like that."

"So?" Darna said. "You can just steer clear of her, like I do. It's not hard."

"She won't like it." The girl squinted to get a better look at the beads in Darna's hand. She was about Darna's size, not the strongest of scrapplings, but it would be nice to have someone with her, to help get under heavy bits of garbage.

"Here." Darna tossed the girl one of the beads. She dove for it. "Meet me at afternoon gate-opening tomorrow, up on Conn's Roost, and we have a deal." The bead dropped and the girl dug for it in the dust. She could see well enough, close-up, Darna observed. It felt strange, throwing that bead away, but if Nira wasted her followers' time with errands like threatening Darna, then she didn't deserve to have them in her gang.

The girl was still looking for the bead when someone else crested the hill. It was the Cerean boy that Darna had seen on her first venture out to the dump. He must have heard them talking. Darna hadn't seen him since then and wondered where he'd been. There hadn't been any new foreign traders in port lately, but there he was. Had he hidden out in one of the near provinces, and walked back to the city? He held a piece of rusty iron in one hand and a scrap of ragged cloth in the other as if he'd been trying his hand at scavenging, too.

"I join your gang!" he shouted.

"Who are you?" Darna asked.

The boy looked confused, as if he didn't know what she had asked. The girl, Nira's follower, squinted at him.

"What is he?" she asked Darna.

"A filthy Cerean," Darna said.

"He doesn't smell bad, at least not from here," the girl said.

"I not dirty!" the boy said. "I join your gang!"

"I don't..." Darna looked at the two of them, side by side. As odd as they were, together they could probably gather more beads, maybe enough to buy them all apprenticeships in the lesser guilds. The Cerean sailors on the harbor were friendlier than most of the natives of Anamat, and here was one her own age, more or less. He was odd, serious. Maybe she could learn more of his language. Anyway, he was an odd one.

"How did you get here?" Darna asked him.

He looked puzzled.

"You, here, how?" she gestured.

"I don't know," he said. "I join your gang?"

"You have a gang?" the girl asked Darna.

"Well, not yet," Darna said, "but with you two... It would be a small one, but sure, it's a gang, if you want. Equal share of the beads. I get half, you get half of the rest, each of you."

"That's great!" the girl said. "Half! I'm with you!"

Darna meant, of course, just a quarter of the take, and she felt a bit bad about the girl's misunderstanding, but consoled herself by the fact that it was a lot more than Nira was giving her.

"Half what?" the Cerean boy asked.

"Half of half," Darna said. That seemed to satisfy him. He also seemed to understand that he'd be getting a quarter share. He came closer. "What are your names?" Darna asked.

"I'm Elna," the scruffy girl said.

"And I... I am Girizit."

"Girizit?" Darna struggled with the unfamiliar sounds. "I'll just call you Giri, that's easier," she said.

"But that is not my name!" he protested.

"It's too hard to say. You want to be in the gang or not?"

"Yes," he said. "I join you." He bowed his head to her.

Elna looked over her shoulder. "Nira said to go back at dusk," she said.

"Well, let's go scavenging now, before she comes looking for you," Darna said.

"Scavenging?" Giri echoed.

Darna grabbed his rusty bit of metal. It crumbled in her grasp. "Scavenge. Find things," she explained.

"Find things. Scavenge," Giri repeated, nodding his head vigorously.

Darna sighed. "Come on."

§

They dug for a while near the cart then made their way to the far side of the dump, where they found some more glass pieces and a sack with a hole in it. Elna surprised Darna by pulling out a needle and twine and fixing it up right there. She shouldered it cheerfully while Giri carried a loose bundle of sticks and metal, inexpertly tied together with twine.

At dusk they went back in through the gates, hiding their loads as well as they could to avoid paying the gate watchmen's tax. Elna suggested that they stash their findings in the potters' yard, which was full of holes, left over from the days when the guild dug their clay right behind the guildhall. Now they used the holes to store their materials, but usually half or more of them stood empty.

As they walked through city, Darna noticed that people were staring at them. Or rather, they were staring at Giri in his scrunched cap.

"Take that thing off!" Darna said, trying to snatch it from his head. "Makes you look like a foreigner."

Elna looked shocked as Giri clutched his cap to his head. "No," he whimpered. "No take off. Curses."

"Curses?" Darna asked.

"Eyes!" he said. "Looking!" He pointed to the top of his head.

"I don't wear any stupid cap! I don't worry about curses." Darna stopped talking as they cut through a group of guildsmen, all of them staring at Giri. If the dragons cursed people – surely they could if they wanted to – Darna didn't think that wearing a cap would hold them back at all. A dragonlet sped past and Giri shivered. Darna usually felt the dragonlets' presence as a kind of warmth, and Elna didn't seem to notice it at all which made it even stranger that Giri, the foreigner, had reacted to it.

"Just take it off," Darna said.

He shook his head.

"Well, have it off by tomorrow," she said. "You can't be in my gang if you wear something that makes people stare at you all the time. Meet us at the breadlines."

"Breadlines?" he asked.

"You know," Elna said, "at the temple."

"No, no temple!" He shivered even more.

"They have good bread," Elna said reassuringly.

"No. Meet you at gate," Giri said.

"Fine, then, the palace market," Darna said. "But you take off that cap."

He nodded. Elna ran ahead in the dusk and found a nice hole near the canal bank. They stashed the things from the afternoon's search.

"I'll guard it!" Elna volunteered. She was small, but better than no guard at all – unless, of course, she took the stash to Nira.

"Just don't tell Nira's gang," Darna said.

"I won't," Elna said. "I sleep here almost every night. I'm the only one around, usually."

She seemed perversely proud of it. There were a lot of hiding holes there but none of them looked comfortable or dry. It seemed odd that Nira's gang didn't gather at night, too.

"Where do you sleep?" Darna asked Giri.

"Sleep?" he asked.

She pantomimed.

"Oh, I sleep..." He gestured vaguely downhill, to the west. "You?" he asked.

"None of your business," Darna said.

It was a while before she could make much sense of Giri, but she did learn a few more Cerean words by listening to him mutter to himself. He spoke enough of Theranis's language to make his way from day to day. Darna almost tried her Cerean greeting on him, once, but then Elna came along, and she thought better of it. Elna was shy around Giri, and Darna didn't want to scare her by making foreign noises. For herself, Darna kept wondering how and why Giri had come to be in Anamat, but Giri wouldn't say.

He insisted that he wouldn't, couldn't go to the breadlines at Ara's Landing. "No" and "Curses!" were all he seemed to say in those first few days. They would all meet up by the palace or near the Northeast Gate then peddle their wares around the city until midday while Nira was out scavenging. Nira sometimes sent one of her followers to trail them and shout threats and Elna trembled but said she didn't mind too much, now that she had beads in her pockets. Darna pretended not to hear them, and if Giri understood what they were saying he didn't worry much about it.

He learned to speak the language of Theranis much more quickly than Darna had learned Cerean in her midday meals with the sailors. That made her even less inclined to tell him what little she knew – she didn't want him thinking that she was an idiot because of her clumsy Cerean, especially since he had started talking more like a real person, even though his speech was still strange and choppy-sounding.

They ranged over the hills of the dump in the afternoons, temporarily unmolested by Nira and her gang, and staying well out of range of the watch. Giri didn't like the watch any more than ordinary scrapplings did, maybe less.

"Why are you so afraid of the watch?" Elna asked him one warm afternoon as they picked through a pile of broken wood. "You didn't do anything really bad, did you?"

"You are also afraid of the watch?" he asked.

"Sure, but not if I don't have anything on me," Elna said. "They can't do anything to you if you're not pickpocketing or stealing or something, or fighting. You're jittery around them all the time."

"I am... what I am?" Giri didn't understand "jittery."

"Never mind," Darna said. "What do you think they're after you for?"

"After me? They could catch me. Take me back," Giri said with a shudder.

"To Cerea?" Darna asked.

His eyes took on a wistful look.

"You miss home?" Elna asked.

"No!" Giri insisted abruptly. "It was bad. Is bad, Look." He lifted his tunic, and they could see purple stripes from old lashes across his back. In Darna's time as a servant at Tiadun keep, she'd been beaten a couple of times but not so badly that they left a mark for years afterward. Elna bit her lip.

"Looks bad," Darna said. "What'd they do it for?"

"I was bad, lazy," Giri said. "I was supposed to scrub –"

"I know all about that," Darna interrupted while he fished for words."I used to have to scrub the kitchen floors at the keep before... before I ran off."

Giri seized the idea. "I ran off also."

"From where?" Darna asked. He sounded like he was echoing her, making up his story.

Elna went back to poking around in the junked wood. She already had a nice piece of polished wood, just a little bit cracked. Darna searched alongside her.

"I was on a boat," Giri said, after a while.

"You're too young to be a sailor," Elna said.

"Not on a Cerean ship." Giri sighed. "I was in the galley, scrub, work. The cook pointed knives at me."

Darna was still thinking about the stripes on his back. "Is it true they have slaves in Cerea?" she asked.

Giri shrugged. "I hear, maybe. But not allowed in Anamat." He looked sulkily at his cap and put it on. Darna let him, since no one else was around.

"But you still miss Cerea?" Darna asked.

He was saved from responding by Elna's sudden exclamation. "Look!"

She held up something which shone in the sun, as wide as her head, a bright copper box with only a little green in its cracks.

"Wow!" Darna marveled. It glowed in the afternoon light, even through its covering of dust. "Let's go sell it now!" She took it from Elna to look more closely. It was a big piece of copper worked into an intricate pattern and only slightly dented. The hinge on the back stuck, but Darna poked at it until it swung open all the way. The wood interior of the box smelled like incense.

"Do you think we can get a lot for it?" Elna asked.

"I'm sure of it!" Darna said, but Giri was silent. They headed back to the city with the box hidden in Darna's bag.

§

The box looked valuable but Darna couldn't seem to sell it. No one even made an offer on it, nothing at all. She clattered down the rocks to the shelter under the bridge and threw her sack into the shadows. The box made a bright pinging noise as it fell.

"What did you get?" Thorat asked her.

"Nothing," she grumbled. "Not something anyone wants to buy, anyway."

"Nira was over in the market yesterday," Thorat said. "She's been hanging around there a lot."

"Hanging on Pannen, you mean?" Darna said.

"Some," Thorat said. "They're together a lot. Nira wants you to stay out of the dump – "

"Sure," Darna said, "and not to deal with the merchants

and the guilds who won't buy anything from me anyway. She shouldn't even care. She still gets first go, and she probably isn't even trying to get an apprenticeship. Besides, why are you carrying messages for her?"

Thorat sighed. "Pannen told me to. I didn't want to. I liked the East Market better before Nira was around."

They all stared into the fire for a while. Darna reached over to pick up her sack. She didn't open it, but she ran her hands over the contours of something inside it, pensively.

"What is in there?" Thorat asked.

"Nothing," Darna said, but she loosened the knot and handed it to him. The bag slumped open, revealing the small copper box. It was inscribed with a scene of a man with a spear standing on a cliff. Patterns of vines decorated the sides. Thorat passed it to Myril

"This is nice," she said.

"I was going to fix it up if I can. The metal-smiths won't buy it back from me."

Myril turned the box over. "Is it from Theranis?"

"Where else would it be from?" Iola wondered. She looked sideways at the box but didn't reach for it.

"It could be from anywhere," Myril said.

"I'll tell you what," Thorat said.

"What?" Darna said.

"I'll try to sell it. Maybe I'll have better luck with the merchants than you've had."

"Nira will be mad," Darna said. "I'll let you keep half the take. More if you want. Do you really want to help me?" It was too much to hope for, but he smiled at her.

"Sure I do. Why not? I need a change from the East Market anyway." He began to smile again, but this time he was looking at Iola again, as usual.

§

Thorat tucked the box into his cloak the next morning. At the breadlines, he told Pannen that he'd passed on Nira's message and that he wouldn't be in the East Market for a day or two.

"Fine," Pannen grumbled, "do what you want." Nira flounced over. Pannen looked at her skeptically, but hungrily, too.

Thorat set out for the West Market with high hopes. It was all the way across the city from his usual haunts and he didn't think that the merchants there would know him. The box was pretty and copper was good tender because it could be made into beads easily. First he went to a granary just north of the west dock. Everyone said that the merchants there had plenty of beads to spare.

"What's that?" the grain-seller said when he saw the box.

"It's a box, a pretty one," Thorat said. "You have a priestess you want to give it to?"

The grain-seller shook his head. "Not my trade," he said. "You got a mill to grind grain in, scrapper?"

Thorat put the box away. It was only the first try, he told himself, and there were plenty of other merchants in the city.

By the time the gate swung shut at midday, he didn't feel quite so optimistic. The vendors were shuttering their stalls and he was hungry. Thorat went to the baker who had given them pancakes when they'd first arrived. The baker seemed to be taking a little longer to close up his shop than the others.

"What do you have there, boy?" he asked as Thorat approached.

"Just a box," Thorat said. "A nice copper box. Only a little dented and—"

"Let's see it." The baker stretched out his hand, which

was wide and had thick calluses at the bases of the fingers. "You shouldn't have any trouble selling a copper box around here."

Even as far away as the East Market, Thorat had heard that this baker was sharper than most shopkeepers, not worth the trouble to try to steal a cake. Thorat didn't know how he'd gotten that reputation, but his gaze had followed Thorat all morning as he walked up to one shop after another. Still, the baker had helped them on that first day and he seemed friendly.

"You're out of your usual territory, and trade," the baker observed.

Thorat unwrapped the box and handed it to the baker.

"Ah, there's the trouble right there."

"What? Is there something wrong with it?" Thorat asked.

"Well, it all depends on what you call wrong, I suppose." He handed the box back to Thorat.

"What is it?"

"I need to close my shop right now," the baker said, pointedly ignoring the question. "Come around back and I'll give you a bowl of stew and explain a few things to you."

"A bowl of stew?" Thorat said. He wouldn't turn that down.

The baker nodded. "Good mutton stew."

"You don't want to buy the box?" Thorat asked.

"No," the baker said, "but I can explain why you can't sell it, if you want to know." He pulled his shutters closed. Thorat hesitated. "Now circle around to the back," the baker said through the shutters. "I'll see you there."

Thorat followed the quiet alleys around to the back of the shop and entered a narrow courtyard with a donkey's stall to one side and an open fireplace in the middle. The baker's wife stirred a pot over the coals, wiping the sweat from her brow. She smiled at Thorat. She reminded him of one of his aunts, lukewarm in her greeting, ready to feed him but just as happy to send him away. She handed him a bowl of stew so thick that it mounded in the middle. It was rich with oil and spices.

"Don't feed him too much," the baker warned as he emerged from the building. "The boy's not used to it. Are you?"

"I don't mind," Thorat said.

The baker laughed. "You might not, but your stomach will. I don't want to make you sick."

"I've never heard of being sick from too much good food."

"I trust that someday you will." The baker had a bit of a paunch at his waist that bulged as he settled onto a stool. "Now, about that box of yours. Where did you get it?"

Thorat explained that he'd gotten it from a friend, who'd gotten it from the dump, or maybe from a scrap pile.

"Why do you think someone would put a good box like that on a scrap pile?"

"I don't know," Thorat said.

"Well, some things are just bad luck," the baker said. He spoke slowly, chewing between sentences. "This isn't one of them, but I can see how people might think it is. You see, this isn't from one of our Anamat metal-smiths, or even from the provinces. It could be from Enomae. I'm not sure though. Let me see it again."

Thorat handed him the box.

"You see that man with the spear? That's a strange figure. He's a warrior, not a hunter. Only a few of the princes keep spears for their warriors."

"I thought warriors only carried swords," Thorat said.

"Spears are for hunting boar."

The baker smiled and nodded. "Not this spear, though," he said. "There's no boar in the scene, so a person might think that this box told the story of a failed hunt." Thorat began to see why people might not want it despite the good copper.

"But this isn't the story of a failed hunt, it's something else," the baker said, tracing the lines of the illustration. "You see these waves at the base of the cliff? There's a dragon out just here," he pointed, "and here. Almost invisible. This is the story of an old hero of Enomae who drove back the sea dragons."

"Drove back... but why would a hero do that?" Thorat asked. "He wouldn't be a hero then, would he? Heroes are friends of the dragons."

"They should be, and always have been here in Anamat," the baker said. "People are different in other lands, though. I don't know how this box came to be on an Anamat scrap pile, but the best thing for it is to go to another foreigner, or to be melted down."

Thorat could see the sense in that. He nodded. He didn't want to keep the box any more. "I don't know any foreigners," he said.

"Good, that's sensible, safer for you," the baker said, handing the box back to Thorat.

"But I know a girl who does," Thorat said.

The baker raised his eyebrows.

"It's just one foreigner," Thorat explained. "He's trying to be a scrappling."

"A foreigner trying to be a scrappling?" the baker frowned. "That's troubling."

"I don't really know anything about it," Thorat said hurriedly, regretting that he had said too much. "It's just a rumor."

"There are lots of rumors," the baker said. "Would you tell me if you hear more of him?"

"I can't do that," Thorat said. "I shouldn't have said anything. He's my friend's friend, maybe." The Cerean boy might not be a real scrappling, but he was in Darna's tiny gang and that counted for something.

"I suppose I'll have to do my own listening, then," the baker said. "Don't worry, I won't tell where I heard it from. Now finish your stew."

Thorat looked down to discover that he'd left a good quarter of the bowl full. He'd been so distracted by the baker's story that he'd forgotten his meal. He wolfed the rest down so hungrily that he didn't hear the baker slip away. When he looked up, the baker's wife was standing in the doorway, watching. She silently took his empty bowl and shooed him away.

Thorat gave the box back to Darna that night and told her what he'd learned, leaving out the fact that he'd mentioned of her foreign friend.

§

Nira and her gang, helped along by Pannen and his boys, made sure that Darna couldn't sell anything in the eastern quarter of the city. When anyone asked how it was going, she said she was saving her stashes for Midsummer, even though it wasn't true. At least the baker's story explained how hard it had been to sell the box. Darna and Elna went from shack to tavern to guild with the choicest of their finds, and sometimes it took all morning to sell one little piece of metal. Giri often went out on his own and came back with a bead or two, not telling Darna where he'd sold the things he'd taken with him. The way things were going, she wouldn't even be able to buy an apprenticeship with the ropers.

All around them, the trading season gathered pace. Merchants dusted off their baskets and cranes and re-arranged their warehouses. A lone ship came in, carrying horses from Enomae that were delivered straight to the governor's palace. The ship sailed away again, leaving the harbor to the fishermen.

Darna sold enough to buy a little extra food, mostly for Giri and Elna. She looked at her growing stash of scavenged pickings in despair.

Giri refused to eat temple bread even when he couldn't get anything else. He would hide behind a hedge at the dump with his begged bread and mutter strange words over it then eat it quickly, hiding it from any person or bird who might see him eating. Darna could almost understand about the birds. Gulls circled around, crying their menacing call and waiting for the crumbs. Sometimes they even dove in to tear a piece from a scrappling's hand.

"Why don't you eat in the temple courtyard like everyone else?" Darna asked Giri one day.

"Eat? There?" Giri startled.

"Well, it's what everyone does," Darna said.

"But there are all those eyes!" Giri said. "Eyes! All over everything."

"Everyone's looking at their own bread," Darna said.

"But those..." he gestured up and around, clamping his lips.

"The statues? Of the dragonlets?" Darna said.

He nodded emphatically and turned away from her to steal another covert bite of his own bread.

"The dragonlets are not going to steal your bread!" Darna said. "Definitely not in the temple courtyard!"

Giri tucked his bread back under his cloak. "But curses," he said. "They have curses!"

"Oh, go back to Cerea!" Darna said.

"But I can't," he whimpered.

Elna was coming over the hill just then. She'd found something. "Look at this!" she said, showing off a nice long piece of shiny wood. It might have been part of a wealthy merchant's cart or a ship once.

When Giri finished chewing his crust he joined Darna and Elna in puzzling over the piece. "What is it?"

"It looks like it could be from a ship," Darna said.

"We could go to the harbor, find out," Giri suggested. "A new Cerean ship is coming in. I could ask them, they want it?"

"How do you know that?" Darna asked.

"I... I just heard," Giri said quickly. "Heard a merchant saying something about it."

Darna hadn't heard anything, but she didn't hear everything, unlike Myril. She would have to ask Myril if she'd heard, but she might not say because she was so worried about foreigners. "Could we sell it to them?" she asked.

Elna's lip trembled with worry. "But they're foreigners."

"So's Giri," Darna said. "He can translate."

Giri nodded eagerly, as if he were looking forward to that Cerean ship coming in despite what he said about his home country.

"Giri's different," Elna insisted, as if she never noticed how strange he acted around food and the temples.

"I thought you were trying to get away from Cerea," Darna said.

"I am," he said nervously. "It's just most merchants, they won't care, they won't know me. I'm just from a small village. Just – "

"As long as we get our beads it will be all right," Darna
said. She was tired of getting turned away. If she had to trade
with foreigners to get her apprenticeship then she would. It
gave them a way around Nira's schemes to keep them out of
the scrap dealers' quarter. For a moment, Darna wondered if
the dragonlets would mind, then she decided not to think
about it. The dragonlets had led her to plenty of fine places
when she first arrived, prodding her this way and that. She
hadn't seen many lately apart from Iola's pet dragonlet under
the bridge. Giri might be a liar, but the Cereans could hardly
catch her for a slave in broad daylight, in plain sight of Anara's
gate.

§

Chapter 7: Cereans

Anamat city, o'er flowing with bounty:
Come to me, never leave me.
Touch not the hand of the man across the sea,
for he is the dragons' enemy.

- A song

fter dark, they brought the piece of polished wood in through a culvert under the north wall. The next morning, the first of the Cerean merchants from the new ship stepped ashore.

"Are you sure you want to do this?" Darna asked Giri.

He shook his head as a sailor sauntered past, giving them – especially Giri – an odd look.

"Take off your stupid hat!" Darna was so nervous she hadn't even noticed that Giri was wearing it again. It marked him as one of them, and they would ask questions. Elna snatched it off his head before he could protest and stuck it inside her cloak. He tried to get it back, but she kept it just out of his reach.

"I'll talk to them," Darna said as they reached the end of Merchants' Wharf. If Giri wondered how she could speak the language, he didn't say anything about it, he only pushed past, making Darna stumble and fall off the dock. She landed on the wet sand with a soft thump, but at least it was only a short fall, and she knew she wasn't hurt, only annoyed. Giri was holding the piece of wood. He started up the dock without her.

"Wait!" Darna bellowed. Cerean or no, Giri was the lousiest bargainer she'd ever seen and Elna was almost as bad. She didn't want them taking matters into their own hands.

Giri turned around slowly, swiveling his head from side to side, blinking. "Darna?" he said. "Where is she?"

"I'm here, you donkey!" Darna said.

Elna, stock still, looked down from the dock with her thumb in her mouth.

"Help me up!" Darna said. By the time Elna reached down she was halfway to her feet. tromped back to the end of the dock and climbed up there, on her own.

Things improved after that inauspicious beginning. Giri and Elna followed Darna up the dock, keeping close together.

"Goods for sale! Goods for sale!" she called as they came alongside the ship. The sailors peered over the rail at them, talking with one another.

"What are they saying?" Darna asked Giri. She couldn't quite make it out.

He startled at the question. "Saying?" he echoed. "They're saying, 'Look, it's an Anamat scrappling like we heard about.' Someone else said he'd seen ones like us before. Another says it's too strange, Anamat, we would never do that in Cerea."

"Why not?" Darna asked him.

"I don't know, maybe they do, the sailor just doesn't know everything." Giri bit his lip and shuffled away from her.

"Come on, let's just sell this thing," she said. "Goods for sale!"

Finally one of them came to the rail. "What you have?" he asked in the language of Theranis.

Darna showed him contents of her sack one by one. A gaggle of other sailors joined the first one, whispering among themselves. She wished that Giri could tell her what they were saying, but she didn't want to let him start translating before she had a better sense of what the sailors might want. Darna brought out a length of rope that she'd spliced together, but Giri waved it away. There was a piece of misshapen iron that Darna hadn't been able to figure out. It didn't have the feel of a farm implement. After a moment's hesitation, she showed it to the sailor at the front of the crowd.

He inspected it closely then waved one of the other sailors closer.

"How much?" he asked.

"What's it for?" Darna asked in return.

He looked at her blankly. Darna looked back at Giri, questioning.

Giri translated, and the sailors huddled closer.

"What do they say?" Darna whispered.

He pulled himself away slowly. "It's for the... something in the kitchen, something for cooking."

They must have said more than that, Darna thought, they'd been talking so long. "And what did they say about you?" she asked.

Giri just shrugged. "They say... I tell them I wait for another boat, that I go home soon."

"Oh. That's what you tell them, is it?" She looked at the piece of iron again. "How about two large blue beads?" she said.

Giri translated. It went back and forth a few times, Giri and the Cereans showing sizes and numbers with their hands as they argued. Darna began to remember what she'd learned from the other Cereans before she'd let Giri join her gang, especially the words for numbers.

"They say, they give you one large, three small," Giri said after a while.

"One large and five small," Darna said, "all Anamat beads."

They conferred more quickly then nodded, agreeing to Darna's terms. A paunchy man counted out beads and handed them over. It was the best sale they'd made since Nira had told the merchants to stop buying from them. Elna hopped up and down excitedly but Giri looked so calm that he might have been seeing beads like that every day. One of the Cereans slipped him yet another bead. Darna didn't let him see that she'd noticed.

Elna thrust the piece of polished wood forward too quickly, before the beads had hit the bottom of Darna's pocket. Darna scanned the boat's rigging for the third time since they'd reached the harbor that morning and for the first time since they'd gotten close. She still couldn't see anything that looked quite like the piece of wood but there was something toward the bow that looked a bit like it, only shorter and thinner. One of the sailors jumped onto the dock to look more carefully. Elna startled away from him and stuck her thumb in her mouth.

The sailors gathered around, discussing the piece loudly.

"How much d'you think we can get?" Darna asked Giri.

He shrugged. "I do not know."

It had to be worth at least as much as the metal thing, they'd just sold, Darna figured.

"They say it's missing a piece," Giri whispered, "that it's broken."

"But it's better than the one they have, isn't it?" Darna asked.

"How'd you know?" Giri asked.

"I can see things," Darna said, raising her eyebrows at him.

Giri looked spooked. He still thought Anamat had curses. Darna wondered how he couldn't see how ridiculous his fears were, how silly they made him look.

"Five large yellow-striped beads," she proposed. "A bargain."

The paunchy man laughed and held up three fingers.

Darna frowned, trying not to show how glad she was to get even one mid-sized bead for anything. "Three large," she said, "and two middling tailor beads."

The paunchy man didn't quite understand, so Giri translated again. After a little back and forth, he held out his offer – three large beads and a silver one that Darna didn't recognize, a bit bigger than a tailor's bead.

"Fine," she said. The paunchy man handed over the beads and one of the sailors hauled the piece of wood on board. They carried it to the bow and set it beside the similar piece Darna had noticed. They pointed and prodded and rolled one piece over next to the other, chewing on the bits of dark rope that they kept tucked in their pockets.

"More?" the paunchy man asked, drawing Darna's attention back.

"Ah." Darna looked hurriedly through her bag. "No, nothing special, just some bits of junk." She had the copper box, but wasn't convinced that the Cereans would like it any more than the Anamat merchants had. Maybe it was just bad luck all around. She could trade it to Nira. That would be a good joke.

"What about that – " Elna started. Darna elbowed her. The man was talking and Darna couldn't understand him at all. He sounded different from the other Cereans.

Once more, Giri translated. "He says, bring your good things."

"Yes." Darna nodded vigorously at the merchant. "I will. Bring good things." She was pretty sure they'd said something else, too, something Giri hadn't translated.

The paunchy man reached toward Darna. She looked at his hand, not sure what to do.

"He want you..." Giri's brow wrinkled. "He wants your hand in his."

Darna thought, why not? She might be dealing with the dragons' enemies, but they were putting good Anamat beads in her pocket. She set her hand in his, lightly. Her fingers sank into the deep creases between his calluses as he gripped it. It was a strange sensation. He moved his hand up, with Darna's in it, then dropped it, smiling all the time. The sailors she'd met before hadn't done anything like that.

Darna forced herself to smile, but it was a strain. Giri should have warned her about the odd custom. She didn't like it at all.

They hurried away down the dock. "Is that how you Cereans pass your curses around?" Darna hissed.

"Curses?" Giri said. "No, we don't curse! That is sign of friends!"

Darna hoped that he was telling the truth. "You could have warned me," she said.

"Next time, I tell you," Giri said.

She didn't bother to tell him that she already knew about *that* now, but what else did the Cereans have in store? Would he really warn her? She wasn't so sure.

§

Darna's gang spent the rest of the day making the rounds

of the markets where they hadn't been entirely turned away, and a few merchants even bought things for a small bead, or a tiny one. By the end of the day their sack was almost empty. They ate their afternoon supper at a place called the Thirst of Conn, washed down with weak ale. Scrapplings usually kept clear of that tavern since it was a favorite with the watch, but Darna and her gang had their own fairly gained beads that day, so she figured they could go everywhere they wished, even right under the watchmen's warty noses.

Giri and Elna gorged themselves on the soup like it was the best thing in the world. The ale made all three of them a little tipsy, and they rolled away from the table giggling and still counting their beads. Elna said she might try to buy an apprenticeship at the tailors' guild – if their luck held, she might have enough.

Outside, storm clouds gathered and a fresh breeze blew up from the harbor. An anxious dragonlet paced in front of a corner shrine. Darna had plenty of beads in her pocket, so she slipped one into the offering tray, just to be on the safe side. The dragonlet looked sideways at her, but took her bead and ran off with it. It was the first one she'd seen in days, not counting Iola's pet under the bridge. Darna hoped that meant that everything would be all right with her new dealings.

Giri and Elna wandered off to wherever they slept, and Darna returned to the fireside under the bridge, stopping along the way to buy a fiagon of ale and a whole plucked duck.

"I got five large beads today!" she announced to Myril. "Well, half of that, after I'd paid off my gang. We're going to be rich!"

"Shh." Myril pointed up, toward the road.

"I..." Darna started loudly again, then got a little quieter. "All right, but we are going to celebrate!"

"Is that a duck?" Iola said, gliding up from her usual perch by the canal where she'd been communing with the dragonlet.

Myril was already chopping onions. The duck would just fit into the pot if she saved some of the greens for later. She trimmed the carcass and soon had it simmering with fragrant roots and a few new herbs to lighten the aroma of fat, dark meat.

"Who are you selling to?" Thorat asked.

"It's a secret. Trade secret," Darna said. She didn't want him blabbing to Pannen who would surely pass the news on to Nira.

§

In the next few days, farmers came in from the hills for the beginning of the Midsummer festivities and every morning brought more green scrapplings to the breadline. After taking the priestesses' bread, Thorat went with the East Market gang while Myril and Iola went begging and Darna went her own way. One day, she would go up to Conn's Roost, the next, out to the dump. Sometimes she met Giri and Elna, sometimes she went on her own, as far as Myril could tell. It was coming on to the last full moon before mid-summer, and it seemed that Nira had decided to leave Darna alone.

Myril and Iola went to their usual begging place, where Myril watched and listened as the crowds grew. A small, dark man with tattoos on his arms came by, hands folded close and casting fearful glances at the people around him. He was from Enomae, if she guessed right, or maybe Ganat. Not one of the people of Theranis, in any case. She tagged along with her basket, not bothering with words. He saw Myril and stopped. He'd understood what she wanted quickly enough, and dug under his arm for what must have been a pocket. From it, he produced one of the tiniest beads she'd ever seen, but it shone brightly and she thanked him before running back to where Iola sat, her empty basket at her knees.

"Did you hear anything?" Iola asked as she sat back down.

Myril shook her head, but she opened her ears until a conversation caught her attention.

"D'you hear about that scrappling with the stick?" someone said.

"The upstart scavenger?" one of the farmers asked.

"Yeah, that one," the first person said – it was a woman from the roper's guild, her belt jingling with tools. "Do you buy from her?" she asked.

"Not yet. Got to keep the other ones happy," said the farmer. "Besides, I don't have much use for scrap."

"Well, I wasn't either," the roper said, "but sometimes she had things, so..."

The pair walked away. For a moment, Myril couldn't hear much over the complaints of an approaching cow. The farmer and the roper were still talking when Myril heard them again.

"I saw her out on the docks, talking to Cereans!" the roper said.

"That's strange," the farmer remarked.

"It's a scandal!" said a third voice, joining the conversation.

"It's a treason," said the farmer.

"We can't have her doing that, she'll cut us right out of work," said the roper. "We trade with the foreigners. It's only to protect the scrappers from foreign slavers, they should know that."

"Surely they wouldn't do that here!" the farmer said.

"They have in Ganat," said the roper.

"Well, they do keep slaves in Ganat, sometimes, least that's what I've heard," reasoned another guildsman as he joined the conversation.

They were talking about Darna. Who else would be so reckless? Everyone knew that the foreigners meant danger and that they had no reverence for the dragons or the dragons' children.

Myril looked over at Iola, gazing beatifically at the shrine. Myril placed a hand on her arm to draw her attention back.

"Darna is trading with foreigners," she said. "We should stop her."

"She can't be," Iola said. "That would bring the dragon's anger on us!" she said.

Myril wondered if she could stop Darna. A knot of worry formed in her gut. "I should stop her," she thought aloud.

Iola shook her head. "Anara will stop her. Don't leave me. This will be a good begging day."

As if to prove Iola's point, another bead dropped into their basket. Myril thanked the farmer who'd dropped it.

"Merchants trade with foreigners all the time, why is it different for scrapplings?" Myril wondered aloud. She was uneasy, but she wasn't sure why.

"Because we're the dragons' own," Iola said, staring off toward Anara's island. Then she shook herself back to the present. Myril leaned away. She didn't want to be pulled in by the trance that came and went so lightly for Iola. "The merchants belong to their guilds, not the dragons."

Myril frowned. The dragons could curse as well as cure. The countryside was full of tales of blighted crops and stolen livestock. It was said that things like that happened when people neglected their offerings, but Myril shied away from believing that the dragons would curse the city, regardless of what Na had said at the bottom of that lake in the mountains. She pushed that out of her mind. Darna was only trading, as many in Anamat did. The foreign boy in Darna's little gang worried her more.

"I should go find her," Myril said. She quieted her thoughts to listen for Darna. "North," she said to herself.

"She's safe for today, then," Iola said, half-entranced by something only she could see. "She's away from them. You don't need to go."

Myril still wanted to find Darna, but she also didn't want to argue with Iola or leave her alone with her visions, so she stayed, watching as a hail of tiny beads fell into their basket.

§

One morning, Darna sent Elna to watch the Northeast Gate to see if any of the greater guilds were sending carts out to the dump. The greater guilds – the glass and metal workers, the chroniclers, and the planners – left the best scrap, even after their garbage-haulers had skimmed the choicest pieces. The chronicler's guild usually left only scraps of parchment too small for practice, but those could be sewn together by a careful hand. Elna was half-blind past her arm's reach, but she worked a needle and thread well. The sword-makers and other smiths left metal scraps. Even Nira's gang knew enough to look out for those. The planners guild had all manner of curious tools which could get a good price with farmers and tradesmen, even when they were bent and broken. Nira's gang usually overlooked those.

Darna and Giri carried their wares down to the docks. They had some scrap metal, a few pieces of broken glass, and one or two prize bits of sheepskin almost good enough for parchment. The Cerean ship was due to leave soon. Darna half worried that Nira might tempt Elna back into her old gang if the trading dried up again. That would be too bad – Elna might be half blind, but she was easier to get along with than Giri, with his fear of curses.

"Why are you so scared of Anara?" Darna asked Giri as they retrieved some of their stash from a hiding place near Watchman's Bridge.

"Everyone is scared of Anara!" he declared. Then he looked at her and bit his lip. "You're not?"

"I haven't crossed her," Darna said. "She's not just terrible, she's beautiful, too, and... They all say that, in the temples anyway," she said. "Listen, Anara's not going to take your arms off for eating temple bread."

"Does she do that?" Giri asked, alarmed. "Take arms off?"

"Well of course she does, she's a dragon!" Darna said. "But not for eating temple bread."

"For what then?" Giri asked.

Village children were told that the dragons kept Theranis safe from foreign invasion, but maybe it was only the foreigners' fears of dragons that kept them away.

"For making war on them, on the dragons," Darna said after a while.

"Who did that?" Giri asked.

"No one did!" Darna answered. At least, they hadn't as far as she knew. Maybe someone had, back in the legends, like the warrior hero on the copper box. "Do you want your arms torn off?"

"No!" Giri trembled as if Anara were circling above him, ready to strike. Darna checked the sky, but Anara wasn't watching Giri, at least not that she could see.

They were getting near the place where Watchman's

Bridge crossed the West Canal. There, it flowed almost as swiftly as the river outside the city walls. Darna looked up and thought that she saw Anara's wing between two buildings, but she wasn't sure. Then the dragon made herself invisible against the sky, if she had been there at all. Giri had been looking at his feet the whole time. Had he shuddered? Darna wasn't sure.

"Let's go this way," Darna said, just to find out if that glimpse of wing meant anything. She led Giri, slightly befuddled, through a narrow string of alleys. They made it down to the harbor in record time.

§

Chapter 8: Nira

In the months of trading season,
weather's fair and men have reason
to toast companions new and old
and seek new pastures for their fold.

– A ballad fragment

The Cerean ship lay at the end of the dock, busy and jam-packed with barrels. A wispy-looking vintner's agent bargained with the ship's captain while his laborers rolled their casks down the street and out to the ship, rattling all the way. A quantity of beads passed between their hands at the scrapplings' approach. Darna had never seen so many beads in her life, not all at once. Her jaw gaped open.

"Don't look like that!" Giri whispered.

"Mind your own look," Darna groused, but she shut her mouth and pretended not to care. The vintner's agent squinted at their approach.

"No scrapplings on the dock," he said. "Pickpockets!"

"I am not a pickpocket!" Darna protested. She waved her stick and exaggerated her limp.

"Or beggars neither!" the vintner's agent said, his oiled beard quivering.

"Ah, my friends!" the Cerean captain said, brushing the wispy agent out of his way. He wasn't as fat as the paunchy man they'd bargained with that first day, but he still had a wide girth for a seafarer.

The vintner's agent looked so puzzled that he bent sideways. He frowned at Darna and Giri as the captain slapped him on the back and sent him on his way. Even he, accustomed as he was to Cereans, didn't like the touch. Darna noted that. She thought she could deal with their strangeness better than the vintner's agent had. Maybe she could be a merchant some day, if the guilds wouldn't have her and if she could escape whatever the Prince of Tiadun had in mind for her. She imagined being paraded in front of lordlings and chieftains while they sneered at her behind their hands for her limp and did whatever they could to make sure she never saw a dragon again. Had that been Anara that she'd seen earlier?

Giri greeted the captain with the Cereans' odd hand-clasping ritual and they exchanged hurried whispers. Darna stuck out her hand and did her best to smile as the Cerean captain shook it.

"You have goods?" he asked her.

"A few things," Darna said. The captain sat on a piling while they opened up their sacks. He picked out some of Elna's repaired parchment and a few of the finer pieces of scrap-metal.

"How much?" he asked, indicating all of it.

Darna calculated quickly, but he interrupted her with a laugh.

"Good trade!" he said suddenly. Then he put his hand into a pocket - he had more than one, with different bead-values in different places - and produced a dozen silver and glass beads. It was more than Darna would have asked for, and she would have expected the captain to haggle for a lower price. Giri caught his breath.

The captain held the beads out to Darna and she thanked him in the Cerean tongue – that much, she could let Giri know.

"My friend," the captain said in the language of Theranis. "I have a friend, he come soon, big ship, with a..." he paused, trying to recall a word. "A bird, there." He pointed to the bow of the ship. "Wood bird, not real bird."

Darna nodded and beside her, Giri stiffened.

"You come trade with him," the captain said. "He want Anamat things."

"Sure I will!" Darna said. She had been worried that they would have no more Cereans to trade with, that she would have to deal with the dark and oily men of Enomae whose language she didn't understand at all, or the sailors from Ganat who wore swords at their belts like the city watch. Thanks to having Giri around all the time, the Cereans were starting to seem almost familiar.

Giri and the captain exchanged a few more words in hushed tones. Darna couldn't understand most of the little she could hear. All she knew for sure was that the captain was offering Giri something, and Giri was shaking his head. Finally Giri turned back to her.

"We go?" he said.

"Sure," Darna agreed. They repeated the strange hand clasping ritual and said their farewells.

As Darna and Giri walked back down the dock, Darna reflected that Giri was hiding something from her. Between his fear of the dragons, his strange tongue, and the fact that he could undercut her in her dealings with the Cereans, she wanted a better handle on him. She needed to learn to understand more of what he was saying, without him knowing what she was doing. She frowned.

"What's wrong?" he asked.

"Nothing," Darna said, "I'm just thinking."

But then they saw that something else was wrong. Elna was coming toward them at a run, her cloak torn, mud all over her face, and a dark bruise forming around one eye.

"Elna!" Darna ran toward her. "What happened?"

Elna fell into her arms, sobbing. She almost knocked Darna over, but Giri stepped in, too.

"It's Nira! She says – " Elna paused to sob. "She says to tell you get out of the dump, it's her turf."

"Are you all right?" Giri asked.

Elna shrugged. "I guess so. There was a cart, a big one, from the glassblowers. I followed it out into the dump and then... and then Nira and two of the boys got in my way and told me to scram. They said, 'This is our turf, get lost,' and I said, 'I don't have to,' and then they knocked me down and I got my cloak ripped and Nira came and punched me."

"Did she punch you a lot?" Darna asked.

Elna shook her head. "No, just once." She pointed to her eye and winced.

"Looks ugly," Darna said. "You'll be all right?"

Elna nodded, sniffling.

"Well, let's think about it tomorrow," Darna said. "We can't let her do that."

"I don't know," Elna said.

She had a point, Darna thought. The three of them weren't nearly enough to stop Nira and her bullying.

"We go to the water-spout," Giri suggested. "Clean up."

Giri and Darna supported Elna between them. She stopped shaking and snuffling so much. Apart from the black eye, she didn't seem to be badly hurt.

"We can't let Nira scare us," Darna said, as much to

herself as to Elna.

Elna nodded. "No. I have better beads, more bread now."

"Good. And it will only get better." Darna clenched her jaw, determined to make it so. "It will only get better. There's only a moon-round until Midsummer. We can just work around her for now. Maybe at night. Don't worry, we'll get back at her."

Giri went wide-eyed with fear. "Night?"

"Night and moonlight," Darna said. "And none of your stupid talk about curses, either."

"But I can't see anything at night," Elna sobbed.

"And the gates are closed," Giri added, as if that mattered.

"I don't know." Darna sighed. "Let's just let Nira have the stupid glass. I hope she cuts herself on it."

Elna choked back a sob and took a steadying breath. A soothing rain had started to fall, blending with Elna's tears. Darna left her in Giri's care. She was too angry to rake through garbage and her best customers were sailing away on the tide. Only a moon-round until Midsummer, she told herself, and by then she would have enough for an apprenticeship, one way or another, and she could stay in Anamat forever.

§

Back at the bridge that night, there was no sign of Thorat and Myril and Iola hadn't seen him since morning, either. Myril sat very still and listened.

"He's over in the East Market," she said. "He's all right, but he won't be back tonight." She shook herself as she brought her senses back to what was closer at hand.

"Is Nira there, too?" Darna asked.

Myril nodded. They settled in together as well as they

could. They glimpsed him across the temple courtyard the next morning hemmed in on every side by Pannen's East Market boys and Nira's gang. Darna looked away, another friend lost. After the breadlines, she went looking for Elna who wasn't in any of her usual places. Late in the morning she spotted Giri on the shore near Merchant's Wharf and managed to catch up with him before he slipped away. He told her that Elna was resting, and that neither of them much felt like scavenging. Darna didn't want to let Nira drive her off, but she wasn't quite ready to brave the dump on her own, so she sat in the market with Myril and Iola, stick on her lap, scowling at her begging bowl.

On the third night, Thorat finally made it back to the bridge.

"Where have you been?" Darna asked by way of greeting. Myril and Iola were building the fire. Darna dumped her bundle of firewood beside the stones. "Well?" she said.

Thorat turned around to look at her. She raised her eyebrows at the sight of his black eye. "You got one, too?"

"Who else got one?" Thorat asked.

"Elna, that girl who helps me out," Darna said. "Is yours from Nira too?"

Thorat shook his head. "Not exactly, but she had a hand in it."

"She's getting on my nerves," Darna said.

"She's hanging around Pannen a lot," Thorat said. "She doesn't like you much either, but you know that."

"Let's not talk about Nira," Iola complained.

"Fine," Darna and Thorat said in unison.

Myril inspected Thorat's eye then she put bits and pieces together in her small pot for a poultice while their evening meal bubbled on the fire.

§

"Where we going today, boss?" Giri asked the next morning, when they met near the palace hill temple. Giri didn't seem to mind seeing the dragonlet statues as much there, maybe because in Conn's Coop the priestesses were mostly interested in the governor, the princes, and their wealth, not the dragons. He looked tired, but not as bad as Elna did. She stood beside him, nodding absently and staring at Darna's piece of bread from behind her purpled eye. Darna handed it to her. Elna's cloak was still torn halfway up the back.

"You gotta fix your cloak," Darna told her.

Elna just nodded.

"Let's lay low for now. Let Nira think she's scared us." It was all Darna could think of. "We can start looking for another place to scavenge, maybe." She took a bite of the bread. "Let's go get Ara's Landing bread, this stuff is too dry."

"I won't." Giri shook his head so vehemently that Darna thought his little scrunched cap would fly off.

"'Course you can," Elna said. "Let's go!"

"No!" Giri said. He reached out to Elna and grabbed her arm, but tenderly. Elna eased back toward him.

"Will you help me fix my cloak?" she asked him.

"I will," said Giri, "but no dragon-curses."

Elna frowned at Darna, as if sympathizing with Giri's fear of curses. Darna doubted that Elna had ever seen a dragonlet, never mind a full dragon. For the past moon-round, the dragonlets disappeared when Darna looked straight at them. Even under the bridge, Iola blocked the dragonlet from sight most of the time. Was she losing her ability to see the dragons? Had she caught dragon-blindness from the Cereans? She needed to be alone, to think.

Darna walked away from Giri and Elna. They were holding hands like Cereans. "Meet me back here in four days, all right?" she yelled back at them. She was going to get some better bread if there was any left at Ara's Landing. She limped down the hill, keeping to the main streets for a change.

Darna arrived just as Nira's gang was leaving for the dump. They circled around her.

"Your little gang run off?" Nira shouted.

Darna ignored her.

"So?" she yelled. "Answer me, you little cripple."

Darna stopped and wrinkled her nose at Nira. "Go dig up rotten cabbage."

"Ha ha." Nira punched one of her lackeys in the arm. "You got a lot to learn, runt." As she stepped in to take a fistful of Darna's tunic, a clear voice rang out over their heads. Nira paused.

"Children, you must not fight in the holy sanctuary of Anara," a priestess said. She stood beside the gate, blocking Nira's escape. "Come here. Your name is Nira, is it not?"

Nira let go and her followers parted to let the priestess approach. Darna hurried off to ransack the pile of cooling bread while the priestess took Nira a little distance apart and whispered something to her, something Nira didn't want to hear. Darna wished Myril were there to tell her what the priestess had said, what had made Nira's face sour even more than usual. The priestess waved the scrapplings away. Nira ignored Darna as she gathered her gang and made off for the dump.

"What was that all about?" Darna asked the priestess, after Nira had gone.

"I should be asking you that," the priestess said.

"Fine then. Can I get an extra piece?" The others were

mostly gone, and there was still a big stack.

"Who will you take it to?" the priestess asked.

"I don't know. Probably just eat it myself," Darna said.

"You don't know someone who needs it more?" the priestess said.

"Never mind," Darna said, "I... I have to go."

The priestess shoved the bread into Darna's hands. She almost gave it back, but it smelled so, so good. Giri would surely find Elna something better to eat, wouldn't he? He would look after her.

By midday, Darna was back at the bridge, crouching in the cool shadows. The dragonlet was nowhere to be seen, but in the heat of the day anyone would want to hide away. Before long, Myril and Iola climbed down the bank, their beggars' basket clinking with beads. Darna offered them some of her extra bread as they sat down.

"I hope you're staying away from those foreigners," Myril said.

"They're the least of my worries," Darna said. "And they're gone now, the Cereans."

"Anara doesn't like them," Iola said, not looking at Darna.

What difference did it make? Darna wondered.

"Come to the market with us this afternoon," Myril said.

She should consider it, but she just didn't want to. "I'm going to look for new scavenging grounds," Darna said.

"Do you think there are any others?" Myril asked.

Darna sighed. "Not really, but I almost have enough for an apprenticeship, so I have to try. Don't you want your apprenticeships?"

"We're all going to be priestesses," Iola said, sounding impatient. "They don't take fees. The guilds shouldn't either."

Darna sighed. "They do, though. Fine, I'll go begging with you, but just today." She certainly didn't want to be a priestess, but at this point all she needed was a little bit more.

§

A bead landed in the basket. It came from the hand of one of the scrap re-sellers, and he made a warding sign over Darna as he dropped it. Darna nodded her thanks. She didn't think she would last through the afternoon.

A tiny clay bead fell into Iola's basket. The cobblestones poked into Darna's bottom, making her bad leg ache. Surely there were things places she could explore, places where Nira wouldn't find her. There could be some untried scavenging ground near the city, but there was a gang in the West Gate market that did a little scavenging, and there others picked over the guild scrap-heaps. That left the palace. Darna didn't like the idea of digging through their kitchen garbage.

Another bead landed in the basket. Myril elbowed Darna and she joined the other two in thanking the farmer. She felt like she was going to go stark raving mad. She looked out at the harbor. There were no more Cerean trading ships there, but a merchant boat from Enomae sat at the west dock and one from Ganat bobbed out in the waves, along with a new Ganatean merchant ship that had sailed up in the night.

"Don't even think about it!" Myril chided her.

"I'm just looking," Darna said.

"Begging is safer," Iola said.

"Safer?" Darna said. "Is that why you came to Anamat?"

Iola's lip quivered. "No. I came because they wouldn't let me stay."

"Maybe they –"

"Darna!" Myril snapped, cutting off whatever insult Darna had been about to spit out.

"If I could be a priestess now..." Iola sighed. "But they won't have me."

"They will," Myril said. "It's only another moon-round."

"It seems like forever." Iola gazed longingly at the shrine. "You're sure?"

"Mmm. Sure." Myril looked around to get her bearings. "You're not going to trade with those foreigners?" she asked Darna.

"Not today," Darna said. She wondered if Iola and Myril sat around bickering like that most days. She knew that she would if she had to keep sitting there. She started to stand but then she saw one of Nira's lackey green-knees, a boy with a snotty nose, hovering around a roper's makeshift lean-to. She sat back down.

He scuttled toward them. Myril put her arm around Darna who tried to shrug her off. Myril held tight.

The boy put his hands on his hips as if he could tower over Darna. "You stay away from that dump," he said. "We got your friend, that boy..." His eyes moved even closer together as he failed to remember Thorat's name. "His gang, our gang, we're like this!" He waved his fingers in Darna's face. "You stay out of it, Nira says."

" Sure -" Darna started. Myril jabbed her, but she continued. "You tell Nira she can have her stupid dump." Myril elbowed Darna so she didn't go on to tell the boy what a sorry piece he looked.

"We got - East Market gang, Nira's gang, we got our turf," the boy said. "You stay out."

Darna rolled her eyes. "You tell Nira I say, 'Sure.'" She figured that he probably couldn't remember more of a message than that. Nira's lackey slunk off, back to his overgrown gang leader.

As soon as the boy was out of sight Darna got to her feet again. "I have to go somewhere. I'll lose my nut if I keep sitting here."

Myril and Iola sighed in unison.

"Just stay away from those foreigners!" Myril warned.

"I'll see you back at the bridge," Darna said, not making any promises.

Darna walked the length of the harbor front, leaning her stick into the sand and stretching her stride as long as she could make it go. Why did Nira bother Thorat and Elna? Sure, Darna was cutting in on her turf, but there was plenty there she didn't see, and if she'd come straight to Darna apart from sneering at her in the breadlines, then maybe they could have talked. Darna wondered what would happen if they fought, her stick against Nira's much longer reach and shorter wits. What if Darna won? She didn't think there was much chance of it, but it was a nice thought.

Darna strode all the way to where the west wall met the water where she crouched on the wet sand with her back to the wall. She had to have some other plan, not just selling to the Cereans. Myril was right about that much, especially since it left Darna relying on Giri more than she liked. It was time to start looking for an apprenticeship in earnest, even if she didn't have enough for the planners' guild. Maybe she could try her luck with the Anamat merchants. That reminded her: she'd been meaning to go begging in the taverns again and find some other Cereans to see if she could learn more of their language without Giri noticing.

Darna had seen a couple of those scrunched caps on the Ganatean packet that morning. There might be Cereans in its crew, Cereans who didn't know Giri. Maybe they could teach her a few more things, even if they weren't junk buyers. She waited and watched. Before long, a small group of them climbed into a tender and rowed to the shore to take their midday meal in a tavern. Darna followed.

The Cereans pulled their boat onto the sands and left it overturned. She studied it from a distance. It had some metal fittings that she might be able to almost match with dump scrap. Thinking about those, she was so distracted that she didn't see one of them sauntering toward her until his shadow crossed the sand at her feet.

The moment Darna looked up, he shook his fist toward her face. He had thick, tanned forearms covered with pale hair, and he squinted at her through light brown eyes. He put himself between Darna and the boat and pantomimed that she was to stay away. She shook her head. She tried to think of some words in Cerean.

"Greetings," she managed to say.

"Stay away," he said, gesturing madly with his hands.

"I get you good food," Darna tried the words, but they came out all wrong.

"What's that?" said another of the men, coming up behind him. "It can speak?"

Darna stuck out her hand, begging. The first Cerean shook his head, but at the same time he dug in his pocket and produced one of the very tiny beads she'd seen from the last batch of Cerean sailors. She took it and thanked him in their language.

Some of the other sailors in their group called, hurrying them along. They started to walk away, then the second man turned back to Darna.

"Come along?" the second man asked her.

Darna agreed by following. She repeated the man's words under her breath, practicing the sounds.

§

Chapter 9: The Tongues of Anamat

*They came from all directions, the commoners, the nobles,
and traders from across the salty waves. As the year's longest
days lit the sky, they wore out their traveling shoes on the
mountain passes to buy new ones in Anamat, to celebrate the
journey between the worlds, to greet one another, and
perchance to witness the magic of Anara's blessings.*

– The Chronicles of Theranis

For the next few days, Darna followed the Cerean sailors
around to the taverns and helped them make sense of
Anamat when the others were taking their midday rest. She
translated for them, using a lot of sounds and hand gestures to
fill in. She picked up their words as quickly as she could, but
four days wasn't much time. Still, it helped her remember what
she'd learned before and she added a dozen or so new words
most days. She tried to ask them if they'd seen a Cerean boy
around, but they didn't seem to understand the question, no
matter which language she used.

One day, near dusk, she spotted Giri around the west end
of the harbor. He disappeared into a blind alley. He wasn't
there when Darna walked by a short while later. He must have
gone into one of the side doors of the warehouse there. Was he
sleeping in a merchant's warehouse? Darna waited for a while,
but it was late and she was hungry, so she gave up and headed

back to the bridge. It looked like some merchant was keeping a place for Giri. Very strange.

Other than that, Darna didn't see Giri or Elna for a few days, as they had planned. Darna kept to herself except for going to the breadline with the others and her midday meals with the Cereans. When the new moon came, they met again at the palace temple, at the usual time, and got back to business. Darna hadn't found any other good foraging spots so they went back to the dump.

It seemed that Nira had called off her patrols, taken in by Darna's absence, thinking she'd won back her turf. Then again, maybe she was just busy with other things over in Pannen's territory. The scavenging was good. Elna's bruises had faded and she seemed almost cheerful, walking along with Giri. Still, they could barely sell anything so they saved it all for the next Cerean trader.

The moon turned another quarter. Every now and then, when Darna was alone, she thought about Tiadun and wondered when the prince and his retinue would come for Midsummer. She'd already seen the princes of Onarun and Getedun with their guardsmen in the palace market. Rumor had it Lemirun's prince had arrived, too. The others wouldn't be far behind. The princes made trade deals with one another and set up councils to derive new ways of taxing the peasants, or something like that. Darna gazed out over the city as she waited for Giri and Elna to appear.

"There, dearie." An old woman's voice roused Darna from her reverie. "Looking for a trade?"

"Got a trade," Darna said. "I'm a scrap dealer."

The old woman, wearing a greasy apron and her hair pulled back into a stringy bun, shook a finger at her. "No, a real trade. For after Midsummer."

Darna edged away. "I was thinking of the guilds," she said.

"Ha. Aren't all of you? The palace kitchen needs some hands."

Darna sprang to her feet. "Not my hands!" she said.

"Just come calling if you change your mind," the old woman said as Darna hurried away.

The palace kitchen might not be as bad as Tiadun keep, Darna thought, but it would still be far too close to the life she'd fied. Surely Anamat had more than that to offer. She knew it did. She'd seen the guildsmen at their work, the merchants and the valley farmers. She would not peel parsnips again. Besides, in the palace she might see people from Tiadun keep. She shuddered at the thought. She had felt so trapped, so constrained there. She would probably see them if she kept hanging around the Conn's Roost, too.

Darna hurried back down the hill. She thought about knocking at the guild hall gates, but she hadn't heard of any of the scrapplings taking an apprenticeship yet. It was too soon and she didn't have enough beads saved up. Any apprenticeship would have to wait until the last few days before Midsummer.

Her wanderings took her down along the West Canal where she found a bit of bread on the scrap heap behind Thirst of Conn. Back down to the harbor, she found a quiet corner and ate it, listening for any interesting rumors.

A passing sailor, a Theranian of one kind or another, was talking to a young guildswoman.

"Stay away from the harbor unless I'm with you," the sailor said.

"Don't be silly, I'm fine," the guildswoman said. She looked like a tailor or a weaver, but Darna wasn't sure.

"I heard that Ganatean trader takes slaves sometimes," the sailor said.

"Not here in Anamat," the guildswoman said. "We'd never let them back again, and besides, the sea dragons would sink their ships first."

"The sea dragons aren't so choosy," the sailor said sadly.

"Oh, look," the guildswoman said. "There's another prince come to town."

They hurried off to see the prince's procession, taking them out of Darna's hearing. She hoped that the guildswoman was right. The governor might not care much about the scrapplings, but the guilds still did, or maybe they did. Giri had said that the Cereans had never taken slaves in Anamat, just hired on the occasional sailor. The other foreigners were probably the same. Besides, even if the slave traders were more than a rumor, what could they possibly want with Darna?

§

By the time the new Cerean trading ship made port, Darna could make out more of what the Cerean sailors said to each other. It wasn't a lot, but it was a beginning. The new ship had two tall masts and a carved and gilded bird on its bow, just as the other captain had said it would. Darna, Giri and Elna watched it from a lookout spot near Conn's Coop.

"Do you think that's it?" Darna asked.

"Probably," Giri said, "but I don't know." He was losing the strange choppy way he'd had of speaking when she'd first met him and he never asked her to repeat what she'd said any more. He still wore his stupid cap, but standing there next to Elna he looked less foreign than he had a moon-round before.

"I don't want to go too close 'til I'm sure," he said, catching Darna's sleeve, suddenly jittery. "They might know the guy... the guy whose goat I stole. Cerea's not so big, not as big as Theranis. Maybe they know me, maybe they're the ones who kicked me out."

"You stole a goat?" Elna asked. "How?"

"I just..." Giri shrugged.

Darna wondered if he'd really stolen a goat, or if there were some other story. His stories of how he'd left Cerea never quite matched up with each other.

"We can look from the sides then," Darna said. "What are we saving all our best scrap for if we're not going to sell it to them?" She led her two followers down to the harbor, keeping to the back alleys so they would have less chance of crossing paths with Nira's gang, the watch, princes, or any stray foreigners, slave-traders or otherwise. Every now and again, they got a good look at the ship through the gaps between buildings. Elna squinted at it but clearly couldn't make out much.

"What do you see?" she asked. "Is it the one?"

"It's got a bird on the front all right," Darna said. "Big gold bird."

"It's big," Giri said. "I never seen a boat so big. Must have fifty sailors."

"Or more," Darna agreed. "D'you think they'll know you?"

"They might." He affected a shudder.

"If they did, you could just run off into the hills," Darna said.

"But what about our trade?" Elna protested.

"We'd find a way," Darna said. Giri's weird cowardice still bothered her. "You going to go look at that boat or not?"

"I'll go," Giri said. He slipped away before Darna could ask him anything more.

"You think he really was a slave?" Darna asked Elna once

he'd gone.

Elna nodded. "He wants to go back to Cerea anyway, I don't know why."

"You like him?" Darna asked her.

"He helped me, when I was hurt," Elna said.

"Sorry. I didn't know you needed help," Darna said. She wished she'd taken Elna that extra bread, but it was too late.

"It's all right." Elna frowned. "I got more beads with you than I ever would've got from Nira, and you're not as mean. You'd never beat me up."

"No, I guess I wouldn't. Unless you went back over to Nira's." Darna only said that for form's sake, as a kind of a joke, but Elna shrank back.

"I won't." Her voice trembled.

"I was just joking!" Darna said. "Sorry."

"Oh," Elna said, but she didn't come any closer and kept a wary eye on Darna. A moment later Giri reappeared, scuttling up the alley.

"All clear!" he declared. "They're just a merchant ship, just a really big one. They're not from the king." The sound of his voice had changed again. He sounded almost happy. Darna had never heard him sound like that before.

She helped Elna stand up. "As if they'd send a king's ship just for you!" Darna said, and they all laughed at the idea, or at least, Elna and Darna did.

§

The Cerean ship sat at anchor far out in the harbor. The three scrapplings waited most of the morning for it to sail up to Foreigner's Wharf to unload its cargo. Elna tried to pick a few pockets to pass the time but didn't get much. Darna put her beggar's basket down for show. Giri paced in the shadows. Once or twice Darna thought maybe he'd gone back to the warehouse where he slept, but then he would reappear too soon to have gone that far. Some of the governor's men rowed out to the ship then came back again, poling their boat up the West Canal.

"You sure it's not the king's?" Darna asked. "It looks really big."

"Sure," Giri said. "They're just traders."

He seemed nervous. The governor's scribes and guardsmen took boats out to the merchant ship. They never visited regular ships, not that Darna had seen, but this one *was* bigger than most. She left her begging spot to try to eavesdrop but didn't learn much. Near midday, the ship moved up to the dock. A few of the governor's men stood guard as it was tied to the deepest end of the wharf. They lingered for what felt like half the day. Finally, only one of the governor's men was left on the dock, dozing with his back against a piling.

"All right!" Darna decided aloud. "Let's go!"

§

Giri and Elna followed at Darna's heels, carrying sacks full of their second-best junk. Darna didn't have any idea what to say, who to talk to, or even which language to use. She had been planning to spring her command of Cerean on Giri that day, but the fact that he wanted to go back to Cerea made her hesitate. She wanted to keep him working, to see if he really was translating or just making his own deals.

There might have been a hundred sailors on the decks, the ship was so big. Darna didn't think that Giri looked any more jittery than usual, but usually he looked plenty jittery for any occasion. She wondered if it was the king's ship after all, and he'd just said that it wasn't for some mysterious reason of his own.

"Who's in charge?" Darna asked Giri.

Giri pointed to a bloated-looking man sitting under an awning amidships. The men on the other boat had been a little thick in the middle, but this man was enormous.

"Is it always the fat ones in charge?" Darna asked.

Giri nodded. "They eat more, work less," he said in a whisper, as if that explained it all. So did the governor's men, but they didn't look like those absurd, uselessly fat Cerean captains. Darna had only seen Anamat's governor twice, from a distance, but she was sure that he wasn't nearly that fat, and all *he* did was sit around giving orders.

"Seems weird," Darna said, "weird like you."

Giri blushed a bit and Darna made a show of threatening him with her stick. They'd gotten up to the end of the wharf, where the ship's rail touched the dock and a person could step across. Darna hesitated, then pushed Giri forward.

"You talk," she said. "Tell him about that other trader, what he said."

"Ahoy!" Giri yelled. The fat man looked up and called to someone behind him, someone who could walk without jiggling all over the place. The fat man then turned to a box on the arm of his chair and picked through its contents, ignoring the scrapplings.

The man who approached the rail was well-dressed, probably one of the ship's officers. He wore a blue over-cloak and one of those slouched hats with braided trim, very finely made. It would sell for at least three middling tailor's beads, to judge by the cloth. He walked steadily despite the gentle roll of the deck and his high-heeled boots.

"No beggars!" he said in the language of Theranis.

Giri shuffled from one foot to another. He spoke in Cerean. Darna made out what she could, which went more or less like this:

"We are not beggars, but young tradesmen! We offer the best cast-off things of Anamat. Some of these things are treasures in Cerea. You can make many beads, much money reselling these things! Also we have useful things. The captain Venntental said to come to you direct when you arrive in port."

"Are you Cerean?" the man asked Giri.

Giri's answer was guarded, terse, and too quiet for Darna to hear. The ship's officer wasn't satisfied with it, either.

"Loyal to the King?"

Giri hung his head in a way that implied assent.

"Where do you get these goods?"

"They are things that have been thrown away, sometimes by accident," Giri said.

The ship's officer frowned. "Wait here," he said.

Darna watched him go.

"What did he say?" Elna asked, jumping up and down.

"Yes, what did he say?" Darna echoed. Giri was sneaky and no good, particularly if he was still loyal to that Cerean king after that story he'd told her, and not just putting on a show for the men on the new boat.

"He says we should wait here," Giri said. "The captain will decide whether to trade with us."

Under the awning, the ship's officer was having a heated conversation with the captain. The captain looked at the scrapplings from the deep sockets of his eyes, frowned, and argued with the officer. The officer mentioned the name of the other ship's captain, loudly. Finally the captain waved his officer back to the "young tradesmen," his face fixed in a smirk.

The officer nodded to Darna, but addressed Giri.

"Is this lame girl your captain?"

Giri nodded.

"Tell her that we do not deal in junk, in thrown away things. We are the king's ship."

That was it then, the little rat was lying. Darna frowned as if puzzled, but neither of them was looking at her anyway.

"We have other work for you, though," the officer said. "Listening – you understand their tongue?"

"Very well," Giri said.

"You can... enter places?" the man asked.

"Of course," Giri said.

"Take things?"

Giri hesitated.

"Your captain can answer?" The officer asked, his eyes finally lighting on Darna.

Giri turned to her. "Can we steal things?" he asked.

"I'm a scavenger, too clumsy to be a thief," Darna said, indicating her stick.

"There's a lot of rich beads in it, I'm sure. Gold, even," Giri said.

More beads would be good, Darna thought. She looked at Elna. She wasn't clumsy, even if she was half blind. "Would you?" Darna asked her.

"Maybe," she said. "In Nira's gang we used to, from the market stalls. It was easy when they didn't have dogs."

"I don't think this will be market stalls, somehow," Darna muttered.

"What did you say?" Giri asked.

"Nothing. We will consider the job, if it's small," Darna said. "Tell them that we are only small traders, and good citizens of Anamat. We will not cross the guilds or the watch. We will think about it." She nodded to the ship's officer, who smiled in return.

"We can do your stealing!" Giri declared, in Cerean.

Darna bit her lip. She would have known he wasn't translating her words even if she didn't understand any of the Cerean language.

"But only if it is not too difficult," Giri added, making it sound a little better.

"Come back tomorrow, same time," the officer said. He tossed Giri a silver bead, then, almost as an afterthought, threw a gold one to Darna. He didn't reach for Darna's hand, or Giri's, just twitched his lip and walked away.

"What's going on?" Darna demanded as soon as we were out of earshot. "Why didn't he do that hand thing?"

"I thought you didn't like it," Giri said.

"I don't, but you said they always do it, 'sign of friends,' you said. Are they friends?"

Giri looked at his feet and shuffled them back and forth.

"Are they?"

"I don't know," Giri mumbled. "But they have gold, lots of gold. That's what the sailors said, and you can tell, look at them."

That was sure. Judging by the fat captain they had to have a full larder and then some. The governor's men had come to greet them, which they didn't do for every ship, so they must have been an important trading ship at least, if not emissaries of the Cerean king himself, which seemed likelier, by the look of things. She was going to have to find the other Cerean sailors as soon as she sent Giri away.

"Let's go sell some junk anyway," Darna said. "I'm all out of beads, unless you count this gold one. I think it would look weird, a scrappling having a gold bead like this. I don't know about this ship after all."

"We go back tomorrow, don't we?" Giri asked, as shifty

as he'd been on the dock.

"Sure, we can go back tomorrow. Stealing sounds all right," Darna said, trying to sound as if she believed it. The watch was busy with the crowds of Midsummer. A little thieving should be easy enough to hide, but she didn't like it. "There's sure money in it. I could do with a good string of beads," she said. "I can dodge the watch. You two want to dodge the watch?"

Darna could tell that Elna wanted to say no, but she nodded anyway, looking at Giri. None of them wanted to land in jail, especially not so close to Midsummer, but if they weren't caught, what was the harm in it? Giri didn't seem worried about jail now, and that in itself worried Darna.

At least stealing for the Cereans would keep Nira off their backs for a while. They would be out of her territory, but they would have to make sure she didn't get wind of it, just to be safe.

"We're in," Darna said, "but we've got to be quiet about it. I don't want Nira getting jealous."

The other two nodded, shifting uneasily under their loads. They still had two big sacks full of their second-best junk and the rest of the day ahead of them. "Let's go sell some of this loot to the peasants," Darna said, setting out toward the west end of the harbor, about as far from Nira's turf as they could get.

Elna slipped behind as they walked along, clearly unhappy about the prospect of stealing.

"What will they do if we say no?" Darna asked Giri.

Giri got shifty-eyed. "Probably nothing," he said. "I don't know. Maybe find some other scrappling to take their gold."

Darna nodded. Giri was hiding something, maybe more than one thing. "You're with me, right?" she asked him. "So they picked us. And they're rich."

"Yeah," Giri nodded, "rich."

§

Darna left Giri and Elna to their own devices a little while before sundown. They'd lightened their load a little in the west harbor market. She wandered up the harbor then listened at the back door of one of the taverns. There were no Cerean voices that she could hear, so she went on to the next place, keeping under the broad eaves as a light rain began to fall. Giri always hung around the west end of the harbor when he was on his own, and the Cerean sailors still thought that Darna was joking when she said that there was a Cerean boy on the streets of the city. She was becoming more and more sure that he'd been avoiding them, but why would he, if he wanted to go back to Cerea?

Being beaten was nothing unusual, but not the kind of beating he must have had to scar his back. Giri claimed that he'd been exiled for stealing a goat, but that seemed a strange sort of punishment for theft. Laziness in a galley didn't seem like the kind of thing you'd exile anyone for, either. Maybe he hadn't really been exiled, Darna thought. Maybe he had some backhanded deal with Cerean slave-traders, or with their king. He'd seemed unworried with the captain and crew of the first trader, but he seemed to be afraid of the men on the new boat.

Darna smelled an unusual kind of smoke at the next tavern she passed and decided to look in. There were a few Cereans leaning against a side table, but not the ones she'd gotten to know. They were probably from the new ship. She tried to listen to what they were saying from the door, but the barkeep shooed her away.

By that time, Darna was about to give up. She'd gone to every tavern along the west end of the harbor and the only

Cereans she'd seen were the ones from the new ship. The others, back at the bridge, would be asleep soon. Darna yawned. She turned up a side street to cut across toward the East Canal. About two steps further along she saw the small group of Cereans that she knew, coming around the next corner.

"Hey," Darna hailed them.

"It's our little 'scrappling,'" they said. They swerved drunkenly toward her.

"What brings you out so late, little trader?" one of them asked. He was a ruddy-faced man with a scar under his left eye, but he was always smiling and he seemed friendly. He'd been a fisherman in Cerea, before taking employment on the Ganatean trader, at least that's what Darna understood from his pantomimed story.

"Have you seen my friend, the Cerean boy?" Darna asked them. It was the usual thing that she asked.

As usual, they laughed. "What Cerean boy? We still haven't seen him. There's no Cerean boy, it's a big joke." One of them staggered off to the side of the street and relieved himself. The Cereans were rude, as a rule.

"He stays in a warehouse on the west end of the harbor," Darna said, telling them more than she had before. "There's a merchant there, does he trade with the Cerean ships?"

"We don't know," one of the men said. "We keep away."

"Why?" Darna asked.

The scar-eyed one reached out and patted her shoulder drunkenly. "So many questions. Ah, Anamat, where the women are free – "

"For lots of their gold beads, they are," another of them interrupted.

"And the ale is strong."

The men sighed. They agreed on that much. They seemed to have forgotten Darna for a moment in their drunken fantasies.

"What about that boat?" Darna asked. She didn't have to say which one.

They sobered a bit. "It's the king's boat," one of them said. "He doesn't like any Cerean to work for the foreign traders, like we do."

"What about slaves?" she asked. "Are you?"

"No, no. We're not slaves, no, we're free men!" one of them said. He started to bellow a song before the others hushed him.

"You hiding out from them?" Darna asked.

"No, no, no," they all said hurriedly. "Of course not."

"We sail in the morning," the scar-eyed man said. "You can come along?" he invited.

"No way." Darna panicked. What if the Ganateans were slave traders after all? The Cerean sailors doubled over with laughter at the sight of her panic, except for the scar-eyed man.

"I'm sorry, little girl," he said. "I didn't mean that, not that," he gestured vaguely.

"You sure?" She still hung back.

"Sure," he said.

"We got to go back to our ship, good ship from Ganat," said one of the others. "Sailing on the tide."

"But what about that other boat, the big Cerean boat?"

"It's the king's. We don't like the king."

"Does anyone in Cerea like the king?" Darna wondered.

They all looked at each other. Sometimes it seemed like they shared one brain and had to decide who to pass it to, so that one could speak for all of them. Finally the scar-eyed man spoke again.

"I suppose most do," he said, "but he calls our tribes criminal, we follow the old ways, in the hills."

"Like bandits?" Darna asked, in her language because she didn't know the word for hill bandit in Cerean. "Thieves?" she asked in Cerean.

"No, it's the king that steals!" he said. "Taxes."

"Oh." That didn't mean much to Darna. Theranis's farmers paid taxes, too, and so did anyone richer than a scrappling who passed through the city gates. It seemed a strange reason to go into exile, but not quite as strange as Giri's excuses for being in Anamat.

"Are you..." She wanted to ask if they were exiles, but didn't have the word for it. "Can you go back?"

"If we want to go to the dungeons," one of the others answered. "Or pay taxes to the king."

"We must go back to our ship."

"Don't talk to those other Cereans."

"Be careful!"

"Drink Anamat ale to us!"

They all lined up and took Darna's hand, not like the men on the new ship, they raised it and dropped it in the Cerean way before they staggered back to the harbor. She watched them go, sad, and still knowing nothing except that the Cereans had dungeons all the way over the sea and there were men in the hills who left rather than pay taxes.

Darna walked back to the bridge and slipped under the blanket beside Myril, who murmured something in her sleep then rolled over and put her arm around Darna, as if warding all those foreign slavers away.

§

Chapter 10: The Commission

Gather and pilfer beads all day, on streets and markets rolling,
but if you breach the inner walls the watchmen will come
calling.

– Sayings of the Scrapplings

Back home in Helanum, Myril's mother would be harvesting green peas and planting the second crops. Her sister would be learning to tend the gardens, as she had been last year before Myril left for Anamat. Myril missed them, but at least she had some human companionship, even in Anamat. She could bear the loneliness. Sometimes she woke early, though, to be alone, and walked down to the shore to see the sun rise.

She watched as the enormous foreign ship sailed in at dawn under a dragonless cloud. When Myril blinked, the cloud disappeared. She knew that it was a sign, not just an ordinary cloud, but she shied away from thinking of it too much. It hurt to look at. Back at the bridge, she tried to sleep a while longer, but she couldn't stop her mind from circling back around to the dark emptiness over the ship. She lay between Iola and Darna, just waiting for someone else to wake up so that she wouldn't feel so alone with that vision.

Myril wondered if any of the others would understand what she'd seen. She didn't understand it much herself, and she wasn't sure that she wanted to even talk about it. As Midsummer drew closer, Iola had been lingering more and more at the breadlines, talking to whatever priestess glanced her way. Her body was far from ready, but the novitiate lasted years, and maybe she was just small. She didn't understand, couldn't understand, refused to see the corruption in the small temples, though the temple of Ara's Landing was the finest anywhere, and probably the truest place to worship the dragons. Myril would go where Iola went, just as Thorat would do if he were able.

Even though Myril longed for firmer walls to shelter her in the night and a readier supply of food, something about the temple gave her pause. She couldn't quite name it. The priestesses were said to be the consorts of dragons and the lovers of men. She was old enough to know that she didn't want to make her life one of lying down for men, even for the dragons' sake. Even without being able to picture the specifics, the idea made her want to cower under the bridge until she was old, alone and untouched. But Iola needed her, and so she would go, knowing that Iola's gift made her otherworldly, fragile, unable to make her way alone, even in the temple, or maybe especially there.

After the breadlines that day, the two of them went to sit in their usual begging place. They looked out for new scrapplings and peasants coming in from the country. Despite all the newcomers, the begging was slow that day. Myril's eyes lit on the new Cerean boat she'd seen that morning.

"Do you see that boat?" she asked.

Iola peered out at the harbor, right past the boat, and then scanned all the smaller craft around it. "Which one?"

"The new Cerean boat. It's at Foreigner's Wharf, at the end." Myril pointed, and Iola strained her eyes in that direction.

"Oh, that one. It's strange. The dragons don't see it," she said. She looked puzzled, then shook her head, as if shaking water out of her long, glossy hair.

"How?" Myril asked.

"I don't know," Iola said. "I can't even think about it."

She would say nothing more, so that was the end of that. Myril felt the shadow around the boat again, reaching out and chilling her. Iola seemed to be able to ignore it, or maybe she really was blind to it. What unholy magic did the Cereans have?

A bead landed in the basket and Myril absently thanked the person who had dropped it. She faced west all that day, trying to stay out of the shadow of the Cerean ship.

§

Pannen's East Market boys watched the Cerean ship come in that morning, too. It was the talk of the street as the scrapplings waited for the temple gates to open. They didn't talk about the dragon-hating foreigners in front of the priestesses, but they started again as soon as they were back on the street.

"The boat's solid gold!" one boy said.

"It's not," Pannen scoffed. "Just that one part of it is, and they say it's just for show, not solid."

"It's a *big* boat, though," one of the other boys said. Pannen couldn't argue with that.

"I bet they got a lot of gold in there, anyway."

"You think we could get it?"

The conversation stopped suddenly as Nira walked up. Thorat looked away.

"You boys planning anything?" she simpered.

"Thinking about it," Pannen said vaguely. "You want in?"

Nira looked back at her gang. "Maybe we got a plan, too."

Thorat was glad that he wasn't looking at her, because he could tell by the hollow ring in her voice that she didn't have a plan any more than the boys did. He would have laughed if she'd said that to his face.

"What are you looking at?" Nira strode up to Thorat and batted at his head.

Thorat ducked. "Not you!" he said.

"How's your cripple friend?" Nira said. "She learned her lesson yet?"

Pannen interrupted. "We got plans to work on, Nira," he said. "You go work on your own."

"Sure," she said. "See if I come around, then."

Pannen rolled his eyes and Nira huffed and tossed her hair. She rejoined her band of followers and led them off on their daily parade to the city dump, ignoring Pannen as hard as she could.

On the way out to the market, Pannen sulked.

"Are you and her done?" Thorat asked him.

Pannen shrugged. "She's dragging on me."

"Isn't she - you know, a little old to be a scrappling?" Thorat asked.

"Priestesses still let her into the bread lines, don't they?"

They did, but it still seemed strange, even if it was excuse enough for Pannen.

"Hey Pannen!" One of the younger boys ran up from the back of the pack. "We going to go look at that Cerean ship today?"

"It's out of our territory," said one of Pannen's closer friends.

"Yeah, way out," said another. "Nearer West Market."

"That gang's too fat and lazy to try anything," Pannen said. "To much easy living over by Getera's gate."

"I think there's enough gold on there for all of Anamat!"

"Probably enough swords to keep off the whole city watch, too."

"What's that to us?" asked a young, slightly dim-witted boy. "We don't want the watch on there with us. I don't like the watch."

"Those Cereans have enough swords to run all of us through and stick us to their spars for show, besides."

The dim-witted boy bit his lip and nodded. They walked on, not talking about the ship again until they reached the crest of a low hill and could see its masts over the rooftops.

"So, are we going over there?" Pannen's friend asked.

"We're going to go if we can get something off it," Pannen decided. "We'll stake it out tonight. You in?" he asked Thorat.

"Me?" Thorat startled.

"You can swim, can't you?"

Thorat nodded. He hadn't noticed, or planned it, but somehow he had fallen into walking with the small cluster around Pannen. Nira wouldn't be in on this new plot, as far as he could tell. "Sure, I'm in," he said. "When do we go?"

"Midnight," Pannen said, "at midnight bell-toll. Meet us this side of the mouth of the west canal, under the sea wall there."

§

That night Thorat saw Darna come in right before he had to go meet the boys. He waited for her to fall asleep before he crept out on the off chance that she might follow, but she'd limped down the canal bank like she'd walked her feet half off. Soon, she was snoring softly. Thorat wondered if Darna's Cerean friend knew anything about the new ship, but he didn't want to ask her. If news of the East Market gang's plot slipped to that Cerean boy, he might pass the news on to his countrymen. Thorat wondered why Nira considered Darna a threat to her territory. Darna only had the two followers, and neither of them was especially agile. He gave her one last look. She was breathing steadily, as if soundly asleep. He climbed up the canal bank and followed a moonlit side street down to the harbor's edge.

Most of the taverns were already shuttered for the night so the harbor front was quiet apart from a few stragglers and the occasional rat scuttling over the sand for a bit of washed-up fish gut. Thorat found Pannen and three of the others under the shadow of the sea wall, watching the ship.

"They got a guard," one of them whispered.

"'Course they got a guard."

"Two," Pannen said. Then he looked again. "Two on the boat, and another at the end of the dock."

"They have pikes."

"*And* swords."

"There's no way."

"There's never no way," Pannen said, unconvincingly.

Thorat had an idea. "How about their tenders?" he said.

"Tenders?"

"You know," Thorat said. "The little boats they row in to shore. They won't be at the dock the whole time. They'll have to row in sometimes. If they go to the taverns some night we can grab the tender."

"Then what?" Pannen asked.

"Not sure," Thorat said. "We can hide it and use it to raid other boats, later on?"

"Or we can sell it," another boy proposed, "after the Cereans leave."

"But then trading season will be over, won't it?" Thorat asked.

"Maybe they'll leave early," Pannen said.

It seemed to be as good a plan as any.

"It'll be big," Pannen said. "Where can we hide it?"

"One of the culverts up the East Canal," Thorat suggested. "Some of them are probably big enough."

They stared at the ship for a little while longer. Its guards were tall and muscular. They didn't look the least bit drunk or sleepy and they kept their weapons at the ready. The blades were so well polished that they flashed in the torchlight.

On the far side of the harbor sat a Ganatean ship, smaller than the Cerean boat and not nearly as rich-looking. It had been in the harbor for over two months. It hadn't looked worth risking a break-in, since they mostly seemed to be in Anamat to repair their sails and spars. Someone had lit a lamp and hung it on the Ganatean ship's bowsprit. A few sailors shifted around the deck, readying the ropes.

"Ganateans are leaving," Thorat observed.

"I wonder why," Pannen said. Someone yawned, then Thorat yawned, too. Pannen turned his attention back to the Cerean boat. "Anyone else have an idea?"

The boys shook their heads.

"All right then," Pannen declared. "We'll watch them a bit. Figure out when they leave their little boats unwatched, then we'll grab one. It's not breaking in, but it's something."

The sails of the Ganatean ship filled with a light breeze as the boys walked back along the shore. Its chains clanked and its ropes creaked as they weighed anchor. The ship heeled to one side and rode out before the wind.

Thorat stopped at the East Canal. "I'll go off here," he told Pannen.

"You can come back to the market with us," Pannen invited. "We're going to wade around the wall. The water's warm enough now."

Thorat shook his head. "I'll just go to my usual place."

Pannen shrugged. "All right. You know, that was good thinking, a good plan. I'm glad we asked you along, but... don't tell the others. Gotta keep this close."

"Not a word," Thorat promised.

Pannen thudded him on the back. Thorat drifted, yawning, back up to the bridge. He brushed the sand off his feet, slipped under the blanket beside Iola, and fell asleep instantly.

§

In the morning, Darna woke up a little later than the others. Myril was stirring the ashes, looking for live coals. Light bounced off the green water, making patterns on the stone arch above. Thorat sat beside Iola on the canal bank. He put his arm around her shoulder and she leaned into him, closing her eyes. Darna went upstream to splash off her face.

A light breeze rippled across the canal, but in the shallows the water formed clear reflecting pools. Darna glanced down before her hand disturbed the water and caught a glimpse of her hair. The fiery red roots were showing and the walnut dye around them was growing thin and patchy. She looked ragged and conspicuous. The princes would be coming soon if they weren't in Anamat already.

"We're going to get bread," Myril called. "Are you coming?"

Darna shook her head. "Na's blood!" she said to herself. "I can't go up on Conn's Roost looking like this, not near the palace."

Myril waited for her while Iola and Thorat went on

ahead, climbing the canal bank hand in hand.

"I'd better come with you," Darna said. She dried her face on the edge of her tunic. "My hair's showing through," she said as they started out toward the breadlines.

"I noticed," Myril said.

"Would you dye it for me again?"

Myril nodded. "I could do it tonight if you come in before sunset," she said. "But you'll have to go up to the weaver's quarter to find the dye – I haven't seen any walnut bark in the harbor market."

Darna sighed. "Forget the breadlines, then. I'd better go there first." She would have to, if she was going to get the dye before she met Giri and Elna.

"Be careful!" Myril called after her as she hurried away.

Darna made a vague gesture in response. What was worrying Myril now?

Midsummer was less than a moon-round away. The guilds of Anamat had filled their warehouses, dusted their lintels, polished their floors, and opened their halls to traders. If they were starting to take note of future apprentices they didn't show it, not that Darna could see. The streets had seemed busy to the new scrapplings when they first arrived but now they were more crowded than Darna could have imagined then, less than two moon-rounds before. The market squares were thronged with people, even early in the day. Darna hoped she would be able to disappear into the crowds if the men from Tiadun came looking. She hadn't noticed so many gaps in the wall lately. Maybe the dragonlets were shy of crowds, too.

Darna followed the East Canal up as far as the next bridge and through the streets of clothiers' workshops to the weavers' guild. Their hall was a single-story building with high walls along the street side. The opposite side opened onto a work yard by the canal, where cauldrons hung over fire pits for dyeing. There were troughs for washing wool and linen fibers and a wide embankment where finished cloth dried in the sun. Darna would have gone in through the back gate, but her steps had led her to the street-front instead, so she tried it.

The wide double-doors were rolled open a crack, so Darna slipped into the shadowed hall. High clerestory windows let in sunlight, making the place bright enough for the weavers to work, though not as bright as the street outside. It took Darna a moment to get her bearings. The looms had been moved to one side and lengths of cloth lay on tables and hung from racks, making a maze of the center of the room. A guildsman was showing a bolt of cloth to a priestess. The priestess had turned toward the street door and was looking straight at Darna.

Darna froze for a moment. Priestesses mostly looked all the same to Darna, with their smoothly brushed hair and their impeccable robes. The provincial priestesses wore slightly coarser cloth, like this one, except on festival days.

"So. You are in Anamat," the priestess said.

The voice brought it all back to her, that moment in the kitchen, that accusation that the prince was her father, the insinuation that she should care, that she should welcome becoming a pawn in his games.

She would have to do without the dye, or send Elna for it later.

Darna bolted out the door and into the mercifully crowded street. She dodged through the crowds as she ran for the palace hill, up any back passage she could find, using her stick only once every four or five steps, or if she slipped. She looked over her shoulder. The priestess hadn't followed, but she would have to be careful, much more careful now.

§

Giri and Elna were waiting for her behind Conn's Coop. They'd even gotten an extra share of bread for her. Together, they went straight down to the harbor, eating as they walked.

The Cerean ship looked even less friendly than it had the day before. Armed men guarded the end of the dock. Giri explained their mission, in Cerean, and the guards let them through, lowering their blades but keeping their hands on the hilts, their gaze following the scrapplings' progress toward the captain.

"They going to slice us up if we say no?" Elna worried aloud.

Darna shrugged. The guards looked like they'd be happy to use their weapons at any excuse, however slight.

"We just have to go talk to the captain," Darna said.

Giri led the way, frowning. Darna yanked him back. "I'm in charge," she asserted. "You're just the translator, remember?"

Giri repressed a sneer, but not fast enough. Then he got behind her.

"Ahoy!" Darna called.

The captain had spotted them. The fat rolls on his neck jiggled as he turned his head. He beckoned for them to come on board the ship. Darna hesitated.

"Go on!" Giri said.

She didn't want to. They'd never been on the other ship. Even if she didn't believe all that talk of the Cerean dungeons and slave trading, it seemed foolish to ignore the rumors completely. Giri even said that he'd been a slave, and he made it sound a lot worse than Tiadun keep. "Do they want to make us slaves?" Darna whispered.

"No!" Giri's brows pushed together. "No. Captain

wouldn't talk to us if they were going to, they'd just stick us in the hold."

"All right then, but we're not going below-decks where they could shut us up," Darna said.

Giri frowned.

"Ever. Do you agree?" Darna asked both of them. Her hands were sweating so much they were slippery on her stick. It was bad enough that they were going onto the ship, but at least on deck, people from the shore or the dock could see if anything happened. Whether they would or could do anything was another matter, but Darna didn't want to disappear into that ship.

Elna nodded, eyes wide. Giri agreed, too, but less convincingly. Darna led the way onto the deck. It swayed under them, not much, but Darna had never been on a boat before and she had to catch herself with her stick, to lean on it a lot more than she did on the steady streets of the city. The captain eyed her progress scornfully.

The ship's officer they'd spoken to the day before emerged from below decks with another man, not quite as richly clad. The second man looked carefully at them, particularly at Giri.

"We bring our own translator," the ship's officer explained to Giri.

Giri frowned and nodded.

"How have you been progressing?" the translator asked Giri.

"Well, I think," Giri said.

The rat. "What are they saying?" Darna asked him.

"We extend our greetings," the translator smiled. He was an oily one. Giri was slippery, too, but he helped her find a way around Nira when she needed that, and he'd helped Elna when she was hurt.

The captain spoke, and his voice rumbled and mumbled so that Darna couldn't make out a word, but the translator nodded.

"We have a ... small job for you." He smiled his oily smile, thin lips just curling up at the edges, his fingers fidgeting with a rolled leaf from his pocket. He stuck the leaf in his mouth and chewed as the captain spoke again.

"We have been to your governor's palace and seen many fine things there," the translator said. "There is one that the governor will not miss, but has great value to our king. It is only a small thing. You can fit it under your cloak."

"Why don't you take it yourselves?" Darna asked.

The translator twitched his lip and told the captain what she had said. The captain grunted. "We have..." He paused. "We have a reputation to maintain. We are a government. You have seen the governor's men here? They watch us carefully when we visit. You? Not so much. You are beneath their notice."

It was true, the governor hardly thought of the scrapplings at all, let alone any particular one of them. He wouldn't think anything of her at all unless the prince of Tiadun put his guardsmen on the hunt for her, and maybe not even then.

"The governor can jail us if we're caught," Darna said.

The translator shrugged and conferred with the fat captain in whispers. He turned back to Darna with a thin smile. "We will make it worth the risk, and in every country jailers can be bribed." He opened a purse and showed the scrapplings an array of beads, more than they'd gotten from the other ship all together. Darna counted. There were too many to count, but there had to be at least twenty in there, probably thirty or more, all gold. More than enough to buy an apprenticeship if the guilds would take Cerean beads, if they were real.

"Where is this thing?" Darna asked. "What is it?"

Again, the translator spoke to the captain for a while, arguing in whispers. "It is a small Cerean amulet," he said, "which once belonged to an important man in our land. An unscrupulous Anamat merchant stole it a generation ago. The heirs only seek its return. It has great...sentimental value." He paused to chew on his leaf, which smelled sweet, like some kind of olive. "The governor keeps it in a meeting room, a rarely used chamber, not far from the kitchens. You can go in there. It is under the window, in a box on the table there. Leave the box, take the amulet."

"What does it look like?" Darna asked.

They said that it was about two hand-spans long, and made of clear crystal with silver bands around it.

"Tell me more about the room," Darna said. She formed a picture in her mind of the thing, this amulet. The silver bands would shine brightly against the crystal, the smooth polished stone would shine as if from within. She pictured how easy it would be to walk away with the prize, if she chose to, or if they didn't let her say no.

"You can go in through the kitchens," the translator said. "You can do that, can't you? Beg for scraps?" His lip curled with scorn.

"We don't beg at the palace kitchens," Elna said.

"Well, you can begin, then," the translator snapped.

Darna didn't bother to clarify. She didn't even like begging for beads much, but no one begged for scraps. That was why they were scraps. You could just take them. That was how Anamat worked, even in the governor's palace.

The translator continued his description of the job. It wouldn't be an easy task, he said, but it could probably be done and look, he said, all this gold can be yours. All this gold, Darna thought, enough for her and Elna and maybe even Giri.

Darna had never been inside the palace, but she'd gone all around the outside of it, and that old woman had asked her to come work in the kitchens. Maybe she could pretend that she would go back to her old scrubbing and carrying. The translator described a room with a tall ceiling and a painted window. The table, the box, the amulet, all were under the window. He concluded with another sneer and stuck the leaf back in his mouth.

"That should be enough, I think?" the translator said, chewing.

The captain waved them away, saying something in Cerean about getting the vermin off his deck, from what little Darna could make out. "Is that all?" she whispered to Giri.

He nodded and tugged her away. She stumbled and had to concentrate to regain her footing, but she caught Giri looking back to the ship's officer.

"Make sure it's done, and done right," the officer told Giri in Cerean. "Or else!"

Or else what? Darna wondered. "What did he say?" she asked.

"He bids fare-well, until we meet again," Giri said.

Darna nodded. Giri looked narrowly at her, as if he was going to ask her a question, but then he didn't. Elna slunk along. She looked as unnerved by it all as Darna felt, but she wasn't trying to hide her fear.

As soon as they stepped up onto the dock, Darna felt better. She could get her grounding. There was something strange about being on that ship, even stranger than she'd thought it would be. She'd forgotten to ask them something important.

"How long do you think they'll give us?" she asked Giri.

Giri's eyes widened. "I don't know. Until Midsummer?"

"Go back and ask," Darna said.

She watched as he jumped back on board. He looked comfortable on that boat, a lot more comfortable than Darna would be if she were on the run from the king who so obviously owned that ship. She also had the feeling that the men on the ship hadn't been at all surprised to find Giri in Anamat. Darna couldn't hear what he said to the translator, but one thing she was sure of: it was more than she'd asked him to find out. Giri wasn't afraid of the king, not like he'd said he was. He was probably just making side-deals with them, but at least he was helping her get a lot of gold in the meantime.

"Elna," Darna said quietly. "Can you keep an eye on Giri for me? Let me know if he comes down here without us, will you?"

Elna nodded. "But I don't know where he goes at night, not most times. I don't want to argue with him, or with you, but I don't want to go on that ship again."

"Neither do I, but we might have to."

"But the other..." Elna stopped abruptly as Giri returned.

"A half-moon," Giri announced as he climbed back onto the dock. "That means we have until two nights before Midsummer. We have time, they say, plenty of time. You know how to get into the palace?" he asked Darna.

"How hard can it be?" she said. "The governor's men are idiots, just like the watch. Let's go see if we can sell some junk to the drudges at the palace kitchen."

She had the beginnings of a plan, but she didn't like the assignment. It would land them in jail or worse if it went

wrong or if the Cereans were lying. They probably were lying.
They didn't seem like they thought much of the dragons' truth.
The guards at the end of the dock let them pass, looking no less
dangerous than they had on the way in. As the crowds of the
market closed around them, Darna relaxed some, but she kept
a wary eye out for the priestess or anyone else from Tiadun.

She had a strange impulse to go looking for Anara. She
wasn't some dewy-eyed beggar like Iola, but she wanted to see
Anara, wherever she was, as soon as she could.

"I've got to think," Darna told her hangers-on. "You two
go sell some junk in the West Market or wherever. Bring me
your take at sundown. I'll be at the Corana's gate."

"What about the palace?" Giri demanded.

"It's not too far from there," she said. "I'm going to have
a look around. Go on, sell some junk."

Giri and Elna nodded and scurried off together. Darna
walked out along the beach, scanning the skies for any sign of
the dragon of Anamat.

§

Not a single bead landed in the girls' baskets all morning,
even though Anara was everywhere in the skies. Iola had been
watching the dragon for almost two moons now. Anara was
closer to humanity than Tegana had been, or at least she
seemed so. The city was like a jewel the dragon cherished in
concert with its people. She guarded her people like a cat
watched her kittens. Today she was troubled, fiitting this way
and that, never settling in one spot, not even gliding peacefully.
She didn't come close enough for Iola to see her eyes.

Iola looked down for a moment and noticed that Myril
was peering down the shore toward the west canal. She shook
her head.

"What is it?" Iola asked.

"I thought I saw Darna." Myril said. Unease troubled Myril's eyes, like the clouds around Anara.

"Where did you see her?" Iola asked. She had to strain a little to readjust her vision to the human world after gazing after the dragons. The city was such a confusing place. She wished she could stay with Anara, or at least under the bridge with the dragonlet until the temple let her in.

"On that boat, near it, anyway," Myril said.

"What boat?"

Myril pointed and Iola looked again. Just like the day before, she didn't see it at first, but when she concentrated she could blink away the strange fog around it. It sat in the midst of a soul-cold emptiness on the waves.

"I can't see it very well. There's something strange about it. Can you see it all the time?" she asked Myril.

Myril nodded. "It's not always clear, but I can see it."

Iola tried to look again, but it made her tired, so tired, and soon another sight caught her eye – another sight which faded in and out of her vision, but only because of the crowds milling on the shore. Darna strode up along the shore, stick poking into the sand, weaving in and out.

"There's Darna," Iola said.

Myril watched Darna approach as Iola turned back to the sky. Anara circled her island out in the harbor, as far away as she could get from the half-invisible boat while still staying near her own fleet, the Anamat fishermen's boats. Iola couldn't stand to look back at that boat again, let alone measure Darna's agitation against it.

Darna almost tripped over their begging basket, as if she, too, had been looking toward the dragon's island.

"What are you doing here?" Darna asked, startled.

Iola drew herself back to where they were sitting. Myril

had slipped into one of her listening trances again. "It's our usual begging spot," she said. "Right by the shrine."

"Lousy market," Darna muttered. "Didn't think I'd come over this far." She didn't look at Iola, or even at Myril.

"Where did you think you were?" Myril asked, returning from whatever she'd been thinking.

"I don't know," Darna said. "Have you seen Anara?"

She looked at Iola and Iola was forced to look into her eyes. Darna was afraid of something. That was new. She hadn't seen Darna afraid before.

"Anara was right there, over the island," Iola said.

"I was looking," Darna moaned. Then she shook herself. "Never mind. I don't see her anyway, you know."

Iola couldn't answer that. When she looked again, she couldn't find Anara either. "Maybe she's gone down to rest," she mused aloud. "She'll be back. She always comes back."

"She has to," Darna said. Then she shook herself. "I have to go!"

Myril grabbed her by the arm before she could storm off. "Darna, you were out on that dock, by that ship."

Darna waved her hand noncommittally, pulling away.

"What if I was? They have a job for me. I'm going to get some good beads, gold."

"You don't need beads to be a priestess," Iola said.

"I don't want to be a priestess!" Darna freed herself from Myril's grip. "Besides, it's just a little errand."

"There's something not right about them," Myril said.

"How would you know?" Darna sniffed. "You don't know anything about them."

"I..." Myril began.

"And where is Anara?" Darna demanded of Iola.

"I don't know, she's gone since you came along."

Darna scanned the sky frantically again, looked at Iola, then back at the sky. Her eyes followed something that Iola couldn't see.

Iola braced herself to look at the ship once more. "They're against the dragons," she said.

"They're just greedy foreigners," Darna said. "You're just scared of them like every other green-knee in the city, afraid because they're strange." She turned to walk away, but then she looked back.

"By the way," she said to Myril. "I couldn't get the dye. There was a priestess at the weavers' guild, she recognized me. I had to go."

Myril stared down into her empty basket.

"The dragons don't see the ship," Iola said.

Darna hesitated. "At all?" Then she shook her head. "Never mind. I'm going. Maybe I'll see you later."

"Well, don't..." Iola started, but Myril rested a hand on her shoulder to stop her. Darna walked on up past Fisherman's Wharf to the east jetty, not looking back, not toward the girls in the market, not toward the Cerean ship, and certainly not toward the governor's palace.

§

Chapter 11: In the Governor's Palace

The mighty Conn took his people and set to the sea in rafts.
He ruled with might and wisdom, but those did not defeat the
dragons. Ara gained him foothold on Anara's shore. His
descendants owe her homage forever.

– From a temple teaching text

D arna didn't find Anara that afternoon. The dragon wasn't by the harbor and she wasn't by the castle and she felt stupid for even talking to Iola and Myril about it. Why had Iola said that the dragons didn't see the Cerean ship?

She wished she could ask Anara herself about that, but she wasn't anywhere, at least, not for her. Even if Anara did appear, Darna wasn't Iola, chatting with dragons as if they were people. The palace was the least dragon-loving place in all of Anamat. It couldn't mean anything, so why was Anara's absence so loud? Darna paced the city, searching and thinking.

She met Giri and Elna by the North Gate in the midst of a crowd sprinkled with fat, unguarded pockets. Elna picked one and got a pair of large cobalt glass beads. Giri didn't even look at all those bulging pockets. The sun sank toward the western hills, the bandits' hills. Darna wondered what it would be like to go there, maybe alone, certainly without Myril and Iola, though she wouldn't mind traveling with Thorat if he would leave Iola, which he wouldn't.

"So what will it be?" Elna asked.

Darna blinked at her. "What?" she said. "Oh, the palace." She looked over her shoulder at the gate.

"Yeah, boss," Giri said. "What will it be?"

"I have to think," Darna said. She'd given herself half a day to think but it hadn't done any good. Her nerves were jumping around like fleas. The kitchen yard of the palace was practically butt up against a gate in the city walls. A pair of sleepy-looking guards played dice in front of the little guard-booth by the kitchen entrance that also led to the palace stables. The guard booth had just enough room in it for the two of them to stand out of the rain or the midday sun and they were leaning against the wall.

"I don't think we can sneak past them," Darna said. "We'll have to state our business."

Through the inner gate, Darna spotted a gray haired woman going by. She turned to Elna. "What guild do you want to join, Elna?" Darna asked.

"I don't think they'd have me, but I'd like to be a weaver."

"You might be a good weaver," Giri said approvingly.

Darna frowned. "Do you think you could pretend to try to get work at the palace, like in the kitchens? An old woman wanted me to, but I hate kitchens."

"So do I," Giri said.

"Why?" Elna asked.

Darna grimaced. Clearly Elna had never worked in a kitchen.

"I like kitchens," Elna protested. "Palace kitchen probably has good food, too. I'd work there."

The orange sun perched just over the black-shadowed hills and the sky was streaked with purple, but the daylight was still plenty bright enough to show Darna's red hair growing out. She led the other two down a back alley, away from the palace. She paused at a corner where she could see if anyone was coming.

"All right," she said, "here's the plan. We go to the palace temple breadlines tomorrow morning and then Elna tells the guards that we want work in the kitchens, and also maybe we have some scrap to sell. I'm not sure about that part."

Giri shook his head. "No kitchens!" he said, just as if he were saying "Curses!"

Darna took a deep breath. "Elna can work in the kitchens, then. We'll just come along selling scrap."

"But I don't want to be alone!" Elna complained.

"Fine!" Darna said. "Let's just come here after the breadlines and make something up then. I'm getting my bread at Ara's Landing. I don't like the dry stuff the governor's priestesses make."

Giri and Elna grumbled and went off to wherever they slept. Darna ambled down the main streets toward the East Canal bridge then detoured over to the weavers' guild. The doors had been rolled almost shut, but there was a tiny crack still open. She poked her nose in. It was dark inside but she could see a fire in the canal-side work yard, its light licking through the open doors on the opposite wall. A big dog slept just inside, growling at something in its dreams.

Darna listened. The guildsmen and women tending the fire were talking and laughing. They probably would tell her to lose herself, but she couldn't go into the palace with her red hair showing through, not with the princes coming. At least the priestess from Tiadun wasn't in the guild hall and it seemed unlikely that anyone from the palace would venture down to the guild halls so late in the day. Darna stirred herself back into motion and slipped around to the canal bank.

Three men and a woman of the weavers' guild sat on low stools around an open fire. A second woman stirred the pot, poking something down in it from time to time. Whatever was in the pot smelled acrid and bitter, but the fire danced and threw off cheering sparks. The weavers spoke quietly but they noticed almost immediately when Darna came into their yard.

"Who goes there?" said one of the men.

Darna took a deep breath and approached. "I'm just a scrappling," she said. "I want to buy some dye, or some walnut bark."

The woman at the cauldron leaned on her stirring-stick. "This is guild property," she said. "Initiates only."

"And customers," Darna said. "You had customers here this morning."

"So we did," said the woman who'd been sitting by the fire. She wore a kerchief over her head and held her hands in a bowl of salve. "They had beads to pay with. Do you, scrappling?"

Darna nodded. "I'm sure I have enough, just for a jar of walnut dye."

"And what would you be wanting walnut dye for, girl?" asked the oldest of the men. He had grizzled hair and hunched a little closer to the fire than the others, warming his slippers.

Darna held out a bunch of her hair.

One of the younger men laughed, and the woman with her hands in the salve elbowed him.

"Red's a fine color for hair," he said apologetically.

"I want to dye it. I just need a little and I'll be gone."

The woman took her hands out of the bowl and dried them. "But who will put it on for you?" she asked.

"I have a friend," Darna said. "I'll be fine."

"Luka," said the older man, "we can't just sell her the dye. She might sell it along to the foreigners."

"I won't!" Darna said. "I'll go. I'm sorry!" She started away, but Luka leaped up from her place at the fire and grasped her gently by the wrist. Her hands were slippery with the salve. Darna almost jerked away.

"Wait, wait," she said. "I will help you. Your friend's country dye is wearing off, and the next batch won't stick any better, I'm sure."

"It will last until Midsummer, won't it?"

"I can do better," the guildswoman said. "Come with me, scrappling girl."

"Into the guild hall?"

"No, just one of the sheds, the dye shed. Come along." Luka put her hand on Darna's shoulder and steered her away from the fire.

"I'm sorry to come barging in," Darna said, "but I tried to come this morning and I didn't –"

"Didn't want to interrupt our trade, I'm sure." Luka unlatched a small door in the side of the guild hall and used a burning twig to light the wick of a small lamp. Inside, rows of jars lined the shelves. More mysterious liquids filled vats on the floor. From a shadowed corner, Luka produced a small basin and a ladle.

"I... Can't you just sell me some and I'll go?" Darna asked again.

"And have it peel away like that just when you're trying to convince the priestesses you're pretty enough to be one of them," Luka said, inspecting a strand of Darna's hair in the lamplight. Close to the flame, it gave off an almost putrid smell.

"I don't want to be a priestess," Darna said. "I'm sure

I'm not pretty enough and I'm a cripple anyway."

The woman ignored her and searched among the jars. "Who dyed your hair before?" she asked.

"Just a friend, another girl," Darna said. "She said she learned it from her mother, in her village back home."

"Interesting," the woman said distractedly. "It's not a bad job for a village midwife's daughter."

"I don't know if she is a midwife's daughter," Darna said.

"She must be. In the villages, they're the only ones who would know something like that unless she was raised in a provincial temple."

Darna shook her head. "I don't think so."

Luka found the jar she'd been looking for and motioned for Darna to sit. "Your friend," she said, "is she seeking an apprenticeship? Are you?"

"I don't know," Darna said. "I think she's going to the priestesses, but I have another friend, she said she wanted to be a weaver, or a servant in the palace kitchens." Darna shook her head.

"Stay still," Luka ordered. "I have to strip this old dye off before we start over," she said, pulling Darna's head into position over the basin and running her fingers through the hair. "Close your eyes."

The smell was overpowering. Darna clamped her eyes shut. Her scalp burned. She stayed as still as she could while the woman worked some awful stuff through her hair then poured something warm over it. She peeked once, but then closed her eyes again. After what seemed like half the night, Luka wrapped a cloth around Darna's head and tipped her head up.

"You'll have to rest with that on for a little while. There's a bench here, or you can come back out by the fire."

Darna yawned. "How late is it?" she asked.

Luka stepped outside for a moment. "It's near midnight," she said when she returned. "You can sleep here, if you need to."

"No, I can go," Darna said. "How much?"

"A few small beads, if you have them."

Darna nodded. "I do. But tell me, how much does an apprenticeship here cost?"

Luka sat down on the bench. "It depends," she said. "For an Anamat-born child, not much if their parents are guild members in good standing, maybe ten large beads."

"Gold beads?" Darna gasped.

"No, not as much as that," Luka said. "Five large and a few middlings would do for a farmer's child, if she had any talent."

"And we're all farmer's children," Darna thought aloud.

"Scrapplings? Not after a season in Anamat. Some try to come in straight from the farms. If a scrappling can prove their worth, they can earn their apprentice fee in time."

"Oh," Darna said. "When I first got here someone told me the guilds hardly ever took on scrapplings." She yawned again, and took out three small beads to give to the weaver. "What color will it be?" Darna asked.

Luka pocketed the beads. "You'll see it better in the morning light," she said. "For now, you should sleep."

Despite her intentions, Darna slept. She woke to the cacophonous birdsong of early morning. She sprang awake, almost knocking over a jar on the floor beside the bench where she'd slept. The weavers had given her a blanket, thick and warm, but not new. She folded it and looked around for a place to see her reflection, but it was too dark to see much in the dye shed.

Outside, the stars were fading from the sky and the weavers who had been sitting around the fire at midnight were gone. The main hall doors were latched from the inside. Darna wandered over to the canal bank and looked down.

The spot she'd found was not a still pool by any means. It was just a place at the bank where the breezes lapped the water onto the shore. She couldn't see the separate features of her face, but she could see her hair color. Which was red. Redder than it had ever been before, on fire in the sun. She willed herself to wake up from the nightmare, but the smells, the sounds, all of it belonged to the waking world. She stormed back to the guild hall and banged on the door. The dog started barking and lunged at the door, growling. Darna felt him thud against the wood, but the door was too heavy for a dog, or a girl, to break down. Someone whistled to the dog and then opened the door a tiny crack. Darna stuck her stick in, wedging it open. A boy apprentice, scarcely older than a scrappling, peered out.

"What do you want?" he said.

"I want this fixed!" Darna tugged at her hair.

"Fixed?" the apprentice said. "Luka told me it was fixed, now you can go to the guilds looking like your true self."

"I don't want to look like myself!" Darna protested. "They'll drag me back to the provinces! I want my hair brown!"

"Then you'd better find a brown wig or a veil or something," the apprentice said. "Now get your stick out of the door before the dog comes and breaks it off for you."

Darna retreated. She hurried straight down the canal, wading where she needed to, even though the stones were slick and the water stank, just staying as far as she could from any streets where a watchman or a provincial guardsman might wander.

When she got back to the bridge, Myril was just waking up. Thorat slept with one arm over Iola. Her face was placid as she dreamed, probably of dragons and priestesses.

"Your hair!" Myril said as she sat up.

"I went to the weavers for dye again and look!" Darna wailed. "This is what they did to me!"

"But it's beautiful," Myril said. "It's really... I think it's beautiful."

"But you've seen it before," Darna said, more quietly.

Myril shook her head. "No, not like this. It was matted and full of leaves and twigs and dusty. Now it's like fire."

Darna hid her face in her hands. "What will I do? You were the only one here in Anamat who'd seen it, who really knew, or noticed, and now they'll all know me."

"There might be other girls with red hair," Myril said.

"Not with red hair and a limp," Darna said. "Besides, there aren't many, just that one over in the West Gate market, but she's bigger, and that one who hangs around with Nira, with all the freckles and the dull eyes."

Myril looked at her. "I'll make you a hood," she said, "or a hat or something. Wait here. I'll be back."

Darna was never sure where Myril had found the kind of cloth that Ganatean sailors wrapped around their heads, but when she put it on she looked as foreign as Giri did when he wore his little scrunched cap.

§

On the way up through the city, Darna kept her stick close, hiding it as well as she could and only using it on the steeper hills and in the shadows. She arrived late to her rendezvous with Giri and Elna. Giri's eyes popped.

"You look... you look like a young man of Ganat!" he

said.

"Maybe a woman of Ganat?" Elna offered.

"No," Giri insisted. "Women do not wear such things on their head." He rolled his eyes.

"Well, I do, now," Darna said. "My hair would look even worse."

"Why?" Elna asked, frankly puzzled.

"It's red," Darna said.

"But that's all right," Elna said. "Isn't it?"

Darna shook her head. "Come on, let's go see if we can sell some good scraps in the kitchens, or get a job." She urged Elna forward and the near-sighted girl reluctantly led the way.

The single guardsman on duty didn't even glance up at their approach. Elna made a noise that might have been the beginning of a word. The guardsman raised an eyebrow.

"I heard the kitchen, I heard they need, servants, help, apprentices," Elna stammered.

The guardsman yawned. "Go ask the cook," he said. "But no foreigners – they can work in the stables."

Darna shuddered, not just at being taken for a foreigner, but at the idea of working in the stables.

"With horses?" she asked.

The guardsman nodded. "Are you Theranis born or foreign?"

"What?" Darna said.

Giri pulled her away into the kitchen yard. "Don't tell them anything!" he hissed an Elna looked at her reproachfully.

Darna caught her by the arm. "Don't promise them that you'll stay to work. I think you could join the weavers guild, if you wanted. They only ask for a few large beads. We can get enough by Midsummer, I'm sure we can."

"What about the weavers?" Giri interrupted. "We are

thieves now."

"No," Darna grumbled, "we are servants now."

She thought of her hair, and of her stashes of loot from the dump all over Anamat city, and she cursed the Cereans, Nira, the prince of Tiadun, the priestesses, and the weavers, too, every last one of them as she followed Giri to the stables.

"I've never been around horses," she whispered. "What are we supposed to do?"

"Just don't go behind them," Giri said. "I saw one kick a boy straight through a wall once."

Suddenly, working in the kitchens didn't sound so bad. "Maybe I should go see how Elna's doing," Darna said.

Giri shook his head. They were at the inner door of the stables. The horses only passed through the palace's kitchen yard to go into their stalls. Every day, the stable boys led them out to graze in the pastures outside the city walls. Darna had seen them from a distance, from the outermost corner of the city dump. She did not want to get so near as to actually touch the beasts.

A broad-shouldered man of middle years stood at the entrance to the stables. Darna hadn't seen him before, but he seemed to be the stable-master. He raised his eyebrows at Giri and Darna.

"What have we here?" he asked.

Giri stepped forward. "We seek work, in your stables," he said.

Darna nodded.

The man looked at the two of them closely. "Cerean, are you?" he asked Giri.

Giri nodded.

"And you?" he asked Darna.

Darna bit her lip and thought.

"Mute. Are you mute?" he shouted.

Darna nodded. She didn't think the turban was much of a disguise, but it seemed to be enough to throw off the man's perception of her, to not recognize her as the scrap-seller she might have seen in the market. She didn't want to spoil the effect by speaking.

"We've got no use for redheads inside the stables," the man said. "Frighten the horses. Explain that to your friend," he said to Giri.

A young man emerged from the stables. "Where shall I put Onarun's horses?" he asked.

"Pasture, for now," the stable-master said. "Then take this boy and show him how to prepare the stalls and feed." He ushered Giri forward, but Darna reached out to tug on Giri's sleeve.

The stable-master shooed her away. Just then, a tall squire led a horse through the gate. It stopped and raised its tail, depositing a pile of manure in the middle of the courtyard. Darna stepped around it as she went out. Someone grabbed her shoulder. She swung around, stopping just short of clipping the stable-master with her stick. He held a shovel out to her.

"Clean that," he said. "Into the cart there." He pointed to a cart by the stable door, already half full of dung and clouded by a swarm of flies. "You can wait here and clean up the messes, but don't let the beasts see your hair. Keep it covered."

Darna nodded enthusiastically.

"Do you understand?" he asked.

Darna practically had to bite her tongue to keep herself from blurting out something about not being mute, not simple-minded, but she just nodded.

"You'll get soup from the kitchen at midday if you do your work, and a small bead at the end of the day."

Again, Darna nodded. The stable-master handed her the shovel.

§

Midday brought welcome respite, but Darna had to keep up the charade of being a mute. She soon discovered that the people passing through acted as if she were deaf as well and didn't care if she could overhear them. She wondered if that was how Myril heard so much, by speaking so little. The palace servants took little notice of the new stable hands and shooed them all back out onto the street at the end of the day.

After a few days, Darna, Giri, and Elna had settled into their new routine. With all of the green-knees flooding in from the farms, Darna began to see how the settled people of Anamat wouldn't look very carefully at new scrapplings. In the evenings, instead of going straight back to the East Canal, Darna would walk around the outside of the palace, trying to discover how it was laid out and learned even more by listening to the palace servants giving directions to their visitors. The palace was laid out in a pattern, with the guards' quarters at the front, the servants at the back, guests to the east, and the governor's own quarters more or less in the center, but abutting Conn's Coop to the west. Darna could see bits of the interior gardens, glimpses of trees poking over the outer walls. One of them might be near that meeting room they were supposed to look for. She mapped it in her head as well as she could.

In the space of just seven days Darna felt that they had blended in completely. The princes and a few important village chiefs arrived from the provinces, but not the prince of Tiadun, not yet. He would have to be there in time for the Midsummer councils, though, at least for the final quarter-moon before Midsummer night.

One midday, Darna, Giri, and Elna sat in the kitchen yard sipping their soup while the older servants rested. The soldiers were changing their guard. A lingering servant yawned and settled down for a nap in the shade. Giri and Elna looked around empty-headed.

"I've got to go to the privies," Darna whispered. "Wait here for me."

She hadn't been planning anything, but there was an opening. The new guard had just taken his post and the former one was walking away from them. Darna followed his path downhill to the privies at the northeast corner of the palace, not too far from the room where the amulet supposedly rested. She walked right past them and up a passage. She heard someone coming and ducked behind a tapestry, into the cover of a hidden doorway. She wondered where the door led, but she wasn't far enough into the palace to have reached the place she looking for. Besides, she was wearing a turban that made her look like some kind of Ganatean boy. The footsteps rounded the corner. Darna peered through the gap between the curtains. It was just a maid carrying a pile of rumpled linens, humming a sowing song under her breath.

Darna waited a while after the maid had gone and considered her options. She couldn't keep her turban on, not with the smell of dung clinging to her. Even with all twelve provincial princes and their hangers-on crowding the palace halls, she still felt the stink pouring off her. She didn't like smelling like horses or like the men who rode them. She clearly wasn't the kind of foreigner to be allowed inside the palace. It might be better if they saw her for herself, minus her stick, of course. She unwound her head covering and bundled it under her arm. For good measure, she tore off a bit and covered the end of her stick to muffle its sound on the stone floors.

She slipped back out into the corridor and continued on her way, counting her steps to calculate the distance she'd traveled. She was almost there. Then there was the door. She stopped to listen. No one was coming. She pushed. It was latched. Darna had a medium-sized knife, its blade about as long as her hand. She slipped it into the crack and felt around for the latch then set the dull edge of it against the bottom of the bar and pushed up. She strained – it was stiffer than she thought it should be. She looked at the keyhole. If she'd had a smaller knife she would have been able to put it in there and turn it, but she didn't. She thought she heard footsteps coming and pushed harder.

The bar jerked up and Darna stumbled as the door swung open. She fell against the swinging door and just barely stopped it from banging against the wall. She didn't manage to stop the knife from sliding down and putting a good slice into her finger. She shut the door carefully behind her and leaned against it, sucking her cut finger as the footsteps of a sword-rattling guard clunked by, even louder than her beating heart. Darna thought she heard him mutter to himself but maybe it was just the rush of blood in her ears.

The room had a vaulted ceiling and a table under the window. Darna walked over to it. There was the box, just as the Cerean king's men had described. The box was locked, but she couldn't just take it, someone would see right away that it was missing. Darna hadn't picked many locks, but she'd broken the tops off of a few small boxes that she'd found in the dump. This was finer than those, but maybe the mechanism of the lock would be similar. She scanned the room. An ornament of twisted wire hung beside the fireplace. It would be about the right size. She unbent a piece of it and thrust it into the keyhole. Nothing happened. It wiggled around loosely. She pulled it out, hands sweating, and bent the end of it to an angle. She felt around. It caught against something.

Outside in the corridor, an armed man clomped by. She held her breath. As soon as the steps had faded she pulled the bent wire back out and studied the lock. She peered at it again then closed her eyes, trying to picture the mechanism inside. She bent the wire a little more, pushed it in, and popped open the lock.

She paused and listened for a moment to make sure there was no one coming before she lifted the lid. All was quiet. She opened the box and there was the amulet. It didn't look Cerean. It looked like an Anamat amulet, an abstract image of a sea dragon, the kind of thing that a merchant's boat might carry to curry the dragons' favor. Darna hesitated. If the Cereans didn't see dragons, and the dragons didn't see them, she wasn't sure what they would want with it, but she didn't have much time to think so she stuffed it under her cloak and locked the box, re-bent the wire ornament and put everything back in its place.

Darna stood by the door, wondering how she would latch it again. Another set of footsteps paced by. She decided to just go and hope to get out again unnoticed the same way she'd come in. She opened the door and stepped out into the hall.

Her heart pounded. Her palms sweated, slippery on her stick as she tucked the amulet into her belt, turned the corner...

– and walked straight into a man. A tall nobleman with a sword belt on and a familiar-looking tunic of fine linen. Her eyes traced up, past the band of gold embroidery at his neckline, past the beard and into eyes that were the same pale color as her own. His hair was auburn in the dim indoor light, rather than red. It tended toward gray at the hairline and in his beard. He did not look much like her, Darna thought, but then she had only rarely seen herself in Tiadun keep's mirrors, and hadn't looked at any reflection clearer than the canal water since she arrived in Anamat.

The man stepped back, hand on the hilt of his sword, and looked at the ragged girl. He opened his mouth to speak, then looked at her more closely.

"It is... why did you leave?" the Prince of Tiadun demanded.

The amulet burned against her. It tugged toward the power of Anara, coursing through the land. It was not a Cerean amulet.

"I am Tiada's daughter, and no one else's," Darna said.

"You must return with me."

"No," Darna said, taking one step backward.

"You will do as I command!" the prince said.

Darna bolted. With nowhere else to go, she turned back into the room where she'd found the amulet. It was warm, almost burning in her hand. She barred the door from inside and cast her eyes about as the Prince of Tiadun pounded on it from outside.

"Let me in! I can give you anything you ask!"

The pounding stopped for a moment, as if he were listening for anyone who might come upon him, shouting at a barred door like a beggar or a peasant. For a heartbeat, Darna considered opening the door. She could go back to Tiadun, and leave the stone there in that room for Anara, leave it safely where it was. The Cereans would not risk crossing a prince of the land, would they? They would have to find some other scrappling to do their stealing, if they could.

Darna put her hand on the barred door.

"Open, I say!" the prince hissed.

Giri and Elna were waiting. They thought she'd only gone

to the privies. If she opened that door to the prince, she would be a cosseted prisoner in that lonely keep forever. She would have to leave Anamat. No, she would not leave it, even if this was the price of staying. She took out the amulet and looked at it. It was a piece of Anara, or she was no scrappling. She would have to be as dragon-blind as the prince himself to think the Cereans had any rights to it, and yet she'd agreed to bring it to them. It would buy her an apprenticeship, and she would have that gold, if she couldn't get away. The only alternative seemed to be to turn herself over to the prince.

Unlike Tiadun keep, the governor's palace was a part of Anamat city, planned by skilled craftsmen who sensed the dragon's energy in the land. She could not see the dragon, but she could feel hints of her presence and the amulet pulled at her like a dowsing rod. Darna spotted a narrow door beside the fireplace, maybe a servants' door. It was latched from inside the room, so she opened it easily. She slipped into the dark passage behind it. With shaking hands, she used her knife to put the bar back in place.

The prince's voice faded as she set off down the narrow stair. Soon, she could no longer hear his words. She followed the passage as quickly as she could. It emerged into a cellar where a guardsman slept by a wine barrel and a dark stone stairway led upward, landing her beside the kitchen hearth. She ducked back inside the passage and hastily re-wrapped the cloth to cover her hair.

The amulet warmed Darna's belly. Maybe she could tell the Cereans that she hadn't been able to find it after all. She wanted to return it to the place where it had been, but the prince was there. She burst out into the courtyard, with the clear sky above and Anamat city all around. She could feel the place in her bones. This was where she was meant to be. No prince could steal her from it.

The Cereans would have to go on their way, leaving her to this place, and to Anara. The image of Giri's scars came back to her, and the tales of slave-trading. She hoped they wouldn't steal any of her fellow scrapplings.

Darna found Giri and Elna lazing around as if nothing had happened.

"That took a long time, for going to the privies," Elna commented.

Giri blushed.

"What, don't they have privies in... where you come from?" Elna said.

"Stop it," Darna said. "We have to go. Now."

"You going to eat your bread?" Elna asked her.

Darna's mouth was bone dry. "Just take it," she said, throwing the bread at Elna, who caught it and began to eat almost immediately.

Giri got to his feet and peered at Darna, shifting impatiently from one foot to the other.

"Got anything?" he whispered.

§

Chapter 12: On the Run

What is opened can be closed, what is closed, opened.

– A scrappling saying

"We need to leave now!" Darna hissed.

Giri got the idea, but Darna had to grab the bread right out of Elna's hands to make her listen. Eventually she caught on, too.

They waited for the guard to pass then Giri led the way into the stables. Darna was so worried about being seen that she didn't even have time to be afraid of the horses stomping in their stalls. She followed Giri, climbing up into the hay loft. A big door at the back opened to the outside of the city wall so that farmers could load in their hay and grain without going through the market. No guard was posted there, but a foreign stable boy napped in a pile of hay. Giri unlatched the door and one by one they dropped to the ground outside. Giri and Elna went first. Darna threw down her stick and sack to them.

"Ready?" she asked. She dangled her legs out and jumped. They had to catch her as she landed, unsteady on her feet.

"You got it?" Giri asked, holding her up longer than he really needed to.

"Shut up!" Darna said, jerking herself away. The hay-door swung open above them. A strong gust of wind came down the valley. It banged shut, then there was a footstep. The stable boy had woken up. "Let's get out of here!"

"But I didn't get my bead for today," Elna complained.

"Shush," Giri said.

They ran.

They didn't stop until they reached a little grove by the dump, just in sight of Corana's Gate.

"Did that stable boy see us?" Darna demanded.

"I don't know," Giri said, exaggerating his gasps for breath. "I just ran. He won't say anything."

Giri lied. Darna had seen him look back at least twice. He was sure to have seen the boy, if he was there. "At least you took off your stupid cap," she said.

"Yeah, but you still had your turban, and your stick," Elna pointed out. "You really got it?"

"Since when do you know everything?" Darna demanded. "Yes!" Then she took a couple of deep breaths. "Someone saw me. They know who I am. I have to hide. Really hide."

"You maybe can hide on the Cerean ship," Giri suggested.

Darna shuddered. "No," she said. "Not that." She led them further along the city walls toward the shabby north market and the dumping grounds.

"Where is it?" Giri asked. "Show me."

"Not here," Darna said. "You'll have to just believe me, I got it."

Giri frowned. He panted as he hurried to keep up with Darna, who was moving as fast as she could go.

"Was it hard to find?" he asked.

"That part wasn't hard," Darna said. "It was practically just sitting there."

"It wasn't locked?" Giri asked, wide-eyed.

"Sure, I had to pick a couple of locks," Darna said with a shrug. "That wasn't any problem."

"You know how to pick locks?" Elna asked.

"Of course I do! I'll show you sometime," she promised. It was a thing she had learned something about at Tiadun keep then refined in her early days digging up old boxes in the dump. Behind them, the palace rooftops looked small behind the city walls. They were getting further into the guilds' quarter.

"I want to see it." Giri reached toward her rolled belt.

"No! I mean, we have to keep it hidden, right?" Darna said. "Just in case."

"We going to take it to them now?" he asked. It wasn't really a question. He was just telling her what to do, dropping the whole act of taking her as his "captain."

She frowned. The city would be full of the guardsmen from Tiadun now that the prince knew she was in Anamat. "Not today," Darna said as calmly as she could. She needed to think. Still, she needed to think. "I want to make them wait. We don't want them to think it was too easy."

"But they might have more work for us," Giri argued, "more gold!"

Darna shrugged. She wasn't sure she wanted to do more stealing for the Cereans, or any other kind of work they devised. She wanted to know what it was that she had, wrapped in her belt. She couldn't take it back to the palace. They would catch her for sure. She couldn't keep the amulet, not for long. She couldn't be caught with it, she couldn't let it out of her sight. It was so warm.

"All right, first thing tomorrow, then," Darna said. "You two meet me by the docks, right after the breadlines."

"Giri doesn't go to the breadlines," Elna pointed out.

"We're meeting by the docks. And no tattling, either of you. Heck, you can even go back and scrub the palace kitchen for all I care!"

She waved her stick in their faces and stalked away from them, but they followed. Nira was the last thing on Darna's mind as she wandered toward Corana's Gate, the one by the dump. She loitered in the closed-down market as if she were waiting for the stalls to open. She tried to ignore Giri and Elna as they trailed behind her in the shadows, whispering to each other.

"Stop it!" Darna said, finally confronting them. "Go... go do something else!"

"But..." Elna pouted. "But we haven't *seen* it."

There were so many people in the market. She couldn't unwrap it, and she had the strange feeling that she didn't want to share it yet. She shook her head.

"Why don't you just go see if you can find anything in the dump."

"But Nira..." Elna trembled.

"Oh, I don't care!" Darna said. "Just go away."

Giri and Elna looked at each other then wandered off, back toward the gate. Darna sat down in the shadows of a farmer's stall, leaning on a basket of cabbage, feeling the amulet tucked in her belt and not daring to bring it out into the light. She felt strangely peaceful, being near it. She touched her hand to it surreptitiously. It made her feel light, and strong. No wonder the Cereans wanted it. She wasn't looking around at all.

"Hey cripple!" Suddenly, Nira loomed over her. She was wearing her usual sneer. "Where'd your little gang go? They decide to go get a real gang? Like mine?"

Darna did not appreciate the interruption of her musings. She stood up, letting her stick drag behind her, but she kept one hand on the amulet.

Nira's eyes focused on Darna's hand, holding onto what was tucked into her belt.

"C'mon, cripple," she said. "Give it here!"

"No!" Darna shouted. She jabbed her stick in Nira's direction, just enough to unbalance her, then hurried away. Behind her, Nira laughed and called after her.

"You ever want be part of a real gang, you come out here and let me know!" Nira taunted.

Darna paused and turned to face Nira. "Oh yeah?" she started. "I – " She felt the amulet warm against her belly and remembered that she had other things to worry about. "Never mind," Darna muttered under her breath, then she ducked into the bushes that hid the entrance to the East Canal and slipped back into the city unseen.

§

Myril and Iola sat with their beggars' basket in the market that had just reopened after the midday rest. Iola looked forlornly at the sky. A couple of small clay beads came her way. A palace guard passed through the market and looked critically at them before moving on. Palace guards rarely came as far as the harbor in their official duties, and this one looked a bit confused. He didn't give them a bead.

Myril started to hear the rumors in the late afternoon that someone, possibly a scrappling who might or might not have a limp, but was certainly a bit on the small side, had stolen a valuable jewel from the palace, and was wanted for something else besides. Before nightfall the markets buzzed with rumors, even down by the harbor. People said that the governor's consort, a former priestess, had noticed that something was missing. A city watchman came by with another palace guard as the market was closing down.

"What about them?" the palace guard said.

"No, they've been there all day, they're there every day," the watchman said.

"Who else?"

"I don't know, not many thieves in this quarter. Hardly worth the trouble."

The palace guard nodded. "Let's move on, then."

Iola watched them go. "What's happening?" she asked Myril.

"You didn't hear?" Myril asked. Iola *would* have heard if she'd been paying any attention. The guard and the watchman had made no effort to speak quietly. She explained the rumor.

"From the palace?" Iola said. "Why would Anara..."

"What does..." Myril began. There were too many ears in the marketplace. "Let's get back to the bridge."

"All right," Iola shrugged.

They picked up their basket and walked back to the bridge, listening as they went. They passed two more groups of watchmen who looked them over critically.

"What does Anara have to do with it?" Myril asked at last, as they climbed down the canal side.

"I don't know," Iola said, "I just saw her over that way earlier. I don't know why she was there."

"Nothing to do with – " Myril cut herself off as her eyes adjusted to the darkness. Darna crouched in the far corner of the hollow. When she saw the others, she pushed the dragonlet roughly off her lap. Myril had never seen the dragonlet on Darna's lap before. What's more, it didn't run straight to Iola as it usually did, but hovered near Darna.

"What are you doing here?" Darna asked.

"It's almost night," Myril said. "We're always here around now. It's you that's back early."

Iola ran over to the dragonlet, who hesitated a moment before curling under her outstretched hand.

"What have you done to her?" she half-sobbed at Darna.

"What have I done to her? It's a him!" Darna picked herself up and dusted herself off, grasping at something which looked like it was heavy, something which glowed a little under her cloak.

Iola soothed the dragonlet's ruffled spine and pouted.

"I haven't done anything to him! I just..."

"What do you have?" Myril asked quietly. "Have you heard the rumors?"

"Rumors?" Darna asked.

"About the theft from the palace? The watch is out. They're looking for a smallish scrappling. Maybe a cripple."

"Cursed blood of—"

"Don't *say* that!" Iola interrupted. "And don't *push* dragonlet."

Darna rolled her eyes. "The dragonlet's fine."

Despite Iola's tears, Myril could see that Darna was right. The dragonlet was acting just as it usually did, except that it was looking at Darna for a change, not Iola.

"No thanks to you!" Iola said. "Get out of here!"

"I think I will!" Darna said. "Just you wait!" She started toward the steps.

"Don't!" Myril said. "Don't go. They're looking for you!"

"I can take care of myself!" Darna insisted. She disappeared into the gathering dusk.

§

Thorat didn't return until late that night. Myril and Iola were under the blankets, but Myril sat up when he arrived.

"Where's Darna?" he asked her.

Myril didn't have the heart to feel for her presence, to find out how far she'd gone. "Iola made her leave," she said. "It was something about the dragonlet."

"Why should she be jealous of..."

"I am not jealous!" Iola said, waking up abruptly. "She hurt him!"

"The dragonlet isn't hurt," Myril said, as soothingly as she could. Iola was jealous, though. She saw the dragonlet as her own, as if she could have that piece of Anara for herself.

"Darna probably would have gone anyway," Myril said. "She's hiding from the watch and the palace guards, too."

Thorat sat down by the embers of the cooking fire and ate the last few spoonfuls of soup, then they settled in for the night, without Darna.

§

Darna hid a little further up the canal, in the culvert she'd discovered during her first days in Anamat. She supposed that she must have slept, though she was still tired when dawn woke her. She should have been sore and chilled, too, but she'd slept curled around the amulet and it had warmed her bones. As she stood up, she felt none of the usual pain in her hip. She crept low along the canal bank. She didn't need to use her stick at all. She even thought of leaving it, for a moment. She followed a hidden alley to the back of Ara's Landing and almost stepped out into the street before she saw a trio of palace guards conversing with the priestess at the back gate. One of them was the one who'd been on watch outside the palace kitchen the previous morning. She cursed under her breath and retreated back into the alley.

She watched the others pass by on their way to the breadlines. Myril wasn't even trying to find her. At least Myril wouldn't give her away to the watch. She wasn't so sure about Iola, or even Thorat, especially not if they heard about the prince. So far, the guards said that they were just looking for a thief. Thanks be to Anara, Darna thought. She followed hidden ways all the way across the city to the Cereans' dock. No one saw her.

Eventually, Elna and Giri joined her in the hidden alley.

"We should have taken it to them yesterday," Giri scolded, not even asking if she'd had her morning bread, which she hadn't.

"Oh, shut up. It doesn't make any difference," Darna said. "We'll get it to the cursed Cereans, and that's that. I've got to keep low, out of the way of the watch."

"That... They're looking for us," Elna said.

"Looking for me, you mean," Darna said. "No one would know you from anyone."

"But..." Elna looked upset.

"That's a good thing for you," Darna said. "Listen. Right now we just need to get them this thing."

Giri rested his hand on Elna's shoulder and glared at Darna. "They will look for us, too. You made us run. They don't know who took it."

Darna closed her eyes. "They do, though." She sighed. At least, the prince of Tiadun knew.

The ship was tied up to the wharf but Darna didn't feel like going out there. With the amulet in her hand, she felt strange. She'd felt strange since she first grabbed it. It didn't feel as warm in the morning as it had the night before. When Iola was talking to her dragonlet and accusing Darna of hurting the creature, she'd almost been able to understand what they said to each other. The amulet had power, the power of the dragons. She wondered how it had come to be in the palace to begin with, and how the Cereans had known where to find it. In the culvert, in her half-sleep, Darna had dreamed of dragons taking her down toward their secret places under the earth. She shivered at the thought.

"They say it was a Cerean amulet?" she asked Giri.

"I don't remember," he lied.

The ship's officer came out on deck and looked up and down the shore, searching for them.

"You go talk to him." Darna prodded Giri. "Bring him here."

"You don't want to come?" he asked. "Make the deal on the ship?"

"No! I told you, I'm not going on that boat," Darna said. Once had been enough.

He shrugged and started off.

"Don't you go making any secret deals with them, either!" Darna warned, though she knew there was nothing she could do to stop him.

Giri rolled his eyes at her then walked out the dock. He stepped onto the ship. For a half a heartbeat, she couldn't see him. It was as if he disappeared but then he was back, hailing the ship's officer like an old friend, not at all the way he'd greeted the sailors the first time they'd approached the ship. Giri lounged on the deck while the officer went below. A long time passed. Darna felt the shadows shift around her. Crowds hurried by. A city watchman passed, looking into every dark alley, including the one where she and Elna hid. They were well back in the shadows, though, so he didn't see them. Finally the officer and the translator emerged from below decks. The officer carried a large box under his cloak. He had to strain to carry its weight, and paused to rest it at least five times as he made his way up the dock.

Giri led them to Darna and Elna. The translator kept his hand at his dagger as they walked up the shore and into the mouth of the alley. When the Cereans saw that Darna and Elna were alone, they relaxed a little.

"I see that this amulet is worth a lot," Darna said.

The translator nodded and translated.

"It certainly is," the ship's officer replied. "We would see it, confirm that you have the right one."

"How much will you give us?" Darna asked. She had forgotten, and had spoken in Cerean.

Giri gaped at her. He scowled and stomped. The ship's officer gave Giri a slow smile. "You have a lot to learn, young man," he said. Then he spoke to Darna directly.

"How much of our tongue do you understand?"

"Very little," Darna said.

"Maybe not so little," he mused. "Well, you have the amulet?"

"How much?" Darna asked again.

"Does she have it?" the officer asked Giri.

The translator was eyed Darna with a new expression. For a moment, she'd made him nervous. Good.

"I'm sure," Giri said. "I felt it, yesterday, when I helped her get out of the palace."

"Did it feel as we told you it would? Like the cur –" he cut himself off and glanced at Darna and Elna. He could tell that Darna had understood.

Giri nodded again.

The ship's officer held out a bag of gold pieces. Darna counted thirty flattened beads, each as big as an eye. "I want ten more," she said.

The officer sneered. "You'll get your ten more, and another twenty more, when you do our next job."

"And what's that?" Darna asked.

"We make this trade first," the officer said.

Darna nodded and unwrapped the amulet. It was as long as a man's hand, made of intricately carved crystal. As she unwrapped it from her belt, she felt it echo against the ocean beyond. It might belong to Anara, or maybe to a sea dragon, some close kin of hers. It did not belong to the Cereans, with their long knives; cruel, sharp, and pointed at her throat.

"Excellent," the officer's face glowed a sickly green in the amulet's light. "This will make the king's little man strong." He chortled weakly. Giri grew pale, too, but Elna looked so rosy-faced that she might have been blushing. None of them were breathing, they were all just looking at the amulet, even the Cereans. Was that what it was for? An aphrodisiac? Why would the Cereans need a thing like that? They didn't even have priestesses – or dragons. It couldn't be part of the power of their land. Darna held the amulet for one last moment, but the Cereans would slice her open with their knives if she ran with it now. The amulet could heal, could heal something or someone, but she didn't know if it would save her from bleeding to death. Besides, there was all that gold. If she was caught with the amulet the watch would throw her into the deepest pit of the jail, and she'd be run out of Anamat and into the hills with no chance at all to get an apprenticeship.

The ship's officer blinked and brought himself back to his role. He thrust out the box he'd brought with him. It was nothing like the box the amulet had been kept in at the palace. That had been an ordinary wooden box, a fine one, tooled around with intricate metal work. This box was made of a kind of stone Darna had never seen before, a stone which clamped to itself under its own power.

"Put it in here," the officer said.

Darna did. Her hands felt weak and thin as they approached the box. It sucked up the light of the amulet, negating it, erasing its power. The box clamped shut, and it was as if all the amulet's magic had never been. Darna might have cried if she hadn't had those knives pointed at her and the pile of gold about to fall into her hands. As it was, she was just angry. She felt as if she'd been duped.

The officer tossed Giri the bag of gold pieces.

"Our next assignment," the officer said.

"I didn't say I wanted another assignment," Darna said.

"You will take it," the officer growled. "You will do this for us."

The presence of the box seemed to shut out the light of the sun itself. Darna felt like a part of her mind was missing now that the amulet was gone, with the box closed around it. The dragons. This box was the thing that the dragons couldn't see, what made the ship invisible, as Iola and Myril had said when the Cereans sailed in, when Darna still thought that she would just sell them some junk, that it would mean nothing to steal this amulet.

"You will go into the temple, the harbor temple," the translator was saying, in Theranis's language. "In the back courtyard, where all of you runts gather for feedings, there is a statue. It is only half as tall as yourself, and even thinner. It is, they say, near one of the passageway entrances. It depicts one of your demo—dragons, a runt among your dragons."

"I know the one." Darna frowned. There was only one statue of that size in the courtyard. It was a depiction of one of the provincial dragons. She didn't even know its name yet.

"Bring it, and we will take you to Cerea and see that you are wealthy," the officer said, in Cerean. "You will take it on Midsummer eve, in the morning. If you do not bring it, we will

alert the watch of your previous theft and ensure that you are
dealt with to the full extent of your weak laws. You are already
suspects, are you not? I'm sure we can arrange a little
dismemberment although you are already..." He paused to
sneer.

"Enough," the translator said. "I am sure the beggar
understands."

Elna leaned close to Darna and shivered. Even Giri
seemed uneasy. "What are they saying?" Elna whined.

The translator told her. Darna listened again, to make
sure she'd gotten it right. "You will do this," he concluded.

"I will think about it," Darna said.

"You will do this," the translator repeated. "You
understand that we do not tolerate disobedience in Cerea."

The two men then turned their backs on the scrapplings
and strode out to the ship, clutching their prize. It hardly
mattered to *them* that they weren't in Cerea, but Darna knew
that she was still in Anamat, Anara's own city. Bag of gold
beads or no, she'd been duped. Even if the beads were solid
and real, which she doubted, they weren't worth half the
dragon crystal amulet. It has come from the earth of Theranis,
or from its seas. It didn't belong with the Cereans at all, and
never had. They stepped onto their ship and the air seemed to
change, like a foul wind had blown out of that box.

Giri's mouth opened and closed dumbly. "How did you
learn?" he finally blurted out.

"None of your business, traitor." Darna snatched the bag
of gold out of his hand and strode to the end of the alleyway. A
city watchman was ambling up the shore, hand on his sword,
probably looking for her. She slunk back.

"Get out of my sight!" Darna told Giri once she was
safely hidden again.

Elna blinked. "You can't tell him that!" she said.

"Yes I can," Darna said.

"But he's *nice*," Elna said.

"It's not real," Darna said to her, then she turned to Giri. "You're not really one of us," she said. "You never even were going to try to be, not really. Go back to your limp-dicked Cerean king. I hope he lashes you! Get lost already!"

A strong gust of wind whipped sand into the alley, stinging their faces. The scrapplings pressed themselves back against the wall. The city watchman had walked a bit further up the shore – he had his back to them now. Giri bolted out of the alley, straight for the Cerean ship.

"I hope they take him back to their dungeons," Darna spat.

"I don't," Elna whispered. "He's not that bad." Her voice quivered.

"Yes he is!" Darna said. Why couldn't Elna see it? She dug into the bag. The gold beads were lighter than they should have been, but not too much so. She gave half of them to Elna.

"Keep those," she said. "I don't think Giri needs his share."

"He really wanted to be one of us," Elna said.

Darna shook her head. "It doesn't matter now. He's back with them. I'm not going onto that ship again. I'd rather take my chances with the watch." She didn't need to tell Elna about the prince of Tiadun.

"We've got to hide out until this blows over," she said after a while.

Darna looked up. Rain had started to fall in heavy splats. The watch was after her. Now, at last, she saw something dragon-like behind the clouds, searching, or so she thought. Giri, the rat, was probably still a slave for all his pretense of being a free scrappling. He didn't even escape when he had the chance, and he *had* had a chance. Darna despised him for that. She could tell that the gold was like nothing to these Cereans with the big ship. They had more gold, much more, as much as they wanted, but they didn't have the dragons' power, and now they'd made her steal it for them so they could twist it to their own stupid ends.

The rain gathered into streams and driving sheets. Water poured off the rooftops. Maybe she had offended the dragons. It sometimes rained a little in summer, but not like this. Darna had had no real idea what she was doing until she saw that box, and then she'd been too slow-witted and cowardly to stop herself from doing what the Cereans told her.

She could see Anara now, though, for whatever reason, even though she'd betrayed her. The dragon swooped back and forth across the harbor, whipping up the waves, churning the air, searching. Maybe Anara would dash Darna to the rocks, if she found her. Darna wouldn't mind. Anara could have her. Better to be killed by a dragon than suffer a slow death on the Cerean ship. Anara still couldn't see the ship, either, or her missing amulet. Maybe Giri was hiding from the dragon, maybe that was why he'd gone back onto the ship with his king's men. He was more afraid of Anara than he was of their lashes. He was a fool and he'd tricked her.

Well, Darna wouldn't do anything more for the Cereans ever again, that much she was sure of. She vowed it, from her not-very sheltered spot under a narrow overhang in the alley. Poor dragon-blind Elna just shivered and hid from the rain, too uncertain of Darna's mood to stay close, in the best sheltered spot.

"We've got to hide out," Darna said. At least, she needed to hide out, from the watch, from the Cereans, from the prince of Tiadun, and even from Anara. That meant no going back to the bridge, no talking to anyone, because Iola would tell Anara, and that would be the end of her.

"Where do you sleep?" Darna asked Elna.

Elna hunched her shoulders and stepped out into the rain. Darna followed. They snuck all the way across the muddy, rain-dimmed city to the bleak holes of the potters' yard, where they hid and shivered and hungered while the rain poured down.

§

Elna's hide-out was a wretched hole, not even big enough to lie down in properly. It was damp and stank of mold and piss, and Darna had to crawl to get in. The fact that there were no dragonlets nearby was a strange sort of consolation. It was a desolate place, Darna huddled there all day. When night came, she closed her eyes, but her mind wouldn't let her rest. She kept thinking of Anara, kept thinking of the amulet and the prince and the palace. She could have just left it there. Then they wouldn't have this cold, wintry rain at Midsummer, this cursed rain, a sure sign of Anara's confusion or anger. She tried to sleep. She drifted in and out of consciousness. Elna snored. She was still snoring when dawn came, bringing a little weak light into their hole.

Darna gave up trying to sleep. She needed bread, or something. Even a few bitter greens would be better than nothing and she had her old stash of beads as well as the bag of cursed Cerean gold. Gold beads. She took out the sack and counted them. Elna had a small jar tucked in behind her head where she kept her share. Darna counted the ones in her hand. She was five short, if the planners' guild would even take them. She took five from the jar, as quietly as she could, dropping in almost all of her Anamat beads to make up some of the difference. Elna snored on.

She covered her head as well as she could with what was left of the cloth, but she draped it like a shawl or a scarf so she wouldn't look so much like a "young man of Ganat." Curses on Giri and his curses. She bundled the Cerean gold under her arm and stepped out of the hole.

The potter's yard was empty – it was too early yet for most guildsmen to be at their work, and the rain was still coming down, darkening everything. Darna kept to the shadows. She passed behind a tavern and took a few pieces from the scrap pile there. She ate as much as she could stand to, then made a bundle of a few more pieces to take to Elna, ripping her head cloth to turn part of it into a makeshift satchel. She headed out toward Minstrel's Bridge. At the courtyard there, she laid one of her best Anamat beads in the shrine's offering bowl. She said a prayer as if Anara could hear her.

By the time she reached the planners' hall the city had begun to wake up. She kept out of sight as much as she could. There was a little blind alley just across from the hall's main doors. She sat there and waited. A guildswoman came out, carrying some sort of long measuring instrument. A few men followed, talking about which princes they would meet with that day at the palace. A shopkeeper came, bearing some sort of bill.

At midmorning, she finally spotted the apprentice boy she'd met when she'd first arrived in Anamat. He was carrying a big leather satchel and whistling.

"Hey!" Darna called.

Tevan looked around, not seeing her.

She stepped out of her hiding place.

"Where did you come from?" he asked.

"I want to buy an apprenticeship," Darna said. She thrust the bag at him.

He backed off. "What's in there?"

"Twenty gold beads, like you said," Darna said.

"It's more complicated than that," he said.

"But can't you just ask?" Darna pleaded.

"I don't know," Tevan said. He looked a little bit like Thorat, but with coarser features, a bigger nose. "Why do you want to be a planner?"

"I don't know," Darna said. "I just do. I'm sure. I watched you. Not just you. I've seen other planners in the city. I can see ways through the city, like..." She jerked her thumb toward the hiding place she'd been waiting in.

Tevan squinted. "There's something there!" he said. "Hang on. Can you see dragons?"

Darna froze. She looked down. She looked up at the sky. The rain, which had slowed to a drizzle in the early morning hours, switched back to a sudden downpour. Darna stared at Tevan through the rain running off her eyelashes and dripping from her nose. Tevan held his satchel over his head to keep off the rain. Darna's mouth opened and closed, as if she were a fish washed up on the beach. She couldn't breathe. She couldn't make a sound.

From around the corner came the clomp of watchmen's boots. Darna thrust her bag of beads at Tevan and plunged back into the wall.

"Come back tomorrow!" Tevan called after her, but he couldn't follow her into the wall, couldn't go where Darna went.

The watchmen clomped closer. There were at least six of them, and they had that palace guardsman with them, too, the one from the kitchen entrance.

"Apprentice!" said one of them. "Who are you talking to?"

Tevan shook his head.

"Dragonlet got your tongue?" one of the watchmen said with a chuckle.

"No, sir," Tevan said.

"Well then tell us: has any scrappling girl with a limp and red hair been seen in these parts?"

Tevan looked right toward Darna, but only for a moment. He looked away, puzzled. She tried to go further back in the passageway, but it was blocked where it had been open before.

After a long pause, he answered the watchman. "I don't know."

"Well, if you do find one like that hiding around, bring her up to the palace. There's a reward."

"I have to go," Tevan said. "I'm getting soaked."

"So are we," roared another of the watchmen. "Do your duty to the governor! Recover stolen property!"

"Let's go on!"

The watchmen clomped off.

Tevan darted under the awning at the next door down the street. As soon as the watchmen turned the corner, he went back to the place where Darna was hiding.

"Are you still in there?" he asked.

"Yes," Darna said.

"Take your beads."

"No, I want an apprenticeship. Can you take them to the guild master? Will they have me?"

"You have to talk to one of the masters!" Tevan said, exasperated. "I'm just an apprentice. I'll tell them about you melting into walls, though. I never heard of that before."

"I'm sure I'm not the only one," Darna said. She actually

hoped it was true, as long as the watch couldn't follow her. She didn't really melt into the walls, she just saw gaps in them that no one else seemed to see. Surely there were others who could find the dragons' hidden paths through the city. As long as those people didn't include the watch or Tiadun guardsmen, or Cerean merchants, she would be safe.

"Anyway I don't think we can take criminals," Tevan said.

"I... Never mind," Darna said. She felt behind her. The passage had opened up again.

As she walked away, she heard Tevan call after her one more time. "But what about the beads?" he asked.

She didn't think it would be safe to answer. It would be better not to have them. She should have left them all with Elna. She should have known better. She was a thief – that was what the guilds would see. She did want to be a planner, but she didn't know why, or how. All she could do was to slink back to the potters' yard and give Elna the satchel full of soggy scraps. After that she would try, again, to sleep.

§

Chapter 13: The Boys Take their Share

The earth did not always shake with her wrath. Sometimes it was the sky which quaked, the dark clouds showing fault-lines where lightning flashed, where Anara churned. She rode her anger across the valley. The wind drove the rain, shook loose the roof-tiles, lashed the streets.

– The Darkest Night

Thorat waited all afternoon for the rain to ease up, but finally he left the East Market in the downpour, slipping through the gates as they were closing.

"Where's Darna?" Thorat asked as he reached the cover of the bridge. "I thought she'd be back."

Myril handed him a bowl of soup and shook her head, dimly visible in the firelight. "She's hiding. Even I don't know where she is."

"Is she the one the watch is looking for?" he asked. The watchmen had come around to the East Market, but didn't seem to know quite what or who they were looking for.

"Maybe." Myril shrugged.

"And Anara's angry," Iola added.

"How could that have anything to do with it?" Thorat wondered.

"I don't want to think about it," Myril said. "Just eat."

Thorat shook his head. That was some thieving, if it really

had been done, snatching something from the palace. The boys were impressed with the rumors, but had no idea who had done it. It had to be Darna. Thorat hadn't seen the dragon in days, but then, he never sought that vision when he was with the boys in the market. If they caught him staring at the sky they'd make a laughingstock of him. He wondered if Iola was right, if Anara really was angry. He would look for the dragon himself in the morning.

§

When morning came, the rain wasn't as drenching as it had been the night before, though it still drizzled down. Thorat had seen Anara as a shadow while he and Iola were walking to the breadlines, but he couldn't think too much about it now. The boys' musty clothes steamed as they circled their fire, keeping an eye out for the watch.

"That's a good idea," Pannen said at one point, "stealing from the palace."

"I think it's a lousy idea," Thorat said.

"Why?" one of the other boys asked.

"The whole city watch is on the beat for whoever did it," Thorat said. "It's too much trouble."

"Sure, but you could get rich off one haul," Pannen said.

"Maybe," Thorat said.

"Do you think they found whoever they're looking for?" someone asked.

"Nah," Thorat said, before he'd thought about it.

"Oh?" Pannen said. "How's that?"

"I just figure." Thorat shrugged. "I figure if you're quick enough to get in and out of the palace, you can dodge the city watch all you want. Besides, it's getting crowded, getting on toward Midsummer. The watch have a lot to do."

"Maybe that's what the thief is counting on," Pannen

mused, looking at Thorat.

"That sure took some nerve," one of the boys said.

"I bet whatever they took was worth a lot," another added.

"If they can sell it and not get caught."

The rain dripped down. Now that Darna had disappeared, Thorat was starting to worry about the boys' plan to grab something from the Cerean ship. It was one thing to have a good thieving, another to risk capture by slave traders.

"You know," Thorat said after awhile, "I don't think stealing that tender is such a good idea after all."

"Aw, come on!" One of the boys made clucking noises at him and the rest rolled with laughter.

"What, that palace thief steal your nerve, pretty boy?" They all laughed again.

Pannen guffawed. "Let's do it tonight!" he said.

"But it's raining!" someone protested.

"All the better!" Pannen laughed. "Maybe the Cereans will be hiding under covers, keeping their precious swords dry! Let's do it!"

Thorat sighed. It had been his idea, so he supposed he would have to go along with it.

§

That night, the Cerean ship loomed on its mooring. A small group of boys from the East Market gang crouched in the shadow of Fishermen's Wharf, the same place where Thorat had slept his first night in Anamat. As their sentry ran out to check for the watch, he thought about the time since he'd left home, nearly three moon-rounds. The journey to Anamat had been an adventure and he'd begun to find his way in the world of the city but he still needed to find an apprenticeship. He wasn't ready to go back to the countryside.

Now, waiting with the others under the dock, he couldn't be seen to lose his nerve. Moonlight wavered through the dark clouds above and a light rain drizzled down.

One of the sentries ran back and slid under the dock. "There's one over there!" he whispered, panting.

"Are they watching it?" Pannen asked.

The boy shook his head. A row of tenders and small boats lay along the shore. The tavern doors behind them stood open. Anyone would be able see the boys take it if they happened to look out from those torch lit rooms into the cloudy night at just the right time.

"We'll have to move fast," Pannen said. "Thorat – are you sure you've got a good hiding place?"

Thorat nodded. "Who knows how to row?" he asked.

Most of the boys looked down and shook their heads, but one of Pannen's friends and one of the smaller boys nodded. That made three of them.

"When I saw the foreigners row in the other day it looked like they used the oars differently to what I'm used to," Thorat said. "They're smaller than the oars back home, but I think we can manage."

"You'll show us how," Pannen said.

"All right," Thorat said, doubtful. It was a big tender, they'd never rowed together, and none of them had even been in a boat like that before.

The boys strolled past their target. No one seemed to be watching. Thorat cast a quick glance out to the Cerean ship. Its soldiers' swords glinted in the moonlight, even though they were out at anchor. They had cast off from the dock around midday.

Pannen signaled for the boys to double back. The Cereans' tender was overturned, to keep the rain out. Three boys lined up along one side and tipped back up, then they all started pushing it toward the harbor.

"Stop!" Thorat hissed. "There aren't any oars!"

They stopped to look around. A couple of sets of oars leaned against the sides of taverns further up the shore. They were pretty far away.

"We could just carry it over to the canal, and tow it from there," Thorat proposed.

"Won't we need the oars later, though? To use it? Come on, let's get them." Pannen shooed him along.

"Grab the smaller oars," Thorat told the small boy who'd said that he knew how to row. The others hefted the tender up and dragged it along the sand. Thorat ran back.

"Pannen! Take it into the water and drag it there," he said. "It'll be easier, and they won't be able to see where it went."

They changed their course, and Thorat ran back along by the taverns. He found the oars. There were six of them in all. He could carry two at once, easily. Out on the Cerean ship, one of the armed guards approached the other and leaned in as if to talk. He pointed toward the shore with his gleaming sword, catching the torchlight even though the moon was dipping behind a cloud. Thorat grabbed two oars.

"Run!" he told the boy who was with him. That boy also grabbed two oars and followed as fast as he could. The others had gotten the tender almost halfway over to the East Canal, splashing through the water. They looked over their shoulders, saw Thorat running and doubled their pace, splashing through the shallows.

"Hurry!" Thorat said when he caught up. He threw the oars in and took a handful of rope, tugged, and splashed forward. "They've seen us!" he told Pannen, as quietly as he could manage.

Pannen looked back toward the taverns.

"No, out on the boat!" Thorat hissed.

The guards had left their posts. A couple of men hurried to the side, pointing after the movement on the shore. Another Cerean tender splashed into the waves. Thorat thought it was strange that they kept it on deck instead of in the water, where it would have been easier to use when they were in port. It was strange that they had armed guards, too, even out at anchor. There were a lot of strange things about that ship, he thought. The men jumping into the tender held long, sharp pikes.

"Let's drop it and run!" one of the boys said.

"We're almost to the canal," Pannen countered.

"Come on then."

Thorat gritted his teeth.

The warm, stinky canal water slipped around their ankles, knees, and thighs. Four of them jumped into the boat, Pannen and the three who could row. "Run interference!" Pannen barked at the remainder of the gang. They sprinted back down the beach toward the taverns, shouting, while Thorat, Pannen, and the two other boys pushed the tender into the darker reaches of the canal. The clouds closed over the moon and the drizzle thickened into a real rain again.

They set the oars between their pins and tried to guide the boat up the canal. It was too narrow, though, and the oars acted strangely, so they poled and paddled instead. The covered place Thorat had in mind was only a little distance up, well before Priestess Bridge. The sooner they hid that boat, the better.

"Here," Thorat directed the others as they reached it.

One of the boys leaped to the canal bank, rope in hand. Pannen had brought a length of line with him, just in case, and there was some coiled in the bow, too.

"Where?" the boy on shore asked.

"There!" Thorat pointed at a low-ceilinged culvert of mossy stone.

Pannen whistled. "That is well hidden!" He clapped Thorat on the back and grinned.

They heard the guttural shouts of the Cerean sailors coming up the canal behind them. Maybe they were debating whether to follow the boys further up, Thorat didn't know. Whatever they were saying, they were getting very close.

Quietly, carefully, and as quickly as they could manage, the boys squeezed the boat into the drainpipe. Thorat had found some ancient metal rings there in the daytime, but it took longer to find them in the dark. The boys tied the boat to the rings and held their breath as a heavy man clattered by, fully armed and cursing in his foreign tongue as he slipped on the narrow canal-bank path. Someone choked back a giggle and Thorat heard a punch land with an oof. After that, everyone sat in heart-thumping silence until the Cerean clattered back down to the harbor.

"Let's get out of here," Pannen said. They moved to the mouth of the pipe and looked out at the canal. "One at a time," Pannen said. "Anyone who gives us away is meat for the watch, hear?" They all nodded. "We'll meet in the morning, breadlines. Now scatter!"

Two boys disappeared into the night before Thorat. He got out and went straight up the canal, back to the bridge, safe.

§

Myril and Iola huddled under the overhang of a baker's stall, trying to stay out of the rain.

"Do you see Anara?" Myril asked.

Iola nodded and shivered.

"What's wrong?" Myril asked.

"I don't know," Iola said. "Maybe Anara doesn't know either."

"Let's go back to the bridge."

They sat under the bridge and watched the rain pour down for the rest of the day, sorry for the peasants, the market people, and the scrapplings who had no dry place to hide. Myril wondered how one small theft, if that was what it was, could change Anara's mood – and the weather – so violently. What was it that Darna had stolen? Where had it gone that Anara noted its absence?

Around nightfall, the winds steadied a little and the rain lightened. Myril wondered if Anara had forgiven the theft or if it was only a temporary lull in her upset. What would happen to the ambassadress if she flew when Anara was in such a rage?

Thorat had left early that morning and there was no sign of Darna. The dragonlet was hiding. The image of the Cerean ship loomed in Myril's mind. Sometime during the day, she had sensed it moving further from the shore. She lay awake, feeling Darna's absence and wondering where Thorat had gone.

Myril woke up in the middle of the night. She heard splashing as something came into the mouth of the canal, then muffled, familiar voices. Other sounds followed: the dragonlet ruffling its wings in the darkness, hard footfalls, and then foreign voices questioning, speculating. Soft footfalls, soft enough that she had to strain to hear them, came up the canal bank. That was Thorat. She sat up beside the sleeping Iola,

Thorat looked over his shoulder before ducking into the dark hollow under the bridge and scurrying to the back where they hid the cooking pot.

"Come here and lie with us," Myril whispered. "It'll look

more like you've been here."

The voices came closer, but their approach slowed as the canal bank grew steeper.

"I'm soaked," Thorat whispered. "How do you know I'm hiding?" Myril could hear him starting to take off his wet clothes.

The Cereans were coming closer, and quickly.

Iola woke briefly as Thorat climbed in beside her. "You're cold," she whined sleepily.

"Shh..." Thorat said. "Cereans."

The foreigners shouted back and forth to each other. They carried torches. Myril wished that she could understand their words, that Darna could be there to interpret. She could only listen and guess. She sensed frustration, anger, and not enough stupidity to reassure her. The searchers came close enough to cast their torchlight on the three of them under their shared blanket. Myril felt the warmth of the torchlight on her face and muttered as if disturbed in her dreams. Iola had fallen thoroughly asleep again somehow. Thorat breathed deeply and slowly. The Cereans moved on.

"Is it safe?" Thorat asked a while after the Cereans had clattered back toward the harbor.

"I think so," Myril said. "But maybe we should sleep anyway."

Thorat grunted. "I'm still soaked."

"I can't sleep either," Myril said. "I guess I'll build up the fire."

Iola woke when the other two got out from under the blanket. They sat beside their fire for the rest of the night, staring at the flames and trying to warm up.

"I wish Darna was here," Myril said at one point.

Iola shook her head. "How would that help? She went

over to the foreigners."

"She came back, though," Myril said. "I mean, I don't think she's helping them any more."

"I think we should tell the priestesses what happened."

"The priestesses?" Thorat startled. "What do they have to do with anything?"

"Whatever it was that she stole had some kind of dragon power," Myril said. "It's connected to Anara, but I..." She didn't think that Darna would have knowingly stolen from the dragons.

"You might as well go straight to the watch," Thorat said bitterly.

"I'd rather tell the priestesses," Iola said, "if it's to do with the dragons."

"You can't do that. You can't betray a fellow scrappling," Thorat said.

"I never wanted to be a scrappling," Iola said.

"Just don't tell them," Myril pleaded. "It's the wrong thing to do."

"What's the right thing, then?" Iola said.

"I don't know," Myril said.

"I can't see turning anyone in to the watch, especially not Darna," Thorat said. "Besides, it was at the palace, whatever it was. It didn't belong to the priestesses anyway."

"It should have belonged to the temples," Iola said. "I'm going back to sleep."

Thorat and Myril crawled under the blankets, too, and they slept until late in the morning.

§

The good thing about Elna was that she didn't look like much of anything at all, just a scrappling, no particular scrappling. Her only distinguishing feature was her nearsighted squint. She went out that afternoon to get them a little bread from the scrap piles.

A puddle formed in the middle of the hole. Rain dripped across the entrance. The damp sank into everything. Darna told herself that at least the nights were warm, but then she started coughing and couldn't stop. Every time she heard footsteps coming, she shrank back further, trying not to cough. She didn't dare go out again. Her body ached. Whatever magic the amulet had worked on the pain that made her limp was gone without a trace now, or maybe it had even left a hole in her.

Half way through her second night in Elna's hiding hole, Darna couldn't stand it any more. She was hungry again, and most of the beads – her share and Giri's – were gone. Elna lay with one hand dangling into the puddle, and she snored. Darna could hardly be any damper than she already was, she thought, and she would never be able to sleep with Elna snoring and pushing her into the muddy, jagged walls of her cave. She set out into the drizzle.

Darna wondered if she'd look less conspicuous without her stick, but she only got three steps away from the hiding hole before her bad leg seemed to lose its last bit of strength. She went back for the stick. At first, she tried to walk with it tucked under her cloak but then she gave up and used it normally. She had to follow the street a little way before she got to the entrance to the hidden passage parallel to the East Canal, but whether it was darkness, the rain, her anger, or Anara shutting her out, she couldn't find the telltale chink in the wall.

It was the middle of the night and not too many people were about. In that quarter of the city, there wouldn't usually be any Cereans or palace guards. Darna walked back and forth along the wall, wondering if her memory had failed her. She hid behind a cart when a band of watchmen came along on their nightly rounds. They were heading toward the northeast quarter, toward Elna's hiding hole. They were all over the city. Darna decided that she might as well go on down to the bridge.

She followed the main streets, keeping to the shadows when she could. She was almost at the bridge when she stopped. What if she led the watch to the others, and they were jailed too? Iola and Myril would miss their chance to enter the temple of Ara's Landing and Thorat might miss his chance to join a guild. She wondered what would have happened if she'd stayed in the palace and let the prince keep her prisoner or princess. It would mean no real difference to her, she would be closed up, but it would certainly be more comfortable than limping through the muddy rain. She wondered if she could still go back to Tiadun.

From where she stood, she could see the palace on the hill. It had a tall building at the center, maybe as much as four or five stories high, where the governor kept his private quarters and some of his offices. A lamp – or maybe a torch – shone from up there. She turned herself toward it. Yes, maybe it would be better to go back to Tiadun after all. Maybe next time she could escape with some of the prince's treasure, not just her crippled self, or maybe she could forget the dragons.

She walked up hill as far as the Pentangle, the place where five main thoroughfares met. She was walking on the Auger's Angle, and would cross over to the Palace Path. She would walk up the hill and knock on the palace gate and turn herself in. That, or she could go back to the Cereans and help them steal the dragons' souls, piece by piece. She would not lead the watch to the hollow under the bridge.

There was a shrine at the end of Augur's Angle, just a

street-corner shrine, but a particularly well-tended one because most of the augurs were former priestesses. Darna crossed the street to get as far from it as she could but she clutched a hand to her heart, too. As she passed, the small lamp burning in front of the statue of Anara flared high, like a beacon. She turned to look at it, and as she passed she felt something catch her, like a net, a soft, invisible spiderweb stretched across the end of the street. She could see into the Pentangle square, but she could not enter it. She was stuck there, she could not go forward.

Where once the city had opened itself up to her, now it closed itself off.

She heard the clatter of a patrol of guardsmen coming down the hill of the Palace Path.

"We'll catch that thief tonight and claim the reward," one of them said.

"I'll catch him! That reward is mine."

The guardsmen's voices bounced off the stone-walled buildings of the street and down to Darna's ears. She tried to pull away, to go back down Augur's Angle. Whatever it was that held her back felt sticky. She dragged it with her step by step until the web tore, trailing behind her. The shrine bell clanged brightly, and out of the corner of her eye she thought she saw a dragonlet. The net, or web, had no weight. It drifted away from her as she ran back down the hill to Priestess Bridge. It was as if the city wouldn't let her be a prisoner in the palace, even if she did decide to give herself up to the princes.

The watchmen were coming, so she ran as well as she could.

A few minutes later, Darna climbed down the stones and into the sheltered hollow under the bridge, panting for breath. Myril was sitting up already when she returned, and Iola slept beside her. Thorat was nowhere to be seen.

Darna hesitated. The watchmen had turned off on a side street, down toward the harbor.

"Can I come in?" Darna asked.

"Of course you can," Myril said. "I never said that you couldn't."

"Well, no, but..."

Iola stirred. "Thorat?" she muttered sleepily.

"No, it's me," Darna said.

"I'm just back here." Thorat's voice came from one of the nooks at the back of the hollow.

"Anara's still angry," Iola said.

Myril shushed her.

"Can we light a fire?" Darna asked. She rubbed her arms, but they didn't feel sticky. The web was gone.

"No," Thorat whispered. "Shh..."

Myril went still. "They're coming again. Quick, get in beside me."

Darna scrambled under the covers and feigned slumber. "Who's coming?" she whispered.

"Cereans."

"Fire of Na," Darna said.

"Don't!" Iola whined quietly, then went back to pretending to sleep.

The splash of booted feet echoed up along the canal. The approaching Cereans were making far too much noise for their own good. There were three of them, all big and well-armed. Darna understood some of what they said and she guessed the rest. She could see the flicker of their torches on the stones above through her half-closed eyes.

"Cursed 'scrapplings.'"

"We should make slaves of them all."

"Governor won't let us. We could make him a good trade."

"Where did those buggers go?"

"Boat's too big to hide."

The other one mumbled something that Darna couldn't catch, and they slogged on.

A grunt. "We won't find anything in this dark. We should look in the daylight."

"Captain says no."

"What, you want these people to make a fool of you? We have our pride!"

"That's right. Can't have them know we slipped our watch. Might try to steal from us again. Wretched curse-mongers, all of them."

"It shouldn't be raining like this in summer."

"They say it's the curse of –"

"Don't say that name!"

"It's a curse anyway."

"It wouldn't fit through any further up. We turn back here."

The other two grunted in agreement and the men turned back toward the harbor.

"Wretched place, this demons' hole," one of them said as they splashed away.

"Good ale, though."

"To the taverns then. I could have me one of their priestesses, I could."

"You'd be polluted, bring their curse on the ship. Besides, I'd tell every whore in Cerea, and you'd never have one of them again."

"You know them all, you do!"

Another punch landed, one shouted at the other, then the

third intervened. "Let's get out of this stinking canal," he said. "Bloody rain."

That, they all agreed on, then Darna could hear no more.

§

Chapter 14: Giri, Again

Do not let the foreign thieves return, do not let them in. They would take our blood and drain it. We would die like the dragons of other lands.

– A soothsayer of the dragon Lemira

"Is it safe?" Thorat asked a little while later.

Darna jolted awake. Somehow she'd fallen into a deep sleep.

Myril sat up. "They've gone, but not far," she said. "We can't build a fire, but you can come out of there and get under the blanket. I don't think they'll be coming back tonight."

"Why were they looking for you for?" Darna asked. "A boat? What are they doing here?"

"What were they saying?" Myril asked.

"Just saying we were all cursed," Darna said, "talking about demons, their usual kind of thing. Then they said they were going to a tavern."

"We're safe for a while, then," Thorat sighed.

"Why are they looking for a boat?" Darna asked.

"We took it," Thorat said, then told Darna about the East Market boys' theft.

Thorat gestured down the canal. Darna could guess the place. "That's a good spot," she said. "Good for you and those boys. I hope you keep it, or sell it to someone else. I'd like to plunder those Cereans for all they have."

"So you're hiding from them, too?" Thorat asked. "As well as the watch?"

Darna poured out the whole sorry story, except for the part about the prince of Tiadun. She told them how she'd been paid more gold than she'd ever seen, stolen from the governor's palace itself, and then the Cereans had put the amulet into the box and she'd seen Anara fly into a rage, bringing the unseasonable rain down on the city.

"You were working for them?" Thorat asked, horrified and amazed.

"I'm not any more. That box, I don't know what it was, but it sucked up all the dragonlight around it. I felt cold just being near it. I don't know what they want with that amulet. They gave me a lot of gold."

"How much?" Thorat asked.

"Thirty gold pieces as big as the palm of my hand," Darna said. "It's gone now, though. I tried to buy an apprenticeship, but the watch came and I had to run."

"You tried to buy an apprenticeship with Cerean gold?" Iola whispered, aghast.

"I heard it cost twenty gold beads, if you can't read, just ten if you can," Darna said. "Elna has the rest. She can get her own apprenticeship now."

"What guild?" Thorat asked. "I could go to them and ask for the beads back, if you want."

Darna shook her head. "It's no use. They can keep it. Better they have it than the Cereans."

Iola sat with her knees clutched to her chest. "The thing you stole, it was a piece of her. A piece of Anara. Now it's gone. No wonder it's so cold." Iola shivered.

"I didn't mean to," Darna said. "I didn't know. I mean, I

should have known, I should have been able to tell, but I
didn't, I didn't mean to."

Myril put an arm around her. "Anara's a dragon. I can't
imagine a person could hurt her so easily."

Darna wasn't so sure. The dragon might be more fragile
than they'd imagined. The rain came down harder, but then,
improbably, a bit of cloud blew away, giving them a glimpse of
the stars over the damp, misty city.

"Maybe you should leave the city," Iola said to Darna.

"I don't know where else to go," Darna said. Except
home to Tiadun, but the dragonlets had herded her downhill at
that thought. "If Anara wants to find me, I'll be right here."

"But what if the watch comes?" Iola's voice rose sharply.

"I could go into the hills, maybe. The Cereans can't
follow me there and the watch can't, either."

There was a long silence. Iola chewed on her hair and the
noise kept Darna from falling asleep.

"The priestesses say that foreigners are always stealing
from the dragons, or trying to," Iola said. "That's why they're
not allowed into the temples, or even into the city beyond the
harbor and the governor's palace. Someone forgot, and let that
boy in, that boy who was with you."

"Giri said he didn't want to be a Cerean any more,"
Darna said.

"He was lying," Myril said.

"I know that now."

"I should probably go, too," Thorat said. "The watch will
probably be looking for me and the other boys."

"No they won't," Darna said. "Those Cereans that came
by just now, they said they didn't want anyone to know they'd
been stolen from, so they weren't telling the watch. Keep away
from them and you'll be safe."

"Really?" Thorat said. "I'm going to have to tell the boys. We've all been laying low since last night."

"That was stupid," Darna said. "I wonder if the watch will give up looking for me, too. I don't think the Cereans will."

"Did they ask you to steal anything else?" Myril asked, in a far-away voice.

"A statue from the temple's back courtyard," Darna told her.

"See!" Iola said. "I'm going to go tell them! Also about that boy. What did you say his name is? Giri?" She got up, as if to go over to the temple right then and there.

"No, you can't!" Darna said.

Thorat seemed to be thinking. "Don't go, Iola," he said, reaching out toward her. "Darna? Do you think they might blame the Cerean boy for the theft from the palace?"

Darna shook her head. "I don't care if they do. I mean, we all ran off together, him and me and Elna. I'm sure he'd rat me out if the watch got at him, but now he's on the Cerean ship. They won't look for him there."

"Maybe we should tell the priestesses about the other thing they wanted you to steal," Myril mused.

"They wouldn't believe me," Darna said.

"Maybe the East Market boys can keep a watch on the temple," Thorat suggested, but Iola shook her head.

"They're just thieves, too," she said. "Except for you, of course." She leaned against Thorat.

Myril yawned. "It's almost morning again. Let's sleep."

She didn't need to tell them twice.

§

Darna dreamed of Cerean torture chambers and woke halfway through the morning, drenched with sweat. A short while later, Myril appeared with two shares of bread.

"Where's Iola?" Darna asked. Had she gone and told the priestesses already?

"She's still at the breadlines," Myril said. "She says she wants to guard all the statues herself, but the priestesses won't let her stay past midday. It's three more days until they start taking novices."

"Are you really going to let yourself be cooped up in there?"

Myril threw a crust of bread toward the canal and it disappeared into thin air as the dragonlet caught it.

"I will." Myril sighed. "But you know, I don't see it like that. I don't like sleeping out in the open. The guilds might be better for you, but the priestesses will teach me more about healing, and herbs, and to read. I want that."

Darna considered the place in the air where Myril's crust had disappeared. "I don't like to be inside the walls," she said.

"But you already are," Myril said. "You're inside the city walls. You don't mind that."

"No, they're big enough."

"Maybe the temple walls will be, too," Myril suggested.

Darna shook her head. "I don't know where I'll go," she said, then gave her full attention to eating.

After a little while, Myril looked up at the bridge. "Iola's coming," she announced. "I'd better go to the market to beg with her."

"Let me know if you hear anything," Darna said.

"I will," Myril said, and with that she was gone.

Darna rested and worried. Where was Giri? Not that she cared about him, not if he'd gone back to his dragon-hating king. She needed to get out. She needed to find out. She needed to stay hidden. She should have given Elna all of the gold beads to begin with and told her to do the next thieving if she wanted. She wanted to shake it all off, every word of the Cereans' language she'd ever heard, every sight of them, even that first glimpse of striped sail on the horizon back at Tiadun keep.

She couldn't gather firewood for fear of the watch. Even begging would have been better than just sitting under the bridge, but at least it was drier than Elna's sorry hiding hole.

Darna was so distracted by her thoughts that she almost didn't see the dragonlet. He flitted over the canal, staring at her. He climbed up the canal bank, weaving back and forth along the stones, his eyes fixed on her the whole time. He flicked a tongue of fire. She heard a little peep, like birdsong. She felt a sensation, a warmth very much like what she'd felt from the amulet, but instead of being still and self-contained, it pushed at her. Then the dragonlet withdrew its energy.

It occurred to Darna that she should at least be dragon-blind after offending Anara like that, but still, the dragonlet was trying to tell her something. It came over and rested its head on her knee. Her pain drifted away, from the ever-present ache in her hip to her new bout of chills. She still felt guilty. She deserved all the curses Giri attributed to the dragons. The Cereans were too foolish to see that their own thieving brought on those so-called curses. Darna wanted to destroy that strange box they had, the one that killed dragonfire and dragon-sight, but didn't even know how to reach it. She could do nothing against them. She didn't even have Elna's help any more, not that it would have done her much good.

Somehow, the dragonlet wasn't angry at her. It made no sense.

§

The next day, when the bell had tolled for midday gate

closing, Darna decided to risk leaving the shelter even though Myril had urged her to stay. She still had a few ordinary beads. If Anara let her, she could follow the hidden passages to one of the taverns near the chroniclers' guild and buy something more to eat. The watch and the guardsmen hardly ever went over that way.

Darna bought herself a bowl of stew through a kitchen door, keeping her stick tucked under her cloak and trying to look like a green-knee, which wasn't hard with so many of them in the city. She gulped the meal down then took another hidden passage toward the harbor. If the Cereans still wanted that statue, they would stay at least until Midsummer eve. Sure enough, the ship was still there. Darna saw the darkness around it, eating away at the presence of Anara. Somehow, it was even darker with the amulet on board, closed away in that evil box, as if the box drew power from what was inside it.

She had to get it back somehow, she just had to.

For the rest of the day, Darna watched the Cerean ship from well-hidden places along the harbor and further up in the city. Thorat said it was impossible to get out there, and he was probably right. Thanks to the East Market boys' prank they'd doubled their guard. Still, Darna was glad that the boys had irked the Cereans. It was the least the scrapplings could do for Anara. Hardly anyone came and went from the ship, certainly no one who wasn't a fully-armed Cerean or one of the governor's men. Darna wondered if there might be some way to tell the governor that the Cereans had the amulet, but she wasn't ready to risk that, and they wouldn't believe her any more than the priestesses would. Besides, if the governor let the Cereans run loose in his palace, that was his business.

Darna still wondered why they hadn't just stolen the thing themselves, but then, they'd seemed afraid to touch it. They were cowards, or maybe they just wanted to keep their dirty fingers out of it, pretend that they were friends of the governor, like Giri had pretended that he was Darna's friend. She wondered what the Cereans were doing to him now. She hoped he felt guilty, and that the Cereans' dark magic would sink their shifty ship.

§

Two days before Midsummer night, Darna saw a string of sailors climb into the tender, then one smaller person: Giri.

They rowed to shore and the sailors bunched around Giri for a long few breaths before he shot out, headed straight to the city dump.

§

Myril heard Darna's approach, moving quickly yet aimlessly up the beach. She and Iola were begging in their usual spot, and the crowds were getting busier because Midsummer was so close. Darna's movement across the sand was so unsteady that Myril couldn't guess where she was going until she spoke from behind the wall next to them, keeping out of sight.

"Myril, I need your help!" Darna whispered.

"What is it?"

"Giri. He's off the ship," Darna said breathlessly. "I can't follow him, though. He'll see me. I think he's going to the dump. He's wearing his slouchy cap, just like the other Cereans." She peeked out for a moment then ducked back again. "I know that you can hear from a long way off," she said. "I want to know what he's up to. I'm afraid..."

"I'll go," Myril said.

"But Myril!" Iola protested. "It's dangerous."

"Thanks," Darna said, ignoring Iola.

By the time Myril was on her feet, Darna had disappeared

again.

"I can't stay here alone," Iola complained. "Especially not with..." She gestured toward the spot where the Cerean ship was anchored.

"I'll see you back at the bridge," Myril said, hoping to reassure her. "You can get back there all right."

"But I can't!" Iola protested.

"You'll have to," Myril said. For the moment, Darna needed her help more than Iola did. Then she left.

Myril didn't like walking across the city alone either, but she knew her way well enough, thanks to Darna's reports. There were so many unknown eyes boring into her. In the market, Myril sat in Iola's shadow. Iola drew everyone's gaze to herself, making Myril all but invisible beside her, which suited her well.

Myril stayed on the main thoroughfares, hoping to spot Giri. She'd seen him a few times from a distance, but she hadn't met him and didn't think that he knew her from any other scrappling. Even though Darna said that Giri wasn't very sharp, he must have been clever enough if Darna had been taken in by him and if he'd learned the language of Theranis all on his own. Myril kept looking over her shoulder to see if the watch was following, or the Cereans, but it was only ordinary Anamat guildsmen, people from the palace, farmers, and scrapplings.

She finally spotted Giri near the Corana's gate. He was muttering to himself in his own tongue as he walked, looking back and forth, searching. She tried to listen to his thoughts, but those were as clouded and muddled as the noises coming from his mouth. She stayed on the road to keep him in sight, hoping that he wouldn't notice her.

Giri moved quickly, but his progress was slowed by his

constant looking back over his shoulder. He climbed to the top of the highest mound in the dump. From there, he seemed to spot what he was looking for. Myril hung back, because although there was plenty to hide behind the scrap clattered as she walked over it. She was surprised that Giri didn't hear her, as anxious and jumpy as he was.

"Where's Nira?" Myril heard him ask. He still had the traces of a foreign accent, but if she hadn't known that he was a Cerean, she wouldn't have guessed right away.

She peeked up just enough to see a boy pointing toward the next mound over. She sat very still and listened. Sure enough, she could hear Nira breathing heavily as she moved pieces of garbage around, looking for something salvageable, then she heard Giri's footsteps, sliding and stumbling toward Nira. He muttered as he went.

"Nira!" he called.

She dropped something and cursed. "Get out of here! You're one of Darna's lackeys. I told her, told you all, this is my turf."

Giri kept heading toward her. "Darna's gone," he said, "running from the watch. She's over, done."

"I hope they catch her," Nira chuckled.

"She's not my boss any more," Giri said.

"Even she got sick of you. That's sad," Nira mocked, but Giri didn't move. "What do you want from me?"

Giri lowered his voice. "She got a lot of gold, for that thing she stole."

"She... She's the one? But they said that it was a real good thief. She can't be. She's not even a real scavenger, just a beggar. Not a thief. I told her she'd be a beggar. All cripples are beggars." Nira scratched her head. Myril could hear the scrape of her fingernails against her hard, dry scalp. "If that girl can be a thief it can't be that hard," Nira muttered to herself. She turned back to Giri. "That, or you're a liar. I bet you're a liar."

"It was a good job. Easy," Giri said.

"You say she got gold?" Nira said. "They gave her beads?"

"Big gold beads, like this. Lots of them."

Myril heard the rustle of Giri's hand reaching into his pocket and a faint clinking of beads. She could picture the bead in his outstretched hand, and heard Nira breathe in sharply.

"You know where she kept it?" she demanded. "I'll steal it from her. I'll give you a cut!"

Giri must have shaken his head. He slid the bead back into his pocket.

"Well, you're no use to me then." Nira sighed.

"But I can be!" Giri's voice sounded more foreign, suddenly. "I can be very useful! I can get you even more gold beads! You will be rich!"

"You're a liar," Nira mumbled, but she stayed where she was. There was no clatter of walking away, or even a shifting of her weight. She was thinking. "So how?" she asked. "What's the trick?"

"I heard..." Giri swallowed. "I heard that the man she sold it to, he wants something else. Easy job, much easier than the palace."

"Oh yeah?" Nira said. "So who'd she sell it to? You know who she sold it to? She's dumber than I thought, letting you in on that." Nira paused. "What's he want, the man?"

After a long few breaths, Giri whispered in her ear: "A statue from the temple."

Nira whistled. "That's crazy. No way."

"It's just in the courtyard, right there, easy to get. Just walk in, pick it up, walk out. Priestesses are weak. It's small. They won't even notice. There's lots of gold beads for it. This many. I take half, you take half."

The thought of stealing from the temple made even Nira uneasy. She was terrified of Giri's foreignness and didn't trust him for his association with Darna, either, but more than that, Nira had some small vestige of respect for the priestesses, or gratitude to them for feeding her through her seasons in Anamat. Still, she was greedy, just as Darna and Thorat had said she was.

"I'll think about it," she said, backing one step away.

"No time to think! This is gold!" Giri insisted.

"Gold?" Nira said. "And the watch on my back, hunting me down, I'll bet."

"They won't catch you!" Giri said.

"How come you're so sure?" Nira asked.

"Too busy looking for Darna, governor said to find her first," Giri said. "All clear for you. You're not stealing from the governor, are you?"

Nira snorted out a laugh. She moved a piece of wood then put it back where she'd found it. She fiddled with the jingling, hollow beads in her pocket. "You stick with me, you foreign rat," she said. "I don't want you out of my sight. You better not run back and tell Darna about this. I'll thwack you if you do. Those beads are mine." She paused. "And yours of course. Keep it quiet from the rest of the gang. You stick with me."

§

Iola needed to get away from that empty place on the water. The Cerean ship lurked out there. Why had Darna talked to them? How could she? The Cereans had promised her more for that piece of thieving than a scrappling could hope to beg in a whole season, but the beads weren't the important thing. The dragons chose their fates, whether they went to the priestesses or the guilds or back to the provinces, but Iola knew her fate. She would join the temple, then everything would be all right. She would sit with Anara all day wearing beautiful things to reflect the dragons' glory.

She walked out onto the breakwater at the eastern edge of the harbor. Anara often rested there, close to her island gateway into the dragons' realm. Iola balanced her way from stone to stone, all the way out to the tip, and there was Anara, waiting for her. The dragon blended with the scene behind her, like a brown moth disappears against a tree trunk. Anara was smoky and tired, but definitely present. She looked at Iola. She seemed to be a long way off, even though her clawed feet touched the rocks. Iola couldn't reach all of Anara's thoughts, but she heard some:

Do not let the foreign thieves in.

"I didn't!" Iola said aloud.

Someone in a small boat nearby looked toward her and Anara seemed to fade again.

I could destroy them, as could the land, Anara sighed.

"What about Darna?" Iola asked.

She will live long. I have uses for her. Anara blinked, closing her thoughts, then turned around to fly into the invisible parts of the sky.

The dragon knew and forgave her? Iola wasn't ready to forgive Darna yet, but the dragon had gone so she walked back to shore and dawdled on her way back to the bridge.

Darna was waiting there, picking at a bit of scavenged bread.

"What's going on?" she asked.

"I don't know," Iola said. "Why did you do it?"

Darna stood up and threw half of her bread at the canal. "I don't know!"

The dragonlet swooped up and took the crust. Iola watched until it disappeared, then turned back to Darna.

"It was a challenge, all right?" Darna said, slumping back down. "I hate the stupid governor, and the princes, too. Dragon-blind, all of them. I don't mind stealing from him. I didn't know it was a..." She looked at Iola.

"But you knew once you had it," Iola said.

"They would have found me. I was too afraid of the watch, and the foreigners." She threw the last bit of her bread to the dragonlet. "Is Anara angry at me?"

Iola frowned. "No. She says you'll live a long time."

"I don't want to."

"Of course you do," Iola said. Everyone wanted to live a long time, that was one of the blessings of the dragons.

Darna shook her head. "I've got to get it back," she said.

Iola went over to sit with the dragonlet while Darna paced, waiting for Myril to return.

§

The East Market boys lay low. The West Market gang sent word that the Cereans were sending men up and down both main canals, looking for their missing tender. As far as anyone could tell, they still hadn't alerted the watch. The watch was still busy hunting for whoever had stolen the thing from the palace.

"They say it was a jewel that got stolen from the palace!"

The rumors got better and better as Darna continued to evade the watch.

"Who was it? They say the jewel got snatched right out from under the governor's nose."

"With ten guardsmen looking right at it."

"What do you think about it?" Pannen asked Thorat.

Thorat just shrugged.

"I heard it was a crippled girl," he said.

"I don't know," someone butted in. "I also heard it was a hill bandit with arms longer than a guardsman's whole body."

"No one believes that story," Pannen said.

Another one of the boys broke in. "Whoever it was stole the jewel right off the governor's hand. Off the governor's hand! Can you believe that?"

It wouldn't do to laugh, Thorat thought. They would know that he was nervous, know that he knew something more than they did.

"That's some thief! We've got to have that thief in our gang!"

"Yeah," Thorat said. "Yeah. That's a good idea."

The boys lapsed into silence.

"How are we going to sell that tender?" one of them said. "The Cereans are looking everywhere for it."

"We can wait until they leave," Thorat suggested. "Or maybe we could use it, like at night. Float it up and down the canal. Get out to other boats with it."

"We could," Pannen said. "We could if the trading season were any longer." The market was starting to get dusty again, now that the rain storm had passed. Pannen looked longingly toward the city walls.

"You going to come back next season?" one of the boys asked Pannen.

"I don't know. I might see if I can stay," Pannen said pensively.

They were talking about what to do with the boat again when Nira strode into the market, kicking up sand as she went. Thorat had never seen her look so smug. Darna's foreign hanger-on followed at Nira's heels.

"There's trouble," Pannen said.

Nira came over to him. "How are you boys?" She jutted out a hip. She really was too old to be a scrappling.

"Go get an apprenticeship already," Pannen said.

Nira huffed. "Not me. I'm going to be a rich trader. Not like your little cripple friend."

Thorat raised his eyebrows, but Nira wasn't waiting for a response.

"She'll be rotting in jail and I'll be living free," Nira boasted.

"Was it her? That stole the thing?" Pannen asked.

"I'm not saying it was, or that it wasn't." Nira pouted.

Pannen looked at Thorat but said nothing.

"I don't care, as long as she rots in jail," Nira said.

"You wouldn't turn her in, would you?" Pannen asked, horrified. "We don't call the watch on each other, you know that. I'll call them on you if you call them on her."

"What are you going to call them on me about? My hands are clean!" She stretched them out. They'd been dusted off a bit, but there were fields worth of grime under her nails. "Since when are you that little cripple's friend? She can't limp fast enough to get away from the watch. Ha. I got longer legs."

"So use 'em!" Pannen said. "Get off my turf."

"You'll be sorry!" Nira strode away.

When she was gone, Pannen pulled Thorat aside. "So did your friend steal it?" he asked.

Thorat nodded. "But not from under the governor's nose and definitely not off his hand."

"Too bad. That would've been great," Pannen said. "Still, it's a good thieving. A really good one. Where is she now?"

"I'm not quite sure," Thorat said.

"You know. I can tell," Pannen said. "Listen, I'm not going to turn her into the watch. I'm not Nira." He paused. "Tell her she can join our gang. That was a fine thieving."

"I don't think she would, but I'll tell her," Thorat said.

"You talk to her about it. That Nira." Pannen spat. "Better to see the tail end of her."

"All of it," Thorat laughed.

Pannen frowned, but then he laughed, too. "Go find your friend," he told Thorat. "Tell her we're done with Nira. Tell her she can peddle scrap in our market any time she wants."

"Trading season will be done before the watch lets up on her," Thorat grumbled.

"I forgot about the watch," Pannen said. "Whenever she wants, then."

Thorat said that he would relay the message, and headed back to the bridge as soon as he could.

§

Chapter 15: Iola at the Gates

Anara let her sheltering wings unfurl.
She bowed her mighty head over the harbor shore.
She sought her priestess everywhere.

– from the Ballad of Ara and Enat

Darna waited. She hated waiting. There was nothing to do. Iola had gone out to beg, come back, and wandered off again. Now Iola was returning yet again, while Myril and Thorat - who might actually bring some news - were nowhere to be seen.

Iola climbed gingerly down the rocks and perched on a rock by the dragonlet's favorite pool. She avoided looking at Darna. Darna decided to try to sleep again. There wasn't anything else to do. Just as she was closing her eyes, Iola spoke.

"Anara says you're going to be a priestess," she announced.

Darna gave up trying to sleep. "Why would she say that? I'll probably have to run off to the hills and be a bandit."

Iola didn't say anything for a while. Eventually she got up and poked at the fire.

"The hill bandits have priestesses too, in a way," she said.

So what if the hill bandits had priestesses? That didn't mean she'd be one of them. Soon Iola climbed in beside her under the blankets, not touching her. Darna was thankful for that little bit of distance.

She tried to reassure herself that the foreigners would sail away soon and that the watch and the prince's men couldn't comb the streets forever. Maybe she could come back when everything had been forgotten, when the Cereans' cursed boat had sunk to the bottom of the sea. Maybe Anara could get some sea dragons to whip up a storm to drown them in. Maybe that apprentice had given her beads to the guild master and she would be able to just walk in and claim her apprenticeship. No, he'd probably pocketed them.

It was no use, Darna thought. She had to get the amulet back. It was a piece of Anara and it belonged in Anamat. The governor's palace wasn't the best place for it, but it was better than having it stolen away from Theranis altogether.

Myril was out there, following Giri. Was there some way to make Giri fetch the amulet back to shore? Now that would be a plan, if it had any chance of working, which of course it didn't.

Darna was about to crawl out from under the covers and back up onto the street despite the danger when she heard someone climbing down the canal bank.

"Darna?" It was Myril, panting from exertion.

Darna put a finger over her lips and gestured to Iola, sleeping beside her.

Myril nodded and gasped for breath. "Giri," she whispered. "He's going to have Nira do it. The statue."

"Nira? Nira?!" Darna couldn't keep her voice down and Iola startled awake. "The little rat! I'm going to get him! That is so... so..." She balled her hands into fists and started toward the street.

Myril grabbed her. "Stop!"

"No." Darna tried to squirm free, but Myril was bigger than she was, stronger, and just as determined. "This is the lowest of the low dirty tricks," Darna said, trying to shrug Myril's hands off. It didn't work so Darna hit her.

"Ouch!" Myril exclaimed, but she didn't let go.

"Don't fight!" Iola shrieked.

A sound from the bridge above made them pause. Thorat dropped into view. Darna squirmed again. Myril finally released her. Darna ran straight into Thorat. She had to get that little rat.

"What's going on?" Thorat asked. He put his body in the way, blocking Darna's flight. Darna looked up into his eyes. To him she was just another scrappling – not like Iola. She pulled a little bit away and looked back at Myril, who was rubbing the spot on her side where Darna's punch had landed.

"Is it all right?" Darna asked her.

Myril frowned. "I think so."

"I've got to find that rat," Darna told Thorat.

"You'll have to get through Nira, first," Thorat said.

"She... How did you know?" Darna asked.

"They came to the East Market," Thorat said. "Nira's boasting about getting rich."

"From stealing the statue?" Myril asked.

"She didn't say what from, but that's probably it," Thorat said. "She was bragging about how the watch wasn't going to get her because they were too busy chasing whoever stole the thing from the palace."

Myril sighed. "I'm sorry it took me so long to get back," she said to Darna. "I got a little lost going through the northeast quarter. All the guild halls look alike to me. I kept turning and looking for the main road. I'm sorry I was so slow."

"It's all right," Darna said. "I'm sorry I punched you." She went back to the fire pit. Iola stirred the ashes.

"We're all here now." Thorat gave Iola a sad-eyed look then nodded to Darna. "Pannen wants you to join the East Market gang."

"Me?" Darna laughed. "What about Nira?"

"Pannen's done with her," Thorat said. "Mostly it was about the heist. He thinks you're a great thief."

Darna shook her head. "It was just luck that got me in there, and not quite enough of it."

"And planning," Thorat said.

At the sound of swords clanking, they held their breath. Watchmen were crossing the bridge above them, four or five of them. Darna dove for cover at the base of the bridge. It sounded like the watch were everywhere, pacing back and forth across the bridge, heavy boots clomping over her head. After a little while, Iola climbed up onto the road to see what was happening.

"They're gone," Iola said when she returned. "You can come out."

Darna hesitated. She was covered with dirt and bits of old leaves from the hollow.

"We can all sit back here," Myril suggested. She made an opening in the old brush surrounding Darna's hiding place and they all gathered around. The dragonlet sat nearby, keeping watch.

"So Pannen thinks I'm a great thief?" Darna said. The thought warmed her, not that the reputation would do her much good now.

"He didn't know it was you, at first," Thorat said. "Rumors said you'd stolen the jewel – "

"Amulet," Darna corrected.

"Stolen whatever it was right from under the governor's nose," Thorat said. "Out of his hand, even."

"The governor wasn't anywhere near it," Darna said.

"It doesn't matter. People believe those stories."

Darna considered that for a moment. "Do you think you could row me out to the Cerean ship?" she asked. "Maybe in that tender?"

"No, even if I could, I'm not sure..." Thorat shook his head. "It's a big boat and we can hardly manage the oars. It's supposed to be rowed by six men, and hardly any of the boys know how to row at all. I was going to teach them, but they're no good at it right now. Why? You're not going to turn yourself in to them, are you? Do you think you could find the amulet, or whatever it is?"

"You can't go on the Cereans' boat," Myril said. "They'd take you prisoner. And you'd be in that horrible darkness."

"I don't care," Darna said. "I'm worth nothing to them. I'd be a lousy slave. Even Giri – " She turned to Myril. "Did Giri see you when you followed him?"

Myril shook her head. "I don't think so."

"Do you think he knows that I know he's gone over to Nira?" Darna asked.

Thorat shrugged. "Nira couldn't have been much more obvious about it, but a lot of people think you might have left the city. Maybe he thinks so, too."

"Well, *he* knows that I didn't steal the amulet out of the governor's hand," Darna said.

"He wouldn't tell anyone, though," Thorat said. "No one but you even talks to him. I guess Nira does now, but she won't go bragging about you any more than he would."

"What about the girl?" Myril asked.

"Elna?" Darna thought about Elna sitting in her horrible

little hideout night after night, all alone. "I need to go find her. I shouldn't have just left her in the middle of the night like that. She probably thinks the watch got me."

A pair of hobnailed boots rattled across the bridge above them. Darna waited for them to pass, trying not to think about Iola and Thorat and the moon-eyed gazes that passed between them.

"Maybe Elna can find some renegade guildsman to melt down those beads for her," Darna mused.

"Shouldn't we try to stop Nira from taking the statue?" Myril asked.

"Maybe she won't go through with it?" Darna hoped aloud. "Maybe Giri will scare her off it with all his talk of curses."

"I'll warn the priestesses," Iola said.

"What?" They all said it together, even Thorat.

"We decided not to do that," Myril said.

"But it's in the temple, so it's the priestesses' statue."

"It's Anara's," Darna said. Then the other name came to her. "Actually, I think it's Salara's, here on loan. You could hike over Na's peaks and warn Salara, too."

"They should know," Iola said, ignoring Darna's annoyance.

"They'll just ask how you know, then turn us all over to the watch," Darna said. "Besides, they'll think I'm in on it." She took a deep breath. "Can't we stop Nira, ourselves?"

Thorat frowned pensively. "I can at least make sure no one from the East Market gang helps her," he said. "I don't think they'd like the idea of stealing from the temple."

"I wasn't supposed to take the statue until Midsummer Eve, in the morning," Darna said. "We'll only have to guard it then. The four of us can stand around and *then* you can tell the priestesses if you really want to."

"You'll come back to getting bread at the temple?" Iola said hopefully.

Darna thought again. "Is the watch still there?" she asked.

Myril and Thorat nodded.

"Well, I can't then," Darna said. "Forget it. I can't stop her, I guess."

"We'll help," Thorat said. "It is only Nira, after all."

§

When Darna woke up the next morning, Thorat and Iola had gone but Myril was still sleeping beside her. She wondered if they would really help her try to get the amulet back. She wouldn't blame them if they didn't want to. Chances were they'd never get it, but if Thorat and the East Market boys could row her out to the Cereans' ship then she would try. She might drown trying to get back, but if she could get it away from the Cereans, that would be something. There were worse things than drowning, weren't there?

In the meantime, she had to find Elna. Elna had seen the box of dragon-blindness too. Even if she didn't understand what it did, she knew more about the Cereans than any other scrappling in Anamat apart from herself. She probably knew more than most guild-people, too. Darna rolled out from under the blankets, picked up her stick, and set out for Elna's hiding place.

Mist hung heavy over the city that morning, like clouds in the mountains. Most of the time Darna couldn't see further than the next street corner. She found a back alley headed in the right direction, but then she missed a turn and had to double back to the main thoroughfare. She missed another turn. She never missed a turn. She was grateful for the sheltering mist.

In the potters' yard, the old broken clay and vats loomed like crouching beasts. Darna shuddered. How could Elna live there?

Darna saw movement and hid.

"Remember!" said an all-too familiar voice. "You get this one last chance to be in a real gang again. Come on. I'll get you a real gold bead!" Nira laughed.

Elna must have said something but Darna couldn't hear it. Nira's shadow passed her. Darna waited until she was well clear, far away down the street. She almost missed Elna.

"You?" Elna sniffed. "What do you want?" She was crawling out of her hole, her small bundle of possessions hastily thrown together.

"I don't know," Darna said. "What did Nira want?"

"Wants me to join her gang again." Elna picked up her bundle and stepped out of her hole.

"Did she tell you that Giri's with her?" Darna asked.

Elna nodded and shouldered her bundle. She started across the potters' yard. "She wants to steal for them. Says that I have to do it, too, since I know what it was. Says she'll send the rest of the gang over here after me."

They had reached the middle of the yard and the mist was beginning to thin. Darna needed to get back, to hide. Elna froze, except for her eyes, which flicked around, looking for threats in the mist and shadows.

"Well, we can't let her," Darna said. "You could come with me. I'm going to stop her."

"No! I won't! I'm leaving!" Elna practically sobbed. "I'm done with all of you!"

"Leaving? Where to? You can hide from Nira, you've been doing it for ages now! Besides, you have the beads. The guilds are probably even taking apprentices now, or tomorrow if not today. You can go to the weavers, or wherever you want," Darna said. "Come with me. Nira's done. We'll make sure the watch gets her."

"You'd turn her over to the watch?" Elna said, horrified. "You'd hand me over to the watch, too!"

"I would not!" Darna said.

"You would!"

"Shh." They had reached the street.

Elna sniffed back a sob. "I'm going home."

"Home? What in Na's breath is home?" Darna demanded.

"Lemirun. A village in Lemirun." Elna trembled, looking up at Darna like a frightened rabbit.

"But it's almost Midsummer! You could join the weavers' guild, I'm sure of it." Elna turned away from her and Darna gave up. "Oh, go! I don't care," she said. "I'll be jail-rotting or in the hills with the bandits anyway, go on."

She wouldn't let Elna see her cry, she would not. Even getting beat up by Nira's lackeys had to be better than being stuck in some village in Lemirun. Near-province scrapplings gave up easily. They had such a short walk to Anamat, they were likely to change their minds all the time.

Elna took one last look at Darna and ran.

"You can have all my beads, all of them!" Darna shouted, not caring who heard.

"Quiet out there, scrappers!" A surly guildsman stuck his head out the window and looked at Darna. "Cripple, eh?" He smiled, menacingly. He closed his shutter. He was coming to get her. The watch would be on her. Even Elna knew better than to stick by her. Darna fled into the back passages, all the way home to the bridge.

§

Iola walked to the temple's front gate in the dim light of early morning, long before the back gate opened for the breadline. This was the high, elaborate gate where the petitioners entered with their offerings. Inside the gatehouse sat a green-robed priestess, embroidering. She glanced up at Iola.

"The breadline is at the back of the temple," she said without missing a stitch.

Iola shook her head. Now she wasn't sure what to say. The priestess looked up at her again.

"Would you join us?" the priestess asked. "That, also is –" She began to point then noticed that Iola was still shaking her head. "What is it then, child?" She sighed.

"I have a message," Iola said.

"Ah, a message." The priestess set down her embroidery. "Who is it from?"

"I can't say," Iola said.

The priestess frowned at that. "Well then, what is it?"

"It's just that someone... I've heard that someone is planning to steal something from the temple," Iola blurted out.

The priestess chuckled and shook her head dismissively.

"From the back courtyard," Iola said. "One of the statues. On Midsummer Eve, in the morning."

"I will relay that message as needed," the priestess said.

Iola had the sinking feeling that she wouldn't, and that the others were right about the priestesses not listening to scrapplings. "It's not just a rumor!" she said. "The Cereans are behind it."

"The Cereans would not dare to be so bold," the priestess said. "They have been instructed not to trouble us."

"But they might," Iola said. "They might want to, don't

you think?"

"Thank you." The priestess returned to her embroidery.

"But..." There was something else Iola wanted to know, and hadn't yet dared to ask. "What makes the Cerean ship invisible to the dragons? What is their magic?"

The priestess dropped her needle. Reluctantly, she looked up again. "We don't know," she said. "The Aralel might... but she is very busy now. I will inform her of your question."

The priestess swung her shutter closed.

"But the statue! Tell her about that, too!" Iola said, reaching up and trying to pry the shutters open. The priestesses needed to listen. Where was Anara?

She didn't see Thorat come up the street behind her. She jumped when he set his hand on her shoulder.

"They won't listen!" Iola said.

"You said you wouldn't tell them," Thorat said.

"I didn't promise," Iola said.

"But we all agreed," Thorat said. "I thought you did, too."

"You wouldn't have listened to me, either, just like them." Iola let go of the windowsill. "It doesn't matter anyway."

"Come on," Thorat said. "Let's go back to the bridge before Myril and Darna figure out where you've gone."

"You won't tell?"

"Of course not." Thorat reached out as if to take her in his arms, then stopped. They both looked up to the sky. When they were with each other, they didn't need to say what they were looking for, but this time Anara did not appear. They walked side by side back down to the bridge.

When they returned, Myril was alone.

"Where's Darna?" Thorat asked. He'd made Iola promise

not to say anything to the priestesses again, and in return he'd sworn not to tell the others what she'd done. Myril probably guessed, though. There seemed to be nothing she didn't know.

Myril held up her hand for silence and listened. "Darna's coming. She'll be back soon."

Sure enough, she stumbled in a moment later. "I'm going to turn myself in to the watch," she announced.

"What?" Thorat said.

"You can't do that!" said Myril.

"I can," Darna insisted. "I can turn myself in. I can't keep hiding from them, there are too many of them."

"But you know all of the hiding places," Iola said. "You've hidden so far. Why stop now?"

"It's not just the watch, though," Darna said. "The Cereans and the palace guards are looking for me, too, and – "

"What about getting the amulet back?" Thorat said. "You're the only one who could do it, who knows what to look for."

"You have to try," Myril said.

Iola frowned. "I don't like that the Cereans have anything that belongs to the dragons. They shouldn't. It's wrong."

Darna shook her head. "They'll get me in the end. I had an idea, but it wouldn't work."

"What's the idea? Why won't it work?" Thorat asked.

"I'd need your help," she told Thorat. "You and the whole East Market gang."

"Can we help?" Myril asked.

"No," Darna said, glaring at Iola.

"Let's go get bread," Myril said, tugging Iola to her feet, but Iola waited to hear the plan.

Darna crouched down and chewed over her thoughts for a moment, ignoring the two girls. She looked like she'd been crying. She told Thorat the outlines of the plan, rowing out to the Cerean ship and swimming back by herself, once she'd done what she needed to do.

"Can you swim?" Thorat asked.

"I don't care if I drown," Darna said.

"I'll teach you," Thorat said. The boys would think it was a fine stunt. He resolved to try to teach Darna to swim in the two days remaining before Midsummer night. There was no need for her to drown, he hoped.

§

Myril and Iola brought two extra portions of festival bread back to the bridge. The sun beat hot on the streets above. Myril threw a crust into the water for the fish and gave one to the dragonlet.

"The priestesses start taking novices tomorrow," Iola said. "I'm going as soon as I can."

Thorat stopped eating. Darna's jaw dropped.

"But you need to help bring the amulet back," Myril said.

Iola frowned. "I don't think there's anything I can do. I won't go near that ship. I can't even stand to look at it."

Darna sighed. "I feel the same, but..."

"You do not!" Iola said. "You don't know how I feel!"

"No one asked you to go out to the ship," Darna grumbled.

Thorat was looking at his bread. It was festival bread, sprinkled with dried fruit from the last year's harvests. He couldn't eat. Only one more day with Iola? Less?

"I'll have to find an apprenticeship," Thorat mused.

"Maybe I'll just join the hill bandits," Darna said.

"You can't," Iola said. "Anara said you're going to be a priestess."

"You said they have priestesses too," Darna said.

"Not real priestesses," Iola said.

Myril threw another crumb into the canal. Thorat added the last of his loaf to her offering.

"The guilds probably won't have a cripple or a thief anyway." Darna wouldn't go back to the planners' guild – the watch had nearly caught her there, they would be lying in wait. She'd never get in. She threw a stone into the water, making the biggest splash that she could.

The color of Thorat's eyes deepened from moss- to forest-green as the sky darkened. He shook his head and pulled his knees up to his chin. After a moment, he spoke.

"I think you should come out to the East Market with me," he said to Darna. "Let's plan that heist."

Darna nodded and they set out.

"Anara did say she'd be a priestess. I don't know why," Iola said as they left. "You'll come to the temple with me tomorrow morning, won't you?" she asked Myril.

"Not until Darna gets that amulet back. I'm going to help her. You should, too."

Iola shook her head. She would make herself an offering, as if that might pay the price of Anara's lost gem if Darna and the boys failed.

§

Chapter 16: Darna and the Boys

Here's to the sailors, gone 'cross the sea.
Vessels and crates in their company.
They may return to peace on land,
or sink in the waves and be lost to the sand.

– A song

It had been stupid, asking Thorat to help. He didn't believe they could break into the Cerean ship any more than she did and Pannen had hardly even spoken to her. Maybe there was something she could do alone, without the East Market gang making fun of her for hobbling or dragon-sight or even just for being a girl.

"You're sure they'll help?" she asked Thorat as they crawled under the city wall. They went by the secret way to avoid the watch at the gates.

"Sure I am." Thorat didn't sound convinced.

"It'll never work," Darna said.

Thorat nodded.

"You don't have to agree with me!" Darna crawled out of the tunnel and dusted herself off. Thorat took the lead and brought Darna out around a scraggly bush and into the center of the East Market boys' turf.

When they arrived at the fire pit, Pannen clapped Darna on the back. "Great heist," he said. "The palace! That's real daring!"

He sat her down beside him, and the boys gathered around. They seemed willing to help. They didn't know how easy it had been, breaking into the palace. Getting out had been a little harder, but that didn't have anything to do with the thieving. Getting out to the Cerean ship and back would not be so easy. Darna took a deep breath.

"All right," Darna said. "We've got to keep this quiet."

The boys all nodded, and right away they were into the planning.

Darna described her plan: rowing out to the Cerean ship, climbing aboard, then getting back the amulet and taking whatever else struck their fancy. Pannen thought it was the wildest, best thieving idea he'd ever heard of.

"We've broken onto ships before," Pannen said confidently.

"That was different," Thorat said. "It was at the dock."

"That's just since you've been here," Pannen said. "We did others, last season."

"You were here another season?" Darna asked.

Pannen shrugged. "Some of us go back home, if we don't get an apprenticeship right away."

"Like Nira," Darna mused.

"Forget about her," Pannen said. "We've got bigger ideas now."

"The other boats we raided were at the dock, too," one of the older boys said.

"Sure, but now we have our own boat!" Pannen said.

"And didn't have so many sentries," the boy pointed out.

Despite the skeptics, it was some consolation that the boys were with her for a moment, even if she was going to drown soon.

"Who can swim?" Pannen asked.

Only Thorat and two of the other boys could, the same ones who were able to row.

"We'll do it," Pannen declared. "Let's swear by spirit of Midsummer dawn."

Darna had never really planned a heist before, apart from the almost bungled one that had gotten her into this mess to begin with, and that she had done alone. She listened as Pannen and his gang plotted out their approach to the ship. For every objection and doubt, Pannen had an answer. He asked Darna what she knew about the Cerean ship. It wasn't much, but Pannen claimed that he could figure out how it was all arranged, where they kept their stores, and where the captain slept.

"Most ships are set up more or less the same," he said. Darna hoped he was right. She hadn't liked her moment on the Cerean ship at all. She doubted that she could find anything there, except maybe the captain's cabin. Hopefully that was all she needed to know.

"You won't want your stick on the boat," Pannen said.

"There's lots to grab on to, on a boat."

He had no idea how handy the stick could be, and her skepticism showed.

Thorat elbowed her. "He's right." Thorat winked at her, but didn't notice that she blushed.

Darna refused to leave her trusty stick behind, not on that heaving thing with all those Cereans and their pikes and evil magic.

As Pannen and Thorat worked out which of the boys would help get out to the Cereans' boat and which would stay on shore, most of the gang scattered for a last afternoon of pickpocketing before Midsummer eve. In two days they would all be gone, into guilds or other apprenticeships, or to be servants in the palace, or even back to the villages they'd come from. Darna hoped that Thorat would find an apprenticeship by then, and that he wouldn't be too far away. He would never look at her with the moon-eyed gaze he saved for Iola, but at least they could be friends.

On the way back to the bridge, Thorat and Darna skirted around the end of the city wall where it ran out into the harbor. That was her swimming lesson.

"It's cold!" Darna complained as Thorat urged her forward.

"You'll dry," he said. He pushed her out and out until she couldn't keep her toes on the sand any more. Her mouth went under water. A wave splashed into her face and she coughed. Thorat grabbed her under the arms and pulled her back.

"You've got to kick your legs. Like this." He showed her, and then how to move her arms, and mostly how to float. She moved about as fast as a snail, in terms of forward and back, but at least she didn't drown right away. Not that she would ever be able to make it back to shore from the Cerean ship.

Darna was pretty sure that they'd be fishing her bones off the bottom of the harbor when it was all done, but thanks to Thorat's lesson the drowning might take a little longer. She wasn't sure if that would be a good thing.

§

Iola woke at dawn, warm from dreams, nestled between Myril and Thorat. Darna snored lightly on Myril's other side. Light played across the arch above them. The damp and mossy stones shimmered and shone. Iola took a moment to relish the warmth of the sleeping friends on either side of her, then she wormed her way out, careful not to disturb them.

Today she would enter the temple, she would become a novice priestess. She would leave behind all the dragon-blind scrapplings and the indignity of begging. She looked back at Thorat. She would leave him behind, too. He had no beard yet, but there was a hint of hair on his chin. If she saw him again, when she saw him again, he would be – she wouldn't think of it. Today was the day. She would not deny Anara's call.

An early cart rattled across the bridge. Shapes emerged from the shadows of night along the canal. The dragonlet glided by and disappeared into a curtain of mist. Iola climbed up to the streets, still empty and quiet. Country folk camped in doorways, come for the Midsummer festivities and of course to see the ambassadress fly to the dragons' world.

Iola walked up the cobbled street to the neighborhood waterspout and washed her face. There was no one to see her when she stopped to stare at the sky. Thorat, Darna, and Myril never thought she was strange, not like the people she'd left behind in Teganum. She turned her gaze to the temple's rooftop shining golden over the common buildings and dreamed of what waited for her inside. Would it wait? She could bring Myril with her. No, the temple was calling her, but she returned to the bridge one last time.

A little while later, Myril and Iola left for the breadlines. They wove through the gathering crowds along the main thoroughfare, the street already dusty with the heat of the day. New scrapplings and visiting farmers woke in shadowed doorways and in alleys. Merchants opened their shops.

The temple breadlines were busier than ever. If Iola hadn't been warned, she wouldn't have seen the way Nira lingered in one corner of the courtyard.

Myril and Iola got their bread plus some for Darna and Thorat. The priestesses didn't even look at Nira. All the scrapplings in the world seemed to have gathered for this second-to-last feast of temple bread before the trading season ended, the temple gates closed, and they all went to guilds or temples. The green-knees meandered back and forth, gawping. They kept trailing their cloaks on the stones, pointing out the pavement mosaics to each other, marveling at everything. Iola looked past them all.

"Do you remember the first time we came here?" Myril asked her.

"Of course," Iola said, but she wasn't thinking of the past. She kept looking at the priestesses, trying to catch their attention. They were too busy to notice her.

"It's hard to believe that we could walk back home and only a season would have gone by," Myril said.

"No. I'd never go back," Iola said. "This is home now," she declared, looking at the temple.

Myril was just as distracted. "That's the one," she said, pointing out the statue of Salara.

It was a small statue of a dragon courting the stars. A bit of its soul, a crystal, was frozen inside. The Cereans could have gotten a plain statue without stealing one from the temple. Any goldsmith could have made it for them, but there was something special about the temple statues and even the foreigners seemed to know it. Maybe they wanted a piece of the dragons' magic.

Myril tucked the bread under her arm while keeping an eye on Nira. Finally, Iola spotted an elder priestess standing beside the bread line, looking past the flurry of reaching hands.

"I'm going to talk to the priestesses," she said.

"Wait," Myril said, but Iola barely heard her. She cut straight through the waiting scrapplings.

Iola stood in front of the elder priestess. The chaos around her receded, the clamor faded. The stench of unwashed scrapplings was replaced by the delicate odors of bread and incense. The priestess's face was serene, framed by the gray curls escaping from the edges of her blue head cloth.

"What is it, child?" she asked Iola.

Iola took a deep breath. "I would join you. Now."

The priestess looked past Iola, over the other scrapplings' shoulders. Myril was coming up through the crowd, driven by pure determination but not flying on dragon energies as Iola had been. Nira's lackeys blocked her way.

"Do you have call to remain in the world outside?" the priestess asked Iola, peering at Myril over her shoulder.

Iola shook her head.

"She does!" Myril said over the heads of the scrapplings between her and Iola.

Iola turned to face her. "I don't," she said. "There's nothing I can do. Nothing any of us can do."

Myril pushed through the last of the crowd and up to Iola's side. "We have to try," she begged.

Iola looked to the elder priestess. "Please," she said.

Myril took her hand, holding her back.

The elder priestess looked consideringly at the two girls. "It is my call to bring priestesses to Anara," she said. "You may both come to be examined." The priestess began to show the way to a gate behind her, but she stopped in mid-gesture as a clatter of horses' hooves sounded outside the gate. It was a prince and his retinue with another prince behind him and even more guardsmen.

"Wait here," the priestess said. "I see that the prince of Getedun has come with his tribute. And how interesting. I believe that is Tiadun's prince. How interesting." She left them there, and the other scrapplings surged around them again.

"Get out of the way!" one of the green-knees said. "I want my bread."

Iola moved toward the doorway which led into the priestess's own part of the temple. Myril tugged her back by her hand. "I have to go," Iola said. "I have to."

"Can't it wait until tomorrow?" Myril asked. "I could come with you then."

"I won't wait. I can't wait a moment longer," Iola said. She could feel the temple drawing her in like a living thing. It would be like a shell for a hermit crab. If she could live there, she would be sheltered by it. She couldn't bear to see the dark, blank place on the waves any more. She pulled away from Myril.

As the princes and their retinues paused outside the gate, Thorat slipped through into the courtyard. Iola saw him and hesitated. He made his way toward them, skirting the crush at the breadlines. He looked radiant, on fire, or like the dragonlet on a misty morning. Iola's eyes met his, but the temple seemed to hold her back. Her longing for him hit like a flash of lightning, leaving its traces in the sky above.

Myril released her hand. Thorat took it. "Don't go yet,"

he begged.

Iola said nothing. She only looked down at the pavement and shook her head. She was suspended between Thorat and the future, her life in the temple. She raised her eyes to his. "I know," she said. "I know there is more to come. Farewell for now."

He seized her, embraced her. He took her head in his one hand and tipped her face up. He kissed her, his lips crushing hers.

Iola felt the heat of the earth coursing up through the soles of her feet, through her legs and her loins, through her heart and overwhelming all her limbs. She returned the kiss.

§

Iola would not turn around. Behind her, the morning sun beat on the hot paving stones of the courtyard. Behind her, scrapplings clamored for their morning bread. They yearned for a place to go after Midsummer and for a glimpse of the dragon at dawn. Beyond that, she did not know what they thought of or what they dreamed. She had not merely glimpsed the dragon. She had touched a dragon's flank and heard her voice. She had been a scrappling, too, but not for long. She had only come to Anamat for this moment, to this temple, to become what she'd been made for.

The corridor stretched ahead, leading her into the dragons' greatest sanctuary on the surface of the earth, into the temple of Ara's Landing. The cool shade welcomed her. Frescoed images of the dragons on its walls drew her along with polished bronze lamps lighting the way.

The old priestess gripped Iola's arm so tightly that it hurt. Ahead of them, the passageway turned. It would take them out of sight of the courtyard. At the last moment, Iola twisted out of the priestess's grip to look back. The courtyard – the whole outside world – had receded to a miniature tableau framed by the pinpoint doorway behind her. The scene there was almost washed out by the glare of the morning sun. Thorat was there. Some of the scrappling boys were leading him away. She had not kissed him until that moment. She hadn't known what it could be, with the world falling away all around them, their kiss eclipsing everything else as surely as the dragons did.

"Come." The priestess took her arm again. "You will be a force to reckon with if you can learn to harness that power, but we cannot have you spilling it on the streets."

Iola bowed her head. "I know," she said. "This is what I have come for. To serve the dragons."

"We will see." The priestess steered her deeper into the temple, around the corner, and out of sight of the courtyard.

"I need to warn you..." Iola said. "Someone is planning to steal the statue of Salara from the back courtyard."

The priestess shook her head pityingly and brushed a wisp of gray hair off her forehead. "Is this the same rumor that a girl, perhaps yourself, brought to the front gate?"

Iola nodded. She thought of the statue, of Salara's delicate wings folded against her back as she tipped her head to the sky and reached her claws into the earth.

"No one would dare do such a thing," the priestess said. "We are well protected, as we ever have been."

"I am glad to hear it," Iola said, "but – "

The priestess walked on, ignoring her. Iola followed as the last echoes of the outside world faded away to nothing. The corridor branched then turned again twice before it opened into a garden courtyard. Iola had already lost her bearings. She wondered where they were, but when she turned to ask the priestess who had brought her in, no one was there. Even that thin link to the outer world was gone.

Not that she minded. The garden she'd just entered was the most beautiful place she'd ever seen. Nearly so, anyway. A smooth, paved path wound between mounds of herbs and fiowers. The plants grew so thickly together that they spilled over one another, lush with every shade of green and nearly every other color, too. In a far corner, water spilled over stones, the sound mingling with the ringing of a wind chime and the soft rustle of breezes turning sage leaves to face the morning sun.

A porch stood along the far side of the garden, cluttered with tables and benches, stools and buckets. Garden tools leaned against the wall. It was a kitchen porch, but bigger than any Iola had seen before. A wizened priestess with fiour on her hands squinted from the doorway. Steam billowed out around her and she beckoned for Iola to come forward.

Iola crossed the garden slowly, breathing in the smell of growing things and the aromas from the kitchen. She could smell onions, freshly cut green onions, overpowering the scent of the more delicate herbs.

"So, you want to be a priestess, little one?" asked the old, fiour-dusted priestess as Iola stepped onto the porch. Above them, bundles of herbs hung to dry. A clatter of pots inside startled Iola, then she remembered that she'd been asked a question.

"Yes," she said. "It's all I've ever – "

The old priestess squinted at her so intently that moisture gathered around the edges of her eyes. Iola looked down modestly, but when she looked up the old priestess was still staring at her, eyes boring into her. She turned away. Iola was used to people looking at her – she hardly noticed it most of the time – but this was different.

"Come!" the old priestess coughed. She jerked into

motion and began to steer a course through the herbed waves
of the garden landscape, heading toward the sound of falling
water and wind chimes.

A small movement fluttered in the corner of Iola's vision
and she looked up, but it was only a pigeon roosting on the
temple roof, not the dragon.

The old priestess waited for Iola to follow. As they
crossed the garden, Iola noticed a group of provincial
priestesses gathered on a shaded bench, near the corner of the
kitchen porch, drinking tea from small cups. They stopped
their conversation to look Iola over as she passed. Iola lifted
her chin and straightened her shoulders, trying to make herself
look taller. Then she caught her toe on the gap between two
tiles and stumbled. One of the provincial priestesses giggled
behind her hand. Iola hurried on, blushing and keeping her
eyes cast down.

The old priestess came to rest at the bank of a shaded
pool. On one end, its waters rippled under the falling water,
forming a current which lazed through quiet shallows until it
swirled away into a disappearing stream.

"Which province do you come from?" the old priestess
asked Iola.

Iola wasn't sure how to answer. She'd been told that once
scrapplings entered Anamat, they became people of the city,
Anara's children. No one in the city had even asked her how
far she'd traveled, but she supposed that in the priestess's eyes
she must still be a provincial. For the first time, it occurred to
Iola that she might not be chosen, just as other scrapplings
might fail to find apprenticeships. On the streets, she'd known
that others had had doubts, but she hadn't worried, not about
this. The streets had been only a way-station for her, a place
from which she could glimpse her certain future in this temple.

Could they cast her out?

"Well?" The priestess looked at her as if she might indeed send Iola home to the provinces. Of course Iola thought of Tegana sometimes, but she knew that she would never go back.

"Tegana's," Iola said at last.

"Show me an herb that grows in the dragon-rich places there," the old priestess said. "The herbs and flowers here come from all over Theranis, from every dragon's realm. Choose." She settled herself stiffly onto a marble bench shaded by a small willow tree and watched Iola.

In a corner near the cascading water, Iola found a low, bright green carpet of spade-shaped leaves. She walked towards it.

"This," Iola said. "this grew around the spring where I liked to go before they made me leave."

The old priestess nodded. "Pick a sprig," she told Iola. "Now sit there." She pointed to a paving stone beside a smooth, still corner of the pool.

Iola knelt down and gazed at her reflection in the water. Her dark hair framed a face still pale despite her season of begging in the sunny markets of Anamat. In the reflection, Iola's eyes seemed like hollows going down all the way to the muddy bottom, mere windows into the watery world, disturbed only by sunlit ripples on the water.

A shadow passed over the sky and she looked up, but it was only a cloud. The old priestess pulled a sprig of the leaves out of her apron and tossed them into the pool. She muttered something over the rippling water. Iola felt a little field of energy grow around her, but it faded as quickly as it had gathered. The leaves drifted down to the pool's dark floor.

As the shimmer faded, Iola looked around, hoping to see it echoed in the sky or even elsewhere in the garden, but still there was nothing.

"You will call me Honored Geta," the elder priestess said. "We accept one girl from each of the realms. As the ambassadress flies on Midsummer morning, we try the novices to see which of you Anara will have. I see that you are indeed from Teganum, so it is in question."

Before Iola could ask her why, a green-robed priestess hurried across the garden and to Honored Geta's side. "The prince of Getedun is at the gate with his daughter," she said. Then she, too, looked at Iola for rather longer than Iola was comfortable with. "Where is this one from?"

"Teganum. Let us see if Getedun has anything other than gold to offer."

The green-robed priestess bowed. "As you wish." She frowned at Iola then spoke to Honored Geta again. "I was told that the prince of Teganum might sponsor a novice this year, which means that this one may force us to make an awkward choice."

Iola looked back and forth between the two priestesses. "But surely the dragons make the choice?"

Honored Geta raised her eyebrows. "Now is not the time for that lesson," she said. "Tomorrow will be time enough."

Just then, a novice ran into the courtyard. She was about Iola's age and only a little taller, though Iola herself was quite small. The novice sashayed past the gossiping provincial priestesses and tiptoed along the exact center of the garden path so the hem of her plain, undyed robe would not be dirtied, and so that she stood nearly a hand's breadth taller than she would have if she'd walked on fiat feet.

She reached the pool and and curtsied before the elder priestesses, ignoring Iola.

"Honored Geta," she gasped. "The statue of Salara in the

back courtyard is gone. What are we to do?"

Both elder priestesses looked at Iola. "It seems that your report was not unfounded," said Honored Geta. She turned to the priestess in green, who was staring at the novice, looking bewildered. "Go make your assessment of the damage and send someone to tell the Aralel immediately. I will take this one to the old sanctuary," she said. She took hold of Iola's arm, but not quite so tightly as the other priestess had. "Send the prince's girl here. I will examine her when I return."

"But who would do such a thing?" the green-robed priestess stammered.

Geta's eyes narrowed at Iola. "I'm sure that the Aralel can discover it. Let her decide whether or not to call in the city watch or the governor's men."

"But – "

The old priestess waved the green-robed priestess aside.

"What about me?" the novice said, blocking Honored Geta's path.

"You, Tiagasa, had best hurry back to your duties," Geta said, shouldering past her. "The novice's courtyard will still need to be swept."

The novice, Tiagasa, sighed.

As they were about to go, another white-haired priestess called to Geta from the kitchen door. "Wait here," Geta said, leaving Iola with Tiagasa.

Tiagasa circled her, frowning. She was one of the most beautiful young women Iola had ever seen. She moved with carefully schooled grace. Her chestnut hair shone in the sunlight and her eyes were a deep, dark blue. Iola had only seen blue eyes once or twice before on other people, and that only since coming to Anamat. There certainly hadn't been anyone so exotic in her home village. Tiagasa paused for a moment and struck a pose which showed off her slender limbs and budding curves. She had a delicate nose. Even her ears were pretty.

This gorgeous girl turned to Iola and smiled condescendingly. "Upstart peasant," Tiagasa whispered, wrinkling her perfect nose. "Defiling the temple with your rags. You'll learn who's important here."

Iola looked up to the sky, seeking Anara's guidance. There was not so much as a gull's flight to show her the dragon's ways.

"I'll give you a hint," Tiagasa said, poking Iola in the center of her chest with one hard, insistent finger. "It's not you."

With that, Tiagasa strode out of the garden, swirling the hem of her plain novice's robe as if it were made of the finest silk.

§

Myril did her best to look away from Iola and Thorat as they melded into one being before her eyes. She was embarrassed, or was it something else? The other scrapplings hooted, but those who didn't know Iola and Thorat soon became bored and returned to their festival bread. The kiss went on and on. Myril couldn't help herself. She stared at them, locked in their embrace. Another blue-robed elder priestess arrived and set her hand on Iola's shoulder. Slowly, Iola and Thorat loosened their grip on one another.

"You will come with me now," the priestess said firmly. "You must go virgin to the rite, and that is years away. Come."

Iola took a shuddering breath as her lips broke away. She swallowed, nodded, and gave Thorat's hand a brief squeeze before turning her back on him and disappearing into the temple.

Thorat sank to the ground. He buried his face in his hands, his body shaking. Myril reached out to touch him on the shoulder, but stopped short. It seemed like too much intrusion into whatever had just passed between him and Iola. Iola was gone. Thorat shook with her absence. Myril waited, and as she waited, she listened.

She could hear nothing of Iola from inside the temple, but that did not surprise her. Those places were sacred, secret. From the street, she heard the self-assured voice of a commander, tinged with just a little bit of doubt.

"Is there a girl here," he said, "of scrappling age, with red hair, and a limp?"

"I cannot say," the gray-haired priestess answered.

The prince sighed. The prince of Tiadun, Myril guessed. He looked into the courtyard, seeking the girl he'd described. His fellow prince leaned into a palanquin borne by liveried guardsmen and spoke to the girl inside.

"You will make Galara proud, and me," he said to the girl inside. The girl mumbled a response so quiet that not even Myril could hear it. "And send word, if there is red-haired cripple in the temple."

"I'm sure they wouldn't let a cripple in," the girl sniffed. "Farewell, father."

"Farewell," the prince of Galamun said.

The prince of Tiadun straightened on his mount. A group of younger priestesses emerged and took the palanquin from the guardsmen and onto their own shoulders. They bore it into the temple, to places where no man could follow.

The prince of Tiadun called the priestess back once more and Myril strained to listen.

"If you see her, if she should enter these gates, you will have my tribute with her," he said. "Only send word with my priestess."

The priestess nodded. "I will inform the Aralel," she said.

The princes waited for their guardsmen to move back into formation then rode away, back to the governor's palace.

At Myril's feet, Thorat wiped his hand across his face, sniffed, and stood up.

"We'd better go," Myril said.

Thorat nodded. "I have a heist to carry out and an apprenticeship to find," he said hollowly.

Together, they left the temple gates, trying not to look back too often. Iola was gone.

§

Thorat stumbled out of the temple courtyard toward the alley where some of the other boys were waiting for Giri. He felt foggy and dizzy. Myril trailed him.

"Are you all right?" she asked.

Thorat nodded. "I have to be. You go back in to keep an eye on Nira."

Myril went back to mingle with the scrapplings in the courtyard.

According to Darna, Giri wouldn't go into the temple courtyard for fear of the dragons' curses. The East Market boys were counting on that. Thorat joined them, half hidden in the narrow gap between two houses.

Pannen came along next and slipped in beside Thorat. "Have you seen them?" he asked.

"Nira's in the courtyard," Thorat said. "I don't know about..." The alley swam around him and he had to lean on the wall.

"Are you all right?" Pannen asked.

"Sure, sure I am," Thorat said. He straightened himself up and blinked the fog away. He would not faint, he told himself. He hoped that Myril would be all right without Iola. They had been supposed to stand guard around the statue with a few of the boys. He hoped that they would be able to hold Nira back. One of the older boys sauntered up the street toward Thorat and Pannen and slipped into the alley when no one was looking. A couple of others hid in another alley just across the street.

"Who's going in to watch the statue?" Thorat asked.

"A couple of the new boys." Pannen said.

"You think they'll be enough?"

"Sure, it's just... There he is!" The boys ducked back. Sure enough, there was the little Cerean. Nira emerged from the courtyard for a moment and bent down to confer with him, then barked an order to her ragged band of thin-kneed followers.

"You know what to do!" she told them.

Thorat barely had time to wonder what that was. Some of the rest of the East Market gang had just arrived. Those boys pushed into the crowd from the back as Nira cut around to the front with her followers close behind. She seemed to be aiming for someone. Giri was headed straight toward Thorat and Pannen.

Pannen jerked Thorat back into the shadows. "Careful!" he said. Giri turned into the next alley. Pannen signaled to the boys across the way.

Thorat might have felt sorry for Giri if he hadn't double-crossed Darna. The boys let all their fear of foreigners and hatred of the Cereans pound down on Giri until he buckled under and confessed. It didn't take long.

"It's on the boat," he choked out. "It's in the captain's box, in his cabin. He's going to use it tonight?" Now Giri seemed to be making things up, so someone punched him in the stomach.

"For what?"

"He – " Giri gasped. "A priestess. He..." Giri gestured helplessly toward his undoubtedly small prick.

"Phh. Who needs an amulet for that!" Pannen said. The boys all nodded in agreement.

"Let me go!" Giri pleaded, straining toward the light at the end of the alley. He had a cut lip and he was clutching the bridge of his nose with one hand. His scrunched cap lay trampled underfoot. Still, he didn't seem to be too badly hurt.

"Not a chance!" Pannen said. "You're coming with us!"

§

On the morning before Midsummer night, the priestesses of Ara's Landing laid out an abundance of bread, more than anyone could eat in two days, even with the festival. They stuffed it with fruit and some loaves had meat inside, too. Every scrappling in the city came for it, even the new ones and those who kept to the far quarters of town. Many had brought sacks and cloaks to pack full for the feast night and for the following days, in case they weren't chosen by the temple, or a guild, and they had to leave the city once the Ambassadress went under the earth. The foreigners had planned well. No one would notice a cloak with an extra bulge that morning.

Nira was nowhere to be seen and Myril was too nervous to listen as closely as usual. Her ears strained toward the quiet of the inner temple, toward wherever Iola had gone.

Finally Myril spotted Nira shouldering her way through the crowded courtyard, right toward her.

"Where's your little crippled friend?" she sneered. "Gone running back to the provinces?"

Myril shook her head slightly, but Nira didn't even wait for an answer. She was fixated on her goal. She set out across the crowded courtyard to that corner niche, oblivious to everything else. It was a wonder that the priestesses didn't notice her strange direction, but there were so many scrapplings clamoring for bread, and then another prince along with a chieftain and a dozen guards arrived outside the gate. Myril wished that Iola were with her, but it was too late for that.

A few of the East Market boys were supposed to be standing near the statue, but Myril couldn't see them. Then she lost sight of Nira even though she and Nira were both taller than most other scrapplings. She hoped that Thorat's friends would arrive soon. She started off across the courtyard.

"You there!" It was one of Nira's followers. He launched himself at Myril.

Myril felt herself hit the paving stones before she quite realized what was happening. She almost caught her breath but then the boy landed a punch. Myril tried to hit back. She missed and then the boy was looking at something else. She heaved herself to one side and pried the boy off just before another one jumped on top of her.

It only took a moment for a stern, tall priestess to reach the spot, but it was too late. When Myril looked up, the statue's niche was empty and Nira had disappeared.

§

Darna's job was to wait down by the harbor and track any Cerean movements. She made her way along the harbor, ducking behind temporary market stalls and encampments of peasants as she went. People crowded the shore, too many people. Farmers and green scrapplings camped in almost every doorway and alley. The only one that remained unoccupied was the one where Darna had made her last deal with the Cereans. It had a clear line of sight out to their ship and almost no back way out except for a small passage, an opening which would disappear if you didn't look for it with dragon-sight. She hid there.

Myril was supposed to get bread for her, but she was too nervous to eat anyway. She wondered if Iola had been any help, what with all her staring at the sky. Looking at the way Iola acted, it was no wonder that even here in Anamat people were scornful of those touched by the dragons. Darna was glad that no one seemed to notice that about her beside Iola who was so much more obviously dragon-touched.

She waited for the Cereans to discover that Nira had skipped out on them, or else to watch what happened if somehow Nira had scored the theft for them after all.

A little while after the bread line opened on the other side of the city, a small boat rowed away from the Cerean ship. There were eight men on board, six oarsmen, the ship's officer, and the translator. They rowed straight toward Darna. The ship's officer stepped on shore first. Darna heard him order four of the oarsmen to go down the beach to look for their missing tender, and to be ready to report back at a signal.

The translator stood just behind the officer. Both wore long, gleaming knives at their belts. They rested their hands on the hilts and looked both ways, up and down the beach, then sidled into the alley where Darna hid. She flattened herself against the back wall of the alley then pressed herself into the hidden passage and sat just inside it, listening. Her Cerean wasn't good enough – she still had to guess half of what they said.

"When will they come?" the officer asked as he paced.

"Soon," the translator said. "The boy says that they will take it at the beginning."

The officer grumbled something. The two men lapsed into

silence and the translator inspected the hilt of his knife and brushed dust off the braid on his shirt. Darna breathed as quietly as she could but it still seemed too loud. The sound of her beating heart echoed in her ears like storm waves on the shore at Tiadun keep.

"This one is much better suited than the other girl, a little older, prettier. Do you think she will come willingly?" the officer said after a while.

"How would I know?" the translator grumbled. Then he added: "They're all whores here."

"Be sure you haven't tried them," the officer said. Then he stopped pacing. "She's coming."

"The boy's not with her," the officer said. "Where is he, by the king's horse?"

Nira dashed into the alley. "Here it is!" she panted. "Where's my gold?"

Darna couldn't see the statue, but she could sense its presence. This time, the Cereans didn't have a box with them. She wondered if they only had the one, if it was a very rare kind of thing. She hoped that it was rare. She wished it didn't exist at all.

The translator didn't answer right away. When he did, he spoke quietly. "You seem to have forgotten our little friend," he said.

"Oh, Giri?" Nira acted surprised. She edged away a step or two. "He's coming. He must have gotten lost, taken a wrong turn."

So the East Market boys had gotten him, Darna thought. At least that part had worked. Too bad they hadn't bothered to stop Nira first; the Cereans had most of what they wanted.

"The gold is on our ship," the translator said. "You will come with us."

"Oh, no," Nira said. "You're supposed to give it to me here. See, I won't give you the statue."

Darna heard a knife slide out of its sheath, a brief scuffle, and a whistle from the mouth of the alley. Then they were gone. Gone across the beach and halfway over the harbor before she could make her feet move and run in the opposite direction.

§

Chapter 17: Midsummer Night

When Anara flies she lights the skies,
She lights the rivers and the earth;
She lights the crossings, death and birth.

– Source unknown

Giri looked pitiful, but he'd told Thorat and Pannen's gang everything they needed to know about the Cerean boat and its routines.

"We'll let you back on your boat if you tell us all about it," Pannen had said. "Otherwise we'll turn you in to the city watch. Did you steal that thing from the palace?"

Giri shook his head.

"The watch don't know that!" Pannen said.

The rest of the boys laughed with him.

"Now about this box," Thorat said. "What does it do?"

"It keeps away the curses, keeps in the..." He searched for a word.

"Power?" Thorat prompted.

"Yes. Yes, power," Giri said.

"What's it made of?" Thorat asked.

"A thing from the mountains. Of dead dragons."

"That's weird," Pannen said. "Foreigners."

"Shh!" one of the other boys hissed. "Someone's coming!"

They stuffed Giri under a blanket and sat back,

pretending that nothing in particular was going on, but it was Darna. She looked wilder-eyed than Thorat had ever seen her.

"Nira! They took Nira." She bent double and clenched her fists over her eyes. She looked like she might cry.

"What's going on?" Thorat asked. He'd never seen Darna cry.

"I thought you hated Nira," Pannen said to Darna.

"Sure, but not that much! She's on the ship with the Cereans. They made her go. They stiffed her. They have the statue, and her! They – " She spotted Giri, who had poked his head from under the blanket where he'd been stuffed. "You rat! You abominable rat! You knew! They were going to take me slave and you knew! You..."

"I didn't, I didn't!" Giri pleaded, unconvincingly. Darna gave him a second black eye before he knew what was happening.

"You're a wreck," she said after she'd checked her knuckles for damage. "I hope you stay a wreck and they sink you in Cerea and you never come back here."

"We're going to let him go back?" Thorat asked.

"That way we won't have to ever have to see him again," Darna said. "King's dungeons, Giri?" She was snarling. Pannen and Thorat were only just catching up to what she'd said about Nira. The other boys were still bewildered.

"They were going to make her a what?" Pannen asked.

"They were going to do it to me, first," Darna said. "Only they said that Nira was better because she's older, and prettier." She spat on the ground.

"We're going now!" Pannen said, jumping to his feet. He didn't wait to see if anyone else was going with him. He might have been tired of Nira but he couldn't sit by and see her taken for a foreigner's bed-slave, either.

Thorat grabbed Pannen before he dashed off. "We'll go once it's full dark," he said. "There's no way you'd get out there now, not alone and not in the daylight. They'd see you and get you before you were even touching their ship. We have a plan. We can still make it work."

Pannen started to shake Thorat off, then gave up with a sigh. "You're right," he conceded. "Right after dark, then. And maybe Nira will help when we get there."

From what Thorat had seen of Nira, he wasn't sure what she would do. Nira had gotten tricked into being captured in the first place, where Darna had dodged it. Even Darna had come perilously close to being taken in by the Cereans. He shuddered at the thought. The boys could easily bungle everything.

Midsummer night took a long time coming that year. With the minstrels and players in the market squares and

garlands of flowers hung from every window, the day should
have flown by. Instead, each beat of a dancer's drum in the
fortune tellers' quarter slowed time to a crawl. It felt as if the
sun hung at midday for a year. Darna and the boys laid low.
Myril begged a bit to see if she could hear anything and got half
a basket full of tiny clay beads but no new rumors. Thorat was
so nervous he couldn't even pick a peasant's pocket.

Finally, the sun began its low, slow drift down into the
western hills.

§

Darna didn't hate Nira half as much as she hated Giri,
and she didn't even hate him as much as she hated the other
Cereans. With Nira, she knew where she stood. She did feel
some satisfaction at the purple bruise growing around Giri's
eye, but the boys gave him water and let him rest, so that when
the time came to go to the ship he could limp along well
enough.

Giri wouldn't even look at her all day. Darna couldn't
stand the sight of him, either. They stayed as far away from
each other as they could while some of the younger boys led
the way down to the mouth of the East Canal. Bonfires lit up
the sands. There was a big fire in the middle of the marketplace
where Myril and Iola had always begged and another further
down the shore in the square where a girl had been singing on
their first afternoon in Anamat. Drums beat in time, and out of
time. Dancers danced. Anamat kept its vigil, waiting for Anara
to fly.

"Here they come," one of the boys said.

Darna looked up the canal to see Thorat piloting the
stolen boat between its stone banks. He brought the boat gently
to the side of the canal and Pannen waved to them to come
aboard.

"You sit there," he told Darna. "Stick the foreign traitor on that bench, too. You're about the same weight."

So Darna found herself sitting beside Giri as the boys splashed their oars, moving them slowly and noisily toward the harbor.

"I didn't know," Giri said. "I would have told you."

"No you wouldn't have," Darna said.

"I didn't know, they didn't tell me anything," Giri protested. "They just said, if I didn't do it, they'd kill me right here, leave me with the..."

"If you say anything about curses again, I'm going to stick your head in the water until you stop sputtering," Darna said. She couldn't believe him, not with Nira in a hold on that ship, mean as she was. She hadn't wanted to believe that Giri was like the other Cereans on that ship, but he was too eager to play their tune. The Cerean sailors from the Ganatean trading ship had seemed all right. Giri had always been a slimy one. Darna didn't want to admit that she'd been wrong to trust him at all, but it was all a big mistake. Now he'd turned Nira into a Cerean slave, or at least that was what it looked like.

"Quiet!" Pannen hissed at the boys splashing their oars.

They did their best to ease the boat along without too much noise. They hung over the edges, pushing the boat along and almost falling in. They stifled their laughter as they got splashed in the face by their own inexpert oarsmen. Giri and Darna hunched in the stern, watching quietly as the boys paddled and poled the boat out through shallows of the moonlit harbor. There were boats spaced here and there at anchor, their masts reaching up to the sky. Darna doubted that Thorat's swimming lesson would do her much good.

It was a wonder they didn't rouse half the harbor and the city watch with their splashing, but it was Midsummer night.

There was drumming around the crackling bonfires and ribald dancing. Even the Cereans had other things on their minds. Only a few men seemed to be on the ship, guarding their stolen goods and their kidnapped bed-slave. Two guards paced the deck, but they kept looking back toward the city's bonfires as if wishing that they could join in on the festival, too.

The boys managed to tangle themselves in an anchor line and rammed into the side of a fishing boat before they were halfway across the harbor. It didn't matter, though. Everyone was on shore apart from a skeleton crew on the Cerean ship. Even the other foreigners were enjoying the fine Midsummer night.

One more boat lay between the scrapplings and the Cereans. They only had a few more lengths to row. Beside the shore, something splashed.

"What was that?" one of the boys whispered.

A small boat was being put into the water. Three men climbed on board. It looked like they were carrying something heavy.

"Paddle over there," Thorat directed. The boys managed to slip into the shadow of a trading vessel. They sat just behind the bow, staying as still and quiet as they could. The small boat rowed up beside the Cerean ship and the guards put down a ladder.

"What are they saying?" someone whispered to Darna.

"Shh," Pannen hissed. The men in the boat handed up what looked like a small cask and shouted something to the guards then rowed back toward shore.

"Ale," Darna whispered. "They said thanks for the ale."

They had left the ladder down. Now that was luck.

The small boat reached the beach and its oarsmen disappeared into the crowds. "Now!" Thorat said.

The boys bent to their oars. Somewhere between the canal and that last stretch of harbor, they seemed to have just about learned to row. They glided up to the side of the ship, unseen. Giri jumped up. Pannen grabbed him. With the help of one of the other boys, Pannen tied a scarf over Giri's mouth.

Darna pulled out her knife. Pannen nodded. She climbed up the ladder, knife in her teeth. At the top she swayed and turned back. She reached down.

"What?" Thorat said.

"My stick."

"Just hang on to things," Pannen whispered.

Darna kept reaching down but Pannen just shook his head and Thorat shrugged. She gave up. She would have to see what she could do without it.

The ship moved uneasily under her but it didn't rock as crazily as the rowboat had. The boys were making a lot of noise. She missed her stick, but she did have the knife. She heard one of the guards coming and crouched behind a pile of rope. The guard was looking back at the shore. She could smell the ale on him – they'd started drinking already. The guard went back below decks, but not to where the captain stayed. Another guard walked by and shouted something to the first one, who laughed. Darna stuck her head back over the side of the boat to talk to the boys.

"They went inside," she said. Pannen looked like he was holding Giri more tightly than necessary, but then he handed him over to the biggest of the other boys, and the rest of them climbed up, while the one big boy stayed to hold Giri down and keep him quiet.

By the time they were all up on deck, Darna stood at the door of the captain's cabin. She pulled on the door. It didn't budge. She found the keyhole and tried to stick her knife into it. It was too thick. She looked around. The cabin had a hatch on top.

The boys swarmed over the deck. Two of them unlatched a different hatch. Giri had said that the one over there was the cargo hold. Darna couldn't shout, but she waved. They didn't see her. She tried the door latch with her knife again.

She jumped at a hand on her shoulder.

"It's just me." It was Thorat.

"I can't … "

Thorat peered at the lock and brought out his own knife plus another tool. He was working at it when Darna heard the heavy thud of a guard stepping onto the deck.

The ship swung around and the moon shone like a torch on all of them. Darna froze.

Pannen whistled. "Over here!" he shouted.

The guard turned toward him. Just then, Thorat's knife released the catch. Darna was in.

The screams and shouts from the deck must have carried all the way back to shore. Darna tried to think, but the noise of the fight broke her concentration. Things smashed on the deck outside, close to the door, then further away. She heard a girl's scream: Nira.

The boys were small and unskilled, with only their knives for weapons, but they outnumbered the Cerean guards by three to one and they hadn't been drinking so much. They called to each other, coordinating to confuse the Cereans.

The cabin smelled of oil, incense, and sweat. Darna heard one of the boys scream in pain. She couldn't see a thing. All of the cabin's surfaces were polished smooth. She felt her way around. A bed with something soft – blankets. That darkness. She felt that horrible darkness. She shook all over and felt like she was going to retch. She was going to fall down. Then she heard another voice on deck: Nira again.

"Leave me alone!" Nira shouted. "I don't want to go back to your lousy gang."

"But Nira!" Pannen said.

"I'm going to get gold and silks and everything in Cerea," Nira said.

"It's a lie, they're all liars," Pannen said.

"So are you! They say the king wants me! A king's even better than some lousy governor, let alone a beggar boy."

Darna heard a thud and Pannen cursed, then there was more scrambling across the deck. Darna didn't have time to think about Nira. More shouts came and then there was a flash of torchlight bouncing off a polished mirror. The Cereans were signaling to their fellows on the shore.

Darna grabbed the box and wormed her knife into the crack. It didn't budge. She put it down on the bed. There had to be something heavy, but if she made noise they would find her. Someone landed in the water, splashing wildly. She heard Giri's voice. She heard the tender's oars clunk into place. Where was Thorat?

The wind must have shifted again, because the boat swung around ever so slightly on its mooring, just enough for a thin ray of moonlight to enter the cabin. Darna could see the box now. She jabbed. The tip of her knife bent. She jabbed again, harder. It gave, snapped, broke, and the box fell open.

There lay the amulet, glowing. Darna put it under her cloak, rolled it into the belt around her tunic again, just as she had when she'd stolen it from the palace. It still lay oddly across her belly. She tied it more tightly. She felt it pull her forward, across the cabin.

"Cursed scrappling thieves!" shouted one of the guards, in Cerean.

Darna heard an inarticulate, answering shout from somewhere across the water.

"At least the girl's still here," one of the Cerean men said.

Darna's heart pounded. They knew that she was there.

"We should go after them," said the other guard.

"And leave that boy here?"

"You stay, then."

The guards bickered about what to do, then she heard Nira shout to them. Had Pannen left her there?

"Let's go see the girl," one of them said. Darna couldn't tell the two guards apart by their voices. The girl, though. They meant Nira, not her!

"You heard the captain," the other said.

"We can look."

That must have been incentive enough. They walked away. The amulet pulled Darna across the captain's cabin. She felt around. There were boxes there, loosely latched. She opened the first one and reached in, and then suddenly she had the statue from the temple courtyard in her hands, too. It more than she'd hoped for. She could see its face in the moonlight, almost smiling at her, though enigmatic, as dragons always are. Though the statue was small, it was a perfect shape. It looked alive in the filtered moonlight, even in that foul, smelly cabin with its silks and heavy perfume.

At the door of the captain's cabin, Darna hesitated. The guards had walked over to where Nira was being kept. They would see her. Nira would see her. This time Nira would turn her over to the Cereans, and that was worse than the watch. But she couldn't stay.

It was time to drown.

Darna grabbed the evil box to get it out of the Cereans' clutches. She shouldered her way through the door, clutching the thing of dead dragons in one hand. She had the living dragon's statue under her other arm and the amulet tucked into her belt.

She tried to sprint to the edge of the deck but she lurched and fell as the boat shifted again. The movement made her slide over to the rail. Water splashed sickeningly against the ship's hull below. She could die in there. Despite herself, she let out a little cry.

"What's that?" one of the Cereans said.

"They're back." Both guards moved toward Darna, pikes low and ready to strike. They would impale her in a moment. The water would drown her, but more slowly. The water. The water could swallow the amulet and the Cereans would never get it back.

Then Darna heard Thorat shout: "Jump overboard!"

"I can't!"

The guard was standing over her with his pike pointed at her face. She side-swiped the pike with the box. The tip of the pike rang like a bell and the box answered with a clang. The guard's eyes went wide. Darna felt a crack ricochet through the box. Somehow, improbably, it had shattered. It split in two, and as it fell the dark pieces splintered further, breaking again and again until they were like shards of broken kindling, lighter than sand. A short gust of wind blew across the deck and the pieces flew over the rail like wind-blown leaves.

The guard stared, horrified. Darna rolled away and fell.

The water hit her and next thing she knew she was choking. She kicked like Thorat had said to do and somehow she got a breath of air. The water slapped at her. The ship's hull swung closer. She wanted to hold on, but there was nothing to grasp. This business of trying to swim was no use, not with one hand not knowing what it was doing and the other clutching the suddenly heavy statue of Salara. The amulet seemed to take on a life of its own, trying to worm its way out of Darna's belt, but for the moment it stayed. She let go of the statue. Something touched her. She heard a commotion far away over the harbor waters.

The statue sank. Darna could see it even in the moonlight, even in the water. It sank, but slowly, and at least the Cereans didn't have it. Then she saw the side of the ship. She was still right up against it. Now that the Cerean's precious box was gone, Darna felt sure that Anara would be able to see their ship, that it had lost its cloak of invisibility.

Anara erupted from the harbor, as if she'd been lying in wait beneath its surface all night, watching the city's tribute to her. She pulled Darna under the surface in a flash of light.

In a volley of color and a swamping wave, Anara dove into the narrow space between Darna and the ship. She took hold of the falling statue of Salara. She ripped through, somehow pushing Darna further from the ship. Darna struggled and flailed against the rising water. She tried to remember what Thorat had said. Be still and float. She reached for air, spread out her arms, and hoped that she wouldn't drown after all.

Darna's ears rested under the water. All she could hear was the heartbeat of the waves, and a gentle, irregular splashing far away. Something nudged her, something hard and wooden.

"Darna? Are you alive?" a voice said.

The East Market boys leaned over the edge of their dinghy. Darna got herself upright and reached for the rail.

"Don't swamp the boat!" Thorat barked. He reached out, grasped her outstretched hand, and started to pull.

"Na's blood." He let her go and she took a mouthful of

water. By the time she'd recovered, the boys were rowing away.

"Hey!" Darna shouted.

"We can't! There's no time! The other Cereans are coming!"

"Take the amulet!" Darna said. "Take it back to the palace."

In a moment, the boat was back beside her. "Hang on to the back, we'll tow you." It was Pannen. Darna worked the amulet free.

"Sure you don't want to keep this?" Pannen asked.

"I'm sure!"

She could hear the splash of the Cereans' oars behind her and their shouts, calling back and forth to the ship. They were getting closer.

"Just take it!" Darna said.

They took it and rowed away, leaving her in the water. There was another ship nearby. She swam toward it.

She held herself up on its anchor rope for a long while. The bonfires in the market squares might as well have been as far away as the stars for all the warmth they gave her. At least she could see their light. Anara circled the harbor, stirring the waters. The Cereans' other guards returned from their foray into Anamat and there was more shouting. Their language sounded like so many empty noises. Darna held on to her rope and shut out the sound, as if that could keep them from seeing her. The Cereans splashed their oars all over the harbor, searching for her as if she still had what they wanted. Mostly, Darna just tried to hang on. She slipped into the water when she tired and pulled herself up again and again until she shivered so much that she could barely hold on. Finally, the sky began to brighten and she let go.

The water would not let her sink, not far. She moved through the water clumsily at first, then she was buoyed up by something strong, a current in the liquid world beneath her. She saw light in the water, not sunlight, and heard a voice. *You will not leave us, we will not leave you.* She felt as if she were dreaming, or something like that. She could feel the place where the water touched the shore and the land stretching out beyond it as far as the hills of Tiadun, north to the headlands of Teganum and Onarun, west to Slaradun. She could feel the dragons' pulse, rooted deep beneath Na's peaks and spreading all over the land. The shore drew her back, or else some dragonlet of the sea carried her. The shore was her home, the home of the dragons, not just Tiada and Anara, but all the others, too. The dragons had not exiled her from it.

Darna sputtered and flailed until somehow she crawled onto the shore.

It was almost full light by the time Darna came to herself again. The crowds were still waiting to watch the ambassadress's flight, gathered on the shore and on rooftops. The Midsummer sun sailed up from Lemira's low hills, warming her as she lay on the soggy sands. Someone prodded her with a stick.

"Darna? Is that you?"

She opened her eyes. It was her own stick that was prodding her. Or rather, Elna that was prodding her with it. Darna coughed, but she couldn't find her voice.

"Pannen gave it to me," Elna said. "He said I could keep it if you drowned."

Darna coughed and spat some salty liquid onto the sand. She rolled over onto her side.

"What are you doing here?" she said at last.

"I came looking for you," Elna said.

"But you were going home, to Lemirun?"

"I changed my mind. I went to the weavers. I got an apprenticeship!" Elna beamed with pride, but Darna could barely rouse the energy to smile and nod. "I have extra gold, if you want."

Darna shook her head.

Elna looked over her shoulder. "I gotta go," she said. Elna darted up the sand and disappeared into the crowds, leaving Darna's stick behind.

People kept their distance from Darna, wary of her half-drowned form on the sand. She heard snippets of conversation, speculating about whether she was alive or dead, and who could take care of her either way. She kept hearing "priestesses" and "temple." Maybe it got into her dreams, dreams that were just taking shape as someone else called her name.

"Darna?" It was Myril, hurrying over to prop up her head.

Darna coughed out some seawater and tried to sit up. She flopped back into the sand.

"Where is everyone?" she croaked out. "The East Market boys? Thorat?" The effort of speaking triggered a fit of coughing and shivering. Myril put an arm around her.

"Thorat's coming," she said. "He said something about finding an apprenticeship, or a servant job, he's not sure which. He'll be all right. The boys are taking the amulet back. They say there's a reward, and that the governor will call off the watch."

Myril stopped to look up at the sky and Darna followed her gaze. There was Anara, circling over the harbor then gliding up across the city. She had the statue in her claw. She sailed over the temple. The statue plummeted from her grip.

Myril's brow wrinkled.

"Did you hear it land?" Darna asked her.

"I thought I heard a splash, and a crack," Myril said, "but I'm not sure."

Anara's wings widened again and she spiraled up over the city. A few of the people scattered around them could see her too. Some looked up and pretended to see Anara, pointing and shouting with enthusiasm. Even in her half-drowned state Darna could tell that they were pointing at nothing, that they saw only the morning sky. Imagine that, pretending to see the dragon. She closed her eyes, wishing she could rest.

Myril nudged her and Darna reluctantly opened her eyes again. Anara drifted down toward them, her eyes flashing bright. She came so close that Darna's tunic dried in an instant. Darna felt very, very tired, but the shivering was gone. Myril unfolded a blanket and tried to wrap it around her, but Darna couldn't lift herself off the sand.

She took a deep breath and let herself look at the dragon, the being that so many dragon-blind spectators were, for this one day, pretending to see. Anara had saved her life in the harbor that night, even though her own folly had landed her there. What could the dragons possibly want her for?

She scooted herself up a little so she could see some of what was going on around her. She could hear the drums and flutes leading the parade of priestesses. The processional way had been decked with flowers for days now, though she'd scarcely seen them for all her running and hiding.

Myril sighed. "The prince of Tiadun is still looking for you."

Darna said nothing.

"He was at the temple yesterday morning, promising the priestesses tribute if they found you."

"What else?" Darna said.

"I'm going to the temple to be with Iola," Myril said. "It's what I need to do. And you need a healer."

"I'm not so cold now," Darna said. "I'll be able to walk again soon."

"Sooner, if we get you to a healer."

"But..." Darna's mind fogged. "But the healers are in the temple. I'm too tired to walk to the hills today, but I'm not a priestess. I don't want to be."

Myril looked toward the temple. Its spires shone golden in the sun. "You can come to the healers, and maybe that will be all."

Darna shook her head. "What if it's not? What if they want me to stay?"

"You'll have tribute," Myril said. "You won't have to stay after initiation."

"What does that mean?" Darna asked. "How do you know?"

Myril sighed. "I heard the priestesses talking, on and off, and other things. I pieced it together. The prince offered tribute, and the priestesses were talking about sending a girl back to Naramun, now that she could read and write."

"I wouldn't mind that," Darna thought aloud. "Learning to read."

"I'd like to, too," Myril said. "I don't think that the prince will stop looking for you anytime soon."

"What does he want with me?" Darna said.

Myril closed her eyes. "I think it has something to do with..." Her voice trailed off.

Darna reached out to tap her. "Don't faint. Stay with me," she said, then coughed some more.

"If you come to the temple, you can stay in Anamat,"

Myril said.

In her exhaustion, that seemed to be reason enough. "I'll go," she agreed. It wasn't as if she had the power to do anything else. She didn't feel strong enough to be a hill bandit, not yet.

Thorat was making his way down through the crowds. He paused to talk to a woman, a young farmwife by the look of her. Then he hailed someone else and Elna was there, too. Darna heard him coming up behind her and turned her head away.

"Na's curse on the Cereans," Darna said. "If it weren't for..."

"If it weren't for the Cereans, what?" Thorat said.

"I wouldn't have to go to the temple," Darna said.

"Temple's not bad," Elna said. "Best food in Anamat, best food anywhere. And besides, they have the healers."

Darna grunted.

"You'll be all right," Thorat said. He wrapped his arms around Darna to pull her up to a full sitting position. "Thank Anara, you're alive," he said.

Darna felt herself warmed by his touch. She blushed and leaned in closer, her lips almost touching the warm curve of Thorat's neck under the soft curtain of his hair. He broke away.

"Pannen says thanks. We got a lot of loot, most of the boys are fine, too, just a little bruised, and we're used to that."

"Where's Pannen now?" Darna asked.

"You won't believe it," Thorat said.

"Believe what?"

"He took an apprenticeship," Thorat said. "With the watch."

"Na's blood!" Darna sat up. "Maybe he's gone crazy, now

that Nira's gone."

Elna shook her head horrified. "How could she choose to go with the Cereans?"

"I don't know." Myril shivered. She propped Darna up on one side while Thorat helped her on the other. She felt him, up close against her, still radiating heat toward her chilled bones. Elna pushed against her back to help her stand up.

"We're going," Myril declared.

"I think Iola needs you," Thorat said.

Darna snorted and turned away, coughing. "Me? I don't think so, and 'm sure she'd rather *you* came along, except that you can't."

"I'll miss her," Thorat said.

Together, the three of them got Darna up on her feet, at least for a moment.

"Look," Myril said.

The priestesses of Ara's Landing stood on the shore, chanting. Their red and golden robes echoed the fire of the dragons. A long boat poled by masked figures reached the island in the harbor – Anara's gate to the dragons' realm. The gauze-robed ambassadress stepped out of her shelter and the masked figures handed her out, keeping their own feet in the water but delivering her dry-footed to the tiny island's shore. The ambassadress turned to face the crowds. She raised her arms in benediction, bowed to them, then entered the dragon's gate.

Above the human tableau, Anara climbed the heavens. Her shadow passed along the shore. Darna felt forgiven. She had gotten the amulet back. The Cereans were gone. Now all she had to do was to evade the prince of Tiadun or become a priestess like Iola. She was not like Iola, didn't want to be like her, staring at the sky all the time, but the dragons had kept her alive for something. If what Myril had said was true, she would be free when her initiation was done. Three years of priestess training would feel like a long time, but it was not forever. Let the prince squander his gold on her training. There were worse things he could do with it.

Anara tipped her wings and drifted down to the chambered earth where she would live until after the harvest was taken in, until midwinter and the ambassadress's return.

I'll help you up to the temple," Thorat said, "but then I'd better go."

Thorat, Myril, and Elna helped her up through the streets. She noticed the white wall of the temple at the end of one narrow lane. It was a beautiful building. In the upstairs chambers along the street, the denizens of Anamat shook out their blankets and lay down to rest after their long night's vigil. Darna wanted live in a place like that some day, maybe over a shop, near a guild hall. For now, though, only the temple would take her.

In the temple courtyard, something was missing – the smell of bread.

"Go back to your villages," said the priestess at the gate.

Thorat propped Darna up. "She needs to go to the healers."

Darna didn't look up to see how the priestess reacted, but the small gate – the one which would only let one pass through at a time – creaked open. Myril followed her in and the priestess did not object. The gate clanked closed.

"Wait!" Darna called. She twisted around to see Thorat standing there, outside the gate, unreachable for as long as the temple held them. "Where will you go?"

Thorat shook his head. "I can't say, but I'll be in Anamat, I promised her that. I promised that I would stay for her."

Before Darna could think of anything else to say she spotted another figure crossing the street toward them. It was Tevan, the apprentice from the planners' guild.

"Hey!" Darna called to him.

"There you are!" he said. "I was looking for you."

"What, to turn me in –"

"No, no. We have your apprentice fee. You can come to the guild hall."

Darna felt a surge of strength.

The priestess pushed Darna into Myril's hands and shot the bolt home, barring them inside the temple gate, locking them into Ara's Landing.

"This one is promised to us," the priestess said. "The temples take precedence. Besides, she needs a healer."

"But –" Darna coughed. "I don't need a healer! I can go to the guild hall!"

"We will not permit it," the priestess said.

The edges of Darna's vision darkened, clouding in around Thorat, Tevan, and Elna standing on the other side of the impenetrable gates. As she fainted, she heard a voice:

You will be my priestess, too.

She was inside the temple, but she would get out again some day.

§

Epilogue: Entering the temple

Midsummer's gates open wide,
gathering the virgins into the temple,
into the sanctuary of the great ones.

– The Calendar of the Hours

A bell rang, and Darna became dimly aware of her surroundings as Myril and Thorat eased her to the pavement, barely breathing. She wanted to say something but then the world went black.

"She's fainted," someone said.

The ceiling overhead had a curved look to it, with jagged lines running over the arches, or maybe it was only the interference of her half-closed lashes. Darna tried to move.

"Is she awake?"

"I don't think so."

Darna felt something on her hand.

"She's so chilled."

She was in some kind of a stretcher which pinned her arms to her sides. It jostled and bumped along.

"Hurry," said a girl's voice. "I'm hungry."

Darna glanced out through mostly-closed eyes. In the corners of her vision, she could see the smooth dark hair of the girls who were carrying her and the shoulders of their undyed white robes. Novices. Even looking at them was an effort. She tried to sit up.

"We're almost there," one of the girls said, though Darna got the sense that she wasn't talking to her. She didn't have much of a voice.

The curved ceiling ended, they crossed a porch – the rough undersides of roof tiles held up by cedar beams – and then she saw a moment of sky before the girls turned, crossed another porch, and lowered her stretcher onto some kind of bed.

"Run along now," said an old woman's voice. "There's plenty of bread."

Darna's stomach complained.

"There'll be bread for you, too, dearie," the old woman said, "but not yet."

Two white-haired crones bent over her, wearing faded blue robes. Darna took a deep breath.

"I'm supposed to have an apprenticeship!" she said.

"Settle down, now." One of the crones stroked her shoulder forcefully. Darna didn't have the strength to push back. She started coughing again. As her cough subsided, the two old women propped her up, stuffing down pillows behind her back. They handed her a bowl of some kind of broth, which she drank, and soon she was asleep again.

§

While they carried Darna away, another priestess led Myril to an anteroom where she was told to disrobe for the baths. They let her into a low, barrel-vaulted room where two groups of girls sat on marble benches, facing each other across a pool. They were all young and naked, their breasts rounded and high or protruding in sharp points. Beyond that, they had little in common. On one side the girls were dirty and wary, on the other side self-assured girls felt their necks for missing jewels. The bath sent up feathers of steam, smelling slightly of sulfur.

Iola sat between two other scrappling girls. Myril hurried over to take her hand, then squeezed in beside her. A middle-aged priestess who was watching over the girls glared at her, so Myril dropped Iola's hand and stared straight ahead, as the others were doing. That priestess, along with the one who'd brought her in, went back out into the anteroom for a whispered conversation.

"We're still one short," one of the priestesses whispered.

"There's a girl they brought to the infirmary, that cripple girl."

"The prince of Tiadun was looking for a cripple. We'll have his gold yet."

"That one?" There was a pause. "Her hair was wet. It might have been red."

"Fetch her. She'll have to do. We need twelve in the novices' court by sundown."

The middle-aged priestess returned and stood watching them as the steam condensed on the ceiling and dripped slowly down the side walls.

It was impossible to gauge the passage of time. The girls fidgeted but they did not shiver – the benches were warmed by the same heat that made the baths steam. Twice, a younger priestess came to re-fill the oil lamps and trim their wicks, and once she brought water for the girls to drink. Myril counted her breaths but lost track and had to start over. She felt hungry, then only tired and faint. Finally, they brought Darna in. Myril heard them coming: the clatter of poles as they put the stretcher down, Darna's complaint as they hauled her to her feet, and the shushing of the priestesses who helped her forward into the baths.

Darna was thin – she always had been – but without clothes her bones and ribs stood out for all to see, making her look like a haggard child. She wasn't putting any weight at all on her bad foot, and she grimaced every time she moved. The priestesses on either side of her hesitated, then took Darna to sit on the bench opposite the scrapplings, among the girls with the oiled hair, the ones who didn't mind going without their clothes but who desperately missed their jewels.

As soon as Darna sat, the doorway filled with clouds of incense. A young priestess entered, swinging a censer full of burning cedar and a pungent herb Myril could not recognize. She circled the bath, wreathing the fragrant smoke around all of them. An elder priestess entered into this haze wearing long purple robes of fine wool embroidered with yellow flames. She surveyed the young women and glanced down at the scroll in her hand.

"You will enter the bath as I name you," she said, "then proceed to the next chamber, and the one after that. When you have gathered at the end, you will go to the novices' court and break your fast with bread and water."

The girls with the oiled hair made faces of distaste.

"You may find that you are hungry," the priestess rebuked them. She cleared her throat. "As Aralel, it is my charge to call you forward."

So this was the Aralel, Myril thought, the successor of Ara who ruled not only the harbor temple but also all of the temples beyond it. She was dignified, but apart from the richness of her robes she looked very much like the other elder priestesses. The Aralel looked straight back at her and Myril dropped her gaze to the floor. The tiles were mostly rough white marble, but there was a snake of glazed blue tiles coiling across it.

"Darnasa of Tiadun," she began. Darna opened her mouth to protest, but a glance from the Aralel silenced her. The two priestesses who had brought her in led her to her feet and walked into the bath with her, robes and all. They emerged, dripping, on the far side, and disappeared into the next chamber.

"Velasa of Slaradun," the Aralel called. Another girl who looked out of place on the far side of the room stood and hurried into the bath, slipping on the second step down and splashing awkwardly. Some of the other girls giggled. The Aralel waited for silence.

"Lenasa of Getedun," she said.

A tall girl with fair hair stood and strolled into the bath as though she had bathed in such splendor every day of her life.

"Ganie of Anamat," the Aralel said.

The girl on the other side of Iola got up, gave her fellow scrapplings a quick smile, and entered the bath.

"Myril of Na's country." A whisper of puzzlement ran around the room. The Aralel was staring at her, though. She had to go.

The room swam around Myril for a moment but she steadied herself as well as she could and stepped down into the bath. The water was scalding at first touch, but she pushed on through. Halfway across the pool she glanced over at Iola.

Iola, who was always so beautiful, peered at Myril with a strange glint in her eye, almost angry, though that was so unlike her usual self that Myril thought she must be mistaken. The remaining scrappling girl beside Iola nudged her. That small movement brought Myril back to her goal and she continued across the pool. Her feet stuck to the surface of the tiles as if she were walking through thick mud, but the rest of her body floated, caressed by healing waters. The fatigue of her sleepless night faded away. She forgot her hunger and walked on into the next bath and the next, warm waters, then cold, until finally the steps led up to the surface again, where an older novice greeted her with sun-warmed linen towels and a cup of cool mint tea.

§

The Cereans had sailed out on the tide some time before sunrise. Darna hoped they would never find the powers they wanted from the dragons' relics, that they would be limp-pricked forever.

They didn't go back empty handed, though. They had Nira, a girl of Theranis, for their king's harem. Years later, Myril heard a rumor that the king of Cerea kept Nira in a tower and claimed she was a captured priestess. Perhaps she thought herself well-off, even in her captivity.

Everyone admired Pannen's daring, but he mourned for Nira, even though she'd said that she wanted to go with the Cereans. Otherwise, he didn't make out too badly. The boys got quite a bit of other loot from the Cerean ship. A few of them passed it off, selling it slowly in the market through the next trading season, and Pannen had his apprenticeship with the watch.

Giri went back to Cerea and remained there for many years, in the king's court.

Thorat turned his back on the closed and secret world of the temple walked deep into the inner quarters of Anamat, to another secret world and his own path to the dragons' realm.

§§§

Author's Note

Dear Reader,

I began writing this series over a decade ago. For five and a half years, I drafted several volumes, edited, re-wrote, edited again, and sent dozens of query letters off to agents. I leaned on a small set of beta readers, including Natasha Lepore, Beckie Scotten Finn, and Helen O'Brien, who encouraged me to keep going. Thank you for putting up with my early efforts!

I joined several writers' groups, both online and in real life. The now-defunct Fantasy Writer's Dream Yahoo group was a warm and supportive community, my online writing home for many years. I'm thankful to all of my fellow writers there for being on this journey with me. I attended the Viable Paradise Writers' Workshop in 2003. There, I connected fellow writers in the genre there and learned about the publishing industry. I've enjoyed keeping up with the instructors and staff of VP as I get to visit them almost every year.

Then I had children. I set the Anamat project aside for a full six years. When I came back to it, I could see why all those agents had rejected my earlier efforts. Meanwhile, self-publishing had emerged as a relatively legitimate alternative for writers of genre fiction, so I picked up those old manuscripts and reworked them again.

The following spring, I fired off a re-worked version of *Scrapplings* to several beta readers. I exchanged feedback with Pauline Ross and Kaysa, who were working on their novels at the same time. My other beta readers included Matti Raine, Christine Ryes, Victoria Goddard, Emily Smith, and Sheila. Each reader and fellow writer contributed insights which have helped me strengthen this book. Susanna Sturgis edited the opening chapters twice and shared her valuable editorial insights. My mother, Leah Smith, volunteered to proof read the original print edition of this book.

I published the original version of this story in the fall of 2014. At the time, my family was busy with another project as the subject of a short-lived reality TV series, Big Giant Swords. My gig as a reality TV side character came and went and I turned back to this series. A few years later, it was all done, but I'd learned a lot in the process and I realized that *Scrapplings* needed some more work. I revised it again based on what I'd learned writing the rest of the series, the style sheet I had from my last editor, and on reader comments, then turned it over to another beta reader, Andrei Cherascu, for a final round of feedback. One more revision and here it is again!

Please visit my website at www.ameliasmith.net to learn more about me and my work or sign up for my mailing list. You'll also find a full library of my books there, including the next volume of this series, *Priestess of the Dragons' Temple*.

Thank you for reading.